A Love Most Dangerous

BOOKS BY MARTIN LAKE

Resistance: The Lost King Book 1

Wasteland: The Lost King Book 2

Blood of Ironside: The Lost King Book 3

Outcasts: Crusades Book 1

Artful

A Love Most Dangerous

Martin Lake

LAKE UNION
PUBLISHING

Published by Lake Union Publishing, Seattle

www.apub.com

Amazon, the Amazon logo, and Lake Union Publishing are trademarks of Amazon.com, Inc., or its affiliates.

ISBN-13: 9781477821923

ISBN-10: 1477821929

Cover design by Kerrie Robertson

Library of Congress Control Number: 2014916225

Printed in the United States of America

For Janine, my wife, my love and my inspiration.

The Court of
King Henry VIII 1537

To be a servant at the Court of King Henry is to live with your heart in your mouth. This is so whether you are young or old, male or female. Some, of course, have more cause for concern than others. I am young and I am female. So the danger to me is considerable.

The danger is the more acute because I am pretty and the Queen is in the last month of her confinement.

Henry has divorced one wife and executed the second. But that is far from the whole story. A string of shattered hearts lies strewn across the land like pearls from a necklace broken in rage. Aye, it's true that complicit fathers, brothers, uncles and even husbands have got rich by leading their women like heifers to the courtly market. It is the women who give the most and suffer the most grievously.

Unless, of course, they are clever.

It does not do to be too clever, though. Anne Boleyn taught us this. For make no mistake, King Henry is more clever than any man in the Kingdom. And he is as subtle and wily as even the most cunning of women. Anne's head rolling from the block was testimony to that.

The trick is to show your cleverness to just such a degree that Henry is intrigued by it but not threatened. The second trick is to intimate that your cleverness is at his disposal even more than your own. And the third trick? Ah, the third trick is to be willing to bed the great beast of appetites and to know when to do it.

My name is Alice Petherton and I am seventeen years of age. I came to Court as a simple servant but I caught the eye of Anne Boleyn when she was newly crowned. I was good at singing, could dance like an elf, and made her laugh and think. She took me as one of her Maids of Honor and my slow approach to the furnace began.

I was very fond of Anne. She was not pretty but there was something alluring about her, some promise of carnality which affected all who knew her, King and subject, man and woman. I must confess that on more than one night I awoke hot with sweat, having dreamed I had been bedded by the Queen, worn out and used by her, alive and half-deadened, exultant and dismayed.

There came one morning when she stroked my cheek and kissed me swiftly on the lips. I gazed into her eyes that day, telling her that I was willing. But she merely laughed and told me to get on with my sewing. So are we played with by those we must call our betters.

I will become one of these betters, I determined. I will be fawned upon and bowed to some day.

Not that I aspire to be a queen, you must understand. That is too deadly by far. King Henry appears to be in love with Jane Seymour. He would, of course, for she carries his child. His greatest lust is for a male successor, even more than for any pretty face or shapely form. There is no sense in seeking to usurp Seymour's place as Queen, no hope. If she proves to be a good brood mare he will rest content for a little while. But in the meanwhile, he hungers. The furnace grows hotter by the hour.

Chapter One

Pretty Maids All in a Row

It started almost six months ago. I woke early in the morning to see the sun kissing the hills to the east. I hugged myself. It was May Day and great festivities were planned at the Court. It was also my seventeenth birthday. I loved May Day and I loved my birthday.

But first there was the obligatory session of needlework. No matter that it was May Day, Queen Jane insisted that we do a few hours' toil at the needle. I hurried into the Maids' Sitting Room and found Philippa Wicks and Dorothy Bray waiting for me.

Philippa was by far the prettiest of the Maids of Honor. The story at Court was that she was twenty-two years old although she never admitted her age to anyone. She was a particular favorite of Queen Jane. She had beautiful red hair with a luster that glowed like gold. Her cheekbones were high and distinct, making her look a little like a cat. Her lips were pink and full and they invariably wore a smile. She was said to have the most exquisite nose in Court although I cannot recall who told me that. I think it may, in fact, have been her. She was elegant and exciting. When I first came to Court I was glad to be her friend. But nowadays, I am not quite so certain.

Philippa's closest friend was Dorothy Bray. I often wondered that they were so close, for where Philippa was pretty, Dorothy was plain. I could not call her ugly; that would be unfair. But plain suited her well. She had a square face with deep-set eyes and tiny little mouth. Where Philippa skipped along the corridors of Hampton Court Palace, Dorothy trudged. I do not know how old she was. She might have been thirty; she might have been forty or even older.

"Alice, where have you been?" Philippa asked.

I decided not to tell them that it was my birthday. Surely they would remember.

"I couldn't find my bonnet," I said. "It had fallen behind the chair."

"It looks it," Philippa said. She reached up and pushed the bonnet more securely upon my head. "In fact it looks as though you've been using it as a chair."

I forced a smile at her jest.

"Her hair escapes the bonnet," said Dorothy Bray.

Philippa examined me carefully. "You're right, Dorothy. It would never do to have Alice's hair all bedraggled across her head."

She tucked the errant locks firmly back beneath the bonnet. I sighed to myself. I hated that my hair was forced into trammels. Philippa, I noticed, always left a small fringe of her hair showing. But it was a lovely color so I could see why she did this. Dorothy was all forehead.

Philippa grasped my shoulders and pushed me back from her so that she could examine me more carefully. "You'll do," she said brightly. "Come, we must not be late."

I followed Philippa and Dorothy along the corridor. I was grateful they had waited for me, although I could see that Dorothy was fretful at the delay.

Philippa, of course, seemed less concerned. She did not dawdle but nor did she hurry. I smiled quietly to myself, smug that she had chosen to befriend me.

The Queen's chamber was crowded when we arrived. Jane Seymour sat close to the window, working, as always, at her embroidery. She was said to be the finest needlewoman at Court, and not merely by syco-phants. I admired her work and knew that no matter how hard I tried I would never produce anything close to its quality.

This was partly because I loathed working with needle and thread. I much preferred to spend my hours in reading, or even writing. But Jane liked to do neither and so all her Ladies and Maids had to bend themselves and their minds to the constant poke and stitch of needlework. Sometimes, at the end of the day, my fingers felt like pin-cushions.

Jane gave a frosty glance as I entered the room. Then she saw Philippa and gave a little smile. She signaled for Philippa and Dorothy to approach. I wondered whether to follow but thought better of it. Susan Dunster and Mary Zouche sat close to the door and glanced up at me. I went to the chair they had kept for me and pulled out my needlework.

"You're late, Alice Petherton," Susan whispered. "Tut-tut, that will never do." She raised her eyebrows mischievously and gave a little chuckle.

I gave her a little pinch on the arm, which made her laugh still more. Mary smiled gently and continued with her sewing. I watched her for a moment and realized why the Court Painter, Master Holbein, once said that she looked like a painting produced by the Italian Botticelli. With her delicate oval face and hair like summer corn, she could well have been an angel sent to earth. Her dreamy eyes always seemed to be on some distant place, perhaps the clouds an angel is more used to. She was so different from Susan with her mousy-colored hair, sharp nose and wicked smile. If Susan was an angel she was very much a fallen one.

The room fell silent except for the drawing of thread through fabric. You would never have credited that so tiny an act could produce such a volume of noise. It rasped through my brain and the more I listened, the more it seemed like the sharpening of a blade.

Every push and draw of my needle felt like the days of my life running away from me. I shook my head to concentrate. It was so easy to go awry, so easy to make a mistake which would take long hours to unpick. I should be outside, I thought, enjoying this beautiful May Day, enjoying my birthday. I wondered if I'd be given lovely gifts and broke a thread in my excitement. A posy, perhaps, or a book or pretty scarf. I was so enamored of my dreams I could barely see to thread the needle.

Finally, after what seemed many hours, Jane put down her embroidery and nodded to a servant who was standing by the door. The girl rushed out, clapping her hands as she did so. Immediately other servants appeared with trays of refreshments.

I flung down my needlework and looked around the room. Everyone else was still bent at their work, as if they were not distracted by the arrival of the food. Everyone, that is, except for Jane Seymour. She glared across the room at me, her look as cold as her nature. I saw Philippa glance up at me but could not read the expression on her face.

My cheeks flushed hot and I wondered whether to pluck up my work right away. The more Jane stared at me the more humiliated I felt. And along with the humiliation came a fierce resentment. I looked back at her as if I had not noticed that her face was growing angrier by the moment. I gave her the sweetest smile I could force upon my lips.

I might regret doing this, I thought, *but I'm glad I did so nonetheless.*

Jane clapped her hands and the rest of the Ladies put aside their work. They rose like docile children and stood in line to collect their possets and honey cakes. I was hungry and wished to take two of the dainty little cakes but I caught Dorothy Bray staring at me and took only one.

I returned to my friends. Mary had two cakes. Susan had three. She looked pointedly at my solitary cake and without a word gave me one of hers.

"You've worked hard," Susan said. "You deserve it." She picked up my embroidery and examined it carefully. "My goodness, you must have done almost quarter of a border."

"Don't mock her," Mary said. "You know she's better at making shirts and chemises."

It was true but I took no pleasure from Mary's praise. I could perform the more basic work of making clothes; my life had given me plenty of practice at that. But the finer work of the Court seemed still to elude me.

Chapter Two

May Day

We were dismissed by the Queen and were now finally free to join the May Day celebrations. As I prepared to leave the room I got a very pleasant surprise. Philippa Wicks, Dorothy Bray and Mary Zouche were waiting for me outside in the corridor. They each bore a gift, wrapped in green cloth. Susan Dunster was nowhere to be seen, which disappointed me a little.

"Happy birthday, Alice," Philippa said, giving me a peck on the cheek. "We have birthday gifts for you."

I unwrapped Dorothy's gift first. It was a necklace with a little locket. I opened it to see a miniature portrait of Jane Seymour. Tiny though the image was, it seemed that she was glaring reproachfully at me.

"That's wonderful," I said, making haste to wrap it in the cloth once again.

"You must wear it," Dorothy said, wresting the necklace from my grasp. She looped it over my neck and clamped it shut, stepping back to examine her handiwork.

"Now your gift, Mary," said Philippa.

Mary handed me her gift, her eyes wide with excitement. It was a recorder of exquisite design.

"It's made of rosewood," Mary said. "You said you wanted to learn how to play. I shall teach you."

It was a beautiful instrument, polished smooth and glistening like morning dew.

"Smell it," Mary said.

I put the recorder to my nose. It had the sweetest fragrance, very like a rose.

"It's lovely," I said in surprise.

"And it's ten years old or more," Mary said. "Rosewood keeps its bloom and scent."

I embraced Mary and gave her a kiss upon the cheek. "I look forward to my first lesson," I said. Mary was a wonderful musician, the finest of all the Maids and Ladies of the Court. I blew a little note on the recorder and giggled. Mary clapped her hands with pleasure.

I turned to Philippa, who gave me a winning smile. My heart beat faster at this and I wondered what gift she had chosen for me. Countless ideas flashed through my mind. I tried to control their wayward careering and wait patiently.

Philippa held out her gift; it was larger than those my other friends had given and felt soft to the touch. I unwrapped it with undisguised haste.

It was an embroidery sampler that Philippa had begun but left unfinished.

"Oh," I said. I could not think of anything else to say.

"I have started it for you," Philippa said. "Practice makes perfect. Your needlework leaves a lot to be desired. And it's not only me who says this."

I nodded, knowing full well who else had been saying it.

"It's lovely," I said at last. "I shall treasure it."

"It's not to be treasured," Philippa said, patting me on the arm, as if I were a little dog. "It's to be used."

We said farewell to one another, so keen were we to be out of doors and enjoying the celebrations. I hurried to my chamber and put away my gifts, wondering for a moment what to do with the locket Dorothy had given to me. I knew it would be sensible to wear it but I could not bear to think of Jane Seymour hanging round my neck, peering at everything I did on my very own day. So I pulled it off and flung it on a table before hurrying down to join my friends.

Dorothy saw that I was not wearing my locket and was about to speak when Philippa touched her on the arm to stop her. I was glad of that. I had no wish to explain or excuse myself at all today.

It was a beautiful morning. The sun was beaming from a sky of washed blue, a sky dotted with clouds as soft as syllabub. A gentle breeze danced in trees shimmering with the green shoots of spring. I glanced up at the old castle on the bluff to the south. It was very small with no great walls and only one tower but it looked the very image of a romantic castle to me. I wondered what it would be like to be a princess living in such a lovely place.

But then my gaze was torn from the castle by diversions closer to hand. The lawns stretching behind the Palace were filled with all manner of delights. There were scores of little booths and stalls, tables readied for the feast, outdoor ovens with cooks already attending, spits of various sizes loaded up with pork and boar and ox. Most of the Court was already here with only a few latecomers hurrying from the Palace.

Musicians played light melodies upon a stage while jugglers and acrobats cavorted on either side. Children screamed with delight at jesters who danced and jigged. A small choir sang songs but the noise surrounding them was so loud their voices could hardly be heard.

A large Maypole had been erected in the middle of the lawn. I gasped when I saw it, for I had never seen a Maypole so tall and handsome. It was decorated with garlands, flags and flowers. Little purses hung from it, filled no doubt with coins and charms.

"Gifts from King Henry and Queen Jane," explained Philippa.

I wanted to tell her I had already guessed this but thought better of it. Philippa liked to explain things to me, as was her right, having been at Court much longer than me.

At that moment Susan Dunster appeared and waved to me to join her.

I rushed across to her and she smiled and led me a few steps farther still from the others. She kissed me on the cheek and pressed a gift into my hand.

It was a little book covered with soft leather, decorated with flowers and hearts.

"It's beautiful," I said with a gasp.

"I hoped you'd like it."

"I do," I said, hugging her joyfully.

I looked again at the little book. "What's inside?"

"Nothing," Susan answered. "Yet."

I opened the cover. The book consisted of empty pages, cream and clean, without a single word upon them. I glanced at her in surprise.

"There's nothing in the book until you write in it," she said. "It's for your poems. Your very own book of poesy."

Tears filled my eyes and I could barely see her face. I hugged her tight and kissed her.

"Oh, Susan," I cried. "It is the best of gifts."

At that moment the rest of our friends approached.

"Let me look at your gift," Philippa said, holding out her hand.

I passed it to her and she flicked through the pages.

"There's nothing in it," said Dorothy with a laugh. "What a curious gift, Susan."

I smarted at her words and was just about to speak to defend Susan when Philippa held up her hand.

"It's beautiful," she said. "It's a charming little thing. You will be able to press flowers in it, Alice."

I smiled. I don't know why but I decided at that moment not to tell them it was intended for my own poems.

I was just about to give Philippa some neutral comment when I realized that she no longer seemed concerned with me at all. Her attention had been taken by something in the middle distance. She grew straighter and a little ill at ease, almost fretful. It was not like her at all. I followed her gaze.

Standing close to one of the temporary kitchens was a man of middle years. He was pale of face and wore a large, fawn-colored cap. I took him for one of the cooks, or perhaps a baker.

He appeared to be watching us. Yet the moment he saw that we were looking at him he averted his eyes and swiftly checked the crowd nearby. Only when he had completed a good scrutiny did he begin to make his way towards us.

He was a pleasant enough looking man with a square face growing a little pudgy round the cheeks. His forehead was broad and unblemished, fringed by light brown curls that hung below his hat. He had a straight, rather refined nose, gently curving lips above a little chin and was clean-shaven. There was nothing remarkable or noteworthy about the man, I thought, nothing to make him stand out in a crowd or draw a second glance.

But then I saw his eyes.

I gazed into them and could barely suppress a shudder. They were set deep in their sockets and grey in color. But what had startled me was that they looked dead. They were not unintelligent, in fact quite the opposite. Nevertheless, they looked inert and torpid. I had a fleeting memory of when I had previously seen eyes like this and the recollection came to me with a sense of unease. Once, at a fishmonger's, I had seen a swordfish laid out on the slab. This man had similar eyes. Sharp, clever, far-seeing. Yet, despite this, they seemed to be dead, quite dead.

As he approached he broke into a smile. It was a broad smile which lit up his face. Except for his eyes. They continued to stare at us without a trace of life or humanity. I moved behind my friends in order to watch him without it being obvious.

"Sir Richard," Philippa said, giving a low curtsy.

He inclined his head towards her and she rose. As she did so I saw her hand touch his, a fleeting touch which would have been easy to overlook.

"Good morning, Philippa," he said. "I trust that you are well." His voice was quiet and low with no music in it.

"I am indeed," she answered. "And you?" Then she gave a little smile showing teeth. "And your wife?"

He sighed. "I am in perfect health, dear child. My wife, alas, is unwell. She abides at home and will not be able to attend the May festivities."

He stared at Philippa as if his words were fuller of meaning than might rightly be ascribed to them. She stared back at him as if she were drinking in his every feature.

"So," he continued, "I am on my own. Or at least I was until I happened to spy you good ladies."

Dorothy Bray gazed at Sir Richard with a smug look like a fat old dog just given the juiciest of bones. Mary looked uncomfortable. Susan wore an amused smile.

Philippa Wicks, on the other hand, continued to stare into the man's face as if she were totally smitten by him.

I realized at that moment that she was.

Her cheeks had flushed a little and her breast was moving with fast, shallow breaths. I could see nothing about Sir Richard to cause such a reaction in a woman as radiant as Philippa.

"If only I had bought more than one May Day gift," he said, looking towards me with appraising eyes. I lowered my gaze to avoid his glance.

"But I have at least brought this beautiful day," he said with a chuckle. "A fair May Day for even fairer maidens."

"I thought it God who bears responsibility for each day," Susan said. "Not the assistant to Sir Thomas Cromwell."

My ears pricked up. So this was Sir Richard Rich, a man I knew chiefly from the angry songs chanted against him. The second-most-hated man in the Kingdom. The man Cromwell employed to destroy monasteries and holy places. The man said to have stuffed his pockets with the ancient treasures of the church while stripping the monks and the nuns of their livelihoods. It was whispered that the Pope in Rome prayed daily for his damnation.

"Indeed the Lord God does," said Rich pleasantly, though he could not hide a flash of anger which made his dead eyes come alive with fleeting menace. "I stand corrected by . . ." He paused, expecting Susan to offer up her name. She remained silent and smiled instead.

"Susan Dunster," Dorothy said quickly.

"Susan Dunster," Rich repeated, as if he wanted to fix it firmly in his mind. He gave a plump smile then made a swift dart and snatched Susan's hand. I jumped at the speed of his move, but then he lifted her hand slowly to his lips and kissed it gently. She did not respond at all, which much impressed me.

Next he kissed Dorothy's hand, making her preen and giggle like a lovesick child. Then Mary, who inclined her head in the smallest of bows. Diplomatic but not warm, I thought.

His hand reached out for mine. It was soft and hot, as if he had spent many years churning butter without recourse to a paddle. He took my hand to his lips and then, with his other, took hold of my chin and tilted it so that he could take a better look at my face.

His eyes displayed a sudden life once more. He squeezed my hand more firmly.

"I do not think we have met," he said.

"I'm certain we have not, Sir Richard," I said, removing my hand from his grasp.

He stared at me for long moments more and I realized that in all that time his eyes never once blinked. The tip of his tongue peeked out of his mouth, like a mouse out of its hole, and wet his lips.

"I am delighted to meet such a charming young woman," he said. I wanted to avert my gaze but found that his eyes held mine as strongly as if they were under lock and key. A sense of panic began to seize me.

"She has not been long at Court," Susan said quickly, "and you are such a seldom visitor, Sir Richard."

"She?" he said, still feasting his eyes upon my face. "She has a name, I trust?"

"Alice Petherton," Dorothy said.

"Don't burden Sir Richard with names he does not need to know," I heard Philippa say sharply.

Her voice broke the spell in which I was being snared. I turned towards her, shocked by the coldness of her tone.

Her face had lost its flush and was now cold and grey.

Rich smiled at her, a smile I thought somewhat mocking.

"Well I for one am pleased to know you, Alice Petherton," he said, turning back to me. He paused. "What age are you, my child?"

"Seventeen," said Dorothy. "It is her birthday this very day."

"Is it?" Rich said. "How appropriate for such a lovely child to share her birthday with the newborn spring."

He reached inside his tunic.

"I said I had but one May Day gift," he said. "I think it should do double service as a birthday gift."

He pulled out a silver ring with a tiny ruby in its clasp. Before I could move, he had caught hold of my left hand and was putting the ring upon my finger.

"Not that finger, pray," said Mary. "That finger is reserved for marriage."

"Of course," said Rich. "I had not thought."

He removed the ring and placed it on my index finger.

"I must protest," I said, hurriedly pulling the ring off again.

"But no," he said. "It is my gift to you."

"It is his gift to you," Philippa said in a tone that took the warmth from the day. "You must keep it, Alice dear. It is, no doubt, a ring once worn by a dead Abbot and therefore full of potency."

She turned and hurried off without another word.

Susan took the ring from me, forced it back into Rich's hand and steered me away into the crowd.

I looked back towards Philippa.

"She is upset with me," I said. "I should go and speak with her."

"Don't be so foolish," Susan said. "I would not go near Philippa Wicks for a long while now."

"But she is my friend," I said.

Susan and Mary exchanged glances. Their look said more than words could tell. I bit my lip in sudden anxiety.

"You are so naive," Mary said. "That ring was intended as a gift for Philippa and she knew it."

"And the ruby is a symbol of love," Susan said. "Philippa Wicks will not lightly forget or forgive this."

My eyes went to where Philippa and Dorothy were disappearing into the crowd. I felt a chill swirl round my insides.

A loud fanfare sounded from the direction of the Palace.

We turned and saw the King and Queen, hand in hand, making a slow progress towards the Maypole. I also saw Richard Rich pushing his way through the crowd towards us.

"The festivities commence," he said. He offered me his arm. "Alice."

I gave a little curtsy. "Thank you for the offer," I said. "I am hale and hearty enough to make my own way to see King Henry."

He gave a tight little smile in response before turning and looking towards the approaching King. Susan pulled a face, showing her disquiet at what had happened.

"We'd best stay with him," Mary whispered. "He's a powerful man and not the sort to anger."

"But how dare he look at me like that?" I said. "And how dare he try to foist his tawdry gift upon me so?"

Mary shrugged. "You are right to be annoyed, Alice. But he is a powerful man."

"And a cunning one," Susan said. "He could easily say that his offer of a gift was a generous and a natural one, considering it is your birthday."

"Nevertheless," I said, "I will not go anywhere near him."

A line had formed all the way from the Palace to the Maypole and, at my insistence, we joined it a dozen yards from Sir Richard Rich, closer to the Maypole. But we were no sooner settled than I found to my consternation that Rich had left where he had been standing and pushed his way next to me. I did not acknowledge him but craned my neck to watch the approach of the King.

A ripple of applause ran down the line and I joined it with more enthusiasm than I felt. My mind was still raging about Sir Richard Rich and the reaction his behavior had caused in Philippa. I glanced at the line opposite but she was nowhere to be seen. She must have been distraught indeed to absent herself from the presence of the King.

At this point I felt a nudge in my ribs from Susan. The King and Queen were only a few yards away. We joined the rest of the line in bowing or curtsying. We straightened up as they passed but then they stopped right in front of us.

"Dear Mary," Jane Seymour said. "I have been talking with His Majesty about your wonderful skills at playing music. I would have you play for us later today."

"I am honored, Majesty," Mary said, blushing red and doing another curtsy.

"I compose music," the King said. "Perhaps you have played some of my works."

"I have indeed, Your Majesty," Mary said. "And loved them."

I marveled at how easily the lie came to her. She had played his compositions right enough but said she found them tedious and mannered. I bit the inside of my lips to try to prevent myself from smiling.

"Something amuses you?" the King said, glancing at me.

"No indeed, Your Majesty," I answered, shocked that he had noticed.

"But you smiled."

My heart missed a beat. "I smiled at the memory of Mary playing your compositions. She is a wonderful musician."

"And my songs?" said the King. "Are they not wonderful as well?"

"They are indeed, Your Majesty. They are truly wonderful."

A look of doubt crossed his face but he quickly hid it. At that moment, to my relief, Sir Richard Rich moved and the King's gaze turned to him.

"Ah, Rich," he said. "You embody your name today." His voice sounded cool and distant.

"Your Majesty?"

"You are rich in the company you keep. You are surrounded by beautiful maidens."

He spoke the words to Rich but as he did so, I felt his eyes stray back to me. He gazed upon me a moment longer then turned to Jane Seymour and said, "What a beautiful May Day."

She smiled and did not answer. Perhaps the King's words were proving too difficult for her to comprehend.

The King and Queen resumed their walk towards the Maypole. I turned to Mary to see how she fared after her discussion with the King. She looked even paler than normal.

And just beside her I saw Richard Rich staring at me, a thoughtful smile upon his face.

Chapter Three

Pursued

From that day onward, Philippa Wicks turned against me. I was distraught and did not know how to respond. I tried to talk to her as I had of old but she merely turned her head and pretended I was not there. Oftentimes she would get up and walk away. I felt so humiliated I could have wept.

Her accomplice, Dorothy Bray, was equally cutting but I did not mind that as much. I had never liked her, merely tolerating her as a friend of Philippa. Besides, she was as ugly as a toad and who wants to have acquaintance of a toad?

But the loss of my friendship with Philippa hit me hard. I could not understand what I had done. In fact, in giving the proffered ring back to Sir Richard Rich, I deemed I had done all I could to prove my regard for Philippa. From the way she was acting I might just as well have stuck it on my finger and flaunted it in front of her face.

"I don't know why you react like this," Susan said to me one morning. She had witnessed Philippa Wicks ignore me and seen how upset I was at her behavior.

"Wouldn't you?" I answered. "Philippa was my friend and now she treats me vilely."

"She was never your friend," Susan said. "You were her plaything, a little toy with which to entertain herself."

"How dare you say that?"

"I dare say it because it's the truth."

She took my hands in hers and stared into my eyes. "Philippa Wicks is a capricious woman who delights to win the hearts of the younger Maids and add them to her entourage. But if any cross her or seem to prefer others, she turns on them savagely. You are not the first to suffer her spleen, Alice. Nor will you be the last."

I pulled my hands free of hers.

"I am not such a dupe," I said coldly.

"Indeed you're not. But that doesn't mean that you haven't been duped. Don't underestimate Philippa Wicks. And in the future, whatever she does, don't trust her."

I was stung by her words, got to my feet and walked out of the room, marching along the corridor to seek fresh air. But as I did so I realized that I was doing to Susan what Philippa had done to me. My steps faltered. I turned and hurried back to the room. Susan was still sitting there, gazing into space. I sat beside her and took her hand.

"Thank you," I said. "You are a good friend, Susan."

I did not like Sir Richard Rich but I liked his lover Philippa Wicks even less now that she had turned against me so violently. I resolved to teach her a lesson.

Whenever Rich came near I pretended to be totally disinterested in him. But when he turned away I would give a quick glance, a glance I intended him to see. Whenever he did, he would become confused and flustered. I enjoyed this. It left him uncertain and at a loss. It left me very much in control. And it fueled Philippa Wicks's jealousy, as I intended.

Unfortunately, it had another effect, one I don't believe I fully realized. Richard Rich, despite having a wife at home and Wicks as his mistress, was becoming infatuated with me.

Wherever I went, I saw him. It was only gradually that it dawned on me this was because he was following me. In the Great Hall, in the corridors, in the gardens and even in the Chapel. He haunted my steps.

I began to get unnerved and ceased my pretense of interest in him, hoping this would make him lose interest in me. Instead, it made things worse. He was more than interested in me now, more than fascinated. He had become besotted, violently and uncontrollably besotted. I began to fear the worst.

Thanks to Sir Richard, the next three months became a nightmare for me.

He was a married man with a house near the Temple in London. But he was chief assistant to Thomas Cromwell, the Lord Privy Seal, and because of this he was often a visitor to the Court.

I swear I became able to sense his presence even as he descended from a boat at the Palace landing stage. He was like the blackest of clouds squatting on the edge of summer skies. Wherever I turned I would bump into him. He was always polite, always attentive. He made me shudder as much as if a plague rat had scurried up my arm.

It was the last week of August that the worst happened.

The weather was hot and sultry and thick clouds were building in the sky. It promised a thunderstorm and I hoped it would come, for this would clear the air. We had eaten lunch in the part of the Great Hall reserved for the Maids of Honor. It was Friday so we had dined on fish—river perch, which tasted unusually dull and muddy. I could not finish my meal, partly because it was unappetizing, chiefly because I had no appetite. The air was close and sticky and it seemed enough of a struggle to breathe let alone to eat.

"I think I'll go to my room," I said. "I'm sure there'll be a storm and I'll be able to watch it from my window."

Most of the Maids shared rooms. I was fortunate in that only one room was available when I first came to Hampton Court. It was very little bigger than a closet and had been shoehorned into a space above a turn in the stairs leading up from the Great Hall. Its little door was hidden by a pillar and if you did not know it was there you would never have found it.

My chamber was less than half the size of most of the Maids' chambers. A tiny bed had been jammed between two walls, without an inch to spare. The only other furniture were a wobbly table, a squat little chair and a chest consisting of three small drawers that could not possibly take even my few clothes. I had to hang my dresses from hooks on the walls. If I brushed past them too quickly I would knock them to the floor.

It was a tiny room and most people who came into it were quick to leave, feeling too hemmed in, I suppose. But I loved that room more than I can say.

I hurried from the table and made my way to my chamber. A small window above my bed gave a wonderful view across the countryside to the north of the Palace. I had left the casement open and a little breeze blew gently about the room. It was still hot, however, and I closed the door and slipped out of my top-gown, hanging it from a hook. I climbed onto the bed and rested my arms upon the windowsill. I had been right. Huge storm clouds were piling up in the sky and already I could see the occasional flash of lightning. The air felt charged with excitement. I rested my chin on my arms, gasped at a huge flash of lightning and turned my ear to catch the boom of thunder.

At that moment the door to my chamber opened. I turned immediately, thinking it would be Susan or Mary. Instead I saw Sir Richard Rich.

He was framed in the doorway, a cold and knowing look upon his face. Slowly and with utmost deliberation he stepped into my room and closed the door behind him.

"What do you think you are doing?" I cried. "I have not asked you into my chamber. You must leave immediately."

He did not answer but his eyes roamed from my face to my breast. I gasped, remembering that I had removed my outer garment and was in my undergown. He examined my body and his eyes grew big with appetite.

"You must leave," I repeated. "You have no business here."

"Don't I?" he said quietly. "I think I do, Alice Petherton."

He smiled and leaned against the table. "And I think that your state of undress signifies you were expecting me."

"How dare you?" I cried. My heart began to race and I felt my face flush red.

He chuckled. "I can see a blush upon your face, dear Alice. A maidenly blush. That's very appealing, very seductive." He gazed downward. "And see how your breast heaves," he said. "You must desire me every bit as much as I desire you."

"Get out," I cried. I could feel the tears begin to well in my eyes. "Get out before I scream."

He shook his head and as he did so a thunderclap sounded and the storm began to hammer upon the ground. "No one will hear you," he said. "Although a few squeals and gasps from you will season the meal for me."

He opened his hand and placed a thin coil of leather upon the table. I stared at it, my eyes wide.

"This serves two purposes," he said, picking it up and part uncoiling it. "I can use it to tie up your hands. Or I can use it to lash you. I am happy to do either. I would prefer to do both."

I tried to answer but no words came.

He leapt towards me, the leather rope swinging in his hand. He wrapped it swiftly around my wrists and flung me back upon the bed. Then he lunged and ripped open my blouse.

"Beautiful," he said. "Just as I expected." He bent his head and began to suck upon my nipple.

I cried aloud in terror and in shame. He chuckled as I did so and he pressed his weight upon me. His hand grappled with my skirts and tugged at my underclothes, pulling them down to reveal my thighs.

"I'll break your maidenhead, Alice," he said. "There's nothing better for a man than to hear the squeal of pain and feel the rush of blood."

I gasped and shook my head.

He pressed his mouth upon mine, his tongue pushing itself between my lips. I almost bit down upon it but stopped myself. A better idea came to me.

I clutched him by the hair and stared into his eyes.

"The leather lash," I breathed. "Do you reserve that only for the worst of girls?"

He frowned.

"It seems a waste to have it round my wrists," I said. "I thought you said it had another use."

I smiled like a wanton and licked my lips slowly as if they were cream.

"I did," he answered with a voice thick as mud. "I could whip you with it."

"I will not cry out," I said with a challenging look. "I will not cry out until your arm is aching."

He looked surprised for a moment but then swiftly undid the leash. I stared into his eyes and gave a little moan of pleasure before half turning my rear towards him.

"Uncover me," I commanded.

He scrabbled for my drawers and as he did so I reached up to the windowsill and grabbed my embroidery bodkin. I plunged it into his neck with all my force, drawing blood.

He cried out and I plunged it in once more.

"You bitch," he cried.

I held the bodkin against his eye. And then I pressed.

"I've stabbed you twice already," I said. "Don't think I won't stick it in your eye."

He gulped and pulled back, slipping to the floor as he struggled away from me.

"You filthy little whore," he snarled. "All summer long you've been teasing me, acting like a trollop. And now I come into your chamber and find you half-undressed and lustful for me." He spat on my arm. "And then you get frightened like a tiny child and threaten me with a bodkin."

His hand went to his neck and came away crimson with blood.

"You have made a big mistake today, Alice Petherton," he said. "The biggest mistake of your young life."

He retreated from my chamber. I collapsed in tears. I had made an enemy of the second-most-hated man in the Kingdom. Where on earth could I find protection from such a man? Who in the Kingdom was powerful enough?

And then I realized.

Chapter Four

The King of England

19 September 1537

It was the third week in September but the weather continued unseasonably warm. King Henry had been walking in the garden with some gentlemen attendants but must have wished for some solitude, for he gestured them to move some distance from him. He walked over to a bower of roses shriveling on the branch. The autumn winds blew fallen petals about his feet, hither and thither, skittish as a filly.

I opened up my book of verse and strolled across the lawn, reading from the book as I did so.

The King had some small acquaintance of me, although he had only spoken to me once, on May Day. He wished me good day. I did him a curtsy and made to walk on.

"You have a book, Alice Petherton," he called. "Is this for decoration or education?"

I curtsied once more and glanced up at him before looking at the ground demurely.

"For education, Your Majesty," I said in a low voice. "I seek to improve myself."

Out of the corner of my eye I saw his eyes slide from the book to my breasts and then to my hair.

"Don't bend your head to the ground, child," he said. "Your King will not harm you by his gaze."

I took a breath and raised my head. His chest rose, as if a wind of passion were surging within. He held out his hand for the book.

"Poems by Sir Thomas Wyatt," he said, perusing the title. He flipped open the pages. "Do you like the Sir Thomas's poems, Alice Petherton?"

"I do, Your Majesty. They are ably written."

Henry's eyes narrowed and his head turned as if he could not believe his ears. "Ably written?" he said. "A chit of a girl talks of my foremost poet, a knight of the Kingdom, in such a manner?"

I curtsied again. "I meant no disrespect," I said.

"Perhaps what you mean and what you say are very different matters, Alice Petherton?"

"They are not designed so, Your Majesty. It must be my youthful ignorance."

He said nothing but continued to stare at me. "You have very dark eyes," the King said. "Very dark. And yet your hair is blonde and your complexion pale."

"Many have remarked upon this, Majesty."

"Your eyes are the color of damsons," he continued. He gestured me closer, tilted my head and looked into my eyes. I felt the heat of him beating down upon me, or perhaps it was my own heat, gusting like a wind in summer.

"Yes, very like damsons," he murmured. "Dark eyes are hard to read, don't you think, Alice Petherton?"

"Not as hard as the poems of Sir Thomas Wyatt, Your Majesty."

He looked at me more searchingly, a quizzical look upon his face. I saw his emotions battling, his thoughts flying. Then he tilted back his head and laughed. It was a pleasant laugh, not loud, not soft, as natural a laugh as a King could make. Yet as he laughed his eyes locked fast upon me.

I smiled, a gentle smile, as if I did so not at my own words but at my lord's pleasure.

His laughter stopped. He stared at me as if he had not properly seen me until this moment.

When he spoke again his voice was changed, deeper and cloying.

"I would know you better, Alice Petherton," he said. "I would read poems with you."

"I am at Your Majesty's pleasure," I said, giving another curtsy. But as I did so I made sure that my eyes never left his face.

Despite his words, the King did not summon me for eleven days, until the last day of September. I counted them off with care. I was ever wary of meeting Richard Rich but he was not about the Palace. I thought for a brief time that I had frightened him off, not realizing that men such as he do not scare easily. Nor are they put off seeking what they crave. I guessed that he had been sent to despoil some nunnery and enrich himself in the process. I was glad of this although I realized it would only offer me temporary respite. I needed my protector.

The warm weather waned and an autumn chill crept across the Palace. I began to think that the King had forgotten our meeting and pondered how best to arrange a second one.

No good ideas came to me and I did not want to tarry in halls and chambers like some lovesick maiden anxious to meet her beloved. I cudgeled my brain for ways in which to meet him, to no avail. Then, one evening, when a fierce wind rattled the windows and a storm could be seen growing in the west, a Pageboy appeared in the Maids' chamber.

There were half a dozen of us in the room. The Queen's favorites were not here as she had summoned them to her bedchamber. Her time was near and she would not rise again until she had given issue. I was not one of her favorites.

I fiddled with an embroidery, a scene of hounds and hares as I recall, but I could not focus my attention on it. My thoughts were far away, veering between the memory of my meeting with the King and the plight of the Queen in her chamber. I did not care for Jane Seymour as I had loved Anne Boleyn, but I had some sympathy for what she was going through.

The Page was young, perhaps thirteen or so, but that did not prevent the women in the room from casting appraising eyes upon him. Thirteen-year-old boys became fourteen and fifteen. They grew at a prodigious rate.

"Where can I find Alice Petherton?" he asked. His voice was still that of a boy although I could detect the cracks in it.

I looked up from my embroidery. "I am Alice Petherton."

"You are requested by the King," the Page said. "He awaits you in the King's Study."

He stood back, his duty done, not a bit embarrassed or uncomfortable. A buzz arose in the room, the sound that bees might make when their hive is being robbed.

I feigned more surprise than I felt, although, in truth, I had all but given up on ever receiving such a summons.

"His Majesty requires that you bring the book of poems with you," the Page said.

This unusual request set the hive buzzing again.

"Tell His Majesty that I must fetch it from my bedchamber," I said. "Pray ask that he forgives me for the slight delay."

The boy swayed from side to side, uncertain what to do.

"Well, hurry," I said. "If I must keep him waiting, it were best you did not as well."

The boy blushed, cast a quick look at the Ladies in the room and raced away.

The buzz became laughter, the yelping of hounds in a kennel.

"I bid you good night, dear friends," I said with a bow.

"Read sweetly, dear Alice," said Susan. "Be careful not to make any mistakes."

I gazed at her. She gave nothing away by her look but I knew that she was giving me honest advice.

I hurried to my chamber and found the book of poems. My hand was shaking as I poured a jug of water into a basin. I dabbed a cloth in it and wiped my face. Then, thinking more clearly, I slipped off my garments and swiftly washed my body. I caught up a mix of herbs and spice and chewed upon them ferociously before spitting them out into the basin. Above all my breath must smell fresh and pure.

Chapter Five

Not Love but Verse

I hurried along the corridors of the Palace.

It was growing dark, the sun had just set and the threatening storm was painting the sky a morbid grey. It was not yet twilight but that time of risk and promise was close. Rush lights and candles had been lit by the unseen hands of servants and they flickered in the draught. *Strange*, I thought, *they give less light now than when the night has settled fully*. In the half-light they flickered sickly like will-o'-the-wisps beguiling unwary travelers to their doom.

Even though I had never been near to it I knew how to find the King's Study. Hampton Court Palace was vast and many people got lost within it, even some who had lived here for a while. But I had made a map of the Palace in my head, plotting its warren of chambers and halls and corridors.

My bedroom was on the top floor overlooking the Lower Court. To get to the King's Study was a long walk: down several staircases, along the corridor next to the Kitchens, through the Great Hall and past the Watching Chamber, where the King's Guards were quartered.

I walked as quickly as I could, determined to keep the King waiting for as little time as possible.

My breath was coming fast as I crossed the Great Hall, whether from my speed or from the thought of being alone with the King. I turned left and passed by the Watching Chamber, where I could hear the low conversation of bored men. I forced myself to walk even faster as I passed the Pages' Quarters, for I knew the Pages' eyes were quick and their tongues even quicker. No doubt the boy who the King had sent to summon me was even now the center of attention, basking in temporary notoriety from the gossip he brought to his fellows.

I turned right into the Gallery and slowed my walk. It would not do to arrive at the King's Study with heaving breast and reddened face. I could not afford to tarry long, of course, but I forced myself to stop and take breath. I leaned my face against a window to try to cool it. The gathering wind rattled the glass in its frame and it vibrated against my skin. I waited until I felt the flush leave my face and continued towards my rendezvous. All too soon, I stood outside the door to the Study. I composed myself, patting at my hair and checking my bodice to make sure it was not in disarray.

I knocked upon the door, a knock as quiet and gentle as my heart was loud and hammering. I waited for a moment in the silence and then I heard the single word, "Come."

I entered the Study and curtsied. My eyes blinked in amazement. The walls were lined with books. I had never seen so many in my life, could barely imagine that so many had been written and printed. The smell of old leather was heavy in the air yet not unpleasant. A large table stood in the middle of the room with four chairs placed around it. In the far right was another door, which led, I imagined, to a second chamber. On the longest wall stood a large fireplace with a fierce blaze burning in a deep grate. To one side of this were two easy chairs, with a small table between them. The room was as warm as an August afternoon.

There was no sign of King Henry, or so I thought at first. Then I saw him. He was standing in an alcove in one of the bookshelves, an alcove so deep it almost hid him. If he had kept the figure of his earlier years it would indeed have done so.

"So you have come at last, Alice Petherton," the King said.

What did he mean by this? Was I supposed to come to him the week before, after our meeting in the garden? Had I been expected to come to him without his command?

"I came as immediately as I was summoned," I said.

"We sent our Page to you some while ago," he said. "Your King is surprised he has been kept waiting."

"It is a goodly way from my chamber, Your Majesty," I said. "And it took me a while to find my book of verse."

"It took you a while?" He held out his hand for the volume. "I assumed it would be your constant companion."

"I read many books, Your Majesty."

I paused, wondering whether to risk saying what was in my thoughts. I took a deep breath. "And besides, I had to wash myself."

He stared at me, his eyes suddenly hard. "You kept your monarch waiting while you washed yourself?"

He walked away from the alcove and flung himself into one of the chairs by the fire. I bit my lip, aware that tears were forming in my eyes.

The King saw this and his eyes flickered with amusement.

"The King is glad of it," he said at last. "He applauds you for it. Cleanliness is something the King takes very seriously."

He gestured towards the other chair. "Sit, Alice Petherton, and tell me which of Sir Thomas Wyatt's poems you best like."

I sat down but for a moment could not find my tongue. I found my body shaking as if with ague and my wits appeared to have quite deserted me. How would I answer him now?

The King appeared not to have noticed my confusion; he flicked swiftly through the book, barely pausing at any page.

"We did not know Sir Thomas had made a book of his poems," he said.

My tongue was suddenly released. "He did not have it made, Your Majesty. His friend took a fancy to have some of his verses printed. The book contains a dozen or so, I believe."

"Then how have you to come by such a precious jewel, Alice Petherton?"

"Sir Thomas's friend is second cousin of my mother, Your Majesty. We knew each other a little as children, and we have renewed our acquaintance since we both came to Court."

"Ah, Elizabeth Darrel," the King said. "She is pretty, is she not?"

"I believe she is, Your Majesty."

"Beauty appears to run in the family, wouldn't you say?" His eyes lifted from the book and examined me.

"I don't know what to say, Majesty."

"Come, Alice Petherton, no girlish wiles with us. You know full well you have a good face and figure."

"No man has told me so, Your Majesty," I said. "Until today."

He put his finger to his bottom lip and began to tap it gently. He appeared amused by my words and I thought for a moment he would respond with some quip or comment. But instead he returned to his perusal of the book.

"Let us read together, Alice Petherton," he said at last. "For that is the reason I have summoned you here."

With one hand he lifted the table between the two chairs. He balanced it in the air for a moment, as if he were some acrobat showing me his skill, then dropped it on the floor. I jumped at the sound but jumped even more at what he did next. He leaned towards me, lifted both chair and me and placed me closer to him. I gasped in astonishment.

He laughed when he saw my reaction. "You seem surprised by my strength," he said. "Are you?"

"I am, Your Majesty," I said. My hand went to my mouth.

He laughed once again and patted me on the knee. "I am a man of great strength and great zeal," he said. "You will learn this over time."

He opened the book of poems in the middle. His thick finger jabbed at a page, as if he were a merchant pointing out some piece of cloth on a stall. "Here, Alice Petherton, let us read this poem together."

I glanced down at it and began to read it along with the King. He read in a voice not quite as deep as his normal speech, with a surprising lightness of tone, almost as if he were singing.

> "'They flee from me that sometime did me seek
> With naked foot stalking in my chamber.
> I have seen them gentle, tame, and meek
> That now are wild and do not remember
> That sometime they put themselves in danger
> To take bread at my hand; and now they range
> Busily seeking with a continual change.'"

He paused and glanced at my face. "We like this, Alice Petherton; we like this greatly. And how do you like it?"

I blushed under his fierce scrutiny. "I like it very much as well," I said.

He nodded thoughtfully and then turned his face from me.

"And yet," he said.

I swallowed nervously.

"And yet," he continued, "I like not the thought that lovers can be so cruel as to turn from the hand that feeds them."

He turned towards me, his eyes suddenly sharp and fierce like those of a cat readying itself to catch a bird or mouse. I knew that I could not, must not, dare not argue with him.

But I mustn't give way too soon. That would be fatal. Twenty seconds I must disagree with him, to prove myself not overawed. Fifteen seconds, ten.

"I do not see it that way, Your Majesty," I said, forcing my voice to sound strong.

He looked surprised. It must have been a long time since anyone had dared to contradict him. Perhaps Anne Boleyn had been the last.

"Continue," he said. His voice was cold.

"A lover who is tame is not one to relish," I said. "Far better to have a woman so wild the hunter must hunt for her again and again."

He crossed his arms and regarded me.

"And yet," I said, putting a thoughtful tone to my voice, "I see now what Your Majesty means."

I paused to make certain he had heard me. I felt him watch me as I pretended to gather my thoughts.

"Forgive me for not understanding the words earlier," I continued. "A woman who refuses love from her master is foolish."

I bit my lips.

He nodded his head, very slightly, very slowly.

"I think you are right with both your observations, Alice Petherton," he said at last. He snapped the volume shut. "We will read more. Tomorrow evening. Come to my Study at seven."

He waved his hand to dismiss me. I reached out to take the book.

"Leave this with me," he commanded.

I curtsied and fled the room.

Chapter Six

Envy

I stumbled along the corridor until I turned into the Gallery. I could barely see where I was going. My head was whirling, my thoughts confused.

My mind went back to our conversation. Had I been right to argue against the King, even for the little time that I did?

My head said that I was right, for I must prove to him that I could think for myself and not fall down in some cowardly swoon at his merest frown of displeasure.

But had I argued too long?

And then to talk so foolishly of dead lovers. At best it would have reminded him of Anne Boleyn. At worst the thought I had implanted in his mind might prove father to a future child, might link love and death and me in an embrace that would prove fatal.

I shuddered. Could a girl such as me tend a furnace like the King without being consumed? Perhaps I would have been wiser to deal with Rich's attentions myself when he returned to Court.

I walked back to my chamber and spent a sleepless night, my mind ridden by hags and demons.

The next morning I breakfasted early, for the sleepless night had made me unusually hungry. It was a cold, damp morning. The storm of last night had come and gone but it left behind a dank, drizzly day, which gloomed over the Palace. I wanted to go for a walk to clear my head but the weather looked altogether too wretched to venture forth.

I repaired to the Queen's Ladies' bower at eight. Normally it was fairly quiet at this hour with only one or two of my companions here at most. But today there were half a dozen of them.

I bade them good morning and wondered at the lack of reply. I soon realized why. The Ladies were grouped in a crescent watching the entrance to the room. Philippa Wicks was at the center of the half circle, her bodkin stabbing through her needlework with force and spite.

As soon as she saw me she put down her work and stared at me with wondering eyes.

"Well, look who has deigned to show herself this morning," she said.

I smiled as if not aware of what she meant.

"And look," Wicks continued, "she smiles, content and smug, like a cat that has swallowed its fill of rich cream."

"I do not smile so," I said. "I smile only with pleasure at seeing you, Philippa."

Her eyes narrowed. And she had the gall to call *me* a cat.

"How is His Majesty this morning?" she asked. "We hope he has risen with joy and vigor."

I placed my hand against my breast and feigned bemusement. "I cannot say, in truth." I glanced around. "Are you telling me that the King has been in our quarters this morning? Have you seen him at this early hour, Philippa Wicks?"

One or two of the other Maids giggled at my words but Wicks silenced them with a look.

"You know of what I speak, Alice Petherton," she continued. "The last we saw of you was when you raced away in summons to the King's Chamber. And with the Queen close to her time at that. A common harlot would have more consideration of her mistress." She paused. "But I am mistaken, of course. A common harlot would have most regard for her master. Would she not, Alice Petherton?"

My heart grew icy at her words. "I know nothing of common harlots," I said. "I bow to your superior knowledge of them."

I pointedly looked from her face to her lap.

Her face grew hard and pale. When she spoke again it was in a voice like a saw made blunt from overuse.

"I know you, Alice Petherton. I know well young girls like you—"

"I protest," I interrupted. "I like not ladies in that manner. I am not schooled in it." Mary Zouche held her work up to her face, trying her best to hide her amusement. Wicks gave her an angry glance before addressing me once again.

"A pert miss you have become, Alice Petherton. You think, no doubt, that when the sun shines full upon your form you can frolic and flaunt yourself with impunity. But you are watched, Mistress Petherton, and you are not the first of your ilk to be watched by me."

"Indeed," I answered. "And who have you watched before you began to trouble your mind with me?"

"Bigger and grander fish than you, little girl. Aye, one that believed herself untouchable until she was filleted on the fishmonger's block."

My stomach grew cold at her words but I gave a little laugh. "Don't tell me you have a relative who makes filleting blades, Philippa Wicks. One who hails from France, perchance."

A fearful silence descended upon the chamber. All in the chamber knew that Anne Boleyn had been terrified of the blunt English axe, and the King, in one last indulgence of her, had sent for a swordsman from France to dispatch her.

"I fear contact with one who has so charmed the mighty," she said at last.

I frowned at her words, wondering what they might portend.

She turned to the other Ladies.

"It is not safe for us to hold conversation with one who basks so warmly in the sun but tomorrow may be burned to cinders by it." She stood and started to walk towards the door. "Come, ladies," she called. "The air grows sick and noisome in here."

The rest of the group rose to their feet, as obedient as hounds, and followed her out of the room without a glance at me.

Only Mary remained. She glanced at me but her face gave away nothing of her feelings.

I stared back at her, my face set and cold, although inwardly I wanted to weep with hurt and anguish.

And then I calmed myself. Philippa would certainly take the news of the King's interest to Richard Rich. Losing the friendship of some of the Maids was a price well worth paying for that.

Chapter Seven

The King and His Groom

"What is the King to do? Tell us, if you will, Gregory. What is the King to do? The girl is pretty. There is no denying that. Winsome. A lithe body: slim, taut as a bow and firm, very firm. Long legs, goodly buttocks. Small breasts, like little apples. We imagined their firmness this morning, their softness, their malleability."

Gregory Frost said nothing but he appeared to be hanging upon the King's words, waiting with bated breath for him to continue.

"Her face is interesting. No, that does not do it justice. Her face is beguiling. It seemed to us to be an open book, a book which desired to be read. Yet at the same time much remained hidden in that face. Something seemed to call to us, Gregory, to call.

"Her hair is as fair as wheat in summer. She has a pale complexion yet, I dupe you not, her eyes are as dark as jet, rich as damsons. The contrast is quite remarkable. Soft eyes, sleepy eyes, eyes that watch. Eyes that watch even her King. She was not afraid to regard us in the garden last week or even yesterday in our Study. Oh, she was demure enough, we grant you. She played the innocent wench to perfection. But she watched us every bit as much as Master Cromwell does."

"The girl is little more than a child, Majesty," Gregory Frost said. "Perhaps she truly is innocent."

The King turned from the window and stared at Frost. It was a searching look, a dangerous look, and Frost swallowed hard.

Then the King gave an airy wave. "You may be right, Gregory. Perhaps she is innocent."

The King flung himself into a chair and his eyes sparkled. "But I hope you're wrong." He gave a huge laugh, a bellow, and slapped his leg.

Frost laughed with him, watching all the while to see the impression his own laughter made upon the King. Judging the right degree of amusement was a skill necessary for every servant of the King. Frost had the skill to the highest degree.

"We would know this girl better, Gregory," the King said. "She intrigues us."

He regarded Frost through narrowed eyes. "No one else need know, of course."

Frost bowed in answer.

Chapter Eight

Luncheon and Labor

9 October 1537

"You wished to see me, Your Majesty?"

The King nodded without looking up from the document he was perusing. The room was quiet although I could hear the mumbled words of a service drifting up from the Chapel below.

The King picked up a quill, jabbed it into an inkwell and scribbled his signature upon the scroll before flinging it towards the waiting clerk. The man bent and retrieved it and the King dismissed him with a wave of his hand.

He glanced up at me, his eyes shrewd and appraising.

"You look tired, Alice Petherton."

"I did not sleep well, Your Majesty."

"A young girl, not sleeping well. That will not do at all. Young girls should live life as untroubled as a foal, happy merely to be alive and to enjoy all that life has to offer them."

"That is normally the case with me, Your Majesty."

"But not last night?"

"Not last night."

He picked up a goblet, a golden goblet studded with gems. "Why might that be, do you think, Alice Petherton?"

"I know not, Your Majesty. Maybe it was because of our conversation concerning poetry."

"I thought we talked more of love than of poetry." He saw my confusion and smiled in what I took to be good humor.

"Poetry and love are said to be but two sides of the same coin," I answered.

"Are they indeed? And who said that, pray?"

"I did, Your Majesty."

The King shot a look of surprise at me. Then his head went back and he laughed aloud.

"You did?" he cried. "Not content with reading poetry and disputing with your King, you make up aphorisms. What a girl you are, Alice."

I curtsied and smiled. But I noticed that he mentioned I had disputed with him. My heart fluttered nervous as a chaffinch.

He leaned back in his chair, put his hands behind his head and regarded me. I had seen men fencing for sport and pleasure and often wondered what it must be like to be on guard, to watch your foe, to stab and parry. Now, at last, I knew how it felt.

"I have spent the morning reading a library of documents," he said. "I am wearied with affairs of state."

"Your duties must sometimes be onerous, Your Majesty."

"They are, Alice. And I fret about the Queen. She is close to giving birth to my son."

I gave a sympathetic look. "Her Ladies constantly offer up prayers for her and for the child."

"I am glad of it." He brushed his fingers through his hair and sighed. "I have two daughters, Alice, but I need a boy."

"Your daughters must be a joy to you."

He shook his head as if he were exhausted. "Mary gives me no joy. She is dark with shuttered eyes." He leaned forward. "Do you know I never see her walking anywhere. One moment she is nowhere to be seen and the next she appears. Usually in some shadowed corner of a room. But I never see her walking into the room." He frowned, obviously troubled by the memory.

I nodded, not knowing how to answer.

"And the Lady Elizabeth?" I asked at last.

He gave a sharp laugh. "She is just four years of age but she is already a little menace. She knows her mind well enough. Too well perhaps. Like her mother. She will be headstrong and the sooner I marry her off the better."

"I am sure she will make a good wife to the right man," I said.

He nodded and hummed in agreement although I thought that he had some doubts about the matter.

His lips grew thin, his face troubled. "I fear the Queen is not strong."

He tapped upon the table, a slow rhythm.

"Her doctors are good, of course, the best in the Kingdom. But I fear she is not strong."

I watched him as he stared far away without seeing the things of this world. And after a little time I felt a new emotion surge in my breast. I felt pity for him. Pity for the King.

He glanced over suddenly as if he sensed what I was feeling and, like me, was astonished by it.

"Did you know the Duke of Richmond and Somerset?" he asked quietly. "My son, Henry FitzRoy?" A look of pain flickered upon his face the moment he asked it.

"I met him once, Majesty," I said.

He sighed and walked over to the window, staring out, his hands clasped firmly behind him as if to control them and stop them working of their own volition. "What did you think of my son?" he asked softly.

I swallowed. I did not think anything of him, for he had made little impression upon me. I knew more about his mother, Bessie Blount, who had managed to stay the King's mistress for fifteen years without incurring his wrath, no mean accomplishment. She certainly had more about her than their son had. I searched my mind for an answer that would please the King.

"I thought he was a young man of great potential, Your Majesty," I said. "He had the bearing and manner of the greatest of lords." I struggled in my mind to recall anything more about the King's young bastard, anything that I could plausibly say about him.

The King nodded sorrowfully. "He was taken from me when he was only seventeen," he said. "Younger than you are now."

"It was a tragedy, Your Majesty."

He turned suddenly, his face alight with interest. "It was a tragedy, wasn't it, Alice? For me, for my Court and for the Kingdom. I sometimes thought he had the look and manner of my brother. Arthur was taken from us at the same age." His eyes grew moist and he licked his lips as if they had grown dry.

He returned to his chair, cradled his hands and rested his chin upon them. "Of course, if Arthur had lived, I would not be King. And you would not be here with me, Alice Petherton." He grinned widely now, all sense of sorrow gone.

"Indeed, Majesty. And I would be the poorer for it."

The King smiled. "And so might I, Alice, so might I."

He passed a book to me, my book of poems.

"I read some of the poems last night," he said, "after you left for your chamber. Now I would have you read to me, for my pleasure."

I had not expected such a test. With trembling fingers I opened the volume at the first poem. I began to read but my throat caught and I had to cough to clear it. I apologized and began again. The King seemed barely to have noticed. He put his hands behind his head once more and leaned back, hearkening to my words as if in a trance.

I had to read all of the poems. It took a good long while and as I read the final ones my mouth grew dry and my wits became addled. I read the last verses without true meaning or accurate delivery but this did not seem to concern the King. When I finished I placed the book upon the table, so tired of it I swore never to look at another of Wyatt's poems again.

The King gave a contented sigh. "You read well, Alice; you have quite beguiled me. The last few verses I thought were strained but perhaps you have grown tired."

"Not at all, Your Majesty."

"I think you have," he answered swiftly. "And did you not tell me that you did not sleep well last night?"

I swallowed, caught out in my falsehood. "That's true, Your Majesty."

He nodded, his face grown serious. "Allow me to know what's best for you, child. I am your King, am I not?"

"You are, Majesty. And I am yours to command."

I gave him a long, thoughtful look. His face grew redder and I sensed an inward shiver at my words.

"You are correct, Alice, quite correct. I am the King and you are mine to command." His voice was thick and low.

For more than a week I spent part of every day in the company of the King. We spoke of poetry and of the history of his family and the Kingdom. He asked me if I could play an instrument and I told him I could not, but I was learning from my friend Mary Zouche. I informed him I could read music, though, and was said to have a pleasant singing voice. He had me sing some songs he had written in his youth. They were good songs and I was quick to learn the words by heart. He was pleased by this, flattered.

On the eleventh of October I was with the King in his Dining Chamber. I had dined with him only once before and that had been a light luncheon of broiled chicken and sweet cakes. Today was a rather grander affair. The table had been set with silver plates and fine Venetian glassware. I sat opposite the King while Page after Page brought in silver tureens, covered to keep the food hot. I grew nervous, wondering who was to join us. When everything had been brought to the table, I counted a dozen different tureens. The Pages lifted off the covers, bowed and left the room.

Each tureen contained a different dish. A roast fowl in one, a stew of eels in a second, thick slices of pork, a turbot, a brace of pheasants, stewed cabbage, some pink lamb chops, a dish of white beans, a pie oozing rich brown juice, young rabbits, turnips and a lobster.

The King tore a huge lump of bread from a loaf and began to work his way through the tureens. He offered me the choicest pieces; some I accepted gladly, some I declined. I began to wonder when the King's other guests would join us.

"Here, Alice,'" the King said, carving a slice from one of the rabbits and placing it on my plate. "This is quite delicious." He tore a little piece of it and fed it to me, wiping the juice from my mouth with the utmost delicacy. A tiny shiver ran through me at his touch.

He returned his attention to his own plate and continued to chew and chomp, talking all the while about an audience he had just given to the French ambassador. At that point I realized that no other guests were coming and that the King was going to steadily work his way through every dish.

At the end of the meal he belched with loud satisfaction, groaned a moment and then gave a contented sigh. Most of the food on the table had disappeared.

"Will you walk with me in the garden?" he said. "A good meal and a spot of exercise are the mother and father of good health."

"Of course I will walk with you, Your Majesty. I will be honored to do so." In truth I greatly desired to leave the King's Dining Room. The table looked like a battlefield; carnage everywhere.

He pushed himself to his feet, belched again and plucked up a goblet of wine, which he emptied in one swallow.

I rose and stood aside, giving a slight curtsy, not too low for fear of hurting my overfull stomach. The last thing I felt like was a walk. I would much rather have sought out a couch to collapse upon. At that moment there came a knock upon the door and one of the King's retainers peered in.

"Come, Gregory," the King said.

The man entered the room, planting his feet carefully as if fearful of stepping in the wrong place. He was in his forties by the look of him, clean-shaven and with curling hair, his face long and with a chin like a shovel. His nose was also long and seemed to be designed to sniff ahead of him, compensating, perhaps, for his small, crossed eyes that seemed to be insufficient for their purpose. He was tall and thin with skinny legs which did not look as though they would readily bear his weight. He had the look of a heron.

"This is Gregory Frost, my groom," the King said to me.

I bowed slightly.

"This is Alice Petherton, Gregory."

Frost smiled bleakly and gave an exaggerated bow. "The lady who loves poetry," he said, inclining his head to one side as if to get a better view of me.

He knows about me, I thought, my mind racing. And if he knew, how many others did as well? I wondered what the King had said about me. And what this fawning groom believed.

"I have momentous news, Your Majesty," he said.

The King blinked and stared at him.

"The Queen is in labor. The physicians and midwives are in attendance."

The King stared at the ground a moment, then crossed his arms across his chest. It looked to me as if he were trying to calm his heart.

"Is the Queen well?" he asked in a low tone.

Frost did not answer for a moment but glanced at me. His face composed itself to a more sanguine look.

"She is very well," he said. "One of the midwives said the Queen is joyous at the thought of bringing your son into the world."

"It is a son, then, Gregory? It is a son?"

Frost's pale tongue flickered out and wet his lips. He had said too much and now his eyes goggled. He was presumably thinking what to say to redeem his unwise choice of words.

"The doctors have told me, Your Majesty, that it is still too early to tell."

The King laughed and punched Frost on the shoulder, forcing him to reel back a pace and nearly lose his footing.

"Of course it is too early to tell," he said. "What are you thinking, Frost? Are you seeking a new post as my jester?"

He turned to me and smiled. "The fool thinks he can tell whether my child is a girl or a boy when the Queen has only just gone into labor. Angels save me from foolish servants."

Frost bore a sickly grin upon his face. I could barely hide my smile. He saw this and gave me a sour look.

I thought better of making him an enemy and, while the King was distracted, I adopted an expression which might have been construed as resembling sympathy and solidarity. It worked; the sourness faded from Frost's face. Nevertheless, the smile he dealt out was as cold as his name. He turned once more towards the King, who was busy at a mirror, examining himself with care.

"When will the baby arrive, Frost?" the King asked. "Though why I am asking you, heaven only knows. I would be wiser to seek out a milkmaid in the scullery and ask her."

Frost laughed as if he were thrilled at the King's sharp wit. "I am told it will be a long labor, Sire."

"How long? Two hours, three?"

The groom held out his hands, opening them wide like a priest who wishes to signify the mystery of God.

"I must go to the Queen," the King said. "Now, while her labor is just beginning."

He hurried from the room. Frost hurried after him but paused upon the threshold and glanced back at me. "You are dismissed," he said. "Go back to where you came from."

According to the whispers the Queen's labor was proving a long and difficult one. I wasn't surprised. Spontaneity was not something she valued, certainly not something she would have condoned. I wondered what King Henry saw in her. But it is said that often the most simpering of women are like tigers when they climb into bed.

Of course, I did not know about lovemaking, apart from in theory. Although seventeen years of age and with undoubted good looks, I was still a virgin. I did not yet know whether I would prove a tiger or a turtle between the bedsheets.

I walked across to the little table in my bedroom and picked up my mirror. The reflection staring back at me was indeed pretty and engaging. I was not fool enough or proud enough to pretend otherwise. My looks had been given to me as a gift. There was nothing I could do about this, nothing I could be proud of either. It was a fact of my existence as much as that I was a woman and that my name was Alice Petherton.

I held the mirror closer to my face, examining it for any fault or blemish. I could find none. My skin was clear, my hair shone like blossom in Maytime, my chin well made, fine and dainty. I peered into my eyes. They were dark, as dark as the damsons that King Henry had likened them to. A little smile of self-satisfaction crept over my lips.

That self-satisfaction was soon banished. I felt the presence before I saw it. My heart clenched. Philippa Wicks and Dorothy Bray stood in the doorway of my chamber.

"Preening yourself, Alice?" Philippa said. Her voice was charged with contempt.

"Looking for blemishes, rather," I said.

Dorothy Bray smiled at the thought.

"I found none," I added.

"Then you have not looked enough," cried Wicks, hastening into my room. She grabbed the mirror from my grasp and pushed it close to my face, bending back my nose. I tried to pull away but Bray had leapt in behind her leader and held my head fast in her fishwife paws.

"You're hurting me," I cried.

"What are you going to do about it?" Bray's voice came hot in my ear. "Go running to the King?"

"Little will any complaint avail you," said Wicks. "He has other things to occupy his mind, like a new Prince."

I pretended to look surprised. "He has a son? I thought the Queen was still working on the issue."

I felt a sharp slap upon my face. "Impertinence," Wicks cried. "Hold your tongue or you'll get worse."

The slap gave me renewed vigor and I managed to shrug off Bray's hold and knock away the mirror. No doubt the knock was hard but Wicks allowed the mirror to fly from her hand and smash against the floor. It shattered into a thousand pieces. She put her hand upon her hip and gloated.

"Now what will you preen yourself in?" she said.

I stared aghast at the broken mirror.

"That belonged to my Grandmother," I said. "She died last year."

"Then she won't be needing it," said Bray with a smirk.

I turned to her, seething with cold fury. "How dare you," I said. I was surprised to hear that, despite my rage, my voice remained calm and low. "How dare you speak of my Grandmother in that fashion? At least I know who my Grandmother was, something which you cannot boast, Dorothy Bray."

Bray's face grew red. It was rumored that her mother had been born illegitimate.

I turned to Wicks, sensing that the advantage now lay with me. "And what do you have to say?" I whispered. "Do you wish to join your crony in speaking ill of my poor dead Grandmother?"

She did not reply but her lips moved soundlessly trying to frame some answer which would hurt me yet not make her look as despicable as her friend.

I spoke before she had chance to. "If you have nothing to say to me you may leave my chamber. I do not recall inviting you in."

Wicks turned on her heel and stormed out, followed by the red-faced Bray.

I sat on my bed, drained and empty. I thought I had achieved a victory although it did not really feel like one.

Chapter Nine

An Heir Is Born

12 October 1537

I was woken in the dark of the night by people yelling and bells clanging. I gasped and reached for my clothes. It must have been a fire; nothing else could cause such alarm.

I struggled into my gown, too anxious to seek for a flint to light a candle.

Swift footsteps echoed outside and then the door crashed open.

"Alice?" came a voice.

"Is that you, Lucy?"

"Yes." I heard the rustle of clothes and then a warm body flung itself into my arms. Lucy Burton was only fifteen years of age and now she seemed even younger.

"What's happening, Alice?" she asked. "Is it the French? Have they stormed the Palace?"

"Don't be so foolish," I said. "I think it may be a fire."

"Then we shall be burned alive." Lucy gasped. "Quickly, we must fly."

I squeezed her arm to give her courage.

"Hush, Lucy, do not fear. I'll look after you."

A moment later Susan hurried into the room. She held a candle in her hand; it was just like her to have thought of lighting one. She had dressed as swiftly as I had, for her clothes were all awry. But her face was bright with excitement.

"I think it might be the French," Lucy said, "though Alice thinks it is a fire."

"I'd rather it was the French than a fire," Susan said. "Think about those handsome soldiers."

I glanced along the corridor and saw a light to my left. It was moving in the air, up and down, up and down, and getting closer all the time.

"Arise, arise," shouted a voice. "A son is born; a son is born."

Susan and I exchanged glances. Queen Jane had been in labor now for three days and two nights. We had begun to think that the child would not be brought alive into the world.

The light grew larger and I saw that it was a torch held aloft by one of the King's servants.

"A son is born," he cried as he reached us. "Arise, arise and celebrate. The King has a son, an heir."

He pushed a candle into my hand.

"Go to the Chapel to pray for the babe," he said. He hurried on his way, chanting at the top of his voice while bells rang out in wild exultation.

"The Kingdom is saved," Lucy said. "The King has an heir."

"Let us pray the boy lives," I said. "Only his daughters seem intent on surviving."

"His bastard, FitzRoy, survived until a youth," Susan said.

"The Kingdom needs more than a bastard youth who expires at seventeen," I said. I regretted saying these words the moment they left my mouth. Fortunately, nobody seemed to have heard.

"It's a miracle Jane Seymour has produced a son," Susan said. "She is dry and bitter as a quince."

"Susan Dunster!" I exclaimed in a shocked tone. "How can you say such a thing?" Then I giggled and pinched her arm playfully.

"I say what every one of us is thinking," she said. "You included." She paused. "How do you think the King will react?"

"How should I know?"

Susan touched me upon the arm. "You know why I think this, Alice."

I sighed. "The King and I discuss poetry and music, nothing more."

"Then that little is far more than any other lady of the Court," she said. "Your conduct is whispered of, Alice, and not just by the Queen's Ladies. And why does the King wish to discuss poetry with you, I wonder? He could discuss such matters with any number of poets and scholars. If you continue to see him then people will begin to whisper."

"I cannot help it if people like to think the worst," I said. "I only obey his Majesty's commands."

"And that is what the gossip will be about, Alice. What exactly are his commands?"

I held her hands in mine. "I tell you truth, Susan. We read only poetry and discuss things of the mind. Nothing more."

In the flickering light of the candle I saw her smile. If I could not convince my friend, how could I hope to convince my enemies? Lucy, sweet thing, looked puzzled by our conversation.

I put my arms through theirs. "Come, we must away to the Chapel. It will not do if we arrive late."

The Chapel was freezing cold. The service went on for an hour and was tedious beyond recounting. I sighed with relief when it ended and I could make my way back to my bedroom.

Mary and Susan walked with me. I had always considered them to be my best friends. Now I counted them as my only ones. Since I had been summoned to see the King I had become an outcast amongst the

Queen's Ladies. This was not due to loyalty to the Queen, believe you me. It was due to jealousy of my intimacy with the King.

We walked in silence through the corridors. I glanced out of the window. It was still dark night. The dawn would not arrive for a few hours yet.

"Let's get some rest," Susan said as we left her at her chamber. "Tomorrow will no doubt tax our strength."

"Tomorrow is today," I said. "It will be dawn sooner than we hope. But you're sensible, Susan. We must get what sleep we can."

My hopes for rest proved illusory. I lay in my bed but could not sleep. Thoughts whirled around my head like cats chased by hounds. What would the birth of the King's son mean for me? What would the return of the Queen to full health and to the King's bed? How might I fare when Sir Richard Rich decided to come snooping round once more?

I rose with the dawn and washed myself thoroughly. I chose my second-best gown and dressed myself with greater than usual care. I would not let the likes of Wicks and Bray see that I alone of all the Palace did not celebrate the joyous news of the birth of an heir.

A servant hurried along the corridor crying out that we were to attend on the King in the Great Hall within the hour. Mary and Susan joined me at the top of the staircase and we hurried down to the chamber close to the Kitchen, where we dined. I normally ate little breakfast but today, despite the excitement fluttering in my stomach, my long hours awake had piqued my appetite. I ate two white rolls with butter and conserve and drank a cup of watered-down ale. The kitchen staff brought out some saffron cakes, hot from the oven and smelling enticing. I could not resist and ate one of these as well.

And then the rumors started. The Queen had not had a successful labor and the surgeon had been forced to cut the child from her.

I turned to my friends at this news. "Then Jane is dead, or dying," I said. No surgeon would perform a Cesarean until the mother was close to death or had passed beyond it. My hand went to my stomach. Poor woman. I may not have wanted her to return to the King's bed, yet I still hoped that the whispers were false.

Arm in arm with Mary and Susan, I joined the throng of people making their way to the Great Hall. When we got there we found dozens of the Lord Steward's officers, with the Master of the Household huffing and puffing around them to make sure they performed his orders exactly.

We were asked our names and positions at Court and one of the officers led us to the place designated for us. Most of the Queen's Ladies were there and the rest joined us within ten or so minutes. I made sure that I kept away from Wicks and Bray.

The whole Hall was crowded with other senior servants and courtiers.

We stood there for what must have been an hour while the spaces behind us filled up with those who held lesser offices than ours. A space had been left unfilled, a central corridor dividing the crowd in two.

Suddenly trumpets blared around the Hall. The noise was deafening and all the Ladies put their hands to their ears. The trumpets called on and on and on so that I wondered what sort of monstrous lungs the trumpeters must possess. My head began to spin at the clamor.

Then a great gasp swept across the throng.

I craned my head and saw him.

King Henry stood at the front of the Hall, a tiny baby held high above his head. The King began to walk down the central corridor with slow and measured tread, pausing at each group of courtiers to show the child to them. As he did so each group began to applaud with great enthusiasm. A few called out with joy, but the Steward's officers frowned at such loud demonstrations. Presumably they were fearful for the infant's tiny ears.

The King came close to us. Knowing that we were the Queen's Ladies he did more than merely pause as he had with the other courtiers. He stopped and moved right up to us, holding the baby so close we could have reached out and touched him. A cooing came from our throats, as though we were creatures of a Dovecote and not young women of the Household. The King smiled, delighted at our response.

He turned and continued his progress down the Hall, the applause rippling alongside him and his son like waves breaking upon the shore.

He had not looked at me at all.

It was the afternoon of the birth of the future King. After the midday dinner I, along with most of the Queen's Ladies, had retired to our bedchambers. It had been a long and exhilarating day and we were all exhausted and emotionally drained.

I immediately fell into a deep sleep. I woke once and recalled a dream of white swans upon a rippling pond before falling straight back into unconsciousness.

A loud rapping upon my door awoke me.

"Who is it?" I called.

"Humphrey the Page," called a familiar voice. "You are summoned by the King."

I rose at once, confused that the day was waning and the evening coming on. I washed swiftly, dressed myself and glanced around for a book of poems. The King and I had been reading a variety of works over the last few days and a number of volumes were scattered about the room. The King, no doubt, would be weary and would require entertaining.

I hurried down the staircase and along the corridors. The route had become familiar to me, but when I'd found out the Queen had given birth this morning I thought I might never take it again.

I paused outside the King's Study, took a deep breath and knocked on the door.

I stood with my fingers resting on the handle, waiting for his usual command to enter. To my surprise no voice sounded. Instead the door opened to reveal the King, standing in the doorframe. I was astonished that he had opened the door himself. He was wearing hose but not a doublet and his shirt was open at the neck.

He nodded at me and stepped back into the room, beckoning me to follow. I entered, shut the door behind me and approached him.

He took the book from my hand, flung it on a chair and smiled.

"I have an heir, Alice," he said. "I wish to celebrate."

He took my hand and led me towards a door in the corner of the Study. We walked into a second chamber. It was the King's Bedroom. My heart began to hammer.

In the center of the room stood a large bed. Plump, soft pillows were piled high upon it. A red cloth emblazoned with the Arms of England had been pulled back to reveal smooth white sheets.

The King gestured me closer.

"Slip off your clothes, Alice," he said quietly.

I gulped and hastened to do as he commanded. My fingers became clumsy, as useless as raw sausages. I struggled to undo my fastenings and cursed myself for my slowness. I glanced up at the King and saw that my delay, instead of angering him, was actually exciting him. His face shone and his eyes watched my every movement with hungry intensity.

I slowed down a little while his eyes feasted upon me. Finally I stood in only my chemise. I lowered my eyes and allowed it to slip to the floor. I stepped out of it as naked as if about to take a bath. I knew I had a fine body and I stood tall in order to show myself off the better.

"You are beautiful, Alice Petherton," the King said. His voice was heavy with lust. "The King is well pleased with you."

He indicated I was to get into the bed and immediately climbed in after me.

I touched him softly on his arm and gazed up into his eyes.

"I am a virgin, Majesty," I said. "Forgive me, but I do not know the ways of love."

He grinned with pleasure. I could have said nothing more exciting to his ears.

"Then I shall teach you, Alice Petherton," he said. "And our love-making will celebrate the birth of my son with greater enthusiasm than the ringing of all the bells in the Kingdom."

He pressed his lips on mine and I felt his hot tongue push into my mouth. His breath smelled of egg and onions. His tongue licked around my mouth as though he were tasting a dish of custard.

I must confess that this first experience of lovemaking was more painful than exhilarating. In addition to the pang of the piercing of my maidenhead, I felt borne down by the weight of the King. I came to realize later that he was more enthusiastic a lover than a skillful one. Although he was politeness itself, his only real concern was to take his own pleasure.

But gone was the firm voice of command. He enquired solicitously if he could do certain things to me and rather less solicitously if I would do other things to him. I felt bemused by all the acrobatics and contrivances but did my uttermost to be obliging. At last he gave a deep-seated gasp and collapsed upon me. The breath was thrust from out my body so that I gave an almighty gasp myself.

"Aha," he said. "I see I have satisfied you greatly, Alice Petherton. That is unusual in a young virgin."

Not satisfied, I thought. *Nearly suffocated.*

But I smiled with what I hoped looked like gratitude and prayed to heaven that he would heave himself off me before I expired.

He did, withdrawing from me so swiftly that I winced. He smiled again, taking this for yet another demonstration of my pleasure.

"I feel honored, Your Majesty." I gasped. "Honored and exalted."

The King heaved a sigh. Then I swear he almost purred, like a cat being scratched behind its ears.

"I also feel honored," he said. "You have chosen to give to Your King the greatest gift a woman has to offer."

There was no choice about it, I thought. *No choice at all.* But I smiled once more and fluttered my eyelids. "Your Majesty is more than kind," I murmured.

"Come now," he said. "We have been intimate. I want no more of your calling me 'Your Majesty.'" He clutched my hand and brought it to his lips, where he planted a surprisingly gentle kiss upon my fingers.

"From now on," he continued, "you may call me Your Grace or Your Highness. Even in Court."

Then he fell silent and his eyes moved swiftly from side to side. "Except when the Queen is present," he said. "Then I shall require you to call me Your Majesty."

I thought for a moment of the whispers about the child being cut from her. But as the King did not seem the slightest bit concerned I dismissed the gossip from mind.

"Yes, Your Majesty," I said. Then I smiled and held my fingers to my lips. "Yes, Your Grace."

He squeezed my cheek playfully. "The language of lovers is a wondrous thing, Alice," he said. "A wondrous thing."

He leaned back on the pillows, putting his arms behind his head.

"We shall rest for a half hour," he said. "Then we shall continue to celebrate the birth of my son." He lifted his head from the pillow and stared at me.

"Did I say I was going to call him Edward?" he said.

"A marvelous name, for a marvelous child."

"How very true, Alice Petherton, how very true."

And pray to God His Grace hasn't planted another child in my womb, I thought.

Chapter Ten

Peril and Victory

12 October 1537

It was towards the end of the night that I closed the door to the King's Study behind me and slipped into the corridor. I had the good sense to pluck up my book of poetry, as if we had been engaged in our usual literary pursuits in his Study rather than the more energetic ones in his Bedroom.

The corridors were empty. I leaned against the wall and closed my eyes. My mind went back to when I was ten years old and had first ridden a pony. My thighs and buttocks had ached terribly then. They ached far more now. Even my ribs hurt, so heavy and vigorous was the King in his lovemaking. I rubbed my hand across my forehead. It was hot and clammy from so much exertion. The poets had not written of first love in this manner. Perhaps this was because they were men.

I took a deep breath and made my way towards my own chamber. My thoughts ran faster than my feet. I had turned onto a new path now, one which I doubted I could easily step off.

How wise had I been in all this? I had been prompted to seek the protection of the King from the attentions of Richard Rich. But there was more to it than just that. I had long wanted to advance myself in Court, wanted more for myself than my birth stars had given to me. But how much did I actually want? How far was I prepared to go?

I knew that getting close to the King in any manner was perilous. Becoming his lover might well prove deadly.

In truth, I would have preferred to spend our time reading poetry. But in my heart I knew that it had been a mere shadow play before the real game commenced. Now I was in the midst of this game and I barely knew the rules. Even if I had been conversant with them, I suspected the King would not abide by them, would assume that he could break and bend them with impunity. He did with everything else.

It was common knowledge that many men had grown wealthy by favor of the King. What was less well known, or kept hidden, was that many more had been beggared by him.

Every noble dreaded that the King would invite himself to stay at his home a few days; every gentleman feared a visit of only a few hours. For the King never journeyed anywhere alone. He traveled with much of his Court: servants, retainers, courtiers, Bishops and entertainers. Providing only one meal for this vast entourage would devastate most purses. A stay of two or more days would send even the wealthiest scurrying to the moneylenders or selling land or daughters to the highest bidder.

Some, the unlucky ones, had fallen like Icarus when they got too close to the sun. One day they were the apple of the King's eye, the next like cow dung in the field. These men became something the wise kept sharp watch for, to be shunned lest their new stench came to be associated with them. Some of the fallen men fell still further, of course, to the axman's block.

And for women? For young women without kin or connections? My mind went over the Ladies who had appeared high in the King's favor and those few who were rumored to have shared his bed. None, save Queen Anne Boleyn, had fallen to the sword. But once one woman had been forced across that dreadful line, what safety was there for others? The King executed his friends without a second thought. How long might it be before he did the same to any lover who displeased him?

I reached my room and shut the door behind me, leaning against it as if to block the outside world from entering. I lit a taper and went to pull back the coverlet. I stared at it in surprise. It was ruffled although I always smoothed it flat. I frowned, too tired to wonder further. Perhaps Susan and Mary had been waiting here for me. Yes, that would explain it.

I lay on the bed and pondered what had happened. And then I began to think about what might happen next, the consequences of what I had done. I would be safe from Richard Rich from now on. That at least was certain. I sighed with pleasure at this thought.

But then my mind returned to my earlier thoughts, about the dangers of becoming involved with the King. It seemed to me, though I could not quite pin down the reason why, that the most perilous course was to be Henry's Queen. It was said he had loved them passionately at first but when he began to think they thwarted him his passion turned to bitter wrath and desire for revenge. In which case it seemed likely that to be his mistress might well prove the next-most-dangerous position. It seemed he had grown fearful of anyone getting too close to him, of allowing them to see behind the mask of Kingship. A mistress might become far too close, might learn more than was safe for her to know. Better that I remain a casual lover who would pleasure him on occasion and rise a few steps higher in the Court because of this.

And this, of course, must be a secret kept from the world.

I went down to the Great Hall for breakfast and sat at the table. The Maids near me shuffled away so that a space grew between them and me. I glanced up. Philippa Wicks and Dorothy Bray did not try to hide the looks of triumph on their faces.

"Alice Petherton is here now, Dorothy," Wicks said. "After you had waited to no avail for her to appear in her room last night."

"I grew weary of waiting," Bray said with a shrug.

The other Maids turned to me, agog to see how I would respond to this. It was one thing to spend time with the King in the day, reading poetry. But to spend the night with him was to enter a whole new realm of scandal and tittle-tattle.

My first thought was to act contrary to my resolve of the night before. I would cry out: *Avoid me if you choose, do the worst that you dare, for I am the King's lover and am high in his favor.*

But immediately I thought better of it. For I knew that, were I to say this, I would be the King's harlot in their eyes and as such I would become vulnerable to their venom. Better, I thought, to practice haughty disdain and scorn them even more than they did me. Better to keep my own counsel.

"Perhaps you mistook my chamber for someone else's," I said to Dorothy. "You may have taken a little too much wine with your supper. It would not be the first time."

Bray looked furious but was apparently lost for words.

"This bread is delicious," I said.

My voice echoed in the silent Hall. None of the other Maids answered. Although they had shunned me before, this more blatant and public show of scorn wounded me. I feared to speak again for I felt my voice about to tremble and break. Yet I knew I must continue.

I took a sip of wine and a deeper breath. "The preserve, however, is tart. It is a shame to have things so tart and bitter at the King's Court."

I felt some of the Ladies flutter as my words hit home. A moment later a few nodded in agreement and one or two even muttered at the table.

I shot a glance at Wicks. The triumph in her face had changed to bile.

Susan appeared and glanced around. She pointedly took a seat beside me. I breathed a sigh of relief.

"What was that I heard?" she said brightly. "Is there something distasteful in the room?"

"The preserve," said Lucy Burton. She held up the dish of preserve nervously. "Alice said that it is tart and bitter."

"Then I shall take honey," Susan said. She glanced along the table. "Dorothy, my dear," she said to Bray, "please be so kind as to pass the sweet honey."

Bray paused for a moment, as if debating whether or not to ignore the request. With ill grace she passed the honey down the table.

"Thank you, my dear," Susan said, pretending not to notice Bray's bad humor.

She spread the honey lightly upon her bread and offered the dish to me.

"Do try the honey, Alice. Dorothy has taken the trouble to pass it to us. It is very sweet."

I took the dish and nodded courteously towards Bray. "Thank you so much, dear Dorothy," I said. "I appreciate your kindness. Such thoughtfulness will not go unnoticed."

Bray gave me a vicious look.

A sigh impalpable as a breeze fluttered through the room. A low murmur commenced as the Maids began to chatter quietly.

Philippa Wicks rose to her feet and fanned her hand in front of her nose.

"Come, Dorothy," she said. "It grows hot and unwholesome here. Let us go see how the Queen is faring today."

She swept out of the room without a backward glance, her creature Bray chasing to keep up with her.

One of the cooks brought out a platter of eggs soft scrambled and offered it around. I helped Susan and Lucy to some before spooning a goodly portion upon my own plate. I suddenly realized how hungry I felt. I had undergone fierce exercise this last night and needed much sustenance to restore myself.

After we had breakfasted we went into the Ladies' Sitting Room. It was empty save for Mary, who sat at the window looking at the river below.

"You were not at breakfast," Susan said to her. "Are you unwell?"

Mary smiled. "I'm quite well, thank you. I breakfasted early. I was summoned to the Queen's Chamber in the small hours."

"Is the child ailing?" Lucy asked.

"Not the child," Mary answered, shaking her head. "It is the Queen who is ailing."

Susan and I exchanged looks.

"How so?" Susan asked.

I felt the clammy hand of dread upon the small of my back.

"It was a long labor and a difficult birth," Mary said. "The Queen is exhausted and fretful."

"She sent for you in the night?" Susan said.

Mary nodded. "She wanted me to sing to her, to calm her and lull her to soft slumbers."

Mary had a voice as enchanting as a skylark's.

"And did it work?" Susan asked. "Did your songs conjure her to restfulness?"

Mary nodded. "She slept. I did not." She held her hand to her mouth to hide a yawn. "I must go to my bed shortly, if only for an hour or two."

Then she frowned. "You seem preoccupied. Is anything amiss? Alice, Susan?"

Susan turned to me.

"It was terrible," Lucy said. "Philippa and Dorothy hinted that Alice is doing more than just reading poetry with the King. And some of the other Maids are foolish enough to believe this. It's very cruel of them."

"Not so," I said. "These little storms and quarrels are commonplace at Court. You will grow used to it, Lucy. And, as you say, only two are at the heart of it."

Mary shrugged and stifled another yawn. "If Philippa and Dorothy paid more regard to their duties they would not have such time for mischief."

I hugged myself inwardly. Mary was proving a good friend indeed, and not just to Queen Jane.

Chapter Eleven

King Henry Cannot Help but Hint

12 October 1537

"You slept well, Your Majesty?" Gregory Frost asked.

The King grunted.

"I'm glad to hear it," Frost continued. "A rested King is a happy King."

Frost bent again to the King's left ear and applied the ear-stick to it. He burrowed deep within the ear to clean out the wax but was careful, very careful, not to cause his master any pain or discomfort. This was a twice-weekly ritual. It was one of the few personal duties which Frost could truthfully say he enjoyed. He imagined this was how the Court Painter, Master Holbein, must feel when he conjured the faces of lords and ladies upon the canvas. Painstaking, thoughtful and with the realization that, to a tiny extent, he had some real power and mastery over his patron and master. Just as Holbein had the power to make the King look exalted or grotesque, so he, Gregory Frost, had the power to make the King hear better or to deafen him for life.

Of course, were he to do the second, his own life would end in a spectacularly gruesome manner. It would not be wax which would be picked out of Frost's body; it would be his innards and his vital organs. He paused a moment in his work and regretted that the thought had ever entered his mind.

"I've nearly finished, Your Majesty," he said. He worked away for a few moments more and then stepped back, like a painter, to examine his handiwork.

"I've finished. Shall I get Your Majesty's breakfast now?"

"In a moment, Frost," the King said.

Frost watched as the King rose to his feet and leaned backward, stretching his spine in a most pointed fashion.

"We feel fatigued this morning, Frost," he said. "The fatigue of a huntsman who has ridden over hills and dales until he has cornered his quarry in a deep, dark vale."

He beamed at the groom. "Do we look fatigued?"

"Slightly, Your Majesty. Yet triumphant as well, as a skillful huntsman should."

"That is good. That is how it should be."

Frost looked up with bland expression. *He has slept with her,* he thought. *The young girl, Alice Petherton. That must be the reason for this latest nonsense. Huntsman indeed. Bombastic, conceited monster. Devourer of children. The poor sweet girl, what a trial she has ahead of her.*

"Bring my food," the King cried. "I am hungry this morning, hungrier than I usually am."

"Naturally, Majesty. Hard exercise is good for the digestion. And riding, so the physicians tell me, is the best exercise to prick the digestion."

He gave the King his blandest smile in order to intimate that he had no idea what the talk of huntsmen and riding meant. It was best if the King believed him to be a little ignorant and naive.

Chapter Twelve

Maids with No Honor

13 October 1537

"I hate the bitch," Dorothy Bray said. "I hate her more than I can say."

Philippa Wicks strode down the corridor, ignoring her friend's words, indeed barely hearing them. She was too engrossed in her own fretful thoughts, brooding that the situation she had set up with such care had come undone so swiftly and so spectacularly.

"Shut up, do," she snapped.

"I was only saying how I hate Alice Petherton," Dorothy said in an aggrieved tone. "I thought you hated her as well."

"I'm thinking," Philippa said. "Be silent while I think."

They paced on in silence, Dorothy fretful that she had somehow angered her friend, Philippa fuming with visible intensity. She was intent on planning her revenge but instead her mind's eye kept returning ever and again to the scene at breakfast.

How had the little chit bested her? How had she undone the embargo she had placed on talking to her? So red were her thoughts she could not focus her mind on true analysis of the situation. She could not, in truth, bear to think that Alice Petherton had escaped her clutches by her own devices. So when she replayed the scene in her mind, it was without sufficient examination. She saw how the other Ladies had ignored Alice Petherton as she had required. She saw the slut's discomfort, which she so desired. Then, the next moment, there had been lightness in the room, a reaching out towards Petherton and even conversation.

But wait, something else had occurred. Two people had been the first to talk to Petherton. Two people. Ah yes. Her thoughts whirled like carrion birds around Susan Dunster and Lucy Burton. Aye, they were the cause of this reverse. Susan Dunster and Lucy Burton. She dismissed Susan Dunster from her mind. She would prove too difficult a foe for the moment. But Lucy Burton?

She almost hugged herself. Hurting Lucy Burton would be just punishment for her careless misdemeanor. Better yet, hurting her would hurt Alice Petherton. A smile as thin as a newt's lips broke upon Wicks's face.

"You could tell the Queen," Dorothy said. "You could tell her your suspicions of the trollop."

Philippa gave her friend a withering look.

"You fool," she said, angered that Dorothy's words had intruded upon her lovely plan. "Would the Queen believe us more than she'd believe the King? And if she did, would she dare to anger him by seeking retribution upon his new favorite?"

She hurried off, scheming still more, leaving Dorothy standing alone, wringing her hands piteously.

"Come, Dorothy," Philippa called. "We have work to do."

Dorothy plucked up her skirts and hurried after her.

Lucy settled herself at her flute. She was poor at playing it for she had only just taken up the instrument. Yet she had a love of music and a good voice and ear and presumed she would soon be a reasonable player. She pursed her lips and put the flute to her mouth.

"Quite the little songbird, aren't we?" said a mocking voice behind her.

She turned swiftly and saw Philippa Wicks and Dorothy Bray leaning against the closed door. Her heart fluttered nervously.

"I'm not," Lucy said. "I've only just taken it up. I'm more skilled with the recorder."

"Oh, I'm sure that you'll master it soon enough," Philippa said, coming towards her and pulling the flute from her hand. "I think that you are extremely skilled at playing. Playing instruments, playing games and playing people."

Lucy blinked. "I don't understand."

Dorothy gave a hollow laugh. "I think you do, child. I think you understand us very well."

There was a silence and then Philippa turned to Dorothy.

"I think perhaps you're wrong, dear Dorothy," she said. "Yes, I do believe you may be wrong." She bent towards Lucy. "I think perhaps you don't understand aright after all, my child."

She touched Lucy's hair, stroking it softly, curling the locks in her fingers. "Or perhaps you understand too well."

"I'm sure I don't," said Lucy. Her eyes began to moisten.

"Isn't she a pretty little thing," Philippa said in an indulgent tone. "So very, very pretty."

Dorothy joined her and both stared down at the girl, their faces immobile, their eyes guarded.

"Very pretty," said Dorothy. "But they do say that a person's face comes to resemble her character."

"Do they?" asked Philippa. "So if someone is lovely of nature she will have a lovely face?"

Dorothy nodded. "And if she is ugly of nature . . ."

Philippa put her fingers to Dorothy's lips. "Hush, my dear. We must not talk of such things. We don't want to alarm the child."

She smiled at Lucy but the smile was potent with venom.

At first Lucy did not understand their words. Why would all this talk of faces and nature alarm her? And then, at last, she realized what they were hinting.

"I haven't an ugly nature," Lucy said. "I haven't."

Dorothy placed her hand upon Lucy's shoulder.

"Not yet, you don't," said Dorothy. "But if you continue to play games, then that will surely change, as will your looks."

"But I'm not playing games," cried Lucy. Tears were beginning to form now. She wiped her eyes swiftly, determined she would not be seen crying.

"But you are, my child," said Philippa. "You're not, however, playing them very well."

Lucy shook her head in confusion.

"You were playing games at breakfast this morning," Philippa continued. "Yet you played unwisely. You chose to play on the side of the wrong person."

"Alice Petherton," said Dorothy.

"Quite the wrong person," Philippa said.

"What do you mean?" Lucy asked. "Alice is friendly to me; she is kind."

Dorothy shook her head in a pitying fashion. "Poor child," she said, her voice condescending.

"You have been beguiled," said Philippa, "bewitched. You are not the first, nor will you be the last. Why else would the Queen hate Alice Petherton so?"

"The Queen?" Lucy put her hand to her heart in shock. She had heard no such rumor until now.

"It is not common knowledge," Philippa said. "We tell you because we fear for you."

"Fear for me?" The tears welled in earnest now. Two plump drops coursed down Lucy's cheeks.

"Any friend of Alice Petherton is an enemy of the Queen," Philippa said.

Dorothy grabbed hold of Philippa's arm, feigning haste and concern. "Is it too late to prevent news of Lucy from reaching the Queen's ears?" she asked.

"I fear it may well be." Philippa touched Lucy upon the arm. Her fingers were hot as fire. "You were too public in your support of Alice Petherton, far too public."

Lucy felt her heart turn cold. A bitter taste of fear filled her mouth.

"But can we help her?" Dorothy pleaded.

Lucy turned an anxious gaze from Dorothy to Philippa. Would they help her? Could they?

Philippa placed her chin in her hand and gave great thought to the question.

"Perhaps," she said at last. Then she bent close to Lucy's face. "But I make no promises. The Queen's wrath may be too strong to rein in."

Lucy burst into tears, sobbing uncontrollably.

"I didn't know," she said. "I didn't know about Alice and the Queen."

"Maybe you didn't," Philippa said. "But you know now."

The two older women turned and headed for the door, like foxes who had left the hen coop a charnel house.

Chapter Thirteen

Wanted Once More

14 October 1537

"You're wanted. Look lively."

I glanced up to see Page Humphrey looming over me. He stood with hands on hips, all a-swagger. I shot a quick look around, anxious lest the other Ladies notice him. They were bending over their needlework, completely engrossed. Or pretending to be.

I gathered up my embroidery and hastened after Humphrey, who was even now at the door, walking away without a backward look as if he had no need to check on my compliance.

I stepped through the door. "You need not make so public a show," I hissed.

Humphrey shrugged. A little grin played over his face.

I risked a quick glance into the room from which I'd come. It was as I feared. Every one of the Ladies had dashed down their needlework and were whispering together like rats sniffing for food.

"Look lively," the Page repeated. "He won't be kept waiting."

He led the way through the corridors at a pace I had trouble keeping up with. Skirts are a hindrance in any conspiracy. With their stockings and hose it's no wonder men wield all the power. Perhaps that's why women are made to wear such mountains of clothes. They slow us down, encumber us, make it hard to chase and harder still to escape.

I was breathless by the time we reached the Study. The Page pointed a thumb over his shoulder at the chamber. "In here," he said. Then he grinned. "But you know that already, don't you, miss." He sauntered off, whistling tonelessly.

I stared after him, annoyed and yet amused by his impertinence. I knocked gently upon the door.

It was opened not by the King but by Frost, his groom. This would not have surprised me when I visited before, when I was coming to read poetry. Now it did.

"The King is finishing off some work in his Holy Day Closet," Frost said. He stood aside for me to enter. He half blocked the entrance and I had to brush against him, feeling the pressure of his closeness. I thought I heard a swift intake of breath or perhaps a sniff of his nose.

"Wait there until the King wants you." He pointed to one of the low chairs near the fireplace.

I sat and held my hands out towards the fire. Frost busied himself without another glance towards me. I wondered what kind of man would take and be given such a position. He would need to be as competent as a cathedral builder and secret as a tomb. What he witnessed, what he knew, could cause untold embarrassment to the King. And if he caused such embarrassment, it could mean a potentially hideous death for him. I wondered what had happened to Frost's predecessors, wondered what traps and snares the future held for him.

He was swift and adroit in his work, no doubt about that. He picked up the volumes strewn about the room with smooth, economical movements, scanned the title of each book and set it in a decided place upon the table. There must have been near a dozen of them scattered around the Study but soon all were collected upon the table. He stood back, as if to examine his handiwork. Then he bent, gathered them up with surprising tenderness and slipped along the bookcases as gentle as a breeze, replacing them in their rightful homes.

The last book he did not replace but opened somewhat near the middle and swiftly riffled through the pages as if seeking for one he knew. His face lit up and he leaned against the wall, reading deeply as if a thirsty man slaking himself at a pool. *So, Master Frost, you too have a liking for books.* I stored the knowledge of this close within me.

I watched him as he read for, until now, I had little time to take note of him.

He had a soulful look, like a hound which had never caught a fox and bore this sorrow upon its face. His eyelids drooped as if to hide that his eyes were crossed and his nose was long and thin, making him look cold and disdainful. Below this was a chin cut square as if to say, *Don't cross me; don't risk yourself in doing so.* A remarkable face, I concluded, full of contradiction and enigma.

He looked up suddenly. His nose seemed to scent the air and he composed his face into an impassive visage. He returned the book to its shelf and turned towards the far door.

"The King approaches," he said.

I turned to the door in bewilderment. The King was not yet here, nor could I hear any sound of him approaching.

Frost gestured to me to stand, which I did in some haste and flurry. I craned my ears and still heard nothing. Finally, after long moments, I heard the soft creak of a board and soon after, the distant, purposeful tread of the King.

"How did you know?" I asked Frost in amazement.

"I just know," he answered. "I always do."

The door was flung open and there, filling its space, stood the King. He was dressed in a thick fur coat and wore a little hat upon his head, a tassel of red cord hanging from it and resting upon his brow. He would have looked quite sweet had he been a normal man. But he was King Henry Tudor and the potency beat from him like summer heat.

"Alice, my dear," he cried, holding his hand out for me.

I took his hand and followed him into his bedchamber. Frost quietly closed the door behind us. The King gestured me towards the bed.

I started to undress. The groom might be returning to his book, or so I hoped. Or he might be leaning his ear to the door, waiting breathlessly for noises from the bed.

And what noises were about to sound. The King's potency was no mere adjunct of royalty, I realized. He was burning with desire for me. He flung off his own clothes and almost tore the rest of mine from my body. Within moments I felt his bulk on top of me, his tongue, quick as an eel but hotter, probing every part of my mouth. I felt him force himself inside me. I was still dry and unused to such intrusion and I yelped a little in pain.

"What!" he laughed. "A virgin once more, Alice Petherton?"

"No, Your Grace. It's just that you are so thick and bold this morning. I am quite overawed."

The King grinned with pleasure, like a boy.

"I am the King," he said, "and hot with lust for you."

"And I am glad, Your Grace. My heart sings to know this."

He grunted in satisfaction and went to work with ardor. My heart began not so much to sing but to yammer in complaint. My secret parts were raw and painful and then, all at once, I felt his movement in me become easier and less painful. I breathed in relief at the ceasing of the ache and the King bellowed like a bull, thinking his lovemaking had transported me to some place of joy. It felt more like relief from torment, much as a prisoner must feel when he is taken down from the rack. But the King was delighted with my reaction and that was good.

I gasped a little more in trial and felt the King stiffen even more inside me. I turned my head from side to side as if in abandoned ecstasy and his face grew yet happier. I moaned and licked my lips and he chuckled with excitement at the sight of it.

And then I found myself purring, like a little cat. This was not fabricated. It came from I know not where.

The King cried out with joy and spent himself inside me. The purring continued in my ears, alarming and startling, and then I felt a ripple pulse through me, from my groin right up to my belly. I gasped in earnest now, my mouth opening and pursing of its own accord. At last I shuddered with release and little shivers of delight ran up my skin.

"The King pleases you, dear Alice," his voice boomed in my ear.

The noise broke into my feeling of delight but did not shatter it.

"You do, Your Highness," I whispered. "You do indeed." And for that moment, for that briefest of moments, I truly meant it.

In the months ahead I pondered how those few words, spoken in all innocence, may well have saved me from disaster.

Later that day, after the King had left for an audience with the French Ambassador, I walked towards the Ladies' chamber. It was close to noon and I was famished.

The room was empty save for one person. Lucy was standing at the window, staring out at the view of the river beyond.

"You're here early," I said as I went towards her.

Lucy turned. Her face looked anxious, almost frightened.

"Lucy," I said, "whatever's the matter?"

She moved behind a chair, as if to place it between herself and me.

"There's nothing the matter," she said at last. Her voice was hard and yet shook as much as that of a child shivering in the cold.

"But there must be," I said.

She shook her head, once: an angry, defiant movement.

"Even if there were something wrong," she said at last, "I wouldn't ever tell you. Or tell you anything. I never want to be seen with you again."

She rushed past me and fled the room.

I turned towards the door, my mouth open as if I were about to call her back, though in truth it was because of astonishment.

I cannot say why but my heart felt suddenly desolate. I hardly knew Lucy yet it was as if my closest friend had betrayed me, as if I had been left bereft by a dearest lover. I turned to look at the window where she had stood as if to find there the reason for her strange reaction. A bitter taste came to my mouth, a sip of bile as foul as rotten meat. My heart began to beat faster and I felt light-headed.

Standing thus I was found by Susan and Mary.

"Alice," Susan cried. "What's wrong?"

My friends rushed to my side and stared at me anxiously.

I shook my head as if awaking from a nightmare.

"It's Lucy," I mumbled. "She was . . ." I was about to say she had been cruel to me but I checked myself, searching for other words which would not seem so damning. "She was distant and unfriendly," I said. "She ran from the room when I approached her." I gestured to the door as if they were half-wits who needed to have everything pointed out for them.

"Did she say why?" Mary asked.

I shook my head.

"But did you say anything to offend her?"

I shook my head again.

"I found her here alone," I said, "looking anxious. I asked her what was wrong."

I stared into Mary's face, dreading to find a look of doubt or suspicion there. My sense of what was happening had become upset; I was no longer sure I could trust what I saw or heard. To my relief I could see only concern from Mary. She touched me gently on the shoulder, as if to calm and console me.

That touch was enough to unlock the gates of my emotions. I shuddered and felt suddenly faint.

"I must sit down," I mumbled.

Susan and Mary helped me to a seat and stood over me anxiously.

"I'm all right," I said after a moment. "Just shocked by Lucy's reaction."

Susan drew up a chair and looked into my face. "Tell us exactly what happened."

I pushed my hand through my hair, going over the scene. When I had all right in my head I told them, my words tumbling out in a rush as if I had to speak quickly or I would not be able to speak at all.

"This is most peculiar," said Mary. "It's not like Lucy at all. She is a good child and very fond of you."

"Yes," said Susan. "Perhaps you have it there, Mary."

I turned towards Susan, perplexed.

"Think of the words she used," Susan said. "Especially at the end."

"She wouldn't tell me what was wrong," I said. "Or tell me anything at all."

Susan shook her head. "That's not how you recounted it a moment ago."

She glanced up at Mary before taking my hand in hers. "Lucy's final words, if you recalled them right, were that she did not want to be seen with you again."

"That's true," said Mary. "That's what you told us, Alice."

I cast my mind back to the incident. "You're right," I said at last. "That's exactly what she said. But seen by whom? The King?"

My friends exchanged swift glances, glances I did not wish to know the meaning of.

"Enough of the King," Susan said firmly. "Think not of the King."

"Think only of what may have alarmed Lucy," Mary said.

I shrugged. "I have no idea."

Susan sniffed and sat back in her chair. "Well, I have," she said. "Philippa Wicks. And Dorothy Bray. They have played with Lucy's mind, no doubt, and put the fear of the devil in her."

"But why should they do such a thing?" asked Mary.

"Because they hate me," I said with deadened words.

"That much seems plain," Mary said. "But I don't think we really know the reason."

I looked up at Mary. "It is a long story," I said.

And then I proceeded to tell them about Sir Richard Rich and how I had tormented him.

Chapter Fourteen

Death of a Queen

24 October 1537

Twelve days after she gave birth, Queen Jane gave up the ghost. That's what Susan said at any rate. Cruel, I know, but witty. Susan never had much time for Jane Seymour.

It was not news for anybody in the Court, if truth be told. Jane had never recovered from the battle to give birth to an heir. Her strength of body, unlike that of her ambition, had never been noteworthy.

But still, the Court was a hotbed of conjecture and gossip, even more than it usually was.

The night the Prince was born, rumor had it that the child had only come into the world after the Queen's legs had been stretched so wide her hips were almost dislocated. Nobody could say whether or not this was true. There had been no midwife in her chamber, for the Royal physicians had attended her. These venerable old men were learned in the words of ancient doctors, herbs and astrology. But not one of them had ever before helped a woman give birth. They probably had many Latin and Greek authorities to support the racking of limbs.

Darker voices whispered that the Queen had been cut open while still alive and relatively hale. That she had lingered on her bed, in agony, her life ebbing from her, screaming curses on the King for valuing an heir more than her life.

I doubted Jane would ever have cursed in such a fashion. Her motto had always been, "Bound to obey and serve." She was, despite her fierce ambition, a simpleton, and I thought she would hold to her motto even to her death.

Others said that Jane was very much alive days after the birth of the child. She was said to be strong enough to see the boy immediately after his Christening when he was three days old. However, her weak constitution meant that she was not allowed to leave her chamber. Her non-appearance served only to fuel the more lurid rumors.

At any rate, a week after the Christening, whether from the rigors of natural childbirth, dislocated hips or the cut from the surgeon's knife, the Queen had died.

I received the news with a horror which surprised me.

Jane and I had been friends when I first came to Court, two Maids of Honor to the newly crowned Anne Boleyn. I may have grown to dislike her but there was still that early tie between us. I prayed that her death had been a natural one of gentle sleep and drifting to her end, her mind made easy at having given birth to the King's heir.

I feared that it may have been as the gossipmongers whispered. That the King had, indeed, valued his dynasty more than his wife and had ordered that the child be ripped from her belly. That the gash had never healed and the life had been bled from her as if she were a traitor to the Crown, tortured and left to die a lingering and agonizing death. Yet, all the while, she had continued to send her love to her murderer, rejoicing in her self-sacrifice.

I pressed my forehead to the window to cool it. Hearsay spreads faster than the plague. Any of them might be true, none of them might. Childbirth was a chancy thing at the best of times. It was even more so when the mother was nearing thirty.

I stared out of the window of my chamber. Whichever of the rumors was true, there was one thing for certain now. Henry was a widower once again. Three Queens gone. All lying in their cold, cold graves. The King's supporters had been quick to point out that Catherine of Aragon had died of natural causes. But her friends said that she died of the heart he had so callously broken.

Three Queens. Three deaths. A chill hand seemed to clutch my stomach at the thought.

The Queen's funeral took place on 12th November, the first day after Martinmas. It was an appropriate day for a funeral, the first of St. Martin's Fast. Not that anyone took much notice of this particular Fast in modern times. Certainly not the King.

Or at least not usually. This year, the period of mourning and of Fast coincided most happily and the King commanded that all of his Palaces should become places of sackcloth and ashes for the forty days of the Fast. It seemed that the King had been traumatized by the death of his wife and was genuinely grieving for her.

This surprised almost everyone at Court. He had cast off his two previous wives without a backward glance. His marriage to Anne Boleyn had taken place before his marriage to Catherine had even been annulled. He got engaged to Seymour the day after Anne's execution and walked his new bride down the aisle ten days later. He never allowed a sense of propriety to hinder his hunger to get all that he wanted.

This time it appeared that things might be different.

I had last been with the King two hours before the death of Jane Seymour. Naturally, upon hearing the news of her imminent departure, he had been quick to order me back to my own bedroom.

I assumed there would be a period where he played the grieving husband but fully expected that after a few days he would summon me back to his chamber. No summons came.

For fourteen days I waited for the call, for the appearance of Page Humphrey with all his cheek and lack of respect. I waited in vain.

At last I began to abandon the idea of ever seeing the King again. I came to realize that I had been merely a casual relationship, indeed a very casual one. In his grief he had cast me aside. The death of Jane Seymour had ended all hope of my advancement. More than if she'd remained alive and discovered our liaison.

Or maybe I was fooling myself in this. If she had stayed alive things may have played out very differently.

Jane Seymour had been as shrewd and opportunistic as she was ambitious. Like many others, I suspected she had played a part in the downfall of Anne Boleyn. She had certainly been content to continue with her wedding preparations at the very moment that Anne stepped up to the executioner's block. Adept at cloaking her desires behind a facade of demure primness, she was, I believed, even more devious than Thomas Cromwell, the King's principal adviser, implausible though that notion may be.

If she had survived and discovered my relationship with the King she would have maneuvered as silkily and subtly as a swan and then turned on me with a ferocity which knew no bounds. I would have fallen, like Anne Boleyn, to her lust for power. And my head, like Anne's, may well have fallen from my shoulders and rolled, pitter-patter, across the timbers of the stage.

I shivered at the notion and reached up for a little necklace the King had given me. It was hardly more than a trinket, a poor thing of little value. But at least I still had a neck to wear it on.

On the fourteenth day of waiting, the 26th of November if I recall right, Page Humphrey appeared at my chamber once again. I stood in some agitation, wary of what cheek he would offer me but excited at the thought of returning to the King's favor.

He held out a book for me. Wondering, I took it from his hand. It was my book of Sir Thomas Wyatt's verse.

"Henry told me to bring you this," Humphrey said. "Hard luck, miss. A pity really. You seem like quite a girl."

He blew a kiss at me and hurried back down the corridor.

I stared blankly at the volume.

So this was it. Flung away, like a bone he had gnawed clean. I glanced around warily, as if searching for hounds racing to fight over me and gnaw off what little flesh the King had left behind.

At least Humphrey seems to like me, I thought miserably. Then I groaned. How low had I fallen to seek consolation from the admiration of a roguish Page!

I stayed in my chamber for the next five days, pleading an indisposition. I had already had enough of the mourning and mumbling from the Maids of Honor. Those who had liked Jane Seymour least were now loudest in their praise of her. Those who had been most fond kept their own counsel.

I kept to my own bed. It felt safer there. Some at Court might even have thought my indisposition was caused by grief. In a way, perhaps it was. I grieved that my plans had been thwarted so early.

The day of the funeral came with cold wind and squally rain. Mary Zouche traveled in one of the five carriages but I rode with the remainder of the Maids on horseback. I was a competent horsewoman and preferred to ride rather than be jolted along the bumpy road to Windsor Chapel. In any case, I had no choice in the matter. The Duke of Norfolk had arranged all, even down to the matter of who should ride where. I was not surprised by his diligence. It was said that each evening he checked his wife's needlework to make certain she had done it right.

The funeral service was dreary but then I suppose it should have been. I mulled over thoughts of my own funeral as I stood there. I should like it to be a great and glorious occasion, full of light and laughter. I wanted people to celebrate my life, not to mope over it. Though of course I meant to live a good few years more than Jane Seymour. And I meant to enjoy every one of them, to suck from each hour all its gifts.

I closed my mind to the sighs and the wails. A new time was coming.

I grew suddenly reconciled to the fact that the King had dispensed with me. A feeling of deep relief descended upon me. I would find another way to achieve my destiny than between the sheets of an aging monarch. *Farewell, Your Majesty*, I thought. *Hello to a new life.*

Chapter Fifteen

Christmas Festivities

25 December 1537

The King decided to celebrate Christmas at Greenwich Palace, always one of his favorites. I thought it likely that he also wanted no reminder of Hampton Court, where Jane had died. Despite the fact that she had been in her grave for only six weeks, the Christmas festivities were more extravagant than any I had seen in my four years at Court. Or maybe it was *because* she was in her grave. Her mask of rectitude and piety had begun to taint the very air of the Court and now the inhabitants of the Palace began to sniff a sweeter scent than before.

I joined Susan and Mary and arm in arm we made our way to the Chapel. The crowd of courtiers and servants was already tingling with anticipation of the festivities ahead and not even the thought of listening to the Bishop sermonizing for an hour could quite dampen their spirits.

Wicks and Bray were already seated, with Lucy crammed in between them. Poor child. I was still perplexed about the exact poison that had been dripped into her ears but I had not entirely given up on her. We had been friends, and at Court friends are not to be lightly discarded. One never knows when the humble shall suddenly transmute into the great.

I listened to the beginning of the sermon for I liked the story of Christmas more than most in the Scriptures. But I had heard it told much better and I soon stopped listening. Instead, I spent the sermon as I usually did: thinking of the happiest days I had known and trying to arrange them by degree of happiness. A futile task, I know, and one which gave a different result every time I did it. But it was much better than listening to the mumbling and moralizing of the Bishop.

After the service everyone repaired to the Dining Hall for the Christmas feast. The huge number of people in the Hall gave it a warmth which it did not have when empty. The noise was deafening, with all sense of decorum forgotten in the joy of the moment. The Court had experienced a hard two months since the Queen had died, including the enforcement of the St. Martin's Fast. Now the rigor and constraint were thrown over and everyone seemed determined to squeeze every moment of pleasure they could from the day.

The feast was the most magnificent I had ever seen in my time at Court. It was as if the Master of the Household had grown frenzied in his attempts to make up for the straitened days we had all just endured.

The Hall at Greenwich was normally arranged with two long lines of tables with benches on either side. Today, however, it had been set out differently. The tables had been placed in a square with gaps at each corner by which servants could enter the square and speed up the serving of the food.

In the middle of the Hall was a huge table crammed with bread, fruit, conserves, ale, wine and cheeses. A roast boar lay in the center, the scent of its rich meat wafting across the Hall, enticing the taste buds like no other fare can. Next to the boar was a glistening swan, roasted and embellished with fruit and sweetmeats. I guessed that stuffed inside it would be an aviary of birds: goose, chicken, partridge, pheasant, woodcock, snipe, pigeon, heron, capon and songbirds. But no quail. Queen Jane had become addicted to the eating of quail in her confinement, and since her death the consumption of the bird had been forbidden in all of the Royal Palaces.

On either side of the swan were two huge pies with smaller ones atop, like the turrets of a castle. Inside would be various meats and game: beef, lamb and pork; hare, rabbit and venison; kid, gosling and kidneys.

Platters were already set at each place and once we had said grace the servants hurried from the kitchens laden with fresh roast meats and fowl. There was every conceivable meat available. I took a slice of ham and a leg of hare, Susan chose pork, beef and lamb; Mary could not decide for a moment but finally settled upon capon and pheasant. We also took some cabbage and beans, but not too much, for risk of our digestions.

We set to with a will. The noise of the Hall grew quieter as people bent to their work. I suddenly realized that musicians were playing on a dais on one side of the Hall. I hadn't noticed them at all until this moment.

The first course over, the servants proceeded to carve and hack at the boar, the swan and the pies. I allowed them to load my plate near to overflowing. I had already drained my cup of wine and was determined to have still more. I was intent on banishing the greyness of these weeks of mourning with as much bravado as I could manage.

Halfway through this course, someone pushed in between Susan and me. I turned to see who it was.

"I'm so sorry, Alice," Lucy said. "I'm so sorry, but Philippa and Dorothy told me so many things about you and I've just now found out that most of them were falsehoods."

Her face was crushed with misery, her eyes brimming with tears.

I wanted to slap her.

Instead, I took her in my arms and kissed her upon the cheeks.

"It's over now," I said lightly, although I did not feel ready to forgive her. But even as I thought this, my heart began to thaw. Lucy was a delightful girl and I realized I was glad that we were friends once more.

I glanced across at Wicks and Bray, who could not keep from glaring at me. I gave them a gracious smile and they seemed to hiss back at me like angry geese. I wondered who had enlightened Lucy about the situation. I doubted it was either Susan or Mary; they seemed as surprised as I was at Lucy's return to the fold. Perhaps it was merely that she had thought out the matter for herself and come to her own conclusions.

We finished the food on our platters and I replenished everybody's cup with wine. I raised mine in the air.

"To Christmas," I said, "and to friendship."

Lucy was so swift to clink cups with mine that she spilt much of her wine on the table, some of it splashing on her dress. She barely seemed to notice and gulped at the cup as though it contained milk.

I had to find out. I put my hand on hers and leaned close towards her.

"Tell me, Lucy," I whispered. "Who told you that Philippa and Dorothy were telling you lies?"

"Nobody," she answered.

I frowned. "Then what made you realize that they were?"

"I worked it out," she said. "They told so many tales about you that eventually I noticed the stories had begun to change. Philippa would say one thing if we were alone together and later Dorothy would talk about the same matter but say it quite differently. As soon as I'd noticed this I began to watch out for more discrepancies. Dorothy even contradicted herself a couple of times. It was then I realized they were not recounting the truth. They were lying and sometimes they forgot the tales they'd spun."

"Well, all's mended now," I said, patting her on the arm.

Tears filled her eyes once more and two tiny drops trickled down her cheeks.

"You say that, Alice, but I've been dreadful to you. How can you forgive me?" She snuffled and wiped her eyes with a handkerchief. "How can I make it up to you?"

"There's nothing to make up," I said. "I'm sure you'll always want to be my friend from now on."

I picked up a piece of crackling and crunched upon it. Then I felt a finger prodding me in the back. I turned around in astonishment.

Page Humphrey crouched behind me, a smirk upon his face.

"The King wants you," he whispered. "He's feasting in his Dining Chamber with the high and mighty but he appears to have decided to take his dessert in private."

He jerked his thumb in the direction of the King's Private Chambers and stood up, waiting for me to rise.

I could not believe him for a moment but he nodded his head and gave a knowing little grin.

"I must go," I whispered to my friends.

"Merry Christmas," Susan said, a mischievous smile dancing on her lips. "We'll see you in January."

Humphrey led me to the King's Privy Chambers. It was cold and he put another log on the fire.

"I'm glad you're back, miss. And not only because I won the wager."

"What wager—" I began but Humphrey darted out of the room before I finished my words.

A slow smile came over my face. It appeared I had a champion at Court, albeit a cheeky one.

Clearly, the Pages had been wagering whether or not I would return to favor with the King. I walked back and forth across the carpet, pleased with myself. I had never attracted such notice before.

And nor had I expected to attract the attention of the King again. He had been so fulsome in his grief for Queen Jane, so much the woebegone widower. I assumed he meant to dispense with me once and for all.

My smile deepened. Perhaps he had meant to cast me aside but found himself unable to do so. Perhaps he was so besotted with me that he could not but help summon me back. A thrill of exhilaration swept through me. The King of England was besotted with me.

And then my glee vanished. I was not at all sure I wanted him to become besotted.

I paused in my walking and looked around in order to distract myself. It was the first time I had been alone in the Library. It must have been ten times the size of my chamber at Hampton Court. Bookshelves lined the walls from floor to ceiling. How many books must the Library hold?

My eyes ranged across the shelves, marveling that so many words had been written, that so many clever men had chosen to spend hours and years of their lives in conjuring up ideas from their minds and displaying them for all to see, like merchants laying out their goods in a market.

I moved closer and sniffed at some of the volumes. They smelled of great age and wisdom. A mixture of leather, wood, paper and mildew. I wondered how old they might be. I'd heard that in the past there were very few books, that monks had labored many years to copy and embellish just one. What dedication they must have needed. They must have bound up their hopes and dreams within the book, bound them up until they became as much part of it as the parchment they scribed upon.

Like courtiers really. Bound to the King by silken shackles.

And King's favorites?

At that moment the door opened and Gregory Frost stepped into the room. He gave a wintry smile and crooked a finger at me.

I followed him into the bedchamber. There was no mistaking the King's intentions towards me now. I ran my tongue across my bottom lip. Did I want this? Did I want to spend my days pleasuring this old man? And then I sighed. My hopes and wants were futile; I had no say whatsoever in the matter. The King would get what he desired and for the moment, it seemed, he desired me. I had created the situation, of course. And now I must make the best of it.

A huge fire roared in the hearth, logs cracking in the heat, pine and applewood scenting the smoke with a sweet fragrance. The room felt much warmer than the Library and I stood in front of the fire, allowing its heat to caress me. I loved heat, loved the balmy days of summer. My mother said this was because I'd been born on May Day and sucked in the delight of summer with her milk.

I stared into the fire, watching the flames dance and leap. I used to spend hours staring into our fire when I was a child. I thought the flames were little creatures, sporting for my entertainment. At first, I thought them birds and cats and mice, all creatures I was familiar with. Later, once I had begun to read, I populated the fire with more exotic creatures: dragon, phoenix and salamander. I made up stories about them. Sometimes the creatures hunted me; sometimes they imprisoned me. I was always a Princess and the brightest flame was always the Prince. Always, always, he would defeat my tormentors and carry me away on his white horse.

At that moment, I heard a noise and turned to see the King in the doorway, watching me. He was dressed in his full regalia, a thing I had seen on only a few occasions. He shrugged off the heavy coat with one smooth movement, allowing it to slither to the floor. He took off the weighty gold seal he wore around his neck and flung it onto a table. He never took his eyes from me.

I performed the lowest possible curtsy, remaining low on the ground, my gown spread about me, my arms outstretched as if I were praying for clemency and forgiveness.

"Arise, my dear," the King said, his voice deep with affection.

I looked up and saw his hand held out for mine.

"Have you heard the rumor that your King is dead?" he asked.

I shook my head.

The King sighed. "It is said that someone at Court wrote to the Abbot of Reading informing him of my death."

"That was a wicked thing to say, Your Majesty."

"It was indeed. And the Abbot believed him and gave the news to a colleague. I think they believed it because they wished it to be true." He laughed. "Yet I am still alive. Very much alive. But if Master Cromwell knows his work they will not long be."

And then he grinned and gave me a little courtly bow, all thought of death and execution seemingly forgotten.

"Did you enjoy the Christmas feast, Alice?" he asked.

"Very much," I said.

"And the Bishop's sermon?"

"Very much," I lied.

The King gave me a shrewd little look and shook his head as if I were a wayward little thing.

Then he led me into the bedchamber and, with sweet delicacy, sat me on the bed.

He was not so delicate a few minutes later.

It had been two months since Jane Seymour had died, two months since the King had last slept with me. It seemed as if all his pent-up lust and longing crashed upon me like a storm. I could not believe the passion with which he took me, the fierce intensity, the desperation.

But there was no violence with the roughness. If anything there was a sense of vulnerability that made my heart warm to him.

However, I have to say that the King gave little attention to my wants or needs. He was intent on taking his own pleasure, on releasing the deluge of energy that threatened to overpower him. And release it he did, bellowing out his wild delight with unashamed gusto.

The moment he had finished he flung himself back upon the bed, his eyes staring sightless at the ceiling.

I also stared up at the ceiling, wondering now what the future might bring.

Without intending to, my hand reached out and grasped his tightly.

"I am so glad you called me back to you," I said.

"I had no choice," he answered. "You have seized my body and snared my mind."

Within my breast rose two emotions, contrary ones which chased each other round my heart. One was simple pleasure at his words. The other was cold dread.

Chapter Sixteen

New and Dangerous Men

31 December 1537

Richard Rich peered into the mirror, his stare moody and aggrieved. Something was happening, something concerning the King, and he did not know what it was.

Such a situation made him anxious. He had to know what was happening; he had to know. He stuck out his tongue, examining it nervously. It looked yellow and sour.

He dragged his fingers through his hair, which was slick and tangled. He felt adrift and dangling, without his sure defenses, vulnerable to all his many enemies.

He looked out of the window. The morning was as grey as nightfall and a thick, persistent downpour hammered against the courtyard below. It was the last day in December and his year was ending on a sour note. He must do something about it.

"Mason," he called. He counted in his head the interval between his yell and the arrival of his servant. He listened to the hurrying feet and the cautious knock upon the door.

"Come," he said in a low voice.

Peter Mason opened the door and peered in. He was a young man of twenty-two years but he had aged ten more in the service of Richard Rich.

"You called, master?" he asked, bobbing his head.

"Fifty counts ago," Rich replied. "I summoned you fifty counts ago. Please tell me what detained you."

"Nothing, master." Mason bit his lip, realizing his mistake.

Rich sighed and shook his head as if saddened by the news. "Fifty counts, Mason. You have kept me waiting for fifty counts. And for what? You said it yourself. For nothing. If it had been because you were dealing with a tradesman or hurt your leg or heard that your mother had just died, then a delay of fifty counts may be considered appropriate."

He turned and stared Mason in the eye. "But you, Peter Mason, have kept me waiting for nothing."

Mason wrung his hands in anxiety.

"Unless, of course," Rich continued, "you were doing something but do not wish to admit to it."

He stepped close to Mason and it was all that the young man could do to stop himself from visibly recoiling from the fetid breath of his master.

"Was it the wench?" Rich continued. "Were you sniffing like a hound about her privy parts? Is the bitch in heat again?"

Mason's fist clenched but he forced it to relax. "I was talking to Ellen, yes, master. She was asking what I thought you might require for dinner."

Rich regarded him with disbelieving eyes. But Mason had learned to hide his feelings well over the past eighteen months. He looked back at Rich with as bland a look as he could conjure.

Rich stepped away and stared out of the window. "Just keep your dirty thoughts and fingers off Ellen Coles," he said.

He picked up a document and handed it to Mason. "This is to go immediately to the Lord Privy Seal."

"Sir Thomas Cromwell?"

"Unless you are here to tell me that the King has a new Lord Privy Seal. Of course I mean Sir Thomas Cromwell."

Mason took the document, bowed his head and fled the room.

Rich turned and stared out of the window at the busy street below, his mind weaving a complex net of bait and snares. His yellow tongue darted out and caressed his upper lip. He felt sure that his enigmatic missive would be more than enough to pique Thomas Cromwell's interest.

Thomas Cromwell, Baron Cromwell, Lord Privy Seal and a countless string of other offices which he knew the titles of but disdained to use, took the document from Peter Mason's hand.

"Wait over there," he said, gesturing with his chin to a corner of the room.

He peered at the seal on the document. Master Rich. What could be troubling him? He tapped the document against his thumb, pondering whether to look at it or send it back unopened. Sometimes Richard Rich's correspondence meant little or nothing; too often of late it meant a deal of unnecessary aggravation for the Lord Privy Seal.

He glanced up at Mason, who stood in the corner staring at his feet. *He's scared of me*, Cromwell thought. *And well he might be.* He stared at the young servant for a few moments longer as if he might divine the contents of the document from his demeanor.

Foolishness, of course. Rich would never have discussed such matters with a servant. He loves to hoard his power as a miser hoards his coins. He never lets anyone get as much as a sniff at what he knows.

Save me only. And the King . . . perhaps.

He cleared his throat and broke open the seal, flattening the parchment on the desk.

It read: "What is making the King so happy?"

Cromwell frowned and studied the words. His fingers began to drum upon the desk and he read the message a second and a third time.

He rubbed his tongue along the tips of his teeth, a movement he often made in the past when he was troubled. He had not been troubled for a long while now, such a long while.

What is making the King so happy?

He leaned forward in his chair, his eyes focusing on a space a few feet from him without really seeing it. His fingers brushed his lips as if he were searching for a spot which irritated him. He heard the soft shuffle of Mason's nervous feet, the hiss of a log in the fire.

His mind raced back over his last few meetings with the King.

Rich was right. The King had been extremely happy of late, happier even than when the wealth of the largest monasteries had flooded into his treasury. He had been almost playful recently, as if he had regained his youth. As if he had been returned to the time before the jousting injury had, in an instant, loaded years upon him.

Cromwell's eyes narrowed with suspicion. What business did Rich have in drawing his attention to the King's humor?

A part of his mind clicked out a plan to punish Rich for his temerity while the rest sieved his own dealings with the King to try to find the cause for his newfound levity.

He arranged the events of the past few months upon an interior abacus, each one a little shaped token.

Might it be the death of the Queen? Might her exit to the grave have lightened his spirits so? Did he really love her, indeed could he have loved her, milksop as she seemed?

He worried at his teeth once more. *It's said that demure-seeming women can be voracious in bed. If Jane Seymour had been as passionate as she was prim it should have been the King who expired in bed and not his pallid paramour.*

His fingers beat out a rhythm on the arm of his chair. *Surely not even the King could be so crass. It's only two months since Seymour breathed her last. No, there must be some other reason for it.*

Perhaps Rich knows something—something even I don't know. If that is the case Rich will come to regret this knowledge. And regret even more his boasting of it.

He glanced at Rich's servant and crooked his finger to him.

Mason hurried over to the desk.

"Return to Master Rich," he said and bent once again to his correspondence.

Mason shuffled nervously. At last he summoned up his courage. "Is there a message for him, my lord?"

"No message." He dismissed the boy, who hurried to leave the room with great relief.

But just as Mason opened the door, Cromwell called him back.

"There is a message after all."

The servant turned. "My lord?"

Cromwell's eyes blinked and then opened wide as if they belonged to a toad.

"Give Master Rich this message. Tell him that I send him no message. No message whatsoever."

Chapter Seventeen

New Year Gifts

1 January 1538

It was the first day of January, New Year's Day, the season for the giving of gifts. I loved receiving gifts. Even liked to give them, come to that.

For most people the giving of gifts was a pleasant matter. True, one might worry whether a gift for a special friend would give her the pleasure one hoped it would. And sometimes one was given a gift not to one's liking and so had to smile and dissemble while wondering how to quietly dispose of it. But in the main, most people found the giving and receiving of New Year's gifts a light and pleasant matter.

Not so the lords and great ones of King Henry's Court.

For them, the whole Christmas period was a truly desperate time. No field of battle, no lengthy diplomatic negotiations could be quite so arduous and dangerous. Every day and every festivity was an occasion when they might find their star had risen or fallen. A casual word or a careless gesture might be open to any number of interpretations by the

King and the courtier would awaken next morning appalled at how his standing in the Court had become so abruptly exalted or debased.

The most spectacular rises and chilling descents took place at the New Year's gift giving.

It was a time of sharp elbows, fawning words and backs bent low to the floor. Not even the great god Janus was as two-faced as the nobles of the Kingdom on that day.

And Jupiter, the King of the Gods, was the most duplicitous of them all.

Men would have wracked their minds for months concerning the gift they would give to the King. Some, it was said, even appointed experts to advise them. The value of the gift and the quality had to be calculated to a nicety. It had to be a little more expensive and a little bit finer than the gift given the previous year. It had to be appropriate to one's current position in the King's favor, yet always a tiny bit better in order to indicate that the giver rejoiced to give more than was expected of him.

And needless to say, every gift, whatever its value, would be far more costly than any of the givers could easily bear. Every man begrudged the expense the gift had cost and the King knew it. Every man pretended blitheness of spirit at this cost. And the King knew this pretense also.

The ceremony was always conducted in the Great Hall. The King would sit on his throne upon a dais at one end of the Hall, proclaiming the majesty of his grandeur.

On this chill January day, to everyone's astonishment, the smaller throne, the Queen's throne, had been set beside it. Most of the palace had assumed that this throne would have been discreetly left elsewhere. But the King had decreed otherwise and the empty throne sat silent and cold as if to impress upon people his continuing sorrow and distress at her death.

Four people in the Hall knew this to be a masquerade. The King's Groom, Gregory Frost; the King's go-between, Page Humphrey; and the King himself, of course. And me, Alice Petherton, who had for the past seven nights striven with all my might and main to banish any sorrow the King might still suffer and ease the slightest trace of distress.

Not that the King appeared to me to be experiencing either distemper. Far from it. He romped with me like the fattest and most boisterous puppy in a litter and gazed upon my face with the lovelorn yearning of a country youth. And he made love to me with a heady brew of tenderness and passion as if this were the only way he could keep the advancing years from galloping towards him and trampling him underfoot.

The few hours that we had not been occupied in his chamber had been spent in the riotous entertainments of the Court. And every hour I could snatch from King or festivities I spent in feverish making of my gift to him.

Ladies in Waiting and Maids of Honor gave gifts only to the Queen and to their friends, so I was taking a gamble so huge that my needle quivered in my hand as I sewed. I was making a gift for the King; a thing unheard of for any except a courtier or his Queen. I was making him a shirt and with each stitch, each cut of the cloth, I knew I was making either a gown of glory for myself or my very own shroud.

"What have you got there?" Mary asked as we made our way to the Great Hall in the late afternoon.

I hugged the parcel close to my chest. "It's nothing," I answered.

"A large thing for a nothing," Susan said. I saw her bite her lip a moment, a sure sign of her darting thoughts.

"It is nonetheless nothing for either of you to concern yourselves over," I said.

My friends exchanged glances, which I chose to ignore. I could feel their sudden nervousness. I had been troubled for days about how I would take the gift with me to the Hall without attracting attention.

I had to take it with me, for I knew that the King would most likely summon me to his chamber directly after the gift giving and I did not wish to arrive there empty-handed. But the parcel looked conspicuous, far more conspicuous than I had feared.

We took our seats in the Hall. The giving of gifts to the King was a spectacle of rare quality, a thrilling performance for those who were not obliged to give one. Those who had to participate were sick with apprehension.

The first ten courtiers had an easy time of it.

Each man in turn handed his gift to the Lord Steward, who held it out for the King to examine. The King cast a glance towards it and then smiled, indicating he had accepted the gift with good grace. The courtier retired with a bow. They could now breathe easier, knowing that the year ahead would be manageable. Thomas Cromwell, Lord Privy Seal, approached the King and gave a deep bow. I craned my neck to watch him, for I found myself oddly fascinated by his dark reputation.

"Your Grace," he said. "Felicitations on this glorious day."

He held out a box of wood so dark it was almost black. The Lord Steward opened it and took out a manuscript, which he passed unread to the King. The King broke the seal, beamed with delight and waved the manuscript in the air.

"Master Cromwell has given me lands," he cried. "I have here the deeds of Charterhouse, that nest of vipers and malcontents. And the deeds of Castle Acre Priory."

The Court murmured in appreciation.

"He has also, most generous of all my servants, given me six manors which were formerly in his own possession."

Cromwell bowed low at this. "All that I have is yours, Majesty," he said.

"That is nonsense and you know it," boomed the King with good humor. "And to prove it I give to you two dozen manors, in Sussex and in Essex."

Cromwell bowed still lower and loud applause broke out across the Hall. The conceit was that the applause was in honor of the King's generosity. In reality it was designed to curry favor with Thomas Cromwell. He straightened from his bow and turned to look at the courtiers, his snake eyes sweeping over them, marking out who was clapping with the most enthusiasm and who with least.

Next, the Duke of Norfolk approached the throne. Everybody scrutinized the King's face. The relationship between monarch and premier noble of the land was complex and never easy.

"I have not lands to give you, Majesty," Norfolk said, "unlike friend Sir Thomas." Here he bowed politely to Cromwell, though with only the merest trace of warmth upon his face. "I have instead sent ship to the dark lands of Africa and brought back these."

He turned, held high his arm and the doors of the Hall were flung open.

A few of the women behind me screamed. For walking down the Hall came two big strong black men, thick leashes in their hands. But it was not the sight of the exotic men that had alarmed the women.

It was that they were hauling two lions towards the King. The beasts were more fabulous than any illustration in a book. They were enormous; their manes flamed like clouds of gold, their bodies rippled with power and malice. Suddenly one opened its mouth and bellowed a ferocious roar. Every lady in the room screamed and a few of the more foppish men put their hands to their mouths to stifle their own exclamations.

The King was on his feet, his face aglow, his mouth as wide-open as the lion's, but in delight.

"My humble gift to His Majesty," said the Duke with a bow.

For once the King was speechless. He could not take his eyes from the lions, could not even acknowledge the Duke. For long moments he stared at the beasts. I imagined his eyes becoming wanton, lust-heavy and yearning.

He took his throne once more but he continued to stare upon the lions as if to persuade himself that they were real, that they were here and that they were his.

At last he tore his eyes away and addressed the Duke.

"Such a noble gift deserves a Kingly one in return," he said. He gave the Duke the manuscript Cromwell had only just presented to him.

"I give you Castle Acre Priory, in the County of Norfolk."

Applause thundered across the Hall, making both lions roar with apparent rage.

I glanced at Cromwell. He could not quite hide a momentary spasm at seeing one of his gifts to the King so speedily bestowed upon his rival. But then he smiled like a viper and applauded more loudly than anyone else in the Hall.

The Duke turned to Cromwell and stared at him with a gaze as blank and unfathomable as the moon. The applause across the Hall faltered for a moment and then continued with renewed intensity.

Finally, Thomas Boleyn, father of Anne, approached the throne. He looked bewildered. He had been kept back from offering his gift to the King at the time appropriate to his station. He had, inexplicably, been held to the very end.

He was an old man and he seemed to tremble as he walked, struggling to carry a heavy box, bound with silver and studded with gems.

He approached the King, bowed and presented the box. The Lord Steward took it, opened it and showed the contents to the King. The King turned his face away, without giving the slightest look. He waved his hand to dismiss the gift.

Boleyn fell to his knees. "I beseech you, Your Majesty," he cried.

"I want nothing of yours, Sir Thomas," the King replied. He gave an irritated gesture and the Lord Steward thrust the gift back into Boleyn's hands.

There came an inward sigh from all the spectators which, though silent, surged around the Hall.

The old man struggled to his feet. His hands began to tremble uncontrollably. For him the year ahead meant at best disgrace. At worst it might mean confiscation of his lands, imprisonment in the Tower and perhaps even death.

I suspected that everyone at Court had been anxious that they might see such a terrible thing happen to one of their friends. Yet I also suspected that many had been excited at the thought that it might just happen to somebody, agog with anticipation.

And now it had.

I glanced around. It appeared like every person in the Hall felt more alive for having witnessed it.

I hurried out of the Hall along with the rest of the Court.

"What will this mean for the Boleyn family?" Susan said, her face grown pale.

"Never mind what it might mean for them," said Mary. "What might it mean for you?"

It was well known that Susan had been one of Anne's special favorites and anybody connected with the Boleyns might now be in danger.

"I don't want to think about it," Susan answered. "I feel sick."

I swallowed hard, realizing that I might possibly be able to relieve my friend's fears. But I decided to say nothing of this. For what I was about to do, giving the King my gift, might lead to as deadly a path as Thomas Boleyn had just trod.

"Here," came a low, familiar voice as we walked.

I turned and saw Humphrey leaning out from behind a pillar. He so clearly loved the intrigue provided by his role.

I said good-bye to my friends and stepped across to Humphrey, who put his finger to his lips and ducked into a doorway, beckoning me to follow.

I found myself at the foot of a small set of stairs. They were narrow and steep and with a window so tiny the steps seemed sunk in gloom.

"Now, miss," Humphrey said. "This here staircase is very private, very hush-hush. A few of the King's most trusted servants know it exists." He puffed out his chest before stepping close to me. "But not many of us know. Not many at all. So you must promise—no, you must swear—that you will keep it secret as the grave."

"I swear," I said although it was all I could do to keep my face straight, so comical were his airs and graces.

"Come on, then, miss. His Majesty awaits his pleasure."

Humphrey led the way up the stairs. He moved very swiftly and I struggled to keep up with him. I had the King's gift in my left hand and, for fear of tripping, had to lift up the bottom of my gown with the right. We reached the top and then walked along a narrow corridor that seemed to go the length of the Hall before taking a right turn. We hurried along an even narrower corridor and then stopped at a tiny door.

Humphrey pulled out a key, unlocked the door and disappeared inside. "Come on, Alice," he called. "Don't dawdle."

"Where are we?" I asked.

"The King's Presence Chamber," Humphrey answered. "We've just come through a secret way where the most high and mighty of the land are led. So as the guards don't always see who's coming and going to the King's presence."

"Isn't that a bit risky? For the King, I mean?"

Humphrey jerked a thumb behind him. "That's where the King's guards are stationed. Seventy of 'em at the very least. When the rebels was stirring in the north just recent there were near two hundred of them. So all he has to do is call, even if they don't know that he's got a visitor." He grinned at me. "Anyway, miss, in you go. He's waiting for you."

I wondered why the King had decided to have me visit him by this circuitous route. My heart began to beat more swiftly. Perhaps he had become bored with me and required me to take this clandestine way in order to dispense with me in secret, to banish me from Court without a penny or a testimonial.

I turned to ask Humphrey if he had any inkling of the reason but the boy had disappeared. My heart leapt to my mouth at this. The circumstances seemed ever more sinister.

At that moment a figure appeared in the doorway. It was the King's Groom, Gregory Frost.

"Be quick," he snapped. "His Majesty cannot be kept waiting all day."

I hurried after him, through the Presence Chamber and into the Dining Room. The sideboards were covered with dishes and the air was heavy with the aroma of their contents.

"In there," Frost said. "He's in his Privy Chamber."

I nodded and pushed open the door.

The King was sitting by a huge fire, his foot propped on a small stool. Beside him was a little table with a jug of claret and two glasses. He stared at the window, seemingly lost in his thoughts, but when he realized I had arrived he gave a smile and indicated that I should join him.

"What did you think of the lions, Alice? Weren't they splendid?"

"They were indeed, Your Grace. If a trifle fearsome."

"For women perhaps. And for cowards. Not for me, though. For I am a lion as well. Did you not see how the beasts recognized this in me, how they called out in fellowship?"

"I did, Your Grace, although I thought the cry more one of salutation to their superior."

The King's head tilted to one side as he considered this.

"I do believe you're right," he said after a moment. "You're such a clever girl. All of my wives were clever but your cleverness I much prefer. You see the sense of things better than they did. You see things as I see them."

"I'm glad you think so, Majesty." I had to fight down a sense of rising panic. He had compared me with his wives. Whether the comparison was favorable or ill I wanted none of it. I desired neither to be his Queen nor his victim.

He poured some wine for me and as he did so he said, "What is that you are holding, Alice?"

I took a deep breath. There was no going back now.

"It is for you, Your Grace. It is my New Year's gift to you."

He did not answer for a moment and I thought that I might vomit. Then he smiled.

"Is it indeed?" he said. "Let me have it, then." He held out his hand and I passed the parcel to him.

"Let's hope that I look upon it more fondly than I looked upon the gift Thomas Boleyn proffered," he said.

I gave a sick smile. I dared not speak.

Slowly the King unwrapped the parcel. He held up the shirt and shook it so that its creases fell out. I realized I was holding my breath and exhaled as slowly and as quietly as I was able.

He turned to me and beamed. "It's lovely, Alice. A shirt. But also rather like a nightshirt."

I lowered my head bashfully.

"Did you make it yourself?"

"I did, Your Grace. I wanted it to be from me to you as a personal gift, and what better way to ensure that than to make the shirt myself?"

He nodded and put the shirt upon the table.

"I like it, Alice, and I shall wear it. I shall wear it on Twelfth Night in fact."

He put his finger to his lips and looked about the room as if puzzled. "Now, how might I equal such a kindly gift?"

He chuckled and reached out for a little cloth that I had not noticed upon the table.

Beneath it was a necklace made of gold with jewels and pearls hanging from it. He leaned over and placed it around my neck. "Beauty for beauty; sweets for my sweet."

I blinked in astonishment. The pearls felt cool and heavy upon my neck. I reached up and stroked them gently, marveling at their smoothness. I had never touched anything so beautiful. Nor so costly and extravagant.

"I cannot believe you have given me this," I said.

It was true. I was so shocked by his gift that I found myself speaking the truth.

"But why not?" he asked. "I am the King."

"I know. But it is such a wonderful gift. I do not deserve it."

The King laughed quietly and shook his head as if in wonder.

"You can surprise me yet, Alice Petherton. You speak your mind; you are honest with your Sovereign. That is why I like you so much. And that is why you must accept this gift."

"I do, Your Grace, I do. Please don't misunderstand me. I'm astonished, that is all."

"And in that I like you also." He leaned towards me. "It is a fair gift for a fair woman. And one who has delighted me more than any other woman I have known."

Chapter Eighteen

Sleeping King, Wakeful Servant

6 January 1538

You would have thought that the twelve long feast days of Christmas could be exhausting. You would be right. They were particularly exhausting when, like me, you had spent almost every waking day playing close attention to King Henry's needs. And a good many of those hours involved lying beneath or on top of him, trying in vain to quench his torrent of love.

I turned to look at him now. He was still asleep, the back of his hand lying upon his forehead as if he were struggling to remember something. Or readying himself to ward off a sudden attack.

The first light of morning was peeping through the window. A little shaft of sunlight fell upon the King's face. It looked different in sleep.

When awake, his face was square and strong as if it had been made by a blacksmith. His nose was big, the beak of a bird of prey. Beneath it was a mouth surprisingly small for such a large face. But it was his eyes which people noticed most.

His eyes appeared half-asleep yet watchful, as if he were doubting and distrustful of everyone who approached him. Wary eyes, weary eyes. Sardonic, calculating and cruel eyes. Eyes that could unman the bravest heart with a glance.

But in sleep the King was different. The sunbeam seemed to caress him now, as if it were a gentle mother soothing a petulant child. His face lost all its granite, all its grandeur. Without that fierce mind to sculpt them, his features took back a gentler look. A dreamer, an enthusiast, a soul keen to please.

I realized then why Catherine of Aragon, a woman of maturity, had fallen in love with her ardent boy. And why she'd been so dreadfully desperate to keep him even though she knew he no longer loved her.

He stirred in his sleep, lost in a dream. Sleep must be the only time he was truly alone, I realized. At every other time he was on show, with gentlemen to dress him, courtiers to flatter him, politicians to try to play him. He rarely ate alone and even then his servants stood watching. He never walked alone, for guards always paced close by and he usually had an ambassador or great lord beside him. Perhaps he was alone during prayer, but even then he was in converse with God. A God who he now seemed to believe was like some distant cousin or uncle.

With Gregory Frost, his Groom, he seemed most at ease.

No, not most.

He seemed most at ease with me. Despite the frantic lust that gripped him, despite the even more frantic coupling, I sensed he was at peace with me. And when we had finished making love he would lie back and sigh, like a child who had finished every last morsel of pudding, to his own great amazement. And then he would turn to me and a loving smile would play about his lips and he would reach out for me and silently squeeze my hand.

That was when I felt most close to him. When I felt safest. And most afraid.

I rose from the bed without waking the King and took myself to the little privy. How grand it was not to have to use a chamber pot or go to the public privy and sit and talk with thirteen others. I would have a bath this morning, I thought. The King's bath chamber was the thing I marveled at most in all of Hampton Court. It was a fairyland of pleasure, with hot water, steam and soft and yielding towels.

I washed my hands and hummed to myself a song which kept echoing in my mind. I did not know its title nor all the words but it was a pretty tune and it made me feel light in heart. I replaced the soft towel on the rack and stepped out into the bedchamber. I almost screamed in shock.

Gregory Frost was standing in the doorway. He appraised me for the briefest moment while I hastened to cover my breasts and private parts with my hands. He cast his eyes downward in a humble manner although I thought that he had feasted them upon me in that twinkling.

"I beg your pardon, madam. But the Lord Privy Seal desires to speak with you. At your earliest convenience." He turned to go and then paused. "My advice would be to go immediately," he said.

Thomas Cromwell, Lord Privy Seal. *What on earth could he want with me?*

I knocked upon the door, wondering that he had chosen to summon me at this time. The Twelfth Night feast was due to start at noon and all the Court were expected to be there.

A voice called to me to enter.

The January sun made no impression on the shadowiness of the room. I doubt even the midsummer sun would have been allowed to do so. A small fire burned in the grate but it seemed to cast little light and less warmth. I gazed around, my eyes struggling with the dimness of the chamber, searching for the whereabouts of the man who had commanded me to enter.

"Come, child," came a voice in front of me. "I will not eat you."

My eyes focused on the direction from which the sound came.

Sitting behind a desk, as immobile as that piece of furniture, was the Lord Privy Seal.

As my eyes got used to the dimness, his appearance solidified from out of the shadows; he seemed to coalesce, as if from stuff of legend, and settled into the palpable figure before me.

He was dressed in a coat of very dark green, darker even than the wall behind him, darker than the oak chair upon which he sat. A tight, grey hat was pressed upon his head and beneath it he wore his hair well cut, like a younger gentleman might, although the black was tinged with silver.

He gestured to me to come closer, his thick hand adorned with a single ring set with an immense green stone.

I approached the desk and he pointed to a chair in front of it.

I sat, keeping my face averted from his. But my eyes flicked across in order to see what manner of man was Thomas Cromwell. He was in his late middle age with a face as broad and pale as a haunch of pork. His nose was sharp and questing, the nose a little hunting dog might choose for itself if it were to become a human. His mouth was small and well formed, the furrow above it the exact mirror of the cleft upon his chin.

But it was his eyes which held me. Beneath eyebrows perpetually raised in question and doubt, deep sockets cradled unfathomable eyes. They watched me now, gimlet sharp, as immobile as those of a cat waiting on a mouse desperate to make a run for safety.

"You are Alice Petherton," he said.

His voice was like a river of honey sliding over stones. I felt the hairs on the back of my neck rise at the sound of it. Soft as balm, cruel as a scourge.

Raw power beat down upon me, as palpable as the heat from a forge, and I wondered whether it came from the man himself or from his authority and the rumor of his malice.

"I am Alice Petherton, my lord."

He cradled his fingers and rested his chin upon them, staring at me with eyes he must have trained not to blink. Little wonder they called him the King's Basilisk.

He gave a little sigh and picked up a document as though it were one he had been long studying and was suddenly wearied by.

"I am led to believe," he said, "that you are His Majesty's current favorite."

I nodded. "We read poetry together and go for little walks when the weather is clement."

He gave a sudden smile, one that seemed made up of pure delight and good humor.

"You read poetry and go for walks? How pleasant for the King, how fine a solace for him in his bereavement and grief."

He poured himself a cup of wine and, partway through, darted a glance at me.

"And when the weather is not clement? How do you entertain the King then?"

My lips lost all their moisture. I was desperate to wet them but something warned me to keep my tongue within my mouth. Better Cromwell did not see the organ that had so enthralled His Majesty.

"He finds my presence a comfort, my lord," I said.

Cromwell nodded. "I'm sure he does, Alice Petherton." He examined me as though I were a document he suspected of being a forgery. Or a piece of meat he had a mind to eat but feared might hide some rottenness inside.

He wiped his lips with his fingertips, as if cleaning away some lingering crumbs of food. His tiny eyes narrowed.

"I suppose not one of His Majesty's subjects would begrudge him taking comfort from someone as beautiful and alluring as you," he said. "A grieving heart can find solace in a heaving chest." His gaze moved to my bosom.

"If I can help His Grace to find solace in any way then I count it a duty well fulfilled."

Thomas Cromwell smiled. "And what would your father feel if he knew that you were whoring yourself in the King's bed?"

"I am not a whore, my lord."

"And I say you are. I say you most definitely are."

His eyes flashed wider suddenly. Their color seemed to change from black to green, wild as a tomcat's when it was readying itself to fight. I knew that I dared not argue with him, for to do so would risk my doom. Yet I also knew with a dread certainty that I could not afford to acquiesce too swiftly. This was a man who was used to people surrendering to him. I knew that I had to be different, if only for a moment. It was a tactic I had used with the King and I prayed that it would work as well with his servant.

"I am not a whore," I repeated. "A whore charges for her labors. I do not."

His eyes flashed even brighter.

"I hear what you are saying, Alice Petherton," he said. His voice was hard and rough now, no longer honey but a heated rasp.

I counted in my head—five, ten, fifteen, twenty—and still I did not back down.

Then I bent my head as if contrite. "But you are right, my lord," I said. "I am not a whore but I am, in truth, whoring myself."

I took a risk and looked him in the face. He had won, or so he thought, and his face softened.

"I am whoring myself," I continued. "But I do so for my King. And as for what my father might think, I cannot say. My father died when I was a child and I have lived my life without the firm hand of a man to guide me."

I held his eyes in mine and this time it was I who did not blink.

He ran his tongue swiftly over the tips of his teeth. His breath seemed to race a little.

"Do you feel the want of a firm hand to guide you?" he asked.

"A hand like His Majesty's?" I murmured.

"Very close to His Majesty's," he answered.

"Perhaps." I gave him the tiniest of smiles. "Though I would not wish to cause displeasure to the King."

He drummed his fingers on the table.

"Sensible child," he said at last, his voice now cooler and more distant.

He poured a second cup of wine and passed it to me. I sipped at it, realizing I was as parched as if I had engaged in furious combat with him.

He plucked up a little knife now, the sort one uses to break open a red wax seal. He turned it over and over in his hands like a conjurer attempting to fool the eye of his audience. Yet I felt that it was not me that he was trying to fool, not me at all. Perhaps he was pondering how to fool the King. Or perhaps he was, without realizing it, intent on fooling himself.

He let the little knife drop and leaned forward.

"Tell me, Alice Petherton, what do you want from King Henry?"

"I do not want anything. Just to serve him."

"Poppycock. What do you really want? Do you want to replace Jane Seymour? Do you want to be the next Queen of England?"

I shuddered involuntarily. "I can think of nothing worse."

"How so?"

I shook my head, realizing I had blundered into a corner. Or been forced into one.

My mind raced, wondering how to answer, wondering what form of words might best please this man of little mercy.

"I do not wish to die," I said quietly.

He leaned back in his chair, astonished by my words.

"You do not wish to die?" he asked.

"No, my lord."

He picked up the knife and held it to his lips.

"And you think that this is what happens to the women who become Queen of England?"

"Show me one who is alive that I might enquire it of her."

His mouth worked but no words came. Then he shook his head and a rumble of laughter escaped from him. He beat his hand upon the desk, once, twice.

"That is very good, Alice Petherton. That is very droll." He bit his bottom lip and pushed the tight hat back off his head. "I cannot recall when I was last so amused."

He stood up, stepped round the table and stood in front of me.

I rose swiftly, all a-flurry, fearing that he would strike me or summon guards to haul me away to some forgotten cell.

But instead he took my hand and kissed it.

"I like you, Alice Petherton," he said. "I like you very much. We shall become firm friends, you and I. And the King will be the better served for it."

Chapter Nineteen

Wives and Mistresses

7 January 1538

The King lounged back against the chair and belched. His hand reached out for a chicken and tore it in two. He took half to his mouth and began to chew on it with a look of half-absorbed content.

"Do you know something, Alice?" he said as he consumed the last of the fowl.

"What, Your Grace?"

He sighed and stared at the window. "I've just realized, this very moment, that I spent the most part of my lusty youth with a woman old enough to be my aunt."

I blinked at him.

"Catherine. My first wife. When I could have sported with pretty young things, made love to the flower of maidenhood, I stayed steadfast and loyal to an aging woman. And a barren woman at that."

"She gave birth to your daughter Mary," I ventured.

"Speak not of Mary," he said, his voice suddenly harsh.

He saw me stiffen and reached out to pat me.

"Pardon my stern voice," he said. "Any mention of that girl moves me to righteous wrath."

I bit my lip. This was the first time that I had seen any hint of the King's bad temper. It was a little show, I came to realize much later, but it was enough to shake my nerves.

I stole a look towards him. His face was set and hard and a red flush streaked both his cheeks. But then he took a deep breath and he smiled on me.

"Enough of such things," he said. "We are put on God's good earth to enjoy ourselves, not to vex our minds with sad musings and what-might-have-beens."

"You're so right, Your Grace."

He nodded. He was always right. Always. I wondered that he did not get sick of being always right.

He picked up a leg of lamb and bit into it. I felt a little hot in the stomach at the way he devoured the flesh so savagely. It seemed clear to me that he had not put away sad musings, far from it. Proof of this came within moments of him throwing the bone on his plate.

"She's as much a pain as her mother was," he cried. "Mary the bas-tard. More of a pain in fact. At least her mother was obedient. Mary is willful and getting more so by the day. It's her Spanish blood. It's hot and sour. Like fruit gone rancid in the heat of the sun."

Which sun was that? I wondered. The King thought of himself as the sun. Was it he who turned young Mary so shriveled and rank? And what of his other daughter, Elizabeth?

"I expect you're wondering what I think of the other bastard?" he asked.

I swallowed hard. How did he know? Should I deny any such thought? I made a swift decision.

"You read my mind, Your Grace. You know my very thoughts."

"That is because I have your heart in thrall, my dear," he said.

He hummed a little to himself. "I prefer Elizabeth to her sister, if truth were told. She has my red hair and my hot heart. A little minx she'll grow to be."

A smile played on his lips. "In fact she's a little minx already and she's not five years of age."

"And what of your son, Your Majesty? What of Edward?"

The King beamed. "He will be a great King, a worthy successor to me. He will stride the globe like a colossus. The Kingdom will flourish in his hands. And in the hands of his children. My grandchildren. My legacy."

He turned in his chair and reached out for a piece of needlework. He became totally absorbed in it, as if by staring at it he might find out some vital truth. They say that soothsayers of old would stare into the entrails of slaughtered animals to read a man's fate. I wondered whose fate the King might ever seek to read. His own perhaps. His son's?

He looked up and saw me watching him.

"It's a pretty piece, is it not?'"

It was not a question. I had already learned that the King's questions were not questions but statements it was best to agree with.

"It's very pretty, Your Grace."

He handed it to me. It was indeed very fine, although I would not have called it pretty.

"Very pretty indeed," I repeated. "And most skillfully done."

He took it back and examined it once again. "The Queen embroidered it. The late Queen. Queen Jane. She was an expert needle-woman."

Very expert with the needle, I thought to myself. *Even more expert with the knife.* I watched him as he turned the embroidery in his hand. I do believe he really doted upon the milksop. It's unbelievable but I do believe it. I would do well to remember this. People have such different opinions about the same person. Sometimes it almost seems they must be talking about someone else, not the person you know at all.

But then again, my opinion can change. I used to like Jane Seymour myself once.

I watched the King moon over the fabric she had left behind. A chill thought came unbidden to me. Would he be so gentle of the shirt I had made if I were dead in my grave? I shivered and dispelled the thought from my mind.

Still the King turned the piece over and over in his hand, examining it minutely. Perhaps he was not, after all, admiring it. Perhaps he was looking for a flaw. He wouldn't find one. Jane Seymour was far too good a needlewoman to leave a flaw. Not that she could do much else. I knew for a fact that she found reading difficult. And writing was a sore trial for her brain.

I smiled to myself. Here was a way in which I would supplant Jane Seymour. The way to this King's heart was through his mind.

He picked up a second piece of embroidery and handed it to me.

"What think you of this piece?" he said.

I examined the embroidery and looked up, puzzled.

"It is not as good as the first, Your Grace."

He seemed to withdraw into himself. He looked a little chagrined, a little hurt.

"It is my piece," he said. "I embroidered it."

"You embroidered it?" I failed to keep the astonishment from my voice.

"What of it?" he said, snatching the fabric back from me. "Jane taught me how to embroider. We used to sit and work at our pieces together."

I sighed inwardly. Perhaps I had a longer hill to climb before I left behind her shadow.

Gregory Frost knocked gently on the door to the Privy Chamber and slid inside.

"The Lord Privy Seal awaits," he said.

The King flung down his book.

"Send him in. Clear this away before you do." He pointed to the table littered with the remnants of his meal. He folded up the embroidery himself and placed the pieces in a chest.

I rose and curtsied. "I take my leave of you," I said.

"What do you mean?" He gave me a truculent look. "I didn't tell you to go."

"But I assumed, my lord, with the Lord Privy Seal desiring audience with you."

"Thomas Cromwell is like my shadow," he said. "You can't leave me every time you see my shadow so why would you leave when you see him?" He laughed suddenly at his own jest and the door opened.

"Hey, Thomas," he said. "I've just told Alice that you're my shadow. How do you like that?"

"A perfect analogy, Your Grace," he said within a heartbeat. "For if I am the shadow then you are the sun which gives me substance."

The King clapped his hands at that. Once.

"Now, that is how to flatter, Alice," he said. "Say something pleasing to me. But make it the truth and make it witty. That is how to flatter."

"You flatter me in saying so," Cromwell said.

"That is not so good, Thomas," said the King.

"Indeed it is not, Your Grace. I stand corrected. My wit, alas, is less good on cold days."

"When the sun does not shine, perchance," I ventured.

Both men turned to me in some surprise.

Then Cromwell laughed. "I do believe the girl has learned the lesson on flattery consummately well," he said.

"Consummately," said the King. "Here, Thomas, do you know Alice Petherton?"

Cromwell bowed his head towards me. "I have had the honor to speak with her, Your Grace."

The King glanced swiftly at his First Minister and for the briefest instance I caught a flash of suspicion in his eyes. Then he hid it and indicated that Cromwell should sit.

Cromwell settled himself in the upright chair next to the writing desk and unloaded a pile of papers upon it.

"You don't mind if Alice stays, do you?" the King asked.

"As Your Grace desires," he answered. "There are no great State secrets to discuss today."

"Then what do we have?" the King said. He picked up a document and tapped it on his palm. "I do not wish to be wearied by trifles today."

Cromwell did not raise his head but began to order the papers on the desk. "The King well knows that it is I who concern myself with trifles on his behalf. I bring only the things that he must make judgement on."

The King flung the document back on Cromwell's ordered pile, dislodging two papers, which fell on the floor.

"I know it, Thomas, I know it." He peered more closely at Cromwell. "I do believe you are going grey, Master Cromwell. You must be aging swiftly in my service."

"I praise the fact, Your Grace, for with advancing age comes greater wisdom. And so the better I may serve you."

The King jerked a thumb towards Cromwell for my benefit. "Another example, Alice. Masterly flattery. Masterly."

I was perplexed by this exchange. Did the King despise Cromwell for such blatant flattery? Did Cromwell feel shamed he was so found out that the King could make a jest of it?

I glanced from King to Minister. No, there were no such undercurrents. Both men were utterly at ease with each other. They both spoke the truth and it did not worry them. It was as if they were playing a game. It may have been a serious game but it was a game nonetheless.

"Some dissidents," Cromwell said, offering the King a list.

The King looked at it, distaste growing on his face.

"I do not wish to look at the names," he said. "You deal with them."

"Very good, Your Grace." Cromwell rolled up the parchment and put it to one side.

The King tapped his finger on his chin. Cromwell paused in his shuffling of papers but did not glance up.

"Anybody I might need to know about?" the King asked casually.

"Nobody, Your Grace."

There was a silence. A less comfortable silence.

"There is Lord Brampton," Cromwell added at last. "I did not think you'd wish to trouble yourself overmuch with him. He was ever a staunch supporter of the late Queen."

Which one? I wondered. *Catherine, Anne or Jane?*

"He was a loyal man in his youth," the King mused. "We hunted much together. Even before I became King."

Cromwell picked up the parchment and dipped a pen in a little bottle of ink. He held the quill above the list, as if waiting for the command to cross the name through.

"Do you think he's a danger, Thomas?" the King asked at last. "Really a danger?"

"I do, Your Grace. Else why would I put his name on the list?"

"The Tower perhaps?"

"Your Grace is being merciful." Cromwell flattened out the parchment carefully.

"Too merciful perhaps?"

Cromwell did not answer but inclined his head the merest fraction.

"Then let it stand," the King said. "But a swift death. We were once good friends."

"And his property, Your Grace. The usual?"

The King nodded. "But do not beggar his family. His wife is a good woman. Leave his wife her home and three or four manors. Enough to live on and bring up a family."

"A new husband for her? Now that she is to become a widow?"

"Is she still good-looking? I recall that she had a comely face."

"She has aged remarkably well, Your Grace."

"Then a new husband, Thomas."

"She will not be requiring so many properties in that case."

"True." The King did a quick calculation. "Leave her just the one, then. The one she lives on."

"Just the one," said Cromwell, making quick marks on a piece of paper.

I saw the King's eyes grow piggy and he leaned forward a little, unable to hide his interest.

"Four thousand acres," Cromwell told him. "Six hundred pounds in cash and effects."

My eyebrows rose. What lessons I was being given today. Flattery was the least of it. I was learning how to rule a Kingdom. How to rule a Minister. How to manage a King.

I was learning the power of life and death.

The King poured himself a cup of wine and gestured to Cromwell to pour himself another. The King watched with brooding eyes as he raised the cup to his lips.

"You have spoken with Alice, Thomas?" he said quietly.

"I have, Your Grace."

"Then you know?" He left the rest of the sentence unsaid.

Cromwell inclined his head.

"Does anybody else know, do you think?"

Cromwell sighed. "Not unless the girl has told anyone of what has transpired."

I felt my mouth go dry. "I have not, Your Grace."

I was going to add, *I swear it,* but thought that would sound too frightened, too desperate, too suspicious.

Cromwell turned his sharp eyes upon me. "No hints, no intimations, no girlish boasts?"

"None, Your Grace."

The silence settled on the room like a watchful beast.

"Should it be known, do you think?" asked the King.

Cromwell rested his chin in his hand. I stared at him. I sensed that behind the bland exterior his mind worked like a ship leaving port, seeking out the currents, sniffing out the wind, tacking this way and that to make the clearest headway.

"I would advise not, Your Majesty," he said at last. "The Queen's death is but recent and she has many who cherish her memory at Court still. Her brothers, for example."

The King seemed to bridle. "Would any dispute my right?"

"Of course not, Majesty." Cromwell's tone was emollient as cream. He paused to find the safest words. "But folk may know a thing and not wish to be reminded of it. Not immediately after some terrible shock like untimely death."

"So I can have my favorite but not announce it?"

Cromwell opened his hands to indicate agreement. But a moment later he said, "Favorite, Majesty? The term may be thought too charged for a good while yet."

"By those who don't want their noses rubbed in it?"

"Exactly."

The King leaned back and Cromwell picked up his wine and sipped at it.

"So," said the King, "we shall keep it private for the time being."

"I think you decide right," Cromwell said.

"I weary of the tittle-tattle of the courtiers in any case," the King said. "I will announce it in my own good time."

"In that case, Majesty," Cromwell murmured, "we must be doubly sure that no one knows."

"Apart from we three there's only Frost."

"I trust him," Cromwell said. His eyes turned to me once more, suspicion igniting in them.

"No one," I repeated. "I swear." I thought of what half the Maids suspected but said not a word of this. "I have told no one." It was fear that made me answer so, fear of the consequences. But the consequences of lying to the King and Cromwell might be far worse.

I wondered if I should tell the truth but it seemed too late to go back on my words now so I pushed my doubts aside and gave my sweetest smile.

"We have it, then," said the King lightly. "Not quite a State secret but private nonetheless."

Cromwell nodded and then paused a tiny fraction. When he spoke once more it was in a voice made conversational and innocent.

"How does Alice know when you require her presence?"

"I send for her," said the King. He sat upright, realizing the import of his words.

"The same messenger, Your Majesty?"

The King frowned, uncertain of who had been sent.

"It is, Your Majesty," I said. "It is always the same Page. Humphrey is his name." I swallowed hard and tried to calm my heart. "He is a saucy boy but not, I think, one to lightly gossip."

"Let us hope not," said Cromwell. "I shall examine him."

The King nodded.

I bit my lip.

Cromwell reminded the King that the Ambassador of France was due at any time. I was told I would not be required for the rest of the day. I took my leave and departed the chamber with Frost leading the way as if to spy out watchful eyes. I sensed that the most watchful eyes had been left behind me and resided in the head of the Lord Privy Seal.

Frost departed once we were safely beyond the King's privy chambers and I slipped past the Kitchens and hurried to my room. I felt no need of food. My stomach was heavy as a rock.

I slumped onto the bed. It felt like I had been on a grueling journey and I fell swiftly into sleep.

Later that day I sat alone in my chamber, my thoughts still racing. I went over in my mind the meeting between the King and Cromwell. There was something strange about it, something unusual about their relationship. Something I could not quite put my finger on.

I gazed out of the window. Snow had fallen while I'd slept and it had laid a mantle of softness upon the hard earth. It looked so beautiful. Even the branches of the trees were decked in white. As I child, I used to think that snowflakes were fairies. Good fairies, white and kind yet strong enough to protect me should I have need.

I pressed my face to the window and sighed with pleasure. It was so peaceful, so innocent and fresh.

Within a moment my thoughts slipped back to Cromwell, who must have long ago forgotten innocence.

Try though I might, I could not fathom the man. Beyond the certain fact that he was utterly loyal to the King, I could not hold on to any one opinion of him. It was as if he were a cloud of smoke, shifting and changing constantly, one moment light and translucent, the next as dense and impenetrable as night.

And yet?

I frowned. Men walked in dread of him. Courageous men blanched at his mere mention.

And yet? And yet I did not feel such fear of him. Why was this? I could sense the menace true enough. But it was as if he had chosen to lock that peril away for me.

Was this because I was the King's lover? I dismissed the notion even as I thought it. I recalled my interview in his Study. Aye, perhaps that meeting had made the difference. Perhaps it was then that he had decided what he thought of me. Or decided his plan concerning me.

At that moment the door to the chamber was flung open and a figure hurtled into my room.

It was Humphrey the Page. He slammed the door shut and leaned against it as if the hounds of hell were chasing him. He was white as the fields outside and his chest was heaving.

"Whatever's the matter?" I cried.

"That devil," he said. "That devil, Baron Cromwell."

I told him to sit down and poured a cup of wine for him.

"He summoned me, he did, m-miss," he stammered. "He summoned me and examined me for an hour. It felt like days. I thought that any moment I'd be taken off and placed upon a rack. That may have been less painful, come to that."

His eyes watered and a little tear fell on his cheek. He brushed it swiftly away, leaving a mark of grime upon his face.

"What did he want of you?" I asked as gently as I could. I knew what Cromwell had wanted but felt it best to ask, if only to calm the boy.

"He wanted to know if I'd told anybody that I'd taken you to the King. If I'd told anybody that I even took a message from the King to you."

"And have you?"

"By the heart of our Savior I have not."

I stared at him. "I always worry when boys such as you swear on the name of our Savior."

"On my mother's life, then." He wiped his nose. "There, that's more the thing for me to swear on."

I hid a smile. I suspected it was. Boys such as Humphrey never stopped worshipping their mothers. "You've told nobody? None of your friends?"

He shook his head.

"Not even to boast of your own importance?"

"Give me some sense," he cried. He pointed to his head. "Do you think I'd risk this for a bit of gossip? Give me more sense than that, miss."

I held up my hands to placate him although I thought that he was, perhaps, protesting his innocence a little too strongly. I seemed to recall that he had bragged to me about winning a wager with the Pages although I had wondered if this was fantasy on his part. For now I thought it best not to remind him of his boast. If he chose to forget it, then why should I make him even more fretful?

"I believe you," I said, as casually as I could. "But did the Lord Privy Seal?"

A little moan came from his chest. "I didn't think so, not for a long while. I'm bound for the chop, I thought to myself, and I'm not fourteen."

"You'd be hanged, Humphrey. The ax is only for gentlemen." I said this with a chuckle to make him calm. It did not work; he scowled at me.

"Well, I thought I was for it, anyway. He questioned me every which way, so many questions that I became confused. I contradicted myself, I told the opposite of what I'd said the second before. I knew I was doing it but I couldn't help myself. He went on and on and on, just like my mum does but worse."

"But did he believe you?"

He shrugged. And then he pulled a scarf from out his pocket, and then another.

"This is what saved my skin, miss."

I reached out for them. They were nothing but rags, one red, one green.

"How could these save your skin?"

Humphrey sat upright, his face suddenly brightening. He reminded me of a youngster cockerel readying itself for its first ever crow.

"Well, finally Mister Cromwell believed I'd told nobody, or so it seemed. But I realized I was still in danger, that just knowing about you and the King might mean my death."

"Don't be so melodramatic," I said.

He sat up still higher and grinned.

"Well, miss. At this point I spoke to him as bold as brass. I realized that the King would still need a go-between, so why risk it being someone else than me?

"I said, bold as gold, 'How will I be able to summon Alice Petherton in the future without people noticing me speaking to the lady concerned? It's risky to talk so often, a Page to one particular Maid of Honor.' I'd stumped the Lord Privy then and he began to ponder it. Then an idea came to me.

"I said I'd got two scarves, one red, one green. I said if the King wanted your presence, I'd go and find you, not say a word to you but wear the green scarf. If he didn't want you, I'd wear the red."

"But why would you ever need the red scarf?" I said. "Surely you'd never come to me unless the King wanted me. A green scarf will be quite sufficient."

Humphrey wriggled in his seat and looked a trifle put out. "Well, he liked the idea. Thomas Cromwell. He liked my idea. He said it was a grand idea and patted me on the knee. I think that's what saved my skin."

I handed back the scarves. "I'm sure it did. He must have thought you were quite like him. Clever and deceitful."

"Is he deceitful, miss?"

"Of course not, Humphrey." I raised one eyebrow. "He is the servant of the King." I smiled at him. "I think it was very clever of you. You saved your skin most definitely. And you may even have saved mine."

I smiled even more widely and he blushed as red as his scarf.

And my smile, and Humphrey's reaction to it, made me finally understand the relationship between the King and Cromwell. It was intimate. More intimate than that between the King and me.

Chapter Twenty

The Hiding of Sin

7 January 1538

My talk with Humphrey had reminded me of the dangers of what I was doing. I had lied to the King and Cromwell about how my liaison was suspected. Now, above all else, I had to quell the slightest hint of gossip.

I hurried to the Maids' Parlor. Mary was playing a lute in the alcove by the window. She always said it sounded best played there. The melody filled the Parlor like a breeze in springtime.

Susan was sitting close by, her nose in a book. There were three more of the Maids in the room. All were busy with their needlework.

I sat beside Susan and glanced at what she was reading.

"Is it interesting?" I asked in as casual a voice as I could manage.

"The subject matter is," she said, "but the words give me a headache. Why can't people write things plainly as they are said?"

"Vanity, I suspect."

"And a desire to seem wiser than they are. I wonder what a book written by a woman would be like?"

"It would depend upon the woman, I suppose. You would say it plainly, Susan; others would be flowery."

"And what about your words?" Susan said. "You have not shown me any of your poems."

I blushed and shook my head. "They're private. And they're not very good." The truth was that my poems spoke rather too much of love and of loving.

"I'm sure they're very good," she said. "You'll let me read them in your own good time." We sat in silence for a while but eventually Susan put her hand upon mine. "Something troubles you," she said.

"Nothing," I said lightly. "But I do feel like a little walk."

"It's still snowing," she answered. "How about a few turns around the Lower Court?"

"That sounds perfect," I said, although I knew it was not. It was not private enough for my liking.

Susan peered a little closer. "Shall Mary come?"

I nodded.

Susan glanced across to Mary, who nodded, brought her melody to a conclusion and laid down her lute. She joined us and without a word we headed towards the Lower Court.

Running round the Court was a covered passageway fifty yards long on each side. When the weather was inclement, the three of us would sometimes stroll there. Little windows looked out onto the Court itself, making the passageway light and pleasant. It would not do to walk alone there, of course. There were rooms for courtiers running along the passage and some of the younger men would seize the chance to seek better acquaintance of any lady they found on her own.

We walked in silence along the passageway. I felt my heart bubbling with anxiety.

"It is quiet for the time of day," Susan said as if by way of conversation.

"It is," I said. I drew closer to them. "I would talk of the King," I whispered, "but not here. Let us walk a little and then go to our chambers."

We took a turn around the Court and then climbed the stairs towards our living area. Susan and Mary spoke of the littlest things as we strolled: the weather, a dress that one was making, the music Mary had been playing. I walked in silence, my heart so in my mouth I dared not open it.

"Let's go to my room," Mary said. It was a good choice. She was perceived by all as a woman not given to tittle-tattle or conspiracies.

We slipped into her room unseen and she closed the door behind us. Her chamber was lovely, bigger than mine, as was fitting for a Maid of her seniority. Several musical instruments lay on her table: a recorder, a flute and a little stringed piece I did not know the name of.

"Now, what's the matter?" said Susan before we had even sat down. She was ever direct like this.

I gulped. "What do you know of the King and me?" I asked.

"We know he has summoned you to his chamber to read poetry," said Mary.

"Just to read poetry?" I asked.

Mary nodded.

"But we suspect something more," said Susan.

I looked at her and the bile rose to my mouth. I did not need to ask what they suspected.

"But have you told these suspicions to anyone else? Anyone at all?"

Susan shook her head. "Do you think we should be so unwise?"

"Or so disloyal?" Mary added.

"And the others?" I asked. "What of the others?"

"A few know that you talked with the King in the garden in the autumn," Susan said. "Perhaps one or two wondered if you had seen him since." She fell silent for a moment and then spoke more softly. "Perhaps some people might have suspicions of something more but no actual word of it has come to my ears."

"Well, it wouldn't, would it?" I said. "People know you are my friend."

"All the more reason why they'd wish to talk to me, then. To find out exactly what's going on."

I glanced at Mary, who nodded in agreement.

"What of Wicks and Bray?"

"They hate you anyway," Susan answered. "Even if they are putting out vile little hints, the Maids will put it down to their spite and take it with a pinch of salt."

Susan squeezed my hand. "If it would put your mind still more at rest, why don't you ask Lucy if she's heard anything amiss? She has no guile and would know of any gossip."

I shook my head. "The fewer who know my fears the better."

Susan glanced at Mary. "Then you do have something to fear?"

I blinked. Tears were beginning to form in my eyes.

"My poetry reading with the King would have been better kept secret," I said. "It came too close to the Queen's confinement and would not look right. He should have been reading poetry with her, not me, some might say."

"That would prove difficult," Susan said. "The woman could barely read."

"She could read," said Mary. "Not well, but she could read."

"But she preferred to sew," I said. "She was the best of us all at needlework. And she loved music more than words. Your singing must have been a great comfort to her at the end, Mary."

Mary nodded and dabbed at her eyes with a handkerchief.

"Thank you," she said with a sigh. Then she looked up and stared at me. "I don't care if you are sleeping with the King," she said. "You must be a comfort to him."

"Nor I," said Susan. "As long as he keeps his wolfish attention from me." She gave a little laugh.

I could not believe what I heard. "So you do know?" I cried.

"Of course we know," said Susan. "We're your best friends."

I put my hand to my mouth.

"But nobody else?" I managed to whisper.

They shook their heads.

"Let's just hope that you don't fall pregnant," Susan said.

"I don't think that is likely. The King has only managed to get four children these past thirty years. And I am careful."

Susan sighed with relief and squeezed my hand.

"Your secret is safe with us," Mary said.

The tears began to course down my cheeks in earnest. "It must stay that way," I said. "Until the King decides otherwise. No gossip, no hints, not the slightest suspicion."

"That will prove harder as time goes by," Mary said. "The occasional absence can be accounted for but how will lots of them be explained?"

"I don't know," I said.

"But I do," said Susan. "Religion."

I shook my head in confusion.

"You shall say you have a sudden interest in the new religion. You will go to the Chapel on your own and pray. You will carry a book on faith with you and study it with fervent eye. You will tell others you must retire to your room for contemplation. You must even talk to them of faith and disputed theology. People will soon tire of you."

Mary giggled. "That is most cunning of you, Susan."

"A cloak of purity is the cloak which covers best."

She's right, I thought. *And Jane Seymour would have endorsed her words.*

I immediately borrowed a book on theology from the youngest of the Palace priests. He blushed a furious red as he gave it to me, and even more when I placed my hand on his as I took the book.

"Would you give me lessons on the new faith?" I asked.

"It is not a new faith," he said, glancing quickly as if the pews had ears. "The King is still his most Catholic Majesty, still Defender of the Faith. He is not a Lutheran."

"But he has supplanted the Pope as head of the church?"

"He has indeed. And that is right and proper."

I sighed loudly and shook my head slowly. "It is confusing for a simple girl," I said. "That is why I ask for lessons from you."

He blushed again.

The poor man will have imminent need of confession, I thought with satisfaction.

"Perhaps Father Ambrose," he said, his voice high. "He is far more knowledgeable than I."

"He is too old and dry," I said. "I am young and fresh. I need my teacher to be so as well." I leaned nearer so that my face was close to his. He fidgeted nervously but did not move away.

"I need a teacher to understand my heart and soul," I breathed.

He made a noise in the back of his throat and struggled to his feet. "I must go now and pray for guidance."

"Do that, Father Luke," I said. "But I pray you, do not desert me in my hour of need."

He turned and fled. I chuckled to myself. I had my cloak of purity now.

Father Luke sent word to me the next day. He had sought guidance from Father Ambrose, who had immediately consented to Luke acting as my spiritual adviser. I wondered at the old man's alacrity. Perhaps he feared for his own soul more than he feared for Luke's.

I hurried down to the Chapel and found Father Luke deep in prayer. Or perhaps not quite so deep, for I saw his eyes flick open as I approached and he mumbled to a speedy end.

"Ah," he said. "You received my message."

"I did indeed. My heart welled up with joy." It was no word of a lie for I knew now that I would have the disguise I needed. But my joy ended almost immediately when Luke pointed to a pile of books beside him.

"These are the tracts which we will study," he said. "And when the new Bible is ready, Miles Coverdale's Bible, we will sit and read that together."

"Is that a big book?" I asked.

"The Bible is a large tome, Alice. As befits its mighty subject."

"I would not be able to rest it on my knees, then," I said.

"No, indeed. We will have to place it on a table and scan it together."

"And when will we be able to read it?"

Luke shrugged. "It is not yet printed. In the meanwhile I shall have to read the Bible to you in the Latin."

"I do not know much Latin," I said.

"Then I shall translate it for you," he said. "I shall be your Coverdale."

"I shall enjoy being Coverdaled by you," I said, placing my hand upon his.

He jumped at my touch but did not move his hand away. I gently withdrew mine. *Not such an innocent after all*, I thought to myself.

Chapter Twenty-One

Why Is the King Happy?

9 January 1538

Richard Rich hurried along the road to the river. He was late and he hated to be late.

Not as much as his servant Ellen Coles hated it, however.

The previous night he had told her to wake him at five. She entered his chamber at six, looking exhausted. No doubt she had been rutting, he thought. So he had struck her hard across the face, raising a red mark, which would give food for thought for her lover, Mason.

Rich could not tolerate wayward servants.

The sharp January air bit at his cheeks. His stomach grumbled and he paused for a moment to buy a meat pie from a stall close to Blackfriars. He crammed it into his mouth as he walked, its scorching heat a welcome relief from the bitter chill. It was only when he had almost finished that he tasted the sharp tang of meat gone rotten. He would seek amends from the seller when he returned.

Half a dozen boats were tied up at the wharf. A few of the water-men turned away when they saw him, more willing to lose a fare than take him on their boat. Pennies did not make up for the penance of his presence.

He clambered aboard a boat with a sturdy-looking fellow who looked as though he could pull fast.

"Hampton Court Palace," he said. "And quick about it."

The waterman hastened to pick up his oars and pulled out into the stream. There was a thick mist upon the water and the sounds of other boats were magnified.

Rich leaned back against the threadbare cushion and thought that this must have been like King Arthur's journey to the Isle of Avalon. Adrift in swirling mists, dislocated from the world, uncertain of what lay ahead.

Rich shuddered. He did not like this feeling.

"Can't you row any faster?" he demanded.

"I could indeed, sir," the waterman said. "But I'd risk collision in this fog. The sound is chancy, you see. Boats that are far away seem close by. Those that are next to your elbow seem far away and safe. But they're not safe. Not necessarily. My father died in his boat in weather like this. I loved him but I've no mind to follow him just yet."

"What do I care of your father?" Rich said. "Save your breath for your rowing."

He peered to his right. The north bank of the river could only just be seen. The south bank was hidden altogether. "And keep your ears sharp," he said. "If we suffer collision I'll have you in front of a magis-trate and beggar you."

The waterman did not answer. A moment later Rich heard the soft plop of the man spitting in the river.

What does Cromwell want so early in the morning? Rich wondered. He cast his mind over recent events. There seemed nothing untoward, nothing to trouble the King overmuch. Had Cromwell put a foot wrong? Had he angered the King?

Rich shook his head at so unlikely a scenario. Cromwell could juggle a dozen balls while walking on a high wire.

A sour taste rose in his mouth. *Is it me who's put a foot wrong? Is Cromwell angry at something I've done or left undone?*

His stomach heaved at the thought and he hung his head over the side of the boat, thinking he might well vomit.

He grasped hold of the timber, trying to recall anything that he had done which might have caused such wrath. Not that Cromwell needed cause to move against a man. No cause beyond his own advancement, at any rate. And the King? The King would strike down a man for no reason whatsoever. Because he could. Because he was King.

Rich dipped his hand in the waters and wiped his face. Then he groaned. The Thames was foul with waste and rotting things and he had dribbled its waters upon himself.

My God, what a day this is proving.

The waterman pulled into the wharf of Hampton Court and helped Rich clamber ashore.

"Should I wait, sir?" he asked.

Rich threw him a coin. "Of course not. I've business with Lord Cromwell."

The man's face gave nothing away, though he had heard of Cromwell sure enough.

"God be with you, in that case," he said. But he spat on the ground next to Rich's foot nonetheless. A spit was the surest proof against devils who supped with Satan.

Rich turned and hurried up the road which led to the Palace. Guards stood at intervals along the way, stamping to force some warmth into frozen feet. The guards at the gate recognized him and allowed him to enter without showing proof of his business. His heart lifted a little at this. The thrill of power still tasted sweeter than a virgin's flesh.

Once inside the Palace such thoughts deserted him. It was little warmer inside than out at this hour, for the roaring fires had not had time to heat the vast expanse of halls and passageways. His own heart grew still colder. *What does Cromwell want of me so suddenly?*

And then it came to him. Cromwell was angry but not at any of his deeds.

He took a deep breath, knocked upon the door and entered on the curt command.

The Lord Privy Seal did not deign to glance up but remained bent at his paperwork, his quill working inexorably upon some document. Rich gave a little cough but still Cromwell did not as much as raise his eyes. Eventually the quill moved, pointing to the chair in front of his desk.

Rich slid into it and waited, his heart in his throat.

The scratch of the pen upon the parchment was the loudest noise by far in that room. The fire in the grate crackled merrily but it was not so loud. Cromwell's breathing was faint and low. Even the pounding of the blood in Rich's head could not drown out the scratching. It was a thing of power, a portent of great majesty. He had known that pen to obliterate men's worlds, to ruin monasteries, to torment flesh. That pen had made great men insects and puny men giants. That pen had even banished the Pope's power from the land, made rogues of holy men and saints of villains. That pen was life and even more, it was death.

"You sent a message to me," Cromwell said, still without looking at Rich. "You asked me why the King was so happy."

"I did, my lord."

"Did you know the answer? Or did you expect me to know?"

Rich licked his lips. *How to answer?* He sensed that Cromwell was livid with fury at him. He cursed the conceit that had made him send the message. *How to answer?*

"I thought that you might know, Your Grace."

Cromwell put down the pen and stared at Rich.

"And if I did, what of it? What business is it of yours? What possible business, Richard, what possible business?"

Rich swallowed. The spittle in his mouth felt like lumps of clay.

"To do my work, my lord," he mumbled, "I need to know."

"No, Richard, you do not."

Rich's mouth opened but he could pluck no word to fill it.

"Do close your mouth, I beg you," Cromwell said. "I can see some pie caught in your teeth."

Cromwell rolled up the parchment and placed it carefully in a box. Rich stared at it as if it were the warrant for his own execution. *Surely I am worth more than this to him? Surely more than this to the King?*

"So," Cromwell continued, "you send me a note without good reason. You seek information from me when you know full well, or *should* know full well, that it is I who send you snouting out information for me."

"I did not mean to offend, my lord."

Cromwell gave a mirthless laugh. "You did not offend me, Richard. A fly offends me when it buzzes around my head; a hound offends me when it shits where I wish to tread. But you did not offend me."

Rich laughed, his voice so tight it sounded like a child's.

"Now you offend me," Cromwell said.

Rich heard a new sound: his own teeth chattering.

"But I have an answer for you," Cromwell said airily. "Help yourself to wine while I tell you what it is. You look in need of a draught to warm you."

Rich poured wine into a cup. Some spilt and spread across the desk like blood. He took the cup to his lip and gulped down the wine.

"The King is so happy," Cromwell said, "because he has got himself a new bed companion."

"A new whore?"

"Tut-tut, Richard. It is not wise to use such words of the King's friends. Especially not this one." He gazed into the distance.

"Why so, my lord?" Rich ventured.

"Because this one is special. Not like his other women, not even like his Queens. She is clever, subtle and of devious mind. Not like his other women at all. No, perhaps I am wrong in this. Maybe she is like Anne Boleyn at least. Yes, maybe she has something of Boleyn about her."

"Is she handsome?"

"Of course she is, you fool. She is more; she is beautiful."

"I wondered," Rich said, "because not all the King's women have been great beauties."

"You're right, Richard. It is a strange thing now you remark upon it." He closed his eyes for a moment and when he opened them again they were tight with malice. "You think he chooses only women who are his inferior in comeliness?"

Rich gulped. "I think nothing of the kind, my lord."

Cromwell pursed his lips. "Some think it of him. Though few would say it.

"But it is not true of this woman," Cromwell continued. "Not Alice Petherton. She is a beauty, Richard, a rare beauty. I am sure that sight of her would gladden even your jaded eye, my friend."

Rich gnawed at his lip. Alice Petherton was the King's lover. Why had he not heard this? He cursed the fact that he had been so long away from Court. His thoughts went from surprise to anger and finally to alarm. What might the bitch have told the King about him?

"If Venus were to take human form," Cromwell said quietly, "she might take form as Alice Petherton."

Richard Rich heard Cromwell say this and wondered if he had been meant to. His windmill mind began to turn, grinding this information to make new flour.

He saw Cromwell watching him and quailed. Of course he had meant him to hear. It was a trap. He could not see the complexity of the trap but realized that his master had laid it for him nonetheless. *Does he really think I'm foolish enough to spread rumor that he lusts after the King's new whore?* The question died in his mind. *Of course he doesn't. He doesn't think I'm foolish enough. But he suspects I am ambitious enough.*

Rich closed his mind for a moment and saw a vast abyss opening up beneath him. *Let me be*, he pleaded silently, *let me be.*

"So now you have it," Cromwell said levelly. "You are as well informed about the King's happiness as you have need to be." He pushed a pile of documents towards Rich.

"I want these priories investigated. No, that is not the right word. I want them closed. See to it."

Rich nodded.

"Oh, and Richard," Cromwell said.

Rich stared at him.

"Breathe not a word of the King's new friend to anyone. Not if you value life."

Rich scrabbled up the papers and scurried from the room.

Chapter Twenty-Two

Sir Thomas Seymour Hunts

6 February 1538

The services in the Chapel were not the highlight of my week. Father Ambrose was a mumbler, dribbling words onto his chin in a dreary monotone. This may have been a mercy, for I imagine his words, could we have actually made them out, would be the very pinnacle of tedium.

It was a freezing February morning and I huddled near the back of the Chapel with Susan, Mary and Lucy. Lucy, good girl that she was, strained to listen to the sermon. Mary was humming a little tune of her own making without realizing that she was doing so. Susan, on the other hand, was listening intently in order to make witty and disparaging comments about Ambrose after the service.

As usual I began to daydream. The old man's droning was like the buzzing of a bee in summertime: soporific and conducive to flights of fancy.

I imagined myself owning my own lands, somewhere in Cornwall or Cumberland for preference, somewhere far away from Court, somewhere I could not be easily found.

I would live in an ancient manor house with sturdy walls and grand entrance. Dotted around the house would be numerous other buildings: a buttery, a stable block, a lodging place for my visitors. And in the farthest part of the manor would be a little building all for me. It would be round, the bottom story of a tower maybe. There would be windows dotted across the wall so that the sun would fill the inside of the tower from morning until night. And there I should write poetry and paint. No one would disturb me save one ancient servant. Manners would be his name, and he would trudge over to the tower to tell me dinner was about to be served. He would always carry my books back to the house, no matter how heavy they were. I would follow him with a light step, brushing my hands against the flowers which fringed the path, releasing their fragrance to the wind.

Most satisfying.

I could never quite decide whether any of my friends would be with me or not. Most of the time I thought I might get lonely on my own so I usually placed Susan and Mary in a house a few miles away where they could visit when I asked them. Or I could call on them and we could walk together and talk and talk.

Susan's elbow prodded me in the arm. "There's Luke," she said.

I dragged myself away from my reverie and focused my eyes. Father Luke had taken the place of Father Ambrose as he did towards the end of each service now. Presumably the old man became tired or his mind began to ramble even more than usual. At any rate, Luke began to read a lesson or a homily, I know not which. He did not mumble; his voice was clear as a bell on a winter morn. But he was, unfortunately, given to great pauses and flourishes, which seemed to alarm the congregation. I think he may have seen too many mummers' plays as a child.

It was at great variance to the Luke I knew. With me he was quiet and nervous. Here he bestrode the altar as if it were a stage.

"Beneath the cloth lurks a man of passion," said Susan dryly.

"I have seen no sign of it," I answered. "He is quite limp if truth were told."

"That is probably a good thing," she answered. "He serves a purpose for you, nothing more."

"I remember it well," I said. "It is a most useful service but the hours do drag with him."

The mere thought of the long talks about religion which I endured with Luke was enough to make me yawn. But they threw a cloak over my whereabouts and this was their only purpose.

The service ended at last and we joined the throng who pushed their way out of the Chapel.

It was a bitter cold day and the courtiers' breath surged around like winter mist. I felt my teeth chatter in their sockets and I stamped my feet to try to keep warm. Of all the months, I hated February most. Short though it was, it seemed to linger like some drear disease that clung to one with grim determination.

"Oh, do hurry," I muttered to myself, as people filtered slowly through the great entrance into the Palace.

Lucy pulled at my arm and nodded towards the edge of the crowd, a worried look upon her face.

"Who is that man?" she asked.

I followed her gaze. A tall man with piercing eyes stared intently at us. He had close-cropped hair, as if he were a soldier, but he made up for this with a long and luxuriant beard. It was as auburn as a fox's tail, neatly trimmed and well cared for, hanging low upon his chest like a weapon.

"I've never seen him before," I said.

"That's Lord Seymour," Mary said.

I turned to her in surprise. "Jane Seymour's brother?"

"One of them. Thomas. He's just come back from France or somewhere."

I examined more closely. He did not look like any relative of Jane's. Where she seemed half-dead long before her death, her brother seemed to exude rude health and energy. His stance was loose and relaxed enough but his eyes darted everywhere. It was as if he were holding himself on a tight rein for fear of exploding. Not a milksop. Not a milksop in the slightest.

"He's looking at us now," said Lucy in alarm.

He was indeed looking at us. He stood forward on his legs, head jutting towards us like a pointer dog indicating game. His left hand reached up and stroked his beard as if it were his favorite pet. I thought at any moment he might sniff the air, raise his head to the sky and bay like a lovelorn hound.

"Pray God he doesn't come over," Susan muttered.

"Is he dangerous?" Lucy gasped.

"Only to your maidenhood," Susan said.

Lucy blushed red from chin to bonnet.

Not dangerous to me, in that case, I thought. *Not dangerous at all.*

But he did not move. He had no need to. The crowd was drifting towards the entrance to the Palace and we were being carried along with the tide.

All too soon we came up level with him.

He bowed and his long beard seemed to move independent of him, as if imbued with its own life force.

"Miss Zouche," he said. "Miss Dunster. It is a pleasure to see two such pretty faces again."

But as he said it he looked at neither of them. His eyes darted from Lucy to me and back again.

"Good day, Lord Seymour," Mary said, doing him a little curtsy. "It is a pleasure to see you but forgive us if we hurry inside in search of warmth."

"It is indeed cold, my dear," he said, giving a courtly bow and pointing out the door as if we were too stupid to realize it was there.

I doubted whether he felt any cold at all, not with that vast blanket of beard to protect him. Nor with the hot lust flooding from his loins.

I felt his hungry eyes slide over me, evaluating and reconnoitering. I stared back, brazen-faced. This seemed to startle him for the briefest moment. Then his eyes seemed to twinkle and he soothed his beard once again with tender brushing.

"I do not seem to have made your acquaintance, my dear," he said, holding out his hand.

"You are correct, Lord Seymour," I said. "You do not."

And I swept past him into the Palace.

"That may not have been too clever," Susan whispered to me once we were inside.

"Perhaps not," I said. "But it was most gratifying."

We strolled together towards the dining room. It was almost noon; the lengthy sermon and the cold had sharpened our appetites.

If I had thought my cutting comment would have ended Thomas Seymour's interest in me I was mistaken. If anything it had whetted it. Some men relish a challenge, and a forthright, confident woman is to them like gold to a miser.

It was the day after the service that I saw him again. Since the death of Jane Seymour the Maids of Honor had much more freedom. We did not have to wait at her command and could go anywhere much as we pleased. It pleased me to walk in the gardens. The open spaces and winding paths were a welcome relief from the morbid atmosphere of the Palace.

The morning had been wet, but by early afternoon a brisk wind had swept the clouds from the sky and the sun was shining a wintry yellow.

Susan and Mary took one look at the coursing wind and declined my suggestion to go out.

"I'll come to the gardens," said Lucy eagerly. She was still at pains to be agreeable to me after her recent short desertion to the Wicks camp.

"Come, then," I said in a cool tone, as if I acquiesced in her company rather than welcomed it. Her face fell and I regretted my words. "But make sure you dress warmly," I added kindly, to make amends. "Looks can be deceptive; it may be cold in the wind."

She hurried off like a puppy fetching its leash. I went to my chamber and put on my thickest jacket and over that a cloak my mother had owned. It still smelled of her, or so I liked to believe. It was worn and threadbare but it was one of the few things I had to connect her with me now. She died twelve years ago and I was beginning to lose the picture of her in my mind.

I met Lucy at the Gatehouse. It was not as cold as in recent days but the wind was searching so I was grateful for my cloak. We hurried to get in the shelter of the Palace walls and made our way to the Knot Garden. In summer it was a place of scent and subtle color. Now, in the middle of winter, it looked forlorn. Fallen leaves were sodden from the rain and snow and seemed to cling together in clumps of sullen misery. I did not wish to stay longer here.

"Come," I said, taking Lucy by the hand, "I know a secret place."

We walked along the path beside the garden and headed to the river. About halfway towards it a path veered off to the left, a narrow path fringed by aspen trees and willows. It was quite unlike the rest of the gardens; it felt as natural as the countryside that lay beyond the Palace. I never knew for sure whether it had been designed in this manner or merely forgotten by the gardeners. As we walked along, I had the sudden thought that it had not been forgotten by them at all, that they had left this wayward corner for their own delight.

The path followed the course of the river and we could glimpse its waters beyond the trees and rippling rushes. At length we saw a circle of osiers straight ahead.

"Here we are," I said. "Here is my secret place."

The branches of the trees already bore the first of their catkins. My heart lifted at this. For me, catkins were the promise of spring.

But I had not brought Lucy here just to see catkins.

"Close your eyes," I said to Lucy. "I'll guide you to the surprise."

She did as I asked and I took her arm firmly in mine. I led her into the circle of trees and whispered, "You can look now."

She opened her eyes and gasped with delight. The circle of trees formed a bower all around us. In the center of that bower was a small mound about four feet high.

It was covered in snowdrops. It was as if a beautiful green scarf had been studded with diamonds.

"It's a fairy town," Lucy said, clutching me by the arm.

I smiled at her fondly.

"No it is, Alice," she said, "believe me. There really are fairies and they live in secret, secluded places far away from people. Some of them live in tiny farmsteads, so small that they remain unseen. But there are a few places, magic places, where fairies love to live. They build a town and weave around it magic webs so it's kept hidden from prying eyes."

She clapped her hands with joy. "And this is one of them."

She bent closer to the mound as if to search for tiny fairy folk. Then she glanced up. Her face was serious. "We are privileged to see this, Alice. We must promise not to breathe a word to anyone."

"I promise," I said. "We'll keep it secret from all the world."

"Even from the King?"

I crossed my heart. "Secret—even from the King."

"What will you keep secret from the King?" a deep voice said behind us.

We jumped in fright.

Standing behind us, hand on hip, was Thomas Seymour. He was wearing a thick wolf-fur coat and a small hat, which fitted snug upon his skull. There were dark stains on his legs as though he had rushed across a muddy patch of land.

"You frightened us, my lord," I said.

He pursed his lips as if he had dropped a precious object on the ground by mistake. "I am sorry," he said. "I would not have done that for the world."

He stood in front of us—too close, I thought—and gave a courtly bow.

"Please accept my apologies for any alarm I may have caused." He glanced around as if he were a landlord taking stock of some property long neglected. "This is a pretty place," he said. "A place most suitable for such pretty ladies."

Lucy giggled with a mixture of pleasure and embarrassment. I noticed he stroked his beard at the sound of her laughter. He would not find it easy to pat himself on his own back, so this fond stroking must suffice instead.

"Are you alone, my lord?" I asked.

"I was until I chanced upon you," he said. "Quite alone."

He grinned and it seemed a gesture fixed halfway between a promise and a threat.

"It is good to walk alone on such a day," I said. "Please do not let us detain you on your journey."

He shook his head and held his hands out wide.

"Do not trouble yourself over this," he said. "I was only strolling, taking the air. I find Hampton Court rather too constricting." He paused and leaned closer towards us. "It seems that maybe you do as well."

"Not at all," I said. "I find the Palace most congenial. We only came here to see the flowers."

"Alice brought me to see them," Lucy said. "It was a surprise."

"So, you are called Alice," he said as if he had won a point in debate. "My name is Thomas."

I could have kicked Lucy.

"I know who you are, Lord Seymour," I answered in a cool voice. "We were Maids of Honor to your sister."

He nodded. "And I am sure that you gave her great service. It seems only fair that I should give you good service in return."

I did not answer.

I noticed that this made him uncomfortable, as if he had not expected his comment to go unanswered.

My mind went back to when I had first met the Lord Privy Seal. Cromwell was the master of silences. It was good to remember this. Most people hated silences and rushed headlong and willy-nilly to fill them. I would learn to be the master of silences and not their servant. It would be a most useful weapon for me to wield.

Lord Seymour seemed to cast about for something to say. And then, as if he had a better idea, he stooped and tore out a clump of snowdrops and presented them to Lucy.

She shied away like a foal. "You shouldn't have done that," she cried.

"But it's a gift," he said, a look of confusion on his face.

Tears sprang to her eyes as she stared in horror at her desecrated little town.

Seymour did not know what to do and proffered the flowers to me instead.

"I am not partial to gifts declined by another lady," I said. "Thank you so very much for the offer but I must refuse."

He flung the flowers on the ground and would have trampled them, I think, but Lucy bent and picked them up, replacing them on the mound with as much reverence as a daughter placing flowers upon her parents' tomb.

Seymour drew himself up and his voice came stronger on the winter air.

"This is no place for ladies to wander on their own," he said. "Come let me escort you to the Palace."

"No place to wander?" I said. "Why so? There is no danger here."

"We are close to the river. There may be all sort of ruffians here: footpads, thieves, men who would prey on two defenseless girls."

"Not every man sees women as their prey, Lord Seymour," I said.

"And certainly not me," he said with emphatic tone.

I did not reply; I essayed my new weapon of silence and watched him squirm.

We stood thus for what seemed an age. The silence seeped around the dell until I came to think I heard the waters lapping on the bank.

"Oh, let's go back, please, Alice," said Lucy. "I want to go back."

Seymour hid a smile of triumph and offered her his arm.

I did not answer her, nor did I move.

"Will you join us?" Seymour asked.

I shook my head.

"I most definitely cannot leave a lady here on her own," he said with a solicitous voice. He gestured to the river. "Footpads, thieves."

He held out his hand to Lucy. "Come, my child," he said.

"But if you take Lucy with you," I said, "it will be you who has left me here alone, my lord."

"But poor Lucy is distressed," he said. "She desires to return to the Palace."

I turned my gaze to Lucy. Her eyes widened, realizing it was she who we tussled over. I wondered whether that made her feel powerless or quite the opposite.

"I'm all right now," she said. "I think it best if Alice and I continue on our walk."

Lord Seymour bowed. "Of course, dear ladies. I will disturb you no longer." He bowed once more and took two steps away. Then he half turned. "I would feel happier if I kept you in my sight, however.

Please allow me this, dear ladies. I will follow you at a distance. You need not be aware of me."

I would with that great beard. I'd see it in my mind's eye every step, slinking after us through the woods like a starving dog-fox.

But there was nothing more we could do about it. "That is most gracious of you, Lord Seymour," I said, feeling that victory had been snatched from me.

I held out my hand to Lucy. "Come, let us continue our walk."

"Have you more secrets to show me?" Lucy asked as we headed towards the river.

"Only those within the hearts of men," I said.

She looked perplexed and shrugged. And so we walked for a good hour more until the cold began to bite hard. And all the while Lord Seymour dogged our steps, a shadowy specter.

Chapter Twenty-Three

A King Is Refreshed

31 March 1538

The last day of March was Mothering Sunday. All of the Palace servants should have been allowed to go home to their mother church and to their mothers. As usual, the King announced that any servant who wished to leave their duties for the day could do so with his blessing. As usual, none of them dared take up the offer.

It was a fortunate thing that none of them left, for on this day the Palace had great need for servants. Mothering Sunday also bore the name Refreshment Sunday and was the one day in Lent when the rigors of fasting were relaxed. Or it would have been if the King had not decided to relax them earlier in the month by proclaiming that white meats could now be eaten. The whole of the nation responded with great loyalty by killing and eating every type of fowl they could lay their hands on.

The official reason for this announcement was that the cold weather had caused a dearth of fish and that people would starve unless the

Lenten ban on meat was relaxed to allow the consumption of chicken, goose and wild-fowl. The real reason was different. The King realized that in religious matters he could now do whatever he chose with no fear of admonishment from the Pope. Like a child with a new toy, he was keen to play with this delightful new power. And he was clever in his choice of how to use it. Allowing people to break their Lenten Fast proved very popular with high and low throughout the Kingdom. And with many fat prelates in the church, of course, who always found Lent the most difficult rite to observe.

The King intended to celebrate this Mothering Sunday with more than his usual abundance. It was the first Mothering Sunday since Prince Edward had been born and the King seemed to have decided that he should make a pretense of grieving while celebrating to surfeit and beyond. As you see, I was getting to know His Majesty very well by this time.

I walked with Susan, Mary and Lucy to the Chapel. My usual low spirits at the thought of a dreary mass were lifted by the knowledge that a fine feast and pleasant entertainments would follow. There were far more than the usual number of people in the Chapel. Courtiers who lived nearby had descended upon the Palace like rats upon an overflowing grain barn.

The Chapel was decked out in rose-colored hangings and Father Ambrose and Luke had swapped their Lenten purple vestments for rose-hued ones. I nodded to Luke when I saw him and gave him the warmest of smiles, for he looked quite handsome. He blushed more scarlet than his vestments and dropped a chalice.

"Good morning, dear ladies," came a familiar but unwelcome voice.

We bobbed our heads as we knew we were expected to in the presence of a lord.

"Good morning, Lord Thomas," Susan said dryly.

"Rose Sunday," Seymour said, rubbing his hands together. "One of my favorite days. I hear that those who get married on this day are especially blessed."

Susan pretended surprise. "Are you to be married on this day, my lord?" she asked.

Seymour smiled like a cat. "Not today. But perhaps later I will advance my suit." He gave me a lascivious grin.

"Lord Seymour has a fancy for you," Susan whispered when he had left to take his seat.

"I know it," I replied. "I have been expressly caustic and rude to put him off."

She laughed at my words. "Then that was foolish of you. I suspect he's the sort of man who relishes a challenge. It would have been better had you seemed meek and mild and then he would have tired of you much quicker."

I nodded, recalling how I'd done the same thing with Richard Rich and that had goaded him even more. Susan Dunster could peer into the darkest crevices of people's minds; I would be sensible to listen to her advice. I seemed to peer into minds and then forget what I had discovered. Or ignore it.

The mass finished eventually and we hurried out of the Chapel like schoolboys fleeing the classroom on a hot summer's day. We made our way towards the Great Hall and, even before we arrived there, the rich smell of the feast sharpened our appetites.

The sight which met our eyes was magnificent. The Hall was filled with tables and on each of them was a huge platter containing a suckling pig, a joint of beef and a haunch of venison. Surrounding this, like courtiers around the throne, were other platters heaped with pheasants, partridge, duck and goose, legs of lamb, hare and venison. Each place setting held a wooden platter with fine white bread beside it and a glass beaker filled with claret.

Susan, Mary, Lucy and I found seats as close to the windows as possible. It was still chill in the Hall but we knew from experience that it would soon become unbearably hot. Then the windows would be thrown open to let in much-needed air and we were determined to benefit from this.

At the top of the Hall was the Royal table. Arrayed upon this was a range of food such as I had never seen at even the grandest feast. If the King had intended this Refreshment Feast to send a signal to the church and Pope, he could not have chosen better. It was as if he had commanded the greediest gluttons in the Kingdom to devise the feast of their dreams and then employed a hundred cooks to make those dreams reality.

The centerpiece of the Royal table was a dolphin in a smooth white sauce. Surrounding this, as if they were swimming in a lake, was a veritable flock of swans.

"They're stuffed with birds," a kitchen lad whispered to us in a proud tone. "Did it myself. Took ages, it did. Started with a wren stuffed inside a sparrow, then a chaffinch, then something else, something else, quails, woodcock, something else, ptarmigan, partridge, pheasant. Anything with wings has been stuffed into them swans."

"Angels," I said. "Angels have wings. Is the King to dine on even them?"

The kitchen boy laughed. "You're one for a good jest, Alice. I'll tell the boys that one."

"As long as you don't tell Father Ambrose," said Susan.

At that moment two trumpeters marched into the Hall and blew a fanfare. Everyone rose from their seats and turned to watch the King enter the Hall. We clapped politely at sight of him and he acknowledged the applause with a wave of his hand. He took his seat, the applause ended and the rumbles of empty stomachs began.

I scrutinized the courtiers who had been placed at the Royal table. It was unusual for the King to dine with anyone sitting close to him, and those few occasions were marked out by extra ritual. Many of the great nobles had ancient claim to a place, a claim which could not be denied even by Henry Tudor. But the place allocated to each of them was decided by the King and illustrated who was currently high and low in his favor. To his right sat the Duke of Norfolk, the premier noble of the Kingdom, and next to him his son, the Earl of Surrey. I had not met him, although it was said that he was wiser in words than in deeds and only his father's firm hand restrained him from performing even more foolish ventures than he was already notorious for.

Beside the Earl of Surrey sat the older brother of the late Queen Jane, Edward Seymour. He was, of course, in the deepest mourning; the sudden demise of his power and influence had been a terrible blow to him. He may even have mourned his sister, though I doubted it.

Seymour was accounted wise beyond his years, a man to watch out for, in more ways than one. His deep-set eyes looked thoughtful yet weary, as if from too much scrutiny of the world. Even at the feast he peered from one man to another as if weighing up each of his rivals upon a scale of his own devising.

His brother, Lord Thomas, leaned back in the seat next to him, as if this was the place where he felt most comfortable. His eyes moved as much as his brother's but without the same sense of weariness. Quite the contrary. His eyes roamed over the ladies of the Court, hungry as a cat watching tiny birds.

He caught sight of me and gave a glimmer of a smile before removing his gaze and continuing his appraisal of the rest of the females.

Mary turned and gave me a wry look. "You need to be wary of Thomas Seymour," she said.

"I've told her so already," said Susan. "He has a reputation for consuming young women."

"I thought he was charming when we met him in the woods," said Lucy.

I reached out and patted her on the arm. "You have much to learn about the wiles and appetites of older men," I said.

Out of the corner of my eye I caught a tiny smile on Susan's lips. Perhaps she thought that I had much to learn myself. Or, perhaps, that I was already so accomplished a scholar I could teach Lucy all she needed to know.

To the King's left sat the Duke of Suffolk. Now here was a man who could teach even Seymour a lesson concerning young women.

The Duke was in his fifties and his fourth wife, Catherine, a pretty nineteen-year-old. He had married her five years before, six weeks after burying his wife. People wondered what on earth a mature man could desire in a sweet fourteen-year-old heiress to the greatest fortune in the Kingdom. The Duke answered that it was love, pure love. Cynics said that too much love with a girl so young and pretty might prove the early death of him.

The King had been mightily angry at the marriage. Catherine had been Suffolk's ward and it appeared unseemly for him to swap the role of guardian for that of lover. But that was not the main cause of the King's wrath. The wife Suffolk had so recently buried and so swiftly forgotten was Mary, Henry's favorite sister. Indecent lust, indecent haste and incautious disregard of Tudor sensibilities were the height of folly for even a Duke.

For many months Suffolk trembled under the wrath of the King, fearing for his liberty and his fortune. But Suffolk was one of Henry's oldest and closest friends and a man of great ability and greater loyalty. The King decided to reconcile with him. All unpleasantness had been forgotten now and he rode high in the King's favor once more. From the smug smile upon his broad features, the Duke also found much favor in his wife. Far from proving the cause of his early demise, her young flesh appeared to have added to his vigor rather than diminished it.

Next to Suffolk sat a clergyman who I had never seen before.

"Is that the Pope?" Lucy asked.

"Hardly," answered Susan. "That is the Archbishop of Canterbury."

His mind seemed elsewhere, his eyes half-closed, a little smile playing upon his lips. He did not look as though he belonged in this company. But he did not look saintly either.

"I wonder where Lord Cromwell is?" Mary whispered.

The chair next to the Archbishop's was the only empty one at the Royal table.

"The King's business waits for no Cromwell," I said lightly.

"The King does not seem to let business interfere with his pleasure," Lucy said.

"Hush, child," I said. "It does not do to utter such remarks when others may easily overhear them."

I glanced down the table to Wicks and Bray. They were engrossed in furtive whispering with each other. But that did not mean their ears were not directed elsewhere.

At that moment, I caught a glimpse of Thomas Cromwell arriving at the table. He gave a swift bow to the King and sidled into his seat. The Duke of Suffolk spoke to him for a few moments while the Archbishop bent to listen. Cromwell shook his head and that was enough to make the Duke fall silent. Suffolk might be sitting on the King's left hand, but, in reality, Cromwell was far more close to him.

The Archbishop seemed to have been waiting on the arrival of Cromwell. He climbed to his feet and held out his hands for silence. The Hall fell quiet and he said a prayer suitable for Lent, mumbled a few words about Jane Seymour and the King's tragic loss, waxed eloquent about the quality of the young Prince and finally asked blessing on the feast.

There was a heartfelt amen and we all flew at the platters with good heart.

It was with contented stomachs that we left the Great Hall and returned to the Chapel for the second service of the day. The first had been concerned with . . . I know not what, to be honest, for the sumptuous feast had quite elbowed out all memory of what the priests had said. My stomach was so preoccupied with food and my head so fuzzy with strong claret that I dozed through much of this afternoon's sermon, rousing myself every so often to kneel and mumble responses but contentedly nodding through the rest.

Because of this I left the Chapel quite refreshed. I felt no embarrassment for I had not been alone in my slumbers and, besides, everyone knew the real purpose for the second service had been less to fill the Chapel and more to empty the Great Hall.

The horde of courtiers drifted back to the Hall and there discovered the transformation. Every table had been cleared away, leaving an empty space in the center; the benches had been pushed back against the wall; the floor swept clean of every trace of food and spilt drink. In place of the Royal table there was now a dais with two steps lined with red cloth. Upon the dais was the King's throne with the King already sitting in it.

Next to him was the Queen's throne. Thankfully there was no sight of the ghost of Jane Seymour, nor either of her two predecessors, come to that. Beside this throne sat Margaret Bryan, Lady Governess of the Court, with the baby Prince in her arms. He was fast asleep and seemed the only creature unaware of what was to take place.

To the left of the dais sat the troupe of Court musicians, decked out in their best finery, wielding lutes, flutes, sackbuts, hautboys, viols and drums as if they were weapons of war. Beside them stood the Master of the King's Music, the Master of the King's Ceremonies and their colleague, the Dancing Master.

The Master of Ceremonies was a courtly, elderly man with the loudest voice I'd ever heard. It was said behind his back that he'd begun his career as a Town Crier in Southwark and had seduced his way to his present position. He resembled a bull in more than one way, apparently.

The Dancing Master was a mincing fellow, as thin as a wand, admiring of his own charms, vain and condescending. He was an Italian from

Verona and when he led the courtiers in a dance was much given to rolling his eyes to indicate his terrible frustration and despair at the heavy hooves of the English.

The Master of Ceremonies bowed before the King and stamped his mace three times upon the floor for silence. Then he opened his mouth and his mighty voice echoed from wall to wall and from floor to ceiling. He had not really needed the silence.

"My Lords and Ladies of the Court, His Majesty King Henry the Eighth, by the Grace of God, King of England, France, Defender of the Faith, Lord of Ireland, and of the Church of England and of Ireland in Earth Supreme Head, has commanded this day a fete of entertainment and dance. Later on you will witness a spectacle of jugglers and acrobats, of conjurers and clowns, of cunning dogs and dancing bears. But first, the celebrations commence with a dance."

He stamped his mace upon the floor once again and the Master of the King's Music turned to the musicians, raised his hands and the music began.

First we danced a pavan. The Dancing Master insisted on showing us the steps with a select group of cronies. I watched with only half my mind upon the demonstration. I loved this dance with its stately measure and gentle intricacies and needed no show to tell me how to dance it.

Eventually, the Dancing Master completed his moves and the real dance started. My heart thrilled as we counted the beats and then began. I let the music fill my ears and flow through my limbs. I snuffed out all thought and gave myself to the dance.

The more the dance progressed the more I felt removed from everyday concerns, held suspended by the spirit of the moves. Some people found the pavan too complex and Susan, in particular, could never master it. She was the clumsiest dancer I have known and the pavan was far beyond her skill and ambition. Mary and Lucy, on the other hand, were adroit and confident and I began to imagine that we looked like the Three Graces as we stepped across the Hall.

Unfortunately it was soon to become apparent that I was not alone in this imagining.

The music stopped and the Master of the Dance announced a galliard.

Lucy clapped her hands with delight. "I've only danced the galliard twice," she said. "Do you think we will be allowed the volta?"

"The Dancing Master is Italian," I said, "so anything is possible."

"But do you like the volta?" she asked, her eyes wide.

"I've only seen it once myself, last Midsummer. It was demonstrated by the Dancing Master but Queen Jane forbade it at the Court."

Lucy bit her bottom lip. "Ooh, I do hope we will be allowed to dance it, or see it at the very least."

We turned and watched the Dancing Master demonstrate the galliard. I understood why he felt the need to demonstrate the pavan, for the moves were complex and easily forgotten. But the galliard was in the blood of every Englishman and woman and we needed no tuition from a southerner. Yet he had to inflict a demonstration upon us, either because of vanity or in order to justify his salary. It was over swiftly, thank goodness, and the musicians began their introduction to the dance.

"I don't suppose we will be allowed a volta," said Lucy sadly.

I glanced at Seymour's empty throne. So, her web of woe reached from beyond the grave.

"No volta," I said. "At least not for the present. But a galliard is splendid enough."

I smiled as Susan approached.

"I hope that I will not put you off the dance," she said. "But I like the galliard greatly and do not think I can spoil it much."

"You will not spoil it," I said. "We shall have fun."

A gaggle of handsome young men approached and sought to partner us in the dance. The youngest, a burly yet pretty boy, pressed his suit upon me and I agreed. But no sooner had we taken up position than a newcomer pushed him aside roughly.

The boy turned angrily towards the man but the words died on his lips and he bowed instead.

"Lord Thomas Seymour," he said, giving up his place and retreating from sight.

I gave Seymour a very cool glance. "You wish to dance?" I asked.

He gave a low chuckle. "With you, Alice Petherton, of course."

The music changed and the dance began.

When Seymour had so brusquely pushed aside my young gallant I had thought for a moment to walk away from him. But that would have been to insult him—something I dared not risk. Besides, the music was getting lively and the spirit of the dance now caught hold of me.

I gave a little curtsy to Seymour and we began.

The galliard was generally much faster than the pavan and the musicians seemed intent on making this the fastest one ever played, for they drove the dance forward at a steady charge.

I glanced at Susan as I danced. Anything was better than staring at the foxtail of a beard drooping from his lordship's face. She was skipping with more gusto than style but her partner managed to keep her in some sort of order. I smiled to myself and thought that maybe I would offer to teach her some steps.

"Something amuses you," Seymour said. His voice sounded a little cold.

"Indeed it does, my lord, but worry not that it is you."

"Then what, pray?"

"My friend," I said. "She is not the finest dancer in the Hall."

He glanced over my shoulder and grinned. "No, she is most certainly not. The honor of finest dancer belongs to you."

I gave a fulsome smile and executed a complex series of jumps and kicks.

"You flatter me, my lord," I said. "I think you well know that the accolade belongs to you."

He did not trouble to argue with me.

We danced across the Hall and with every step he moved a little closer to me and his hand squeezed mine more tightly. It felt hot, like meat left out on a slab in summer, and I was pleased when he released it in order to perform his sequence of moves. He was skilled right enough if far too flamboyant, kicking his toes and strutting like a cockerel in a hen coop. His left hand was placed nonchalantly upon his hip and I could not help notice that his long fingers pointed down to a part of his body which seemed to be of greater concern to him than even his fine legs.

I began my moves in response, skipping most skillfully and lightly. As I did so, I noticed that his eyes watched me with unbridled lust. I faltered in my steps and lost my rhythm. Then he clasped my hand and swung me off towards a different part of the Hall.

"I fear you are a little tired," he said. "Perhaps you wish us to retire to your bedchamber."

I kicked my heels hard in response to these words and my steps became almost a caper.

"Not a bit of it, my lord. I could dance until Midsummer."

He leaned closer to me and I felt his hot breath whisper in my ear.

"This is a charming dance, Alice, but I desire a far more engrossing one with you."

I was searching my mind for a cutting reply when he suddenly stepped back as if struck by palsy. I turned and saw the King at my elbow.

He held out his hand towards me. I took it in a daze.

I sensed the other dancers falter in their moves and even the musicians blew false notes. But then all resumed and the King led me in a promenade across the length of the Hall. The courtiers rippled with applause as we passed.

The King gave his little dance in front of me, and a good deal more elegant it was than Seymour's show of pomposity and preening.

Then it was my turn and, without meaning to, I danced haughty steps for him, all stamp and defiance, while at the same time my eyes never left his face. I sensed every person in the Hall gasp as they watched me, although such gasps never left their throats.

Then Henry cried, "La volta," and the musicians segued into this melody.

The King stepped closer and lifted me in his arms, half turning me while I gazed down at him and he gazed up. I was seized by a thrill almost erotic. We moved closer and our movements became linked and entwined. I could sense the courtiers watching us, wondering that we were so adroit and easy in our moves. Some, I thought, would guess the reason for this.

The music faded, the dance ended and I did a curtsy. Then the King bowed, took my hand, led me to the dais and sat me upon Queen Seymour's throne.

A shiver ran through me. This was not a place I wished to be. Yet at the same time a little worm of pleasure wriggled in my heart, and I was terrified by it.

The courtiers were stunned. But then, after what seemed an age, Thomas Cromwell rose and started to applaud. Everyone else followed immediately, fearing for their necks and their fortunes.

I glanced at the King. He had the most smug look upon his face.

"You are not my Queen, Alice Petherton," he said. "But I am right fond of you."

He nodded in the direction of Thomas Seymour, who looked both stunned and terrified. "And I have that craven fool to thank for helping me realize it."

"I thank you, Your Grace," I whispered, for my throat was dry and constricted.

He chuckled. "No more skulking down corridors for you any longer, Alice. Now the whole world knows I have a favorite."

Chapter Twenty-Four

The Favorite

1 April 1538

Now the whole world knows that I have a favorite. The King's words echoed in my mind throughout the rest of the evening. I danced with the King a number of times and watched the jugglers and listened to the singers. But my mind was in a whirl.

The King had publicly danced with me, taken me by the hand and led me to the Queen's Throne. I was his favorite and now the whole of the Court knew it.

He was right when he said that there was to be no more skulking down corridors for me. He led me by the hand from the Great Hall and we ascended the staircase to his Private Chambers together.

I could feel a thousand eyes boring into my back. Few of them, I knew, would be wishing me well.

The King was boisterous as a pup when we got into his bed.

"That showed that scoundrel Thomas Seymour," he cried. "The effrontery of the man. Dancing with you without a by-your-leave."

He leaned closer to me, a sudden suspicion flashing in his eyes.

"Do you know Thomas Seymour, Alice? Have you met him before?"

My heart missed a beat. It would be best if I told the truth, I realized, and, indeed, I had nothing to hide concerning the man. I told the King all my dealings with him.

He grew angry as he listened and then laughed and waved his hand dismissively.

"So he lusts after you, Alice, just as I thought when I saw him dance with you. Well, I put him in his place tonight. And that's just the start of it."

I slid over his body and began to kiss him. He was aroused in a moment and we performed the act with much noise and gusto. As soon as we had finished, the King gave a huge grin.

"That showed Thomas Seymour," he murmured and promptly fell asleep.

I climbed off the King and lay back in the bed. The candle by the bedside flamed strongly, casting deep shadows across the room.

I took a deep breath and tried to calm my racing heart. This was not what I expected. This was not what I wanted. I found my hand pressed against my lips, like a little girl who realized she had done something her daddy would find disappointing.

No, this was not what I wanted.

I stared at the glow the candle cast upon the ceiling. It pulsed as if it were a living thing, breathing and sighing, strong one moment, weakening the next. I stared into the shadows beyond the glimmering light.

What did I want? What had led me to this dangerous adventure?

I knew what I did not want.

I did not want a life of service to others who I knew to be my inferiors in gifts and spirit. I did not want to be a woman who danced attendance upon a countess, a duchess or a queen.

I did not want a life of penury with the only hope of escape a reluctant marriage to some vain and well-pursed man who would love me for a twelve-month and then lord it over me as though I were a possession, while he seduced the latest pretty girl to catch his eye.

Nor did I wish to live alone for the rest of my days until I became a dry and withered old woman, musing on the years of missed opportunity and counting down the days left to me until an end unnoticed and unmarked.

So what did I want?

The King snuffled in his sleep and then began to snore.

I certainly did not want to be this man's wife, did not want to be Queen of England. My throat constricted and a sour taste sprang into my mouth. Henry had wed three women already and already all three were dead, one giving birth to his child, one in despair at how cruelly he had treated her, and one at his express command.

A draught caught the candle and it guttered for a moment. I shivered slightly, thinking how apt this was. To be a queen was to be forever like a candle, burning steadfastly to illuminate the King, until he chanced upon a brighter flame.

I was happy to be King Henry's favorite, right enough. I had been struck by the notion six months ago now, had dreamed of it, contemplated it, planned and schemed for it. It had been the only thing to keep me safe from that villain Richard Rich.

But I always imagined that I would be the King's close-kept secret, like Bessie Blount before she had given birth to their son. I wanted our relationship to continue as it had started, with private meetings, the occasional meal and secret bedtimes.

I did not wish to be the King's favorite, announced to all the Court, paraded for all onlookers. This was far too perilous a state. Favorites rapidly became the targets of the ambitious. Some men would rush to fawn over me. Others might rush with greater speed to make sure I was dispensed with.

And being the King's favorite would prove such wearisome work. As it was, I felt I was constantly walking upon a tightrope. I had no wish to do so in front of the whole Court.

I sighed and turned to look at the King. He lived in the public eye and never seemed the slightest bit concerned by it. But, I realized with a growing unease, it was not a life I could willingly embrace.

I snuffed out the candle. No matter how I felt, it was a life I might have to accept. Now the die was cast, there could be no going back. I had strayed too close to the furnace. Now I must keep the flames growing bright and strong. But I must make sure that they did not consume me.

The next morning I awoke to find the King staring down at me.

I reached up to touch his cheek but he leaned back as if to avoid my touch.

My heart began to hammer.

"Does something trouble you, Your Grace?" I asked.

He did not answer but turned to look out of the window.

"Have I done anything to upset Your Majesty?"

He continued to stare out of the window before answering in a low, slow voice. "It was Sir Thomas Seymour's fault," he said. "Not yours."

A silence filled the room, a silence as palpable as a corpse which we both had seen but neither wished to acknowledge.

I plucked up my courage and said in a little voice, "Fault, Your Majesty?"

"Yes. If he had not been dancing with you in so lustful and smug a manner I would not have been snared into dancing with you."

He looked at me; his face was set and hard. "And I certainly would not have been seduced into setting you upon my widow's throne."

A lump as hard as stone had filled my throat. It appeared that my life as favorite was going to be short-lived in the extreme.

I sat up in bed, hunching my knees. My mind was in a whirl, desperate to think what to say. How on earth could I retrieve this situation? It seemed clear to me that Thomas Seymour was not the only one the King blamed for his actions. He was not capable of blaming himself, of course. So that left only one other person.

I managed to swallow at last. And as I did so the tears began to form in my eyes and trickled out like melting snowdrops upon my cheeks. I wept silently.

I heard a gasp and then a sigh. The King's hot hand touched me on the chin, lifting my face to stare into his own.

"You're crying, Alice Petherton," he said.

I nodded, unable to say more, and sniffed.

The King's face softened and then his own eyes grew moist. He moved closer towards me and reached for my hand.

"I would not have you weep, dear Alice. You bear no blame for what happened. The fault lies entirely with Sir Thomas Seymour."

"You're sure?" I said. "You don't blame me, don't think I was a bad girl for dancing with him? You don't blame me for making you dance with me and—"

I could not finish, for the King placed his fingers on my lips.

"Hush, hush, my dear," he said. "I would not have you upset yourself."

He leaned back, hands upon my shoulders, and looked at me as a physician might examine a sickly child.

He sighed. "I wish I had not sat you in the throne," he said. "It was not a sensitive thing to do. But I do not regret dancing with you. And I most certainly do not regret that people saw me taking pleasure at doing so."

I managed a little smile and his face brightened.

"There," he said, "that's better. That's more like the Alice I know."

I laughed a little and wiped my nose with my fingers.

The King reached out for his own handkerchief and held it to my nose, dabbing it gently.

"I think we should take some pleasure today," he announced. "I feel like hunting. Do you hunt, Alice? I know you ride like the wind."

"I have hunted, Your Majesty, though I am not skilled at it."

"Your Grace, Alice. You call me Your Grace."

"Your Grace," I mumbled. "I hunted once and fell off my horse. I was not scared, though."

"I'm sure you were not," he said.

He sprang out of bed and clanged on the bell to summon Gregory Frost.

"Go and bathe, Alice," he said, "and make ready for breakfast and then the hunt."

I slipped out of bed and made my way naked to the King's bathroom. I smiled as I passed him for I could see that my appearance had inflamed him again.

"Before you bathe," he said, reaching out for my hand and leading me back to bed. I slid my body over his, soft and gentle as a summer breeze.

The door opened and Gregory Frost appeared. I stopped my sliding.

The King looked up. "Prepare our breakfast," he said. "Then get my hunting clothes."

Frost nodded and made to shut the door.

"And send for the seamstress," the King said. "Have her bring hunting clothes for Alice."

"Very good, Your Majesty." Frost bowed and then regarded me before giving me the most fleeting of smiles and closing the door behind him.

"Who started the applause last night?" the King asked me.

"Sir Thomas Cromwell, Your Grace."

"Ah, quite so." He nodded several times, thoughtfully. "Quite so."

I slid his member into me and gasped softly. A satisfied and hungry grin came to his face.

"Today is going to be a good day, my darling," he said.

I closed my eyes. Not in ecstasy. In relief.

We had an enjoyable hunt with only a couple of gentlemen and servants attending. The King got a mixed bag: a roe deer, a stag, a brace of rabbits and a newborn lamb which seemed to have died of fright when it saw us charging down upon it in pursuit of a fox. The fox got away.

We returned to the Palace tired but in good spirits.

A message soon quelled this. The French ambassador was in the Presence Chamber, anxious for an audience with the King. He grumbled a little at the news for he did not care for the man and kept him kicking his heels half an hour longer while he threw down some food. Then he kissed me and said he would see me later that evening.

The moment he left, Gregory Frost entered the room. He gave a little cough and smiled.

"I suppose you realize that you are not to use the late Queen's apartments," he said.

"Of course not," I answered. "I never imagined I would. I have my own chamber."

"Not any longer," he said. "As King's favorite you shall have a new chamber closer to the King. Come, let me take you there."

I was bemused at this information. I had been given my chamber when I came to Court. It was tiny but it had been the first room I could call my own and I loved it.

I followed the Groom out into the corridor I had first used to visit the King. But instead of turning left into the long Gallery we continued straight on towards the King's new apartments. We passed the

King's private stairs to the garden and then turned left. We stopped a little way along this corridor. Frost pushed open a door and gestured for me to enter.

I gasped with delight. The chamber was six times larger than my own bedroom and had two windows looking east over rolling country-side. The larger window was a half bow. Next to it was a second door.

"That leads to the King's new bedchamber," Frost said in a matter-of-fact tone. "He has not moved into it yet but has plans to."

I nodded and then frowned. Upon a table near the window were my poetry books, my recorder and all my little knickknacks and jewelry.

"Everything has been brought from your old room," Frost explained. "Your personal things, your gowns, everything." He gave a cool smile. "This is your chamber now, Alice. While you remain the King's favorite it is your chamber."

He turned on his heel and left me alone.

I flung myself on the huge bed and hugged the pillow to my breast.

Chapter Twenty-Five

The Howard Family

8 April 1537

A harsh east wind made the windows of Kenninghall Place rattle mournfully. It fitted the mood of its owner. Thomas Howard, third Duke of Norfolk, was a worried man.

He still counted himself a friend of King Henry and knew well that the restoration of the family's fortune was due to his favor. The Howard family understood better than most how fragile is even a Duke's hold upon titles and power.

His grandfather, the first Duke, had been a loyal friend to Richard III. It had proved a costly association. He had paid with his life at the Battle of Bosworth and the family had paid with their land, their honors and much of their wealth. His son, Thomas Howard's father, managed to escape execution but spent four years imprisoned in the Tower. Henry VII sat uneasy on his throne and had a dread of over-powerful lords. He had finally allowed the prisoner his freedom but refused adamantly to reinstate the Dukedom.

Thomas glanced up at the portrait of his father above the fireplace. He had never been an easy man and the portrait captured this exactly. Face like a brick, nose more fitted to a street brawler and eyes which writhed with suspicion.

"I can't say I loved him," Norfolk said, "but we owe everything to him."

His mistress, Bess, glanced up from her embroidery. "If you say so, Thomas." She had heard this many times before.

"He spent his life proving his loyalty to the Tudors," Norfolk continued. "Yet that vile usurper Henry Tudor would not restore him to the Dukedom."

"Your father had been on the opposing side to the old King," Bess said. "You always say that Henry was not a man to forgive and forget his enemies."

Norfolk ignored his mistress and thought back to the dreary days of the previous reign. No matter how much was done for that spider of a King it was never enough. Never enough to regain the Howards' rightful place in the scheme of things.

He had breathed a sigh of relief when the old King died and young Henry became King. Where his father had been all brooding darkness, the young man was like the sun. It was as if the trammels of the Kingdom had been suddenly cut away. But the Howards' hopes for immediate advancement had been dashed. Just as his father had done, so the new King Henry turned his face against them. Until that wonderful day when the Scots invaded. Then Henry had swallowed his pride and come cap in hand to ask the Howards to lead an army north to do battle.

"Thank goodness for the Scottish invasion," Norfolk murmured, more to himself than to Bess.

He thought back to that glorious victory, a victory due to his father and, even more, to his own military skills and courage. The King had finally restored the Dukedom to the Howards. Nevertheless, he made it very clear that the restoration was for honors earned and would be snatched back with equal speed should the family again incur Royal displeasure.

Norfolk raised a glass to his father and drained it swiftly. *At last I understand you better*, he thought. *You spent a lifetime walking a tight-rope between the pillars of honor and disgrace. Now it seems that I walk on that same path.*

Bess put down her embroidery.

"Surely there's no need to worry, Thomas. The King loved your gift of the lions. And he still has need of you. For your military skills and your experience."

Norfolk scowled. "He has no need of military men. Not when he has a brute like Cromwell at his beck and call."

Bess sighed. "You concern yourself too much with Thomas Cromwell."

"Only because he concerns himself too much with me. Indeed, with everything that transpires in the Kingdom."

"He's a commoner, a servant."

"So was Cardinal Wolsey. And look what power he wielded."

Bess sighed. She knew better than to continue such a conversation when he was in this mood.

Norfolk prowled about the chamber, his eyes blazing. She could almost see his mind working, weighing up chance and risk, opportunity and disaster.

A servant appeared in the chamber and bowed. "The Earl and Countess of Surrey," he announced.

Bess breathed a sigh of relief. Frances could usually shake her father-in-law out of any ill humor.

The Earl entered the chamber and gave a broad smile.

"Good day, Father," he said.

"Is it?" Norfolk answered. "What makes it so, pray?"

Surrey glanced at his wife and then at Bess. "Seeing you, Father," he said in an earnest tone. "It is always a joy to see you."

"Don't lie," Norfolk said. "You only call it a joy when you want something from me."

Frances took the Duke's hand in hers and smiled into his face.

"You are like a bear today," she said. "Who has been baiting you?"

"The usual," Bess said. "Thomas Cromwell."

Surrey threw his arm in the air in a gesture of frustration. "Cromwell, of course."

His father turned on him in a fury. "You may mock. But you won't when Cromwell signs your death warrant."

"Cromwell is a guttersnipe," Surrey said. "Why should I fear him? Or you?"

Norfolk gave a vulpine smile. "I wonder did you mean that ambiguity, dear son?"

"I am a poet, Father; of course I did."

The two men stared at each other, bristling, and then the Duke laughed aloud and embraced him.

"We're very different, Harry," he said. "But we're hewn from the same rock. You have the courage to take a risk."

"Too much," said Frances. She crossed the room and kissed Bess.

Bess frowned. "Why? What has he done now?"

Frances sat beside her and glanced up at her husband.

"Carousing with low fellows," she said. "And singing bawdy songs about the Archbishop of Canterbury."

Bess held her hand to her mouth with shock at this lack of respect. But the look of surprise on Norfolk's face almost immediately turned to one of amusement.

"Did you indeed?" he said to Surrey. He tried to hide his glee. "That was foolish of you, and probably unkind. But a little levity does not go amiss. Especially when it concerns pompous rascals like Archbishop Cranmer."

"Levity?" Frances said. "He called Mistress Cranmer a fishwife."

Norfolk shrugged. "She can hardly be termed a wife. It is not right for an Archbishop of Canterbury to take a wife."

"Would you rather he took a mistress?" said Bess.

Norfolk frowned. "It is not seemly for a man of God to take any woman to his bed—wife, mistress or, as my son so charmingly puts it, fishwife."

"Hypocrisy, sir," Bess said. "When you have bedded me this past ten years and put your legal wife aside to do so."

"That's different," he replied, "and you know it."

Bess shrugged and shook her head as if at a wayward child.

"Maybe I shall put you aside," he continued, "and take Elizabeth back."

"I pray you don't," Surrey said. "I couldn't stand the uproar." He poured a glass of wine for himself and another for his father, who drank it down in one gulp.

"And what about the uproar caused by you singing bawdy songs about the Archbishop?" Norfolk asked sharply.

Surrey shrugged. "The magistrate was amenable to reason and a purse of silver. There will be no uproar. No news of it shall carry to the King."

"If it does, I shall disown you," Norfolk said. "I have troubles enough of my own."

Frances got up and took him by the arm. "You said you were being vexed by Thomas Cromwell," she said in a soothing tone. "What is the cause?"

Norfolk poured himself another glass of wine.

"Apart from the fact that I must seek his approval for bringing my own daughter into the presence of the King?" he cried. "To sue for the lands and titles which should be hers by right as widow of the King's own son?"

"You had to ask Cromwell's permission?" asked Frances in surprise.

Norfolk nodded. "That I should have to ask the permission of a common servant." He glanced up at the portrait of his father, who now seemed to wear a sneer of mockery. He shook his head angrily. "And to rub salt into the wound, the knave gave me ambiguous answer."

"Of course he did," Surrey said. "He knows that the King wants to keep FitzRoy's money for himself and not give it into Howard hands."

"There is more," said Norfolk. "Cromwell is seeking a new wife for the King. Already, with the grass on Jane Seymour's grave not yet grown."

"A King must have a Queen," Frances said.

"But Cromwell is determined that the next Queen be a Protestant one. And he, the lewd guttersnipe, wants to be the one to select her."

"Oh, father," Surrey said, "that is your job, surely?" He poured himself another glass of wine. "After all, you chose so well with cousin Boleyn."

"Hush, Harry," Frances said. "Show respect to your father."

"And Anne would still be Queen," thundered Norfolk, "and the Howard influence still higher, if it had not been for Cromwell's determination to dispense with her."

Surrey sipped at his wine; his eyes glittered with amusement. "Alas, it is only in poetry that love proves more powerful than gold."

"You're not suggesting that the King executed Anne for gold?" Frances said in horror.

Surrey shrugged. "She offered Henry her body and her shrewish mind. Cromwell offered him a mountain of gold from the Abbeys. A vast treasure which Anne was determined should go to charities and schools."

"And where did Cromwell wish it to go?" Frances asked.

"Where the King wished it. Into the Royal coffers."

"And with a portion of it going to line Cromwell's nest," said Norfolk. "The peasant."

A silence fell upon the chamber while each considered what had been said. Until this moment, the Howards had held these dark suspicions secretly, not shared even with other members of the family. Now that they were out in the open it felt a relief, almost like a declaration of war ending months of weary stalemate and diplomacy.

"So this is why father is so angry, you see," Surrey explained to his wife. "When my dear cousin Anne's head rolled from the block, father's star was eclipsed by Cromwell's. If Cromwell can arrange a new marriage he fears it will be quite extinguished."

"I do not fear only for myself," Norfolk said. "I fear for the whole family. And that includes you, my dear son. And I fear for Mother Church."

He began to pace up and down the room, muttering aloud the thoughts which had been turning and churning in his head for weeks. "If Cromwell is able to secure a foreign wife for the King, a Protestant, his power will be unbridled. Every noble family in the land will cower beneath his shadow. And then he will be swift to do his master's bidding. He will dismantle the cathedrals and churches and pour their treasure into the open maw of the King. And after, when Henry has frittered away even that vast wealth on vainglory and gaudy palaces, where then will the snake Cromwell go to find more wealth to satisfy the King's insatiable demands?"

He turned to his family and flung his arms wide. "To the nobility. Henry will achieve what fifty years of war and the miserable rule of his father failed to do. He will destroy the old nobility and replace it with indentured serving men like Cromwell and Richard Rich."

No sooner were those words out than he paused.

"Richard Rich," he murmured. "Now there's a thought." He stared out of the window as if his gaze could fly the hundred miles to London.

"What do you mean?" Surrey asked. He gave his father a look which was half-admiring. "What are you plotting?"

Norfolk started pacing once more, waving his finger in front of his face, counting off the arguments in his mind. He was excited now, animated, completely different from how he had been up to this moment.

"Richard Rich would sell his mother to the devil to further his own ambitions," he said. "Perhaps he may prove a fitting instrument for me. Perhaps I will turn Cromwell's most base servant against him."

"It is a dangerous course," Bess said quietly.

"Yes," cried Norfolk. "And who can win a victory if he is not willing to take the dangerous course?"

Sir Richard Rich pulled the cloak even closer to his face and glanced around. No one was in sight; no one had seen him.

His horse whinnied softly in the twilight. Up ahead, the darkening shape of Kenninghall became pinpricked by light as servants lit candles.

He kicked his heels and his weary horse walked on in the gathering gloom. He gave it another kick to speed it up. He was anxious to arrive at his rendezvous.

Rich had never been in Kenninghall before, had rarely had dealings with the Duke of Norfolk or any of his kin. He knew better than to do that.

His master Cromwell and the Duke appeared to enjoy a civil relationship with each other, in fact a cordial one, but Rich knew that this was a charade. Both men smiled to each other's faces and would work together well enough when it suited their own interests. But they both aspired to be the King's sole favorite. And the King could have only one.

The two men were caught in a deadly dance, a desperate masquerade. Everyone at Court knew it. And everyone watched to see which of the two would stumble first. Most believed it would be Norfolk.

Rich was shown into a small chamber with a good fire blazing in the hearth. He was chill from his long ride from Bury St. Edmunds and he snatched the cup of mulled wine a servant brought to him. He stood close to the fire, grateful for the heat that began to warm his stiff limbs. He drained the last drops of wine and examined the room.

Three comfortable chairs were placed to the left of the fire, with a little table beside each. A large sideboard stood beneath the window, with plates, cups and knives arranged upon it. His stomach rumbled at the sight. He had eaten only a small pie of beef and oysters, bought at noon from a bakehouse in Stanton. He hoped that the plates and knives meant that supper would be provided. And more wine, he hoped, placing his empty cup next to the plates.

The chamber was paneled in rich oak with delicate figure work across a frieze. A large tapestry hung upon the wall, depicting a battle between two armies. *No doubt some celebration of the Howard history*, he thought, his face wrinkling in a sneer.

At that moment the door opened and the Duke entered, followed by his son.

"Welcome, Sir Richard," said the Duke, holding out his hands to grip hold of Rich's.

Rich was amazed at the strength in a man of such years. He felt his hands squeezed even tighter, as if the Duke wished to intimate that Rich was caught fast. As if they were in a giant thumbscrew.

"You know my son, the Earl of Surrey?" Norfolk asked, relaxing his hold.

"By reputation, Your Grace."

Surrey laughed. "A good one or a bad?"

Rich smiled but did not answer.

"See what a diplomat the man is," Norfolk said lightly to his son. "It is little wonder that he has advanced so high in the King's service."

He poured two cups of mulled wine and passed them to Rich and his son. He did not take one for himself.

"You have come far, Sir Richard?" Surrey asked.

"I was at Leez Priory three days ago when the Duke's request to visit reached me. I started early the next morning and stayed last night at Bury St. Edmunds, in a goodly inn."

"Two long days in the saddle, then," Surrey said. "Such work is fine for the aristocracy but not I think for commoners unused to horsemanship."

Rich's eyes glittered as if pondering whether or not the Earl had insulted him.

"I travel much in the King's service," he said. "I go where he commands and I fulfill his commands."

"Yet now you have come at my father's summons," Surrey said.

Rich gave a bleak smile. "A request to visit, my lord. Not a summons, surely?"

"But you came nonetheless. Posthaste."

Rich inclined his head a fraction. "I came and am intrigued at the request to visit."

The atmosphere in the room seemed to crackle and spit. Norfolk held up his hand in a little warning gesture to his son. It was a small gesture, but one which Rich took note of while wondering if the Earl had as well.

Norfolk indicated the three chairs beside the fire.

"Riding is weary work for any man," he said in an emollient tone. "Let us take our ease."

The Duke's steward appeared at the door. "Supper is ready, Your Grace. Shall it be served in here?"

The Duke nodded and turned to Rich. "It is warm and comfortable in this chamber. And quiet."

The steward beckoned to two other men, who carried in trays of steaming food and more wine. "Shall we serve you, Your Grace?" the steward asked.

Norfolk nodded and the servants expertly filled three large platters of food, placing each one on the small tables beside the chairs, together with a fine glass and a jug of wine.

Rich's mouth salivated at sight of the food. There were two thick slices of beef, charred on the outside but oozing red within, a large slice of game pie, a small roast fowl, a thick sausage studded with herbs and a chunk of good white bread running with butter. The servants brought smaller plates, each with a wrinkled apple, a pear and a wedge of cheese.

The Duke bowed his head and mumbled Grace before taking up his plate.

"So, Sir Richard," he said, "you are intrigued at my suggestion that you visit us at Kenninghall?"

"Intrigued and honored, Your Grace. I had not thought that a humble man such as myself would have come readily to your notice." He bit on a corner of the pie.

"Come, come," said Surrey. "You are too modest entirely, Sir Richard. Are you not the Lord Privy Seal's terrier?" He stroked his chin as if trying to recall an elusive thought. "What is it they call you? The hammer of the monasteries? Yes, that's it. You are the hammer and Cromwell is the mallet."

"I obey my Sovereign's commands," Rich answered, "no more, no less." He paused for a heartbeat and glanced at the Earl. "As I am sure we all endeavor our utmost to do."

"Naturally," said Norfolk. "The King is the sun who shines upon the realm and gives warmth and sustenance to all men, great and small." He shot a glance at his son. Another warning. Surrey appeared not to notice and lounged back in his seat, watching the proceedings as if at a play.

Norfolk turned to Rich. "It is of the Lord Privy Seal that I desire to speak," he said.

Rich was taken aback at the speed with which the Duke had come to the point of the meeting. He was used to the slower, more subtle ways of his master.

"The Lord Privy Seal?" Rich asked.

"Yes." Norfolk speared a slice of beef on his knife and held it between them. "I am worried about Baron Cromwell."

Rich frowned but kept silent.

"His duties are demanding, are they not?" Norfolk continued. "Onerous, exhausting. Perhaps too much for one man only."

He said nothing more but pushed the meat inside his mouth as if he were a cook stuffing a capon.

"Lord Cromwell is in the best of health," Rich answered. "He appears inexhaustible, as if his service to the King gives him greater sustenance than food or sleep."

"No man is inexhaustible," Norfolk said.

"And none are indispensable," added Surrey.

Rich's breath caught at this. He sneaked a look at Norfolk. He did not seem the slightest bit perturbed by his son's blunt words.

A thin trickle of fear ran down Rich's spine. There was threat here, a threat to his master. Yet surely none would be so rash as to seek to undermine him? He was too high in the King's favor, too dominant. Unassailable.

Rich's mind worked fast. What did these haughty men desire from him? How might he make use of this desire? Excited though he was, he forced himself to put aside immediate speculation. Better to wait and watch, better to sniff out the advantage.

"You must be a great support to the Lord Privy Seal," Norfolk continued. "I doubt he would be quite as effective without your assistance."

Rich bowed his head. "You are too kind, Your Grace."

"And you must know much about his work," Surrey added. "You must be privy to many of his concerns and strategies."

"Some, perhaps," Rich said in a guarded tone.

"More than some, I should think," said Norfolk. "I doubt there is any man closer to Thomas Cromwell or knows better how he fulfills his duties."

"No man in the Kingdom who could better fill his shoes," said Surrey, leaning forward. "Should he fall ill or grow weary of his tasks."

Rich gave a little chuckle. "As I have said already, Lord Cromwell is in the best of health. And he will never, I promise you, grow weary of the King's work."

Surrey's face was too watchful, too intense, as if he had reached the crucial moment of a battle long planned and fretted over. He hid it in an instant, but not before Rich noticed.

Rich glanced at Norfolk. Unlike his son's, his face was bland and inscrutable. He cut a slice of his pie and placed it in his mouth, chewing upon it, giving it his fullest attention. He was not a man to leave any hostages to fortune.

"I am overjoyed to hear what you tell us about the Lord Privy Seal's rude health," he said with a smile. "Overjoyed." He picked up his glass and swilled the wine around his mouth as if to wash away something unpleasant which had lodged there.

"There is no need for Cromwell to hear of our concerns," said Surrey. "Let this inquiry into his health be put down to genuine concern for a dear friend."

"I agree," said Norfolk.

He turned and held Rich's eyes in his own. "Let this meeting be our secret. We would not wish to be derided or talked about for our heartfelt worries."

"No, indeed, Your Grace," Rich said. "You can rely on me to keep our secret." He paused. "As I am sure I can rely on you."

The Duke nodded. "How goes the King's search for a new Queen?" he asked as if to change the subject of the conversation completely. "I hear that the negotiations to wed the Duchess of Milan are going well."

Rich's eyes flickered. The negotiations were a close-guarded secret, the details known to very few. He had no idea how much the Duke knew of the current state of talks, of how bogged down they were.

His mind raced for a moment, seeking the best course to take.

"They go, as these negotiations habitually do, at a slow but steady pace." He paused and wondered whether to cast some bait and see if the Howards bit. He gave a little laugh. "Of course, the delay gives the King more time to sport."

The Duke frowned at this and shot a glance at his son, who shrugged and shook his head.

"Sport?" Norfolk asked. "What sport?"

Rich pretended surprise.

"Surely Your Grace has heard of the King's latest conquest?"

Norfolk did not answer. He had heard nothing of this but did not want to give Rich the pleasure of knowing it. "What is the woman's name again?" he asked casually. "I forget it."

"Alice Petherton," Rich said.

"Ah yes, I recall her name now. A comely creature."

"More than just comely, Your Grace," Rich answered. "She is the very Venus of the Kingdom."

As he said the words his stomach lurched. After all this time she still had the power to unman him. The Duke's indifference to her could mean only one thing: that he had not yet seen her. Either that or he had forgotten he was a man.

Rich glanced at Surrey, who had sat forward at these words. *Ah, here's one young buck whose interest has been piqued*, Rich thought. He had been wrong-footed by the Howards this night. He was glad that, by mentioning Alice, he had done a small amount to wrong-foot them.

Rich was long awake that night. His thoughts turned time and time again to the conversation concerning Cromwell. Sometimes he thought it as inconsequential as the two nobles had claimed it to be at the end of the evening. Sometimes it appeared pregnant with promise and opportunity for himself. Most of the time it seemed dangerous. Deadly dangerous.

He rose early, bleary eyed and tousle haired. He ate a solitary breakfast under the watchful eye of a servant. The sky grew bright, although it looked as if rain was coming in from the west. He ordered his horse saddled and finished off the last of his meal.

The rain began to patter on the ground as his horse was brought to him. He rummaged in his bag and pulled out his heavy traveling cloak. There was no need for it immediately, but the weather was unreliable in April. One minute bright sunshine, the next an unforeseen downpour. Having a cloak at the ready was essential in such fickle times.

He climbed into his saddle and began the long journey back to London. He had gone a couple of hundred yards or so when he heard a voice calling him.

He turned in his saddle and saw the Duke's steward riding after him.

"Your pardon, Sir Richard," the man said, "but I did not realize you were going to leave so early."

"I have business to attend to at Court," Rich answered.

The steward nodded. "His Grace asked me particularly to communicate to you his gratitude at your journeying here to see him." He paused and fiddled with a blanket in front of his saddle. "His Grace is aware of the time you have taken from your duties to visit. And also that you will have incurred expense in coming here."

Rich stared at the man in silence.

"So," the steward continued, pulling back the blanket, "his Grace charged me to give you this in recognition and thanks."

He pushed a strongbox into Rich's hands, bowed swiftly and rode away.

Rich looked at the box. He rubbed his fingers along the side. It was a plain box, made of wood, with a small lock with a key inside it.

He looked around, swiftly turned the key and opened the lid. He gasped. The box was full of gold coins, perhaps a hundred or more. More than he could hope to earn from Royal service in two years.

He slammed the lid shut, as if to prevent the coins from leaping out and making their escape.

Again, he glanced to all sides, nervous that someone might have seen. He searched the windows of Kenninghall to see if anyone was watching. In particular, he searched for any sign of the Duke. There was nobody.

He covered the box with his cloak and kicked his heels. The horse moved into a walk and then, at a second kick, into a fast trot.

Back in Kenninghall, the Duke of Norfolk stared through a slit in the curtains at the rapidly departing Rich. How strangely apt, he thought, that a man should bear as his name what he most desired to be.

"You want me to find out about this Alice Petherton?" Surrey asked, breaking into his thoughts.

Norfolk did not answer for a moment. His son had not been able to hide his interest in this woman who Rich had so highly praised. Ah well, the hungry hound makes the best hunter.

He thought on the situation. He had hoped to tempt the King himself with one of his family's brood of daughters. A beautiful favorite may well undo such plans.

"Yes," he said at last. "Find out all you can."

He placed a hand upon his son's arm to detain him. "But remember that she is the King's favorite. Remember that. If we are to act against her, no trace must come to our family."

Chapter Twenty-Six

On Love and Lust

9 April 1538

If you think that to be proclaimed favorite of the King is appealing, then think again. I was reminded of the King's lions. People were fascinated by them; they feared their power, yet most secretly wished them gone. So it was with the King's favorite.

The moment the King escorted me to Jane Seymour's throne, my life changed forever.

The question I continued to ask myself was, to what extent did I accept it?

I still did not feel any great passion for King Henry. How could I? He was old enough to be my father, more than old enough. In fact, sometimes, when I lay beside him after the act of love, I would do mental arithmetic and conclude that it was just possible that he could have been my grandfather. He would need to have been a forward youth, of course, but what limits are there to royalty?

The winter months did not help. He suffered greatly from the injury he had sustained in a joust a few years previously. It had opened up an earlier wound in his leg and had not healed properly.

I did not discover it for a few weeks and when I did it was because of the smell. The wound would periodically suppurate, becoming red and raw and oozing a viscous fluid which stank of rotting meat. The first time I discovered it, I gagged at the smell and could not altogether hide my revulsion. The King was kind about it; in fact he seemed rather embarrassed. This was a side of him I had not imagined I would ever witness. He told me to think nothing of it, that it was a little problem and would soon pass. I think he was more concerned that it would put me off my lovemaking than that it would disgust and sicken me. It did both, of course, but I kept this from him well enough. I found it best if I pretended more concern than I felt and clucked over him like a nurse. He liked this.

In addition to the smell, the wound sometimes pained him abominably. The cold, damp weather affected it most. There was many a time when I would find him with his leg propped high on a stool, wrapped in hot compresses which his surgeon swore would ease the wound but never seemed to make the slightest difference. The King bore it all rather philosophically, disregarding the pain and inconvenience, although impatient for it to improve.

When it did improve he was like a rutting stag, almost dragging me into bed and making love as if the end of the world was upon us.

One day early in April had been such a day. He summoned me in the late afternoon and we spent two hours grappling like shepherd and nymph. After the third bout we lay back on the bed as hot as new-baked loaves while the King began to talk about the latest problems with the Kings of France and Scotland.

I must have nodded off while he spoke for I suddenly found him tickling me under the arm.

I shrieked with laughter, being susceptible to tickling. This delighted him and he went to it with a will while I giggled until the tears ran and I begged him to stop.

He laughed and leaned back on the bed, his arms behind his head, staring at the ceiling.

"Ah, Alice," he said. "You make me feel young again."

"That is what a young girl should do. She should help you recapture your youth and ardor."

He smiled benignly. "You certainly do that."

"Hush," I said. "It is what a loyal maid should do for her King. I am, as you said, yours to command."

His face became more serious. "I watch you sometimes," he said, "when you do not realize that I am doing so."

I propped myself up on my elbow and stared at him. His voice sounded dreamy, as if recounting something he had done many times.

"I watch you when you are in the Chapel, singing or praying, listening to the priest. I watch you when you are walking with your friends and delight to see you happy with them."

"I hope you look at only me, not at my friends."

"I only have eyes for you, Alice."

"I don't believe that, Your Grace. I am not the only lovely girl in the Palace."

His eyes took on a faraway look. "I disagree, my dear. There is none to compare with you." He paused and pulled at his beard a moment. "There is one, only one, who has sometimes caught my eye."

"And who is she? I would know so that I ask you to send her from the Palace."

He laughed. "A young girl, dark haired, with a pretty mouth. You were with her yesterday in the tennis court."

"That's Lucy Burton, my friend." I watched him more closely. "She is little more than a child. I'm not sure if she is fifteen or sixteen."

The King said nothing.

I traced a finger along his chest. "So, Your Grace, you have cast your eyes at my little friend Lucy?"

He pursed his lips. "I have noticed her, is all."

"Noticed and desired, I shouldn't wonder." I pressed myself closer to him. "How would you like it if I were to invite her into this chamber? How would you like it if I were to command her to undress for you?"

I felt rather than heard his breath begin to quicken.

"Would you like that, Your Grace? Or what if she were reluctant? What if I had to be firm and undress the girl myself?"

His eyelids blinked rapidly at the thought.

"What if I had to take every stitch from her body until she stood naked as a babe in front of us?"

"Would you do that?" He gasped. "For me?"

"You only have to ask," I said. "I would bring her to your bed myself and fold your arms around her."

"And would she be willing?"

"I'm not sure."

All at once I recalled how Anne Boleyn had troubled my dreams. How, had she commanded it, I would have loved her with more than just my heart.

"Perhaps I would have to gentle her myself," I whispered to the King. My words had a strange effect upon him. He began to tremble like a youth new come to love.

"Perhaps," I continued, "I would have to stroke her and console her. Perhaps she would be unsure how to kiss a man and I would have to teach her myself. You could watch while I kissed her, watch while I taught her how to make love."

He gasped and I looked down. He was more excited than I had ever seen him. "My goodness," I cried, grasping hold of him and feeling the heat flaming within. "I shall have to call this His Highness from now on."

He spent himself in my hand, laughing at my jest and swooning at the thought of Lucy Burton and me as lovers.

Chapter Twenty-Seven

The King's Great Cats

20 April 1538

I woke with the King snoring in my ear. It felt like a tempest in my head.

I lay there for a few minutes hoping the cacophony would stop but I waited in vain. Finally I elbowed him softly in the stomach. He woke and spluttered like a baby about to regurgitate its milk.

"Good morning, Alice," he cried.

"Good morning, Majesty. You slept well."

He raised himself on his elbow and stared at me. His breath smelt like horse sweat. I half turned my head, hoping he would not notice.

"I feel as though I slept well," he boomed. "I do indeed. How do you know, sweet child? Were you watching over me?"

"I always watch over you, Your Grace. I'm your guardian angel." I paused, wondering whether to say more. "But I also know because you were snoring."

"Snoring?" He sat upright and clenched his knees. He stared straight ahead and I sensed the petulance beginning to build. I cursed myself for saying it.

"Perhaps it was some dream of battle and war," I said swiftly. "Maybe a joust with you galloping towards your adversary with lance held high."

"Or a wrestling match, perchance," he said. "Like when I wrestled King Francis at the Field of the Cloth of Gold."

He turned to me, all petulance gone, his face bright with excitement. "I beat him, Alice. At wrestling. My nobles advised me to let him win as we were on French soil and at first I meant to do as they advised. But then the joy of battle gripped me. I remember thinking, *Is not a Tudor better than a Valois?*"

He clambered to his knees.

"Oh, you should have been there, Alice. It was a titanic struggle. Why weren't you there?"

"Because I wasn't born, Your Grace."

He looked at me in some surprise. Then he put back his head and roared with laughter.

I put my hands over my ears. "There it goes again. His Majesty the lion." I pretended to look terrified of him and he caught me up and kissed me fiercely.

He broke away, clicking his fingers sharply.

"A lion. That reminds me. I have not seen my lions since Norfolk gave them to me."

He hurled himself out of bed, yelling for Frost to come to dress him.

"Have you ever seen a lion, Alice?" he asked as he paced around the room.

"Only a glimpse," I answered. "When the Duke's servants brought them into the Great Hall. I was terrified."

He turned to me and his eyes took on that strange blank look which so unnerved me.

"Terrified by a lion," he murmured, more to himself than to me. "Yes, they are fearsome beasts. Kingly beasts. The beasts of England."

At that moment, Frost entered the room.

"I need to be dressed," the King cried. "I'm taking Alice to see the lions."

"I shall get your gentlemen to dress you," Frost answered, bowing.

"No time for that," the King said, slapping Frost on the shoulder with such strength that the poor man reeled almost off his feet. "You'll have to dress me today."

Thank goodness, I thought. *The gentlemen who dress the King peer in at the door to watch me.* At least Frost knew me well and did not need to spy. In fact, apart from the King himself he was the only man who'd seen me naked. Did I excite him? He seemed such an unflappable creature. But surely he must have been excited to see me that morning, all naked and flustered as I was. Surely such sight of me would inflame all men?

I watched as Frost began to dress the King. I wondered at how such a touchy man could be so at ease with his servants and his gentlemen. They dressed him, they washed him, they cut his hair and shaved him. The only things he seemed to do for himself were eat, walk and ride. And ride me, of course. He wouldn't let anybody else do that task for him.

I waited until Frost had attired the King before leaving the bed and going to the bath chamber. I suddenly realized that if I were Queen I would no longer dress myself. I would have Ladies to help me. I thought of Mary and Lucy dressing me and thought that this would be pleasant indeed. But then I thought of Wicks and Bray, who I knew for a fact had dressed Jane Seymour. I shuddered at the thought of them gloating over me, examining my skin for any blemishes, then scurrying back to their chambers to note it in a secret book.

Another reason not to be a queen.

I dressed hurriedly and joined the King at the breakfast table. Despite knowing him as I did, I was still astonished at how much he would eat. Even this early in the morning he stuffed himself with a chicken, a cony, a dozen rashers of bacon, a slab of cheese, half a loaf of bread and a slice of pie. I contented myself with some bread and honey cake.

Frost had disappeared, dispatched to ready the Royal Barge for the trip downriver.

He returned with a thick stole for the King and then glanced at me.

"Mistress Petherton has no outside clothes with her. Shall I send to her chamber for some?"

The King paused in adjusting his belt.

"Or perhaps . . ." Frost said tentatively.

"Perhaps what?" asked the King, his mind still working.

"Perhaps she could wear one of the late Queen's outfits."

The King's face grew hard and anger began to rise to his cheeks. I thought that Frost would quail at this, would turn tail and flee. But he stood his ground, knowing perhaps that the King could blow hot as fire but then cool within a moment.

"Not Queen Jane's cloak, Your Majesty," Frost said quietly. "I agree that would not be seemly."

The King cocked an eye at him. "Anne Boleyn's?"

Frost bent his head. "I shall have it sent here immediately."

I watched him slip from the room upon his errand.

So, I was to be garbed as a Queen today. I bit my lip anxiously. Which of those two dead women's cloaks would I prefer to enfold me? The victim's or the martyr's? Not that I had a choice. The King had decided that I would be given Anne's cloak. The victim's.

Frost returned with a wardrobe woman who bore a thick cloak trimmed with white ermine. I knew that this was one of Anne's favorite cloaks and I was suddenly glad of the choice. Nevertheless, I scrutinized it quickly for any sign of blood upon the collar. There was none, thankfully.

The journey downriver was not as cold as I feared. It was partly because the April morning was milder than of late, and partly because of a small charcoal brazier, which gave a surprising heat. But it was mostly because the Queen's cloak was thick and warm. The journey took five hours and would have been very dreary were it not for the minstrels who entertained us with songs and lively tunes.

Interspersed with this, however, was the constant tomfoolery of Will Sommers, the King's Fool.

I did not like Will Sommers, distrusted his coarse, cunning face. He would humiliate anyone to ingratiate himself still further with the King. I was determined not to be the butt of his jests.

His huge hands dipped and dived as he spoke; bigger than the blades of the rowers' oars, they seemed. Ugly hands, powerful hands. Yet, despite their clumsy appearance, they were as adroit as a harpist's.

I found Sommers tedious beyond words but the King loved him and I forced myself to laugh and smile at his wearisome jests. Still, they kept the King entertained so I did not have to dance my usual attendance upon him. I was able to watch the doings of the river for most of the journey and the time passed swiftly.

The Thames was busier than any highway. Boats of all sizes moved along its waters, most going up or down the river, a few darting across the stream as fast as minnows in the spring. There was a constant noise: of boatmen hailing one another, seagulls squealing and the slap and swish of hundreds of oars.

The riverbank was equally busy, with people tramping to and from work, hauling goods from the decks of boats, casting crude fishing lines or merely standing watching the world floating past upon the never-ending tide. I felt as though I were barely moving and the world was drifting past me like a dream. The clamor and hubbub of ordinary life was slowly drifting away from me.

We reached the Tower about an hour before noon and were soon tied up and stepping onto land once more.

I had never seen the Tower before. It was little used by the King. Mary told me the last time he had stayed there was on the night he wed Anne Boleyn. She never stayed there again either. At least not until she was imprisoned there.

I shivered at the thought of this. It was on Tower Green that she had been executed. Her blood must still be lingering somewhere in the soil, a mulch for little flowers and blooms.

We walked through the gatehouse and I turned my head away from where I imagined she might have been slain. The King took my arm and led me to a path beside the battlements. The air was calm and warm, sheltered from the breezes of the river, and I wished I had left Anne's cloak in the Barge. After a few minutes we went through another gatehouse and strolled onto a bridge which spanned the moat. I wondered if she had walked along this path in the days before her death.

The noise broke into my thoughts as soon as we crossed over. It was like no sound I had heard before: a frightful din of screams and cries, shrieks and bellows. I imagined that this must be what two armies sounded like when they clashed in arms.

The King rubbed his hands with joy and put my arm through his, partly to lead me and partly, I suspected, to make me feel less alarmed.

The closer we got to the Menagerie, the louder the savage noise. And then the wind must have changed for we caught a noisome smell. A heavy, musky, dry-as-dust smell, a smell so thick I could almost taste it. I thanked the Lord that we had come in cool spring and not the height of summer. The stench seemed to beat down upon me, battering upon my brow with potent force.

"A heady scent this morning," Sommers said. "It must be the mating season. Do you think that's the case, Henry? It's not a rotting smell, more a rutting one."

"You may be right, Fool," the King answered. "Though I'm half-convinced the stench does hail from you."

"You are too kind, Henry," he said. "Indeed it has been said I have the smell of a bear. Or was it a goat?"

Henry laughed and slapped the Fool upon the back.

A man approached us wringing his hands.

"The Beast Keeper," Sommers said. "He looks worried."

"I had no notice of Your Majesty's visit," said the Keeper anxiously. "If I had I would have prepared a welcome for you."

"Do not fret, Master Pepper," the King replied. "I have come to see my lions, not you."

The Keeper nodded, his face showing sudden relief. "It is near the time when we feed them," he said. "The lions are in their cages."

"Bring two chairs," the King commanded, "and place them where we have the best view."

Pepper bowed and hurried off to a building beside the bridge.

The King was excited now and rushed us on until we came to a great pit in the ground. On the nearest side of the pit was an open space like the courtyard of a Palace, and fringing this a multitude of cages.

The courtyard was empty at the moment save for one young Keeper who was sweeping the ground.

The King stopped and I felt his body tense. He put his fingers to my lips and pointed.

"There, Alice, do you see them?"

At first I could not see what he pointed at. And then, at last, I saw.

The lions were housed in two cages next to each other. The cages were small and the lions could take only a few steps before hitting the bars.

"'Tis sad that they are imprisoned," Will Sommers said. "They must be supporters of the Pope or perhaps French kitties."

"You're right, Fool," said the King. "It is sad. Noble beasts should not be trammeled so."

Sommers leaned over and pointed at the man sweeping the ground. "Do my eyes deceive me, Henry? Is that not Thomas Cromwell sweeping up the lions' shit? Or maybe the Duke of Norfolk? Will he feed the lions next or lead them on a string?"

It was a jest but it hit home, as the Fool intended, no doubt. Only Sommers would dare hint that the King of England was as much a prisoner as the King of Beasts.

The King leaned over the wall and cried out to the young Keeper. The man looked up with angry glare, searching for who was making such a noise. When he realized it was the King he fell to his knees, screwing up his hat as though it had given grave offense and must be punished.

"Unlock the bars to the lions," the King commanded. "I will see my lions."

The man hurried to do his bidding, fumbling with a large key. He unlocked the cages, jerked the doors open and raced away as fast as he could. He had no wish to remain close to two such beasts when they were uncaged.

At first the lions merely stared at the open gates. *They must be stupid creatures*, I thought, *if so reluctant to leave their cells.*

Eventually one pushed its nose outside the cage, sniffing at the wind in a weary fashion. It stepped out into the Bailey and looked around. A moment later the second lion stepped out beside it. They considered each other carefully. They had no females to fight over so they contented themselves with snarling angrily at each other.

They began to pace up and down the Bailey. The other animals fell silent the moment they glimpsed these frightful monsters.

"See," said the King, gripping me by the hand. "See how the other beasts defer to their lords."

The two great cats trod up and down, their bodies low, their muscles rippling. Suddenly one raised its head and let out a roar. It was like the roar it had given at New Year but here it echoed with a new intensity and power.

The noise seemed to incense the other lion for it turned and roared back with equal vehemence. They stood face-to-face and raged dreadfully, each seeking to drown out its rival's noise with its own outpourings. Eventually they must have felt honor was satisfied, for both fell silent at once.

And then we heard it. A little cry. The cry of a child.

My eyes searched frantically for the source of the noise. I saw her, a child of five years or so. She was in the animal pit only thirty feet from the lions, her toys discarded as she stared at the lions in terror.

"Ned Pepper's daughter," cried one of the Animal Keepers. "Ned Pepper's daughter's in the pit and some fool's let out the lions."

There was an immediate hubbub. Men appeared from everywhere, some carrying long poles, others nets and ropes. Three men leapt over the wall, landing close behind the lions and starting towards them wielding poles. The lions turned and glanced at them, seemingly unconcerned at their presence.

Then one roared out and raced away, slinking low to the ground, covering the thirty feet to the child in moments. The girl cried out. The lion snatched her in its jaws and shook her as though she were a little doll. I wanted to look away but I could not do so. The lion shook the little girl again and again and her cries of terror became screams of fearsome agony. It shook its head a final time and the child was thrown ten feet away.

The three Keepers were on the lion now, prodding it fiercely with their poles so that it turned on them, its huge paws sweeping out in angry fight. A fourth man rushed in and flung a net over the beast.

It tried to launch itself at the Keepers but the net entangled it and it crashed to the ground. Another man was trying to herd the other beast back into its cage but it prowled around him as if seeking to escape.

"The child," I cried.

She lay upon the dust, kicking her feet and screaming. It was a dreadful sound. And then I saw why. The lion had torn off her arm at the elbow. Blood poured from her like water from a pump.

I did not think of what I did but ran towards a gate upon the wall. I pulled it open and tore down a steep staircase to the Bailey below.

"No, Alice," cried the King. "The lions are still at large."

His warning was too late. I reached the Bailey and raced over to the child. I picked her up and pulled her to my chest, my hand trying to staunch the blood from her mangled limb. Who would have thought such a tiny child could have so much blood within her? I pulled out a handkerchief and pressed it against the stump to try to stop the flow. The only thing I could see was her dreadful wound; all that I could hear was her shrieks of agony and the roaring of the lions. I found myself weeping as I tried to staunch the blood.

"You'll be all right," I repeated through my tears, "you'll be all right."

I knew she wouldn't, but I had to tell her so.

A Keeper took the child from me and ran with her in his arms up the stairs to seek a surgeon. I knelt upon the ground and wept.

I felt a hand upon my shoulder and knew it was the King.

"That was courageous of you," he said.

I nodded but could not look up. I could focus on one thing only: that Anne Boleyn's cloak was covered with blood and gore.

I sobbed and clung onto Henry's legs as if they were the only thing which kept me from hurtling off the world.

Chapter Twenty-Eight

Confronting the Royal Beast

23 April 1538

I could not leave my chamber for two days after the visit to the Menagerie. The surgeon had worked with feverish skill but had to amputate the little girl's arm above the elbow. She still lived but it was doubtful how long she would last.

I could not shake her screams from my head. Nor the sight of her tiny arm lying in the dust.

The King, enraged, had ordered that the Keeper who had unlocked the cages be thrown into a cell. If the child survived he was to linger there five years. If she died he would be hanged.

His fury was so intemperate that no one dared tell him that the Keeper had been obeying his command. The King was not the man to be reminded of his own folly.

The other one who felt his wrath was Will Sommers. I assumed this was because the King thought him complicit in the opening of the cage. But then I wondered if the Fool's comparing the Lion Keepers to the King's advisers had been too brutally honest. At any rate, he was banished from the King's presence and sent to Richmond Palace to play the Fool for the Lady Mary. A fitting match for both of them, I thought when I heard.

I think it was this news which freed me from my torment. At last my mind grew calm and I was able to leave my chamber. I found Susan with Lucy in the Maids' Sitting Room.

"Are you recovered?" Susan asked gently.

I nodded. "Is there word of the child?"

Susan and Lucy exchanged quick looks and Susan reached for my hand.

"She died this morning," she said. "It is probably a mercy."

Lucy began to weep soft tears.

"And the young Keeper?" I asked. "The one who opened the cages?"

"He is to hang tomorrow," Susan said. "His family have been imprisoned and all their goods confiscated by the King."

I shook my head wearily. How slender do our fingers grip this world.

"And what of the lions?" I asked. "What has happened to them?"

"They have been punished also," Susan said. "They have been starved of food and the one that attacked the girl has been flogged."

"Without so much as a trial?" I asked with grim irony.

Lucy looked perplexed. Susan patted her on the hand. "It is a jest on Alice's part, Lucy. Only a jest."

"And the King's blacksmith has made a wonderful device to control them," Lucy said. "It is a yoke with two poles which can be extended and held by two men to control the animal's head. Strong men I should imagine."

At that moment Wicks and Bray skulked into the room.

They stared at me for a moment and then stepped closer.

"You have been unwell?" Wicks asked. "I can see it in your face."

Bray laughed—a donkey's laugh.

"I hear rumors the plague has returned," Wicks continued.

I raised my eyebrows with weary contempt. "Rest assured, dear Philippa, that if I had the plague I would rush to your arms to seek comfort. To hold you tight as tight can be."

Bray looked confused by my response but Wicks grimaced.

"And be assured that I would shun you, Alice Petherton. Shun you even more than I do now."

"That may make the plague a price worth paying," I said.

Wicks made as if to answer me but could think of no reply as cutting. Her face worked in frustration and she turned towards the door.

"Why would she seek your arms to comfort her?" I heard Bray ask.

Wicks snorted at her in contempt for her stupidity before storming out of the room.

I laughed aloud. "It is goodly to return to the comfort of one's friends," I said.

But then I remembered the little girl screaming in the lion's jaws. How the innocent are punished and how the guilty gain reward.

I sat in silence for a while with my friends for company. Finally I made up my mind.

"I must go and see the King," I said.

He was in his privy chamber with Sir Thomas Cromwell.

Gregory Frost had tried to prevent my entering but I would not be gainsaid. I saw him calculating the scale of my determination against the potential ire of the King and deciding that to agree with my demand might be the lesser of two evils.

"Alice," the King said in surprise. "What brings you here?"

Cromwell looked startled for a moment and covered over the parchment he had been showing to the King. He leaned back in his seat and looked at me with cool regard.

The King rose and took me by the hand, staring searchingly into my eyes. "I trust you have recovered from your indisposition?" he asked.

"I had," I answered. "Until this morning."

"Ah," he said, "you have heard the sad news about the child."

Cromwell sighed. I thought it not from sorrow at the death but more from being interrupted by what he considered such a trivial matter.

"That is one reason for my disquiet," I said, "but not the only one."

I wondered at my bold words and was clearly not alone in this. Cromwell put down his pen and placed his fingers on his lips as if he were the audience of a fascinating play.

A sudden chill clutched my heart but I steeled myself to continue.

"I have heard that the young Keeper is to hang for opening the doors of the cage."

The King's eyes narrowed, all concern for me replaced by a reptile suspicion I had never seen before.

"And what of it?" he asked. "It is my will. I promised as much, as you will recall."

"It will be wrong to execute him," I said.

I noticed Cromwell's look of astonishment at my words. He turned towards the King to see how he would react.

The King's face grew rigid, as if it were transmuting into stone. He seemed to have stopped breathing and his cheeks grew red with rising rage. I gulped in fear as his hands began to tremble with a violent, barely repressed fury.

To my surprise, Cromwell spoke in a soft, emollient tone. "Perhaps, Your Grace, Alice is still troubled by news of the child."

The King did not answer but gave a quick shake of his head. He never took his eyes from me. His rage looked set to explode.

"You question your King?" he cried at last.

I took a step backward. Even if he had not been King I would have been terrified by the thunder of his fury. It was almost a physical blow.

Coming from the King it was almost enough to make me turn and flee the room.

But I stood my ground, though my stomach felt icy and fear shook me like a leaf caught in a gale.

"I do not question you, Henry, but I say you are wrong."

His mouth opened as if he were about to bellow. No words came.

He looked at me in utter disbelief. Cromwell had half risen from his seat, his hand outstretched as if to try to halt time.

"You are wrong to hang this man," I continued, "because it was you who ordered him to open the cage. He was only obeying your command. As a loyal servant should."

I flung myself upon my knees and held my hands up to the King.

"You did not realize the child was there, Your Majesty. You had not seen her and, had you done, would never have ordered the cages opened. The terrible attack must have erased this from your memory. How else would the most loving and just King in all the world order the execution of this poor man?"

I reached for his quivering hand and kissed it. He would have removed it from me but I held firm and at last his shaking began to calm.

Eventually I felt his other hand reach beneath my chin and pressure me to rise.

I chanced a look at his face. It was changed now, quiet and thoughtful.

"You are right, Alice," he said.

I took a little breath.

"You are right," he continued. "I am the most loving and just of Kings. And I had forgotten that I commanded the man to open the cage."

He slumped down, seeming to recall the scene.

I stood anxiously over him, searching his face.

Out of the corner of my eye I saw Cromwell move, signaling me to sit down.

The King began to play with his beard, deep in machination.

At last he looked over to Cromwell. "Is there time to save the man?"

"The execution is due for tomorrow at dawn, Your Grace. Plenty of time to show the world your clemency."

"My clemency, yes."

A silence descended upon the room. The same thought must have come to all of us.

"He must suffer some punishment for his crime, however," Cromwell said. "Fifty lashes." He paused for the slightest moment. "For mistaking your command to keep the cage door shut."

The King turned wolf eyes to his minister.

"And a grant of twenty pounds, perhaps," Cromwell added, "to ensure his silence."

The King waved his hand and Cromwell hastily scribbled a note which he stamped with the King's own seal.

I found myself shaking uncontrollably and thought I would vomit.

"I need the bath chamber." I gasped.

"You know where it is," the King said.

I fled the room and heard Cromwell say, "Remarkable girl, Alice Petherton."

I did not hear the King's reply.

When I returned from the bath chamber to the Privy Chamber it was empty save for Gregory Frost.

"The King has left," he said. "He has gone riding."

I nodded. I could not find my voice.

My head felt light, as if it were floating free from my body, and I leaned against the windowsill to steady myself. I thought I might faint at any moment.

A gentle hand held me by the elbow to steady me. I looked up to see Frost's eyes regarding me.

"Whatever have you done, child?" he asked. There was a look of concern upon his face.

It was that look which did it. I burst into tears; the tears I had been struggling to keep in check. They were born of terror of the King and fear for my life. And they were also born of rage. Rage that the King could contemplate executing a man merely for obeying him. And rage at myself for becoming the King's lover. For becoming close to him.

I felt a handkerchief being pushed into my hand. For a wild moment I thought the King had returned and was comforting me. But it was Frost who was kneeling beside me.

"Hush, Alice," he said gently. "He has gone. You are quite safe." He patted my hand, stood up and poured me a glass of wine.

"Drink this," he said. "And when you are composed and have dried your tears you should return to your chamber."

He gave me a smile like a kindly uncle might and left the room. I gulped down the wine and poured myself a second glass. I found myself shaking uncontrollably; the glass quivered in my hand and some of the wine spilt on my gown. I rubbed at it carelessly, barely aware I was doing so.

I thought back to what had just happened. What had I done? How would the King deal with me now?

I sat for a few minutes and then went into the bath chamber and wiped away my tears. I looked awful, face pale as the moon, eyes red from weeping. The sooner I was in the privacy of my chamber the better.

I slipped out of the King's privy apartment and crept down the hall to my chamber.

A man of arms was standing by the door.

I took a breath and walked towards him.

"You can't go in there, miss," he said.

"What on earth do you mean?" I said. "That is my bedchamber."

"Orders of the King, miss. Direct from him, not from the Lord Privy Seal even. Direct from him. You can't go in, miss. Sorry."

"But my things?"

"They've been taken away."

I shook my head. "I don't understand."

"They've been taken away." He sighed. "The room's just been cleared. Of everything."

I leaned against the wall.

"By order of the King?"

The man nodded.

I swallowed, for a lump had appeared in my throat. The swallow did not dislodge it. Tears welled up in my eyes.

"Where have my things gone?" I managed to whisper.

The man gave me a sympathetic look. "I heard the servants say they were going to take them back to your old chamber."

"Was that on the King's orders?"

The man shrugged. "I couldn't say, miss."

I nodded my thanks and stumbled my way to my old chamber.

I looked inside. The King had given me dozens of gowns, and they had all been dumped upon the bed. Upon the table was only one of the jewels he had given me: a plain little necklace with a locket containing a cameo portrait of him within.

I flicked open the locket. The cameo had been prised out, leaving an empty space. It was sight of that which proved too much for me.

I flung myself onto my bed, heedless of the gowns I was lying on, and began to weep piteously. But even as I did so, I wondered which, of all the things that had happened to me, was the source of the most tears.

Chapter Twenty-Nine

Persecution and Dismissal

23 to 25 April 1538

My friends Susan, Mary and Lucy rallied around immediately. They heard about the King's dismissal of me within the hour and crowded into my chamber with a jug of wine and some honey cakes.

"What will we do with all the gowns?" Mary asked, looking round in consternation. I was sitting on a pile of them; there was no space to put them away.

"I've got room in my wardrobe for some of them," Susan said and turned to the others. "Can you two take some more?"

They nodded. "As long as we can borrow them," Mary said with a smile. I laughed and kissed her and wiped away my tears.

We spent the next quarter of an hour sorting out which gowns I needed to keep with me in the chamber and which could be stored with my friends. They hurried away with armfuls of clothes while I began the job of hanging my diminished collection upon their hangers.

I glanced around my room. It was tiny as a cupboard but felt quite empty. I thought of the large chamber I had enjoyed as the King's favorite. The delightful wall paintings, the beautiful furniture, the large and comfortable bed. I thought of the vase of flowers which was filled with fresh blooms every morning, and the bowl of choice and delicious fruits. I sighed as I recalled the sense of space and the two large windows which looked out to where the sun rose each morning. Oh, how I was going to miss it all.

I took a deep breath and decided there was no merit in continuing to think this way. *This is my room*, I said to myself. *The first room I ever had. I loved it a few months ago; I can love it again.*

I sat upon the lumpy bed and smoothed the rumpled coverlet. My favorite gowns hung upon the walls like silent playmates; my poetry books and recorder had returned to their accustomed place upon the little table. I would make the best of this, and more. I would enjoy my newfound independence.

I knelt in front of the window. To the north I saw the familiar sight of the ridge of land with its line of trees looking like a green crown. I had often walked there on my own and longed to be there now, under the leaves with only the birdsong for company.

Other company made itself known, alas.

"See how the mighty are fallen," came a familiar voice from the doorway.

I turned and, before I could say anything in answer, Philippa Wicks and Dorothy Bray had pushed their way into my chamber, their faces aglow with spiteful triumph.

Bray giggled. "Fallen to her knees, by the look of it."

I gave her a contemptuous look. Was that the best she could come up with?

"She is more used to falling on her back," Wicks said. "Perhaps her back has given out under the strain."

I opened my mouth to reply but decided not to satisfy the vile creatures by arguing with them.

"It's such a pleasure to see you," I said, giving the broadest of smiles. "I have missed you both so much."

"Well, we haven't missed you," Bray said.

I put on an innocent look. "Have you not? Then why else, pray, have you rushed to visit me so soon?"

"You know why," Wicks said.

"I have no idea," I said. "Do tell me. Please."

She did not answer. To admit that she had come to gloat over my downfall would only demean her. I could see her mind working to frame an answer that would let her reclaim ascendancy over me.

"I have come here because I pity you," she said.

I swallowed. She had chosen these words carefully and for a moment I was lost for an answer.

"There is nothing to pity," I said at last. "I was the lover of the foremost man in the realm. A man who had no wife for me to compete with. Especially not a wife I had tried to supplant but failed to. How are Richard Rich and his wife, by the way?"

Wicks's face contorted in fury. She took a step towards me. As she did so, I caught sight of her stomach. She must have been almost six months with child.

"Oh, Philippa, my dear," I said, cutting as a knife. "You are putting on a little weight. Is this the result of too rich a diet?"

Involuntarily her hand went to hide her stomach. "You little bitch," she said.

I smiled.

Wicks nearly bowled Bray over in her hurry to vacate my chamber.

I laughed aloud and was still chuckling when my friends returned a few minutes later.

"I see you've had a little visit already," Susan said. "We met Wicks and Bray in the corridor. They had faces like furies."

"They came to mock," I said. "But they left the more mocked."

"Be careful," Mary said. "Philippa Wicks is high in Sir Richard Rich's favor."

"I noticed," I said. "It was my comment upon her condition which so enraged her."

"She's hoping to use the pregnancy to persuade him to leave his wife."

"And will he?" I asked.

"I'm sure he won't," Susan said. "He's as frightened of his wife as the rest of the country is of him."

Mary gave me a strange look as if she was pondering what to say to me. "Your return from the King's presence may encourage him to sniff round you once again," she said. "He will wish to dispense with Philippa as soon as possible. He changes his clothes to suit every weather so I would not be surprised if he wasn't equally keen to change his mistresses."

Lucy looked uncomfortable at these words. "What a villain he is," she said.

"The worst in the Kingdom," said Susan. "In a Kingdom of villains."

"Not the worst," said Mary. "Surely that accolade belongs to Thomas Cromwell."

I shook my head. "That's not true," I said. "Cromwell is no villain. He is a man of integrity. Strange integrity it may be, but it is integrity nonetheless."

Susan laughed. "We must defer to Lady Alice, who has such acquaintance with the high and mighty of the realm."

For a moment I thought she was mocking me but then I saw the friendship in her look.

"That was timely, Susan," I said. "I pray you all to knock me back if I ever put on airs and graces. Any which I hitherto cherished have been quite banished today."

Susan sat upon the bed. She regarded me for a while, as if pondering whether or not to say what was on her mind. In the end she must have decided. "And why are they banished, Alice? Why did the King dismiss you? Why have you fallen out of favor?"

I sighed. But it was not because of sorrow for me. It was because I could see again the little girl being savaged by the lion.

Mary and Susan were right about Sir Richard Rich. He appeared in my doorway a few days after I'd been dismissed by the King. He held a bunch of roses.

He gave me what he must have believed was a winning smile. It was not.

"Are those flowers for your lover?" I asked. "To celebrate her confinement perhaps?"

"You have a sharp tongue today, Alice," he said.

"I have a sharp tongue every day," I said. "It's very nearly as sharp as my bodkin."

As I spoke, I picked up a needle and was pleased to see that he blanched, no doubt at the memory of my pressing it to his eye.

He smiled still more broadly but his eyes stayed cold and dead. Deadly, should I say.

"An unfortunate occurrence," he said. "A misunderstanding." His hand reached out and touched me on the arm. "I would have us put that all behind us, Alice."

"I would have you put your arm behind you," I said, shrugging it off. I took a step closer to the door but he moved at the same time, blocking my exit.

"I shall cry for help," I said. "And before help comes your eye will suffer."

He shook his head. "There's no one near enough to hear your cry," he said. "I checked before I entered your chamber. Nobody to hear the least little squeal."

"Not my squeal, perhaps. But they will hear yours, I promise you."

He looked doubtful of my words at first. Then he blinked swiftly, the first time I had ever seen him blink. He bent and placed the roses on the bed.

"I had come here to make my peace with you," he said. "I had hoped we might be friends."

"Friends?" I said in disbelief.

"More than friends, in fact." He put his hands upon his hips and silently appraised me. "Some would not wish to chew upon the leftovers of the King, but I have no such compunction. Especially as choice a leftover as you."

I felt bile rise at his words.

"Get out, you slime," I said. "Get out this instant or you will regret it."

He gave a hollow laugh. "I will regret it?" He shook his head. "You have lost the fleeting power you held in Court," he said. "Whereas I maintain all my power; in fact I augment it daily. I hold all the cards, you see, and your hand, Alice, is absolutely empty."

"I hold the needle," I said.

He smiled still more widely, now resembling a fox. "Then that is what I shall leave you."

He took a step towards the door but paused on the threshold and glanced back. "Such a beautiful woman, such an intelligent woman. But one, alas, who has made a very bad choice today."

I slumped on the bed the moment he had gone. My hands shook as if with bitter cold. I felt like I might be sick but mastered the inclination. I went over the conversation in my mind a couple of times. And each time my thoughts returned to the same phrase: *Then that is what I shall leave you.*

What on earth could the monster have meant by that?

❧

I found out the very next day.

I was awoken at seven in the morning by a hammering on the door. "Get dressed, Alice Petherton," came a loud voice. "Get dressed immediately."

I flung a cloak over my nightclothes and opened the door. Two men at arms stood in the corridor. I pulled my cloak still tighter.

"You'll need more than that," the younger of the two men said. "Where you're going you'll need more than that." He gave a shrill, nervous little laugh.

"I don't understand."

"You're to be shipped out of here," said the older man. "We're to escort you from the Palace and put you on a boat to London."

"By whose order? The King's?"

The man shook his head. The look of consternation upon my face seemed to trouble him for he suddenly spoke more gently.

"Not the King's, no. This is by special order of Sir Richard Rich."

He held up a document.

"But can he do this?" I asked, taking the document from him and staring at it.

"Whether he can or he can't is immaterial," he said. "What's material is that he has. You're to be shipped out immediately, without time for drink or sup."

"But what about my things?" I said, turning towards my chamber.

"Confiscated," he said. "You're allowed one suit of clothes and a traveling cloak." He looked embarrassed as he said it.

"And the little purse," said the younger man.

"Oh yes," the older guard said, "and the little purse." He pushed a purse into my hand.

I opened it. The only things in it were the twig of a rose, a twig of many thorns, and a bodkin.

"From Richard Rich?" I asked.

"Afraid so, miss. He's a charmer, right enough."

He glanced swiftly up and down the corridor and then leaned closer towards me. "Get yourself a little bag," he whispered. "Put your special things in there and hide it under your cloak. No one will know. We'll keep it our little secret."

This unexpected kindness hit me harder than the news that I was being banished from my home. I began to weep. The two guards looked around with worried and embarrassed looks.

"Have a care, miss," the older guard said. "It don't do no good to be crying. That will only attract attention. Be a brave girl, now; get your special things together and we'll help you leave as quiet as a mouse."

I wiped my nose and nodded.

"You're very kind," I said.

"This isn't kind," he said. "This is cruel, dreadful cruel."

Chapter Thirty

London

26 April 1538

I sat in a small and leaky boat with an elderly man working the oars. He wheezed like a bellows every time he pulled, and spat a thick wad of phlegm into the Thames. I wondered which would happen first: our arrival at London Bridge or his demise.

How different from the last time I'd journeyed down the river. Then I had been in the King's Royal Barge with the choicest food and wine, minstrels to play soft melodies and that fool Will Sommers to entertain the King and weary me with his drivel. But it had been me who was the fool, I thought bitterly. My intervention to save an innocent man's life had ruined mine.

I put my hand into the water and pulled it out again, just narrowly missing the latest glob of phlegm from the boatman. I cast him a venomous look, which he mistook for a pleasant one. He grinned, revealing a row of teeth like moss-encrusted tombstones. I closed my eyes to hide the sight of them.

I wondered what I could do now. How I could possibly make my way in London and in life?

Did I regret interceding on the Animal Keeper's behalf? I wondered.

I regretted losing my position at the Court. I would miss the fine clothes, the respect from at least a few of the courtiers, the ease of life. But I would not miss being on public show, always having to think about the impression I might be making. I certainly would not miss the constant sexual pleasuring I had to give the King. He gorged on me every bit as much as he gorged on his food. And now, like a bone from a capon, he had cast me aside.

So what would I do now? The kindness of the two guards meant I'd been able to collect the little money I had, my recorder, my poetry book, a little trinket given to me by my mother and the locket from the King. I pushed open the locket and glanced at where the portrait of the King had lain before it had been prised out, presumably on his order. How could he do such a thing? How could he be so cruel after what we had shared together? How could he stoop so low?

Yet I knew that the lord of all he surveyed was a man who could stoop lower than most. No glory was too high for him to reach for, and no base act too squalid if it suited his purpose. He contained within his one mountainous frame all that was noble in a man and all that was vile. A chill washed over me at memory of him.

"It's a lovely morning to be out on the river," said the waterman. He gave me a look which was both lewd and kindly. No doubt he'd have been happy to have me as either daughter or bedmate. I studied his face. He was careworn and beaten down, and yet, as he glanced around, there was still a shred of life about him. Not defeated altogether. Not completely.

"It is lovely," I said and his face lit up with pleasure.

I could do that with men, I realized. With a word, or a glance or a touch, I could make their hearts beat stronger and their lives feel better.

He began to whistle, tunelessly and flat. But it was preferable to his coughing, at any rate.

I thought back to the King. He had less nobility than even this poor old man. And yet, despite all this, and despite my distaste for his imperious nature, I could not deny that I missed him.

I smiled a little at this revelation. What on earth could it be that I missed? And then I knew. It was not the life of ease and pleasure. It was not the grandeur, though there was plenty of that. It was two things. One was that Henry Tudor surged with boisterous life. And the other was that on occasion he had shown he cared for me.

I have had little of caring in my life.

"What you going to London for, miss," said the waterman, "if I may be so bold to ask? It's early for a young lady to be out and about."

I looked over his shoulder at the sun; even now, it was only peeking above the horizon. Despite it being the height of summer, the mists of night still hung about the river here and there.

"I am leaving the Palace," I said. "I go to live in London."

The old man nodded. "Been sacked," he said. "Dismissed from service?" His eyes seemed to get much smaller. "Got with child, miss?"

"That is no concern of yours," I snapped.

He nodded slowly, as if my response had confirmed his suspicions. He could not help but glance at my stomach.

"I am not with child," I said in a firm tone.

"But you have been dismissed," he said.

"Yes," I cried, vexed at his nosiness. "But what business is it of yours?" My tone was harsh and a look of fright came to his eyes.

"None, miss," he said. "Not my business at all." He mumbled to himself a moment and stared at his feet.

I sat thus, for a quarter of an hour, in seething silence.

At last I relented, feeling sorry for the look of fear my words had engendered in the old man.

"It was fair enough for you to ask, I suppose," I said.

"It were only conversation, miss," he said, looking up hopefully.

"I know. I understand."

"And . . ." the waterman began. He paused as if uncertain how to proceed.

"Yes?" I said.

"And I was wondering how you'd make your way in life now you're dismissed. And where you might go to live. Do you have family in London, miss, or friends? It's a lively place. Might be risky for a young lady like you."

"Risky? What do you mean?"

He sighed and stared at the river in silence. I thought he might never speak again. Finally he gave an even bigger sigh and turned to me.

"Men," he said. "Men will look at you and feel lustful. With good luck, a fine young gentleman will seek you for his wife. With bad luck, villains will abuse you and worse."

"How worse?" I said, my chin jutting forward as if I were squaring up to Wicks or Bray.

"You'd fetch a high price for your charms, miss, a very high price. In the brothels of Southwark. Or even worse, you could be shipped off to foreign parts. Those infidels, the French and Turks, they'll pay big for someone like you. For their harems."

I laughed at his words. "Thank you for your warning, kind sir. But I think I can take care of myself."

He studied me for a moment and shook his head. "You think you can, miss. But it strikes me that you don't know London. And you don't know how low folk can stoop."

"I don't know London," I said. "But I know how low men can stoop."

"You mean the King?" he asked.

I gasped in astonishment. "How on earth did you know?"

"We watermen know everything, miss. We're the ears and eyes of the Palace. When people sit themselves in our boats, high-up people, they don't notice we're here and they talk their hearts out in front of us.

I've heard all sorts from all sorts of people. Who's bedding who, secrets of state and plans for mischief and treachery. All sorts of stuff. And we've got eyes, miss, good eyes." He chuckled to himself. "Especially for such lovely girls as you."

I smiled despite myself. "Thank you, kindly," I said, giving a courtly bob of my head.

He laughed aloud at my words. The longer I spent with him the less grotesque he seemed.

"My name is Alice Petherton," I said.

"Walter Scrump, miss. Son of Jacob."

I stared at him and felt the smile growing on my face as I did so.

"You know about me," I said, "but I know nothing about you other than that you have eyes and ears and a wheezing chest. Tell me about yourself."

"Nothing to tell, miss. I'm a waterman."

I leaned forward in the boat, hugging my knees.

"But there must be lots to tell. How old you are, where you live, your friends and family."

He shook his head. "Don't know how old I am, miss, though my mum told me I was born the year the old King Henry killed Richard Crookback. Used to call me her Tudor Prince, when I were a boy. As a jest, you understand, meaning no disrespect."

I nodded and did a quick calculation in my head. He must have been in his early fifties but he looked twenty years older.

"And where do you live, Mr. Scrump? And what about your family?"

He rubbed his hand across his nostrils, squinted at what had settled on his fingers and furtively rinsed them in the river.

"I lives in Offal Pudding Lane, miss. Close to the river. Can get from my door to my boat as fast as a tick come the morning. Them who gets to their boats first gets the most work, you see."

I nodded. "And your family?"

He gave a lopsided grin. "I have a wife. She's called Margery. Margery Scrump. She can be a bit of a roughhouse when she's minded, miss. The neighbors will tell you that. But only to protect her own. That and when I've taken too much ale in the Traitor's Head. Then she's handy with her tongue." He chuckled at the thought.

"And what about children?"

"Fourteen of 'em, miss. Three still living. There's Walter—he was the fourth to bear that name, though we call him Art—Katie and Jane. Good girls, with kids of their own. Art, though, he's a rascal. A litter of kiddies all across London and not one of 'em knows who their father is."

"He must be a very tired man," I said. "What is his work?"

"Waterman, miss," he said as if astonished by my question. "Father, son, father, son. We Scrumps say we've got Thames water in our veins instead of blood."

I laughed aloud and touched his hand. "You've cheered me, Walter Scrump," I said. "I stepped into this boat as melancholy as a winter evening but now I am cheered."

He pursed his lips. "You won't be when I get you to London Bridge," he said. "Where you going to stay?"

I shrugged. "I've got a little money. I'll find some lodgings somewhere."

"Won't your family help?"

I shook my head. "I've got no family. My mother died when I was seven years old. I was brought up by my Grandmother but she died last year. I've lived at Court for the past few years. It's the only home I've got."

"Well, you ain't got it no more."

I frowned at his bluntness but he did not notice. He began to chew on his tongue, blowing out little breaths all the while and mumbling to himself periodically. Deep in thought I assumed. Either that or chomping on a bit of breakfast still lodged in his teeth.

I turned my attention to the river. The sun had extinguished the last of the mists and was sparkling on the water. It was still early so there was less traffic than normal but a score of little boats scurried hither and tither, upriver, downriver and slanting across from bank to bank. These people were making their way in the world, I thought, and without the advantages that I had. I could read and write, I could dance and sing, I could even write poetry. Then a terrible thought came to me. As Walter had said, I was beautiful. I could find a wealthy husband. Or failing that, earn my money on my back. I pushed this thought from my mind; it was not a subject for me to muse upon. There and then I decided I would not launch my new life by relying on my looks.

"We've got a small room." Walter's voice broke into my thoughts. "It's very small and a bit grubby. But it could suit you well, miss."

I stared at him, openmouthed. "That's so kind of you, Mr. Scrump." I could not believe a stranger would be so generous.

A look of alarm crossed his face. "You'd have to pay, miss. Margery ain't an almshouse."

"Of course," I said. "I didn't think otherwise. I told you I've got money and I'm happy to pay a fair rent. I'd rather it went to you than to some villain who might rob me blind."

He grinned the full set of his teeth. "That's mighty trustworthy of you, miss. Foolish, I might add, as you don't know me from the footpads that stalk the streets. But foolish is as foolish does and if you lodge with me and Margery you won't go amiss."

I reached out and squeezed his hand. He blushed a deep red and turned his head as if to see the way ahead, downriver. When he glanced back he gave me a sheepish smile and began to whistle tunelessly as if to say there should be an end to all further talk.

I leaned back in the boat and closed my eyes. Perhaps my new life would not be as awful as I feared. My eyes began to feel heavy and I drifted into sleep.

"London Bridge, miss," came a distant voice and then the grating of wood upon stone.

My eyes snapped open.

"We've arrived, miss," the waterman said. "London Bridge, as required."

I rubbed my eyes awake and glanced at the waterman; I must have been asleep for two hours or more. I fought the urge to reach out and check my purse. He could have done anything in that time—robbed me, molested me, raped me, even slain me and thrown my corpse into the river. Instead he had kept on rowing in careful silence, allowing me to sleep, almost watching over me.

He struggled onto the wharf, moaning and groaning all the while, and tied up the boat. He turned and held out his hand to help me ashore. His grasp was immensely strong and his hand was as hard and callused as the bark of a tree.

"It's close to dinnertime," he said. "Come on, miss, and I'll take you to Mistress Scrump."

He plucked up my bundle from the boat and led me away from the river into a maelstrom of people, all bustling, hurrying as if desperate to get wherever they were going. The noise was horrendous, the stench of waste and bodies truly terrible. I had trouble keeping up with the old waterman. *He's got all my possessions*, I kept thinking to myself. *He could disappear with everything in a moment. He'll get as far from the river as possible and slip into the crowd.* But he stopped at every crossroads to see that I was following. I'd have lost him in moments if he hadn't done so.

Then another thought struck me. He had known much about the brothels of the city, even about the harems of the Turk. Perhaps it was his intention to take me to some secret, desperate den and sell me to a pimp or slaver. My heart missed a beat and my stomach lurched. What had I done? Why had I been such a fool as to allow myself to be deceived by the old villain?

We turned into a narrow street, barely more than an alley. Half a dozen men were walking towards us pushing carts overflowing with offal. The stench was nauseating and I almost gagged. It did not seem to bother the men, though. A couple were happily stuffing meat pies into their mouths, holding the pastries with hands oozing with blood and entrails. Nor did the smell bother Mr. Scrump either. He trudged along, whistling and wheezing, giving greeting to a number of the men and getting answered by pats on his back which left his coat smeared and filthy. I hurried after him, stepping gingerly over the gristle, lights and entrails which dropped off the carts with every jolt and judder. The whole alley was choked with offal.

The waterman stopped and gave me a grin. "Here we are, miss," he said. "My home, and Margery's. And yours for as long as you want it." He paused and his eyes narrowed. "As long as your money lasts out."

He pushed open the door and I followed him in. We came straight into a small room with low and sagging roof. It was crammed with furniture, all higgledy-piggledy and bleached pale as if by sunshine or maybe long periods floating in the river. The smell of cooking wafted from a door in the far wall and I could hear someone clattering about with pans.

"Who's that?" came a deep-throated voice. "Is that Katie?"

"It's me," said Walter. "Your husband." He smiled at me, as if he had made the greatest witticism in all the world.

"What you doing home?" the voice yelled. "You've not gone and crashed the boat?"

A portly little figure hurried into the room, rubbing her hands on a filthy dishcloth. She stopped midstep when she saw me and turned to her husband with an accusing stare.

"What you doing bringing the likes of her here?" she cried, swatting him with the cloth.

Then she advanced upon me, flapping the rag as if she were shooing away a vagrant dog.

"Get out of here," she said. "We don't want your sort here."

She flapped and flapped as she came closer so that I was forced to retreat to the door. "And I'll deal with you later, Walter Scrump," she cried, "daring to bring your tart to my house."

She glared at me. "I don't like whores, never have. Go and take your trade down Eastcheap. You'll find plenty of customers there."

"How dare you," I cried.

She held her cloth in front of her like a shield and brandished her fist at me.

"I dare do anything in my own house," she cried. "I'll box your ears and kick you out on your backside."

Walter hurried over and caught her by the arm.

"It's not like that at all," he said. "Alice Petherton is a lady, one of the Ladies from Court. She's fallen on hard times and I thought that we might let her lodge here."

His wife turned a furious face to him. "You must think I was born yesterday, Walter Scrump. Think you can bring your girlfriend here, your fancy-piece, and lodge her under my roof. That's nice and convenient for you, I must say. Expect me to bring you both breakfast in bed I shouldn't wonder."

"It's not like that," I said. I counted out some coins from my purse and held them out towards her. "I've got money. I'll pay for lodgings. It's as your husband said. I'm in a desperate way and I need somewhere to stay for a few days. I'll be no trouble, honestly."

She looked from the purse to me. Her eyes went from top to toe, appraising me with the utmost scrutiny.

"How many days?" she asked.

"As many as these coins will buy."

She bent and peered closely at the coins. Then she reached out and took them from my hand.

"Quite a few days, they'll buy. I'm not a cheat, but I'm not a fool neither."

"I didn't think you were either cheat or fool," I said.

She nodded and bit at the coin. "You're welcome," she said. "I'll sort out your room; it's not much but it's cozy. And I've got a stew on the boil if you want a bite to eat."

"That would be lovely," I said. I hoped that it was not made up of scrapings from the street outside.

She glanced at her husband. For a moment he appeared anxious, but then a look of relief came over his face. His wife nodded curtly and he grinned, as if with pride.

"She's called Alice Petherton," he said. "She used to be the King's mistress."

"Heaven help us," Margery screamed, flinging her rag high above her head. "You'll have us hanged, drawn and quartered."

She stared at me in horror, as though I had brought the plague into her home.

"Get her out of here, Walter," she wailed. "Get her out before the soldiers come."

She stepped towards me, her breath coming fast, and managed a semblance of a curtsy.

"I don't want to seem rude," she said, "but I'm an honest woman and I don't want no trouble. I don't want my head cut off like poor Queen Anne. Not my head." She jerked her thumb towards her husband. "Nor his head neither, though he's the biggest fool in Christendom."

"You won't lose your head," I promised. "Nothing will happen if I stay here. No one knows that I'm even here."

"It will get out," Margery said. "Lizzie Dibble would sell her soul for seven shillings so I'm sure as sixpence she'll sell me."

"There's nothing to sell and nothing to tell," I said firmly. "Trust me in this, please, Mrs. Scrump."

She eyed me uncertainly for a long minute. "You promise the King won't send his soldiers?"

"I promise. He doesn't even know where I am."

She took a step closer and stared into my face. "You're a beautiful girl," she said. "I can see why the King would want to take you to his bed." She put her hands on her hips and pursed her lips. "But what I can't rightly understand is why he'd kick you out of it."

"That's a long story."

"She's not expecting," Walter said, "if that's what you think."

Mrs. Scrump snorted. "And how would you know, Walter Scrump?"

"I'm not," I said. "I was dismissed from the King because I argued with him."

Mrs. Scrump's eyes widened in disbelief but Walter laughed aloud.

"Hear that, Margery?" he said. "Getting rid of your woman for arguing. What's good for the King is good for his subjects, so from now on you mind and curb your tongue."

"You're no King, Walter Scrump," she answered, "and I ain't no mistress. So you curb *your* tongue before I gets a knife to cut it off."

For a moment I felt quite alarmed but then I saw that the pair were grinning at each other as if this were an oft-repeated scene.

"Now then, miss," said Mrs. Scrump, turning back to me. "Let's show you your room before I get you a bite to eat."

I followed her ample bottom up a rickety old ladder, which led to the floor above. There was one small chamber with a low bed against the window and a wooden trunk green with mildew. It was a squalid little place but bigger than I thought I would have.

"This is a lovely room," I lied.

"It does for the old man and me," she said, stepping towards a door in the corner. "And this will be your room."

I smiled to hide my mistake and bent under the lintel to get into the room. It was half the size of my old room in the Palace.

The ceiling was so low I had to stoop to avoid banging my head. A slit in the wall sufficed for a window; it cast barely a glimmer into the room, which may have been a blessing. The only furnishing was a small platform jammed between two walls. A filthy cover was thrown upon it.

"It's a small bed," called Mrs. Scrump from her own chamber, "but I'm told it's comfy." She made for the ladder. "I'll get you a bit of dinner, miss."

I nodded in answer although, even had she been in the doorway, I doubt she would have been able to see it in the gloom. I pushed the cover into one corner of what I would have to learn to call my bed. It was a wooden platform, nothing more. I lay upon it gingerly. It was so small I had to bend my knees towards my chin. *What have I come to?* I thought. And I began to sob.

Chapter Thirty-One

Taken

27 April 1538

I have no idea how I did it but I managed to get through the first day and night in Offal Pudding Lane. The stew Mrs. Scrump had cooked was bland and insubstantial. I found it no wonder that her husband was so skinny and huge wonder that she was so round. The tiny bedroom I slept in was hot and claustrophobic. For half the night the room echoed with the wheezing snore from Walter next door. The rest of it was filled with the furtive scurry of mice and rats.

But worst of all was the all-pervading stench from the lane outside. How I did not retch up my stomach is a mystery I cannot fathom. The Scrumps didn't appear to notice the smell at all; they may as well have been breathing a breeze from open meadowland for all the impact it made upon them. Perhaps a lifetime of smelling such distasteful odors had destroyed their sense of smell.

When I awoke the next morning, I found that my own nostrils were beginning to get accustomed to the stink. I was appalled. *I'll soon be like a guttersnipe*, I thought. *I may as well go and scrape up the steaming guts from the lane and offer to make them into a stew for the household.*

I went down the ladder and found Mrs. Scrump with a pile of clothes on her lap.

"These belong to my daughters," she said. "You can't go around in fine clothes like you're wearing, miss. You'd be a target for thieves and murderers as soon as you step out the door. You'd best leave your fancy clothes in your room and wear these things from now on."

She held up a brown smock with no trimming and measured it with her eye. "I think this should fit you."

I took the smock and held it against me. It was of coarse material but smelled clean and fresh.

"That's a French bonnet, I warrant," she said, reaching up to touch it.

I nodded. "It's the latest fashion."

She shook her head. "It won't do round here, won't do at all." She passed me a shapeless-looking woolen hat. I pulled off my bonnet and placed the hat on my head, tilting it slightly over my forehead.

Mrs. Scrump smiled. "That looks better on you than it ever did on my Katie."

I breakfasted on a lump of hard brown bread that was unrelenting in its determination not to be swallowed. It tasted of linen but I forced it down. I had just finished when the door was flung open and a young man stepped into the house.

"You've found your way back, then," said Mrs. Scrump. "Where have you been?"

The man did not answer, for his eyes had lit upon me.

"Who is this, dear mother?" he asked, pacing round me as though I were an exotic beast or work of art.

He was about thirty years old, tall and muscular, with broad shoulders and narrow waist. He had a pleasant look, not handsome exactly, though I could imagine some might think him so. An interesting face,

I thought, with high cheekbones and crooked mouth. His eyes flashed as though they saw excitement everywhere.

"This is Alice Petherton," Mrs. Scrump answered. "And you can keep your dirty eyes off her. She's a lady."

The young man blew me a kiss and bowed low to the floor.

"Pray, dear mama," he said, "what is such a beautiful creature doing in the confines of the Scrump hovel?"

"She's a guest," said Mrs. Scrump. She bustled up to the man and glared at him. "She's my guest, so mind your manners."

He smiled and it thawed any pretense of anger in Mrs. Scrump.

"I am charmed to meet you, Alice Petherton," he said, turning back to me. "I am Walter Scrump, fifth of that name in my own family if you count the babes who predeceased me. But I like my friends to call me Art."

"It's a pleasure to meet you, Mr. Scrump," I said.

"Art, please."

"It's a pleasure to meet you, Walter Scrump."

He laughed at my words but I saw the amusement falter as if he were not sure how to take me.

"Why aren't you on the river?" his mother asked. "Your father's been gone three hours since."

"Alas, I was detained."

"By some whore?"

"By a young lady, yes. In fact she's the wife of the Reverend Turnbull."

"You wicked thing. Sleeping with the wife of a vicar. You'll burn in hell."

"She's very pretty," Art said, as if that were explanation enough. "And Turnbull's a dreadfully fat and boring man. He smells of urine."

Mrs. Scrump pushed a piece of bread into her son's hand. "I don't suppose you've eaten this morning."

"Not food," he answered with a complacent smile.

"You filthy beast," she said, whacking him on the head with her dishcloth. "Get out of my sight and bring me back some money or there'll be no more food for you."

He blew her a kiss, cast a sidelong look at me and ducked out of the door.

"He's a rascal," she said, shaking her head. "Always has been. We spoilt him, you see, being as he was the only boy to live beyond five years. Even sent him to a schoolmaster for two years. He learned to read and write."

"Well, that explains it," I said. "He's very gallant. It must be due to all that reading."

I meant it to be sarcastic but Mrs. Scrump took it as a compliment and beamed with pleasure.

"He is that, my dear. Gallant and charming. He quite bewitches all the young ladies and not just the young wives of boring vicars." She started back towards her kitchen and then paused and looked at me.

"Don't get too familiar with Art, miss, if you take my advice. He's a good boy deep down but he can't restrain himself where a pretty face is concerned. And you've got the prettiest face he's ever seen. Mark my words, he'll make a beeline for you. He'll turn his charm on you like a cat that wants its supper. And neither me nor his father will be able to stop him. That will be down to you."

"I'll bear that in mind, Mrs. Scrump," I said. "Thank you for the warning."

She sighed. "Not that I think it will do any good," she said. "He's a heart-winner and a heartbreaker, that son of mine. There's no woman I know of could resist him."

"I think I'll be able to," I said.

Mrs. Scrump looked dubious and blew her nose on the cloth.

I glanced outside. "I think I'll go out for a walk," I said. "I'll go down to the river."

She shook her head and slipped into the kitchen, returning with a little filleting knife.

"Take this," she said. "You probably won't need to use it but take it just in case. Sight of it should keep any villains at bay; just wave it in front of their noses. They'll get the message."

I took the knife and placed it carefully inside my purse.

"And don't be out all day," she said. "Things get lively round here towards evening. It's not a time for a young lady to be out on her own."

"I'll bear that in mind," I said. "And thank you for the knife."

She touched my arm just as I was about to leave.

"So you won't be wanting your dinner today, then?" she asked. There was a hopeful tone to her voice.

"Not today," I said. "But I'm quite happy to be charged for it."

"As you wish, miss, as you wish."

"And do call me Alice," I said. "I would much prefer that."

"As you wish, Miss Alice, as you wish. You can call me Margery when we're on our own. But not in front of the menfolk."

I nodded and stifled a smile.

I stepped out into the noisome lane and immediately recoiled. If I thought that my nostrils had grown accustomed to the stink I had deluded myself. The butchers' carts had passed by in their hordes and the whole lane was drenched in animal parts that no one had any use for. There were intestines, hearts, lungs, diseased livers, gangrenous tumours, broken hoofs, yellowing tongues and every snout imaginable. It was like a charnel house.

The heat of the day had made the stench fouler and more cloying. I held my hand against my nose and breathed through my mouth as I hurried down the lane. I wanted to run at full speed but I dared not; it was vital to watch where I was putting my feet. Even so I stepped into a slew of intestines and slid along the lane for a moment. I only just righted myself from falling into a load of mashed-up brains. I was glad to leave Offal Pudding Lane behind and reach the comparative cleanliness of the road that ran beside the river.

I leaned against a tree and took great gulps of air. And then it caught me. The wind blew from the west and carried with it the stench from the waste barges wallowing on the river. Some were filled with the offal that had been trundled past the Scrumps' house. Others contained human waste, rotting vegetables, animal hides, dead cats and dogs and even a broken-backed donkey.

Rats leapt and burrowed in the barges, fat and bloated and looking fit to burst. Scrawny cats chased after them, and chasing these were huge, malignant dogs: mastiffs, bulldogs, ill-bred mongrels and vicious terriers. Scampering amongst them all were tiny children, black with filth, searching desperately for the smallest scrap which might have some passing value, screaming at the dogs, which barked back with ferocity.

The clamor coming from the barges was enough to knock you out and if that did not, the stench would do for you. As the barges rocked in the tide, the mound of waste was tossed and turned, rolled and mixed, becoming ever more slick, ever more vile.

I could not help myself; I gagged and threw up against a tree. *Welcome to London*, I thought bitterly.

"You'll get used to it," a voice said in my ear.

I wheeled round, wiping the vomit from my mouth. Standing close behind me, hand on hip and grin on face, was Art Scrump.

"You'll get used to the smell," he continued. "It's all part of the tapestry that is London."

He talks more like a courtier than a courtier, I thought to myself. *Where did he learn such tricks?*

"I thought you had gone to work," I said.

"I have." He nodded to the river where a boat was tied up and bobbing in the current. "But then I saw you and could not help but hurry over."

"To see me vomit?"

He shrugged. "The waste barges give off a mighty stink." He handed me a kerchief to wipe my mouth. I took it reluctantly, expecting it to be as filthy as his mother's dishcloth. It was made of finest cotton and dyed a deep scarlet.

"It was a gift from a lady friend," he explained.

He gestured over his shoulder. "The smell will not get any better for our lingering here. Why don't we walk a little way?"

We headed along the river and past the Tower. I could hear the roar of the lions and hid a shudder at the memory. I need not have bothered to hide it from Art for he talked nonstop as we walked. Most of his talk was about himself, given with no sense of embarrassment or propriety. He spoke of what he did when he was not working, his hordes of friends, the women who adored him and those he loved in return. He was every bit as vain as the King.

Not once did he ask me about myself. This rankled at first but then, as I paid half attention to his prattle, I was glad of it. I had feared having to answer endless questions about myself in London but I was beginning to realize that most people were only interested in themselves. This was true to an extent at Court, of course. But members of the Court were so terrified of falling out of favor with the King that they paid obsessive attention to other people and their doings. At least I would be spared this in London.

We walked for over half an hour. I allowed myself to be guided by my companion. He knew the city and all its byways with an easy assurance and I was surprised to find myself brought by a circuitous route to a large street filled to overflowing with people.

"This is Eastcheap," Art said. "The greatest street for meat in all the world."

I could see what he meant. Every shop in the street was a butcher's and the middle of the road was crammed with little carts overflowing with meat. The clamor was tremendous, with men shouting out their wares, people haggling and children shouting. The smell of Pudding Lane and the Thames waste barges was noisome; the smell in Eastcheap was less so, being of fresher meat with only the occasional tang where something had rotted but still been left for sale.

As we sauntered along the street it became clear that Art's high opinion of himself was not totally unjustified. He was almost as popular as he claimed, although I noticed that he also attracted more than his fair number of angry scowls from men. Women, on the other hand, viewed him very differently. Some watched him silently, their eyes following his walk. Others, more bold, smiled or called out to him. He acknowledged all as though their interest was his natural right and due. Very like the King.

One young woman spied us from a doorway, folded her arms across her chest and marched towards us, eyes burning.

"Who's your friend, Art?" she said in a voice like a hiss.

"This is Alice Petherton," he said.

She eyed me up and down as if trying to locate the best place to punch me. She looked to be about my age and was pretty enough if it were not for a frown that seemed to be permanently etched upon her face. Her clothes were tatty and disheveled and she smelled of ale. I stared back at her, determined not to give way to such a low creature.

"And this is Betty Dibble," Art continued. "My first love, although not my last."

"Your best, though," she said, without taking her eyes from my face. "You know it well enough, Art Scrump, and you'll soon be sniffing round me once again."

"Pleased to meet you, I'm sure," I said in a cool tone.

"Pleased to meet you," she mimicked. She gave an exaggerated bow. "They do breed silver-tongued whores in France."

"I'm not a whore," I said. "Nor am I French."

"Well, you're not from round here," she said. "Not with that voice. A whore from Paris, I reckon you, or from Spain."

"She's not a whore," Art said, "and she's as English as you are."

Betty Dibble pulled her arms even tighter across her chest.

"Well, if she wants to scrap she's only to ask. If she wants two black eyes and cheeks scratched to pieces, that is."

"I don't think she wants either," Art said. "And nor do you. Here, let's away to the Shambles and we'll drink to friendship."

Betty glared at me, nodded curtly, and led the way on shaky legs to a tavern a little way along. The sign swinging from the gable bore a crudely drawn picture of a dog running away from a butcher's with a string of sausages in its mouth. Or perhaps a string of intestines.

I had never been in a tavern before and I did not much care for my first sight of the Shambles. It was still the morning but already half of the customers were drunk out of their minds. Some sat with heads bowed as if trying to remember something of the utmost importance. Others beamed at the rest of the room with the fondest of smiles. A handful of men were trying to sing together—trying and failing, because they appeared to be singing different songs and not a one of them could remember the words. Two men snarled at each other, one with fists clenched and a dangerous look in his eyes.

Art took all in with a practiced glance and led us to a little table as far as possible from the songsters and the two angry men.

A barmaid came up and looked me up and down. "Latest conquest, Art?" she asked.

"What's it to you, Amy Pepper?" Betty cried.

"It's nothing to me, Betty," the barmaid answered. "Just having a pleasant chat."

"Well, less chatter and more serving would not go amiss."

"I'll serve you when you've got some coin," the barmaid said. "You spent what little you had when you came in this morning."

"I'm paying," Art said in a soothing tone. "Three pints of ale, Amy, and one for yourself, if you wish."

Betty glared at the barmaid as she went to get our order. I was glad. It was better if she directed her anger at someone else and away from me.

"Well, this is cozy," Art said. "My oldest friend and my newest."

Betty turned towards me but now all sign of antagonism had drained away from her face. She looked weary from drink, her eyes heavy and fluttering. She perked up when Amy brought the ale, however, grabbing it swiftly and downing half of it in one swallow.

"Like a sewer," Amy muttered but Betty was too engrossed to hear, slurping the drink swiftly and murmuring to herself as she did so.

Amy gave Art a broad smile, knowing that Betty was too far gone to react. He reached out and stroked her bottom. Then he caught my glance and removed his hand.

This was my introduction to Art Scrump and his world. He spent the next two weeks trying to entwine me in it.

He made no bones about his desire to get me into bed. And I made no bones about refusing him.

All his life he had been successful with women and my reaction left him bewildered. I often found him staring at me as if not quite sure how to take me. But he was never dismayed by my intransigence for long and would renew his assault as if he had never been rebuffed.

My money was beginning to dwindle and I was forced to eke it out by making and mending shirts. I was accounted a very poor seamstress at Court, but in the back alleys around Offal Pudding Lane I was reckoned accomplished. I soon found myself with almost enough work to make ends meet.

As the weeks drew on towards the middle of May I began to think I would get used to life in London. I missed the Court and I missed the comfort and good grace I had been used to. But I'd always been taught to accept what life offered me and I was determined to make my way in the world. Although I did not intend staying in the Scrumps' home for long, I reconciled myself to living here for a little while.

This sense of familiarity proved my undoing. I got so used to the daily round that I let my guard down. I swear I do not know how it happened, but I found myself allowing Art Scrump into my little bed-room and then into my bed.

And I had been so confident that I would be immune to him. So foolishly confident.

He was a rogue. He knew he was and he reveled in the fact. Once he even proclaimed that he loved me more than all the world.

Oh really? I thought, although his words left me wondering, a tiny bit wondering.

He was charming, considerate and funny. He could even laugh at himself, not something I had much noticed in the men I had known. He was all show and exuberance, mimicking people he knew, telling tales with such intensity that he captivated even himself. And then he would fall silent, staring at a thing I could not see, a childlike innocence upon his face.

It was all done for effect, of course, all done to seduce me.

He was a skillful lover, make no mistake. I had, of course, only the King to compare him with. Art was superior in every way. He discovered the places I loved to be touched, tried and tested the words which excited me, sensed the times to be masterful and the times not to be. He had a way of moving which made my body throb with pleasure and all the time we made love he stared into my eyes as though he had never seen such beauty in his life. I knew that he was enjoying himself, of course, and suspected that his attentiveness to me was only fuel for his own pleasure. In his own mind he was every bit as much Sovereign as the King and I was his loyal and obedient servant.

But I did not care. He made me feel that I was the loveliest woman in all the world. And he took me to a place I had never been before. I held him fast in my arms as we climaxed and I felt the strangest feeling, standing tiptoe on a dangerously high place yet completely safe and secure. I wanted to tell him this but I could not form the words, for my tongue was thick and my throat too tight.

Then he gave the smuggest smile I had ever seen on human face and whistled a careless tune right in my ear. I was glad I had not been able to find my voice, glad I had not given him the satisfaction of sharing what he had made me feel. But I stroked his face, nevertheless, and sighed at how I had been so easily seduced.

We made love twice a day for the next nine days. I knew that Art had other lovers, Betty Dibble and Amy Pepper to name just two. But I did not greatly care. Art Scrump fulfilled a need in me, just as I fulfilled a need in him. It was a game, little more, and one I was prepared to play for as long as I found it pleasurable.

It was on the tenth day that he came to my bedroom and did not take me immediately in his arms.

"Is there something wrong?" I asked.

"There is. But I am not at liberty to say what it is."

I would have thought this the prelude to one of his amusing tales but he seemed unusually serious and subdued.

"You can tell me, surely. I will not breathe a word of it to anyone. Especially not your father and mother."

At this he looked startled and glanced towards the ground as if his eyes would pierce through to the room downstairs. He wiped his hand across his brow and shook his head.

"What is it, Art?" I said, feeling alarmed. "Has something happened to your parents?"

"Not yet," he said. "And not if I can do anything about it."

He fell silent and I grabbed hold of his arm. "You must tell me what is wrong," I said.

He shook his head, his eyes closed as if he were battling some terrible pain. And then he seemed to make up his mind. He took both of my hands in his and stared into my face.

"My father is a terrible gambler," he said. "He's been unlucky at cards and is being dunned for money by his creditors."

I gasped in disbelief. Walter seemed so sensible; I would not have thought him guilty of such folly.

"And can he pay these creditors?" I said at last.

Art sighed. "I have kept the wolves at bay for the last three months. But they want their money and quickly. I'm not sure how to find it."

"How much does your father owe?" I asked.

"Twelve pounds."

I don't know which opened widest, my eyes or my mouth.

"Twelve pounds? How on earth has he racked up such a debt?"

He shrugged. "Too much time in taverns. You've seen how he looks, Alice, much older than a man of his years. That's due to the drink." He paused for a moment before continuing. "But it's mostly down to gambling. The dice have never loved him and nor have the cards. And the cocks that he bets on are not game for the fight."

"But don't you try to stop him?"

"I try but I rarely succeed."

I glared at him, thinking how he should have tried harder.

I could not believe that anybody could accumulate such debt, especially a man of Walter's station. And I could not, for the life of me, see how it would be possible for him to pay it back.

"Father will never pay it back out of his own wages," he said, as if he'd read my thoughts. "I give him what I can but I fear it is not enough."

He looked completely lost and without hope.

"How much do you earn in a year?" I asked.

"I get about sixpence a day, more in the summer."

"So you earn six pounds a year and your father owes twice as much." I could not believe I was hearing this. "And how much does your father earn? And your mother?"

"I will not tell mother," he cried, leaping back from me as though he had been stung. "It would be the death of her."

I reached out to pull him back to me. "Hush," I said. "I will not tell your mother if you do not want me to."

He could not answer, held his hand to his mouth, as if close to tears. But the look in his eyes showed me how grateful he was.

"So what on earth will you do?" I asked at last.

His face became more serious. "That's where I hoped you might come in," he said.

I frowned, not understanding his meaning.

"You're a lady," he said. "You were at Court. Haven't you any money to lend me? So that I can give it to pay off father's debts?"

I shook my head miserably. "Not twelve pounds. Not anything like."

"How much have you got, then?"

"Not enough. I'd like to help, Art, I really would. But I have very little myself."

He looked crestfallen but brightened up in a moment. "You don't have to lend me the full amount, Alice. The men father owes money to won't be expecting the full amount, not right away. Just a little on account, a token. Something to buy them off and give me more time to get together the whole amount."

I felt my reluctance begin to thaw.

"How much? How much is a token?"

Art shrugged. "Three pounds, two. Even ten shillings would be a help."

"Ten shillings?"

He nodded.

I had thirty shillings still in my purse, the sum total of my wealth. But if ten shillings would help keep Walter's creditors at bay . . .

"And it doesn't have to be cash," he added eagerly. "Maybe some jewelry would go down just as well. That silver locket, for example. Perhaps we could pawn that for ready money."

I bit my lip. The locket had been given to me by the King, though he had ordered that his portrait be prised from it when I fell out of favor. If I were to help Walter and Art it would make good sense to pawn it instead of giving up my last reserves of cash. But something made me pause. Partly it was because, if I were to return to Court, the King would demand account of the locket. But also, I realized to my consternation, it was because the locket felt precious to me. And it felt precious because the King had given it to me.

"Or your cloak," Art said, picking it up from my bed and scrutinizing it. "It's well made and should fetch a good price."

"And what am I to do when winter comes?" I said. I snatched it back from him. "Besides, it belonged to my mother. It's the only thing I have of hers."

I undid the locket from my neck and gave it to him. "Take this. And here is ten shillings."

He kissed me hard on the mouth.

"This will save my life," he cried cheerfully as he disappeared.

Only as the sound of his footsteps faded did I wonder what he meant by the money saving his life.

He did not return for the rest of the day.

His father and mother seemed unconcerned at his absence. They were used to his tomcat ways. But at one point as we sat together after dinner, Walter's gaze fell on me and he asked if something was wrong.

"I don't know," I mumbled. I truly didn't. I had been distracted for most of the evening, that was undeniable. I put down the shirt I was mending. I could not get Art's last words out of my head.

"It's Art, no doubt," said Mrs. Scrump. "He's a heart-taker and a heartbreaker."

"He's a good boy really," said his father fondly.

"He takes you in, Walter Scrump," she said. She leaned towards me. "Do you know this morning the old fool lent him fifteen shillings to pay off some gambling debts?"

"I've got plenty more than that saved up," Walter said, chuckling to himself. "What's money for if it's not to help out your son when he's a bit in need?"

The darning needle fell from my hand. So Art had made up the whole story in order to get money from me. Even now he was likely in the Shambles, drinking away my money, gambling and whoring.

I got up and made for the door.

"You're not going out," Walter said. "Not at this time, Alice. It's getting dark. It's no time for a lady to be out on her own."

"Well, I'm going," I said and went out of the door.

"Go after her, Walter," I heard Mrs. Scrump say.

"I'll get a lantern and stick," he said. They were the last words I heard for I was already marching up the lane towards Eastcheap.

I burst into the Shambles and there, sure enough, sat Art. He was not gambling, though; he was sitting drinking quietly with three men. I did not recognize any of them. One of them was so pale he seemed to have no color about him at all. His hair was white as snow and his eyes as cold as winter ice in a pond.

Art looked up as I got closer and smiled broadly. "Alice," he said. "I did not think to see you here at this hour."

The pale man stared at me, his eyes sharp and calculating.

"Is this she?" he asked.

"Yes, Thorne," Art answered and the man picked up his ale without another word.

"Come on," Art said, taking me by the arm. "The Shambles is no place for a lady at this time of day. Let me walk you home."

"All right," I said. "But I need to talk to you when we get there."

He nodded and hurried me out of the door.

We took half a dozen steps and then he paused and touched my hair. "I'm sorry," he said. "You'll be all right, though."

I looked at him in surprise. "What do you mean?" I asked.

And then a hand clamped on my mouth and two strong arms grabbed me round the middle. I kicked out and heard a howl of pain.

"She's a vixen, right enough." Thorne, the pale man with the sharp eyes, held a lantern to my face. "And as beautiful as you claimed, Art. A lovely little vixen, full of fight. She's worth a fortune."

I was hauled off my feet and carried down a dark alley opposite. Out of the corner of my eye I could see the distant shape of Walter Scrump, lantern and stick in hand, hurrying up the lane. Distant, too distant.

Chapter Thirty-Two

Captivity

The men wound a rag tight around my mouth and carried me down dark alleys to the river. I searched for any further sign of Walter Scrump but he had not seen me in time. The two men knew the path well and nobody saw us as we passed.

I was bundled into a tiny boat.

"Don't move," Thorne's harsh voice told me, "and don't try to shout for help. You'll feel the back of my hand if you do."

I shook my head and whimpered in terror. It was the most noise I could make.

The men climbed into the boat and it pulled into the river. I tried to calm my mind in order to think. A tall ship rode at anchor on the far bank. Images of slavery swarmed in my head. Of fierce Turks with razor-sharp swords, cruel Spaniards with neat-cut beards, pomaded Frenchmen with glittering eyes. Of being locked in a harem, a castle, a dungeon dank with water, filled with rats. But then the boat moved past the ship and headed towards the south bank.

Towards Southwark, I thought. Southwark and the filthy brothels and bawdy houses that crammed its streets. I scanned the area, wondering if I would be able to leap away from the men and hide somewhere.

The boat grated against a bank and the moment it did so I was hauled onto the shoulder of one of the men. He wound a strand of my hair around his hand to prevent me trying to flee. I panicked, feeling utterly powerless.

The men moved more slowly now, as if they no longer feared pursuit or any interference. I presumed that women being kidnapped was a common sight in Southwark.

After a few minutes we reached a large building with three storeys. It looked like an inn and lights blazed from every window. I was lowered to the ground and prodded, not towards the main door, but up a narrow alley next to the building. One of the men opened a door and pushed me inside.

Sitting at a small desk was an old man with the gentle face of a kindly priest. He frowned when he saw me. *Thank goodness*, I thought. He would order these men to let me go. It was all some dreadful mistake.

The man placed his quill carefully on the desk and stared at me.

"Is this it?" he asked.

"Yes, Mr. Dale," Thorne said.

The old man stood up and came towards me. He was small, barely up to my chin. He looked me up and down and then seized hold of one of my breasts and squeezed it.

I gasped in horror and snatched for his hand. But he was quicker. He grabbed my hand and squeezed my fingers back on themselves until tears filled my eyes.

"Very nice, Thorne," he murmured, "very nice indeed." He reached up, pulled down the gag and forced my mouth open. He examined my teeth as though I were a horse and then put his nose close to my mouth and sniffed.

"Fresh breath," he said, "like new-baked bread."

Then his hand went round and felt my bottom.

"She's a fighter," Thorne said. "Kicked me in the shins and tried to bite Jim's hand."

The little old man rubbed his hands together with pleasure.

"Excellent," he said. "Many gentlemen like the whores to put up a bit of resistance. As long as I provide them with the means to subdue the bitches, of course. It wouldn't do to go home to their wives with cuts and bite marks."

He gave me the most pleasant of smiles, which almost made me wet myself in terror.

"Take her up to the back room on the third floor," he said. "It's nice and quiet there so if the clients need to get rough no one will hear. I'll be up presently."

The men dragged me up some stairs and to the end of a long corridor. I squealed in terror and tried to kick and slap at them but they laughed with contempt. I tried to quell my panic, tried to think, but I felt as though every thought was being smothered.

The room was small and dark and contained only a double bed, a table and a little cupboard.

"Welcome to your new home," said Thorne. His pale eyes got even colder. "I hope you'll be very happy here."

The door opened and the old man walked in, carrying a glass of wine.

"Strip her," he said. "Let's see if the money Art Scrump demanded was worth paying."

I froze in shock.

Art had sold me? Art, my lover, had sold me to these monsters? I shook my head, refusing to believe such a lie, and as I did so the men began to rip off my clothes. I was stark naked in moments. I tried to hide my private parts from their eyes but one of the men grabbed my hands and held them above my head.

"Very pleasant," said the old man. "And Art says she can make conversation as well as rut like a sow in heat." He gave me that same kindly smile.

"You and your boys can break her in," he continued. "As part payment for bringing her here."

No sooner had he said it than the man who held my hands dragged me to the bed and threw me down upon it. He unbuttoned his hose and clambered onto me. I slapped him round the head with one hand and with the other scratched his cheek so deep it drew blood and he cried aloud.

"She *is* a fighter," the old man said. "Get off her."

The man grumbled but climbed off of me. I shrank back against the wall and the old man stepped towards me. He picked up two objects from the table: one a long, thin cane, the other a paddle like milkmaids use for shaping butter. He placed the paddle on the bed, held the cane up and whipped it in the air.

"Just so you learn," he said. "On her back so she can see," he ordered.

The men grabbed my arms and legs and stretched me out. Thorne reached for the gag and tied it even more tightly around my mouth. I shook my head to try to stop him but he moved too swiftly for that. I felt as though I would be suffocated.

The old man placed the cane upon my lower belly, just above my private parts. Then he lifted his arm and whipped down. The pain ripped through me, like nothing I had ever felt before. It took my breath away. A red line appeared where the cane had bit. He whipped me once more and were it not for the gag I would have screamed the whole building down.

"That's enough," he said, handing the cane to one of the men. "Don't want to mark her too much." Then he picked up the paddle and held it in front of my eyes. "This gives a different type of hurt," he said. "And the beauty of it is that it doesn't mark as much."

He gestured to Thorne, who turned me over on my belly. A weight smashed onto my bottom. I almost fainted at the blow. Again and

again the old man beat me, so that I thought my flesh would be pulver-
ized. I could no longer see anything for the tears in my eyes and then
I was turned on my back and the first of the kidnappers raped me followed by the other two.

"Make the slightest sound," said the old man, leaning close into
my face, "and I will forget my worries about marking you. I'll get these
strong lads here to flog you until the flesh hangs off in tatters."

The men chuckled to themselves, left the room and locked the door.

I fumbled to pull off the gag, bowed my head and sobbed. My tears
fell unabated. The pain was so intense I could not be sure where I felt
it. I stared at the door, unable to believe that anybody could treat me
like this. What had I done? What had I done to deserve this? I felt like
a piece of dirt.

The next morning, as a church nearby was tolling eleven o'clock,
the door opened and Dale and Thorne entered the room. Thorne had
brought with him the heavy paddle and a nasty leer. He ordered me to
strip and then bent me over the bed. Dale sat on the bed and pulled my
head up so that he could look into my face. Then he nodded and I felt
the terrible crash of the paddle beat upon my bottom.

"You didn't beg," he said with a smile.

They left the room and I pulled my knees up onto the bed and
wept. I did not think to put my shift back on for hours.

As the church tolled six that night the two men returned. They
repeated the process of this morning but this time I begged them fer-
vently not to beat me.

It worked. Dale squeezed me on the chin like an old uncle might
and they left. I closed my eyes in thanks. I must have fallen asleep for
when I opened them again there was a cup of ale on the table and a
hunk of bread. I shuddered. I had no idea who had entered the room.

The next morning Dale and Thorne returned at ten and ordered
me to strip. Again I bent over the bed and again Dale lifted my head so
he could gaze at my face.

I begged once again and he smiled indulgently. But then the paddle crashed down so hard that I was buffeted into Dale's stomach.

"But I begged," I protested.

"I know," Dale said. "Life can be so uncertain."

He looked up at his accomplice. "Take her, Mr. Thorne," he said. "But I don't want to risk her getting with child. Take her from behind, in the other place."

Thorne grunted with pleasure and I felt his rough hands pull the cheeks of my bottom apart and then a searing pain as he entered me. I felt dizzy with the agony of it.

"Get used to this, my dear," Dale said. "It's just another trick to add to your repertoire."

They returned early the next morning and again I begged but to no avail. I was beaten and then taken by Thorne.

That night when they came I had made up my mind. I refused to beg. Dale looked bewildered for the briefest of moments and then gestured angrily to Thorne, who beat me three times and then buggered me.

But when they had left, as I lay weeping, I smiled in my heart at the way I had spoilt Dale's plan.

They came next morning and gave me half a dozen strokes. But then six o'clock came in the evening and they paid no visit.

I lay in the bedroom for three more days with only two visitors each day. One was a kindly old matron who brought me a glass of ale and a dried-up hunk of bread. She washed my wounds and rubbed cooling creams into them.

"Such a pretty girl," she said each day. "I don't know why you girls get yourself into such trouble."

I shook my head at her words, not believing that she could think or say it.

The other visitor was a young girl who came to explain how the brothel worked and what was expected of me. She was called Madge and looked to be a few years younger than me.

"Are you a whore?" I asked.

"Mostly a servant," she said. "I do the odd bit of business when my dad threatens me for more money. But I've no wish to be one of the Winchester Geese full-time, thank you. It's too short a life and not a merry one."

"What do you mean, Winchester Geese?"

Madge clapped her hands and laughed. "My, but you are green. The whores in Southwark are called Winchester Geese on account of the brothels being on land owned by the Bishop of Winchester. That's how he lives so well in his fine houses."

She shook her head and looked almost sad. "But you won't stay green for long, Alice, not for long."

Later that morning, when the elderly matron came with my food I grabbed hold of her arm and went down on my knees in front of her.

"Please help me," I begged. And then a wild idea came to me, an idea I'd been too terrified to think of until now.

"I have wealthy friends," I lied. "They'll pay you if you take word to them. More money than you could dream of."

"And then what would happen, my dear?" she said with a smile. "I'd wake up with my throat cut, floating facedown in the river."

She patted me on the head. "You just accustom yourself to your new life," she said. "A girl like you should have four or five years here. And then you'll have learned enough to make a living on the streets or in the poorer stews."

She said it as though revealing a glittering future for me. "Enjoy your luncheon," she said. "But let's have a look at your backside first."

On the next day the old matron returned with Thorne and Dale.

"You're sure she's healed, Mrs. Barleyfield?" the old man asked.

"Well enough," she answered. "I know the better sort of gentleman likes to see a little bit of marking. Seems to give them license to lash out themselves."

"Let's have a look," the old man said. "Strip."

I pulled off my nightgown and the two men scrutinized me. "Bend over," Thorne said.

I obeyed at once, thinking they had brought the paddle. But no wood was placed upon my bottom. Instead I felt Dale's spindly little fingers press into me.

"A bit of bruising," said the old man, "but as Mrs. Barleyfield said, that's all to the good."

He pulled down the gown and told me to sit up.

"She can start today," he said.

"Very good, Mr. Dale," Mrs. Barleyfield said. "I'll take word."

"Give her an hour or two to make herself presentable," the old man said. "Bring up a fancy gown."

Mrs. Barleyfield nodded and made for the door.

The old man smiled at Thorne. "Get a message to Sir Edmund Tint," he said. "He likes a hellcat."

He turned to me with that paternal smile. "You may fight all you like, Alice Petherton. I'll earn more the greater the resistance you put up."

They locked the door behind them and I walked across to the tiny window. In the distance I could just make out the sails of the ships on the river. About three hundred yards I reckoned. But I'd realized on my first day here that the window was too small for even a child to crawl through. And heavy bars meant I could not even reach to try to break the glass to call for help.

Mrs. Barleyfield returned an hour later with a gown and some make-up. Madge followed with a jug of warm water and a plate of hot pie.

"This makes a change for you, miss," she said as she handed me the plate.

Mrs. Barleyfield gave her a look, making her fall silent.

I fell upon the pie and crammed it into my mouth. Mrs. Barleyfield did not seem in the least bit surprised or shocked, merely laying out the gown on the bed.

"It doesn't do up properly, dear," she said. "Just pull on these two cords and you can slip out of it straightaway. Mr. Dale designed it himself." She smiled proudly at the thought.

She shooed Madge out and looked me up and down.

"You're going to get the best of gentlemen," she said. "You just bear that in mind. And don't take Mr. Dale's words too much to heart. He wants you to put up a fight but not to the bitter end. You have to give in and let the gentlemen have their way nice and loving. Makes 'em feel they've tamed you, you see."

She hummed to herself and poured the water into a bowl.

"Oh, and one more bit of advice," she said. "Use the chamber pot before each customer. Best to be good and empty all round, if you take my meaning."

She collected up the empty plate, left the room and locked the door.

I stared at the gown. It was pretty enough but made of poor-quality material and rather grubby. Still, it was better than wearing my nightgown. I slipped this off and washed myself all over. How I longed for the luxury of King Henry's bath chamber at that moment. I dried myself as best I could with the rag of towel I had been given and then put on the gown. It was horrible, coarsely made of poor linen, but I felt much better for wearing it.

An hour later there was a knock at the door and Madge poked her head in. "Gentleman to see you, Alice," she said.

She stood aside and allowed a figure to enter the room. She shut the door behind her.

The man stepped closer. This, presumably, was Sir Edmund Tint. He was a little man, thankfully, dressed in the finest of clothes and with a beautifully cut beard. He was in his late thirties and despite his small stature was developing a paunch. A sword, a dagger and a large purse hung from a fine leather belt. He gave me a broad smile and his eyes smoldered with lust.

"You're every bit as lovely as Dale claimed," he said. He unfastened his sword, dagger and purse. Then he pulled off his belt and ran his fingers along it.

"And he claims you're a hellcat," he continued. "That you've no taste for pain and won't like what's coming to you."

"You'll find out soon enough," I answered.

He laughed and told me to strip off my clothes. I stood naked in front of him, my face burning with shame. I felt like the lowliest creature on earth, something to be despised and mistreated. I had brought this on myself, I thought, and the tears began to form.

But then my heart grew calmer and I gazed at the man who was about to violate me. Why should I feel any shame? It was me who was being abused, me who was being degraded. It was not me who should feel shame but him.

"Very handsome," he said. "Very handsome indeed."

He took off his doublet and pulled down his hose. He wore only his undershirt and that was not sufficient to hide his excitement at the sight of me.

He picked up the belt and placed it carefully on the bed.

"I'll break you, little hellcat," he said. "Break you with my belt. But first let's get a taste of you." He lunged at me, forcing his lips onto mine and his tongue into my mouth.

I needed no encouragement to fight back. I punched him in the face and pulled at his hair. He bit my tongue and pushed me on the bed, throwing himself on top of me so that the air was pushed out of my lungs.

I was up in an instant, scraping my nails down his face and kneeing him in the belly.

He grabbed hold of my hand and slapped me hard on the cheek. He plucked up his belt and slashed at me twice, across my breasts and belly. Then he reached for my throat and began to squeeze.

I gasped in terror and he laughed, still squeezing. Finally, when I thought I might faint, he released me and kissed me again.

That's enough of fighting, I thought. *Now to act like he's tamed me.*

His tongue slithered round my mouth like a filthy earthworm but I pretended to groan with pleasure. He grunted with satisfaction and raised his head to look into my eyes.

"You are a wonderful kisser, Sir Edmund," I said. "Can you kiss as skillfully down below, I wonder? I'm told I taste sweeter than honey."

He grinned at that. "A real gutter-whore," he said. Then he slipped down my body, his tongue licking my belly as he moved.

I opened my legs wide and pulled his head into my crotch. His mouth went to work immediately, his tongue probing, his teeth nipping. I opened my legs still wider and gave a groan which sounded like pleasure and then squeezed my thighs together as though wishing to hold him like this for all eternity.

Then I reached below the bed, grabbed hold of the chamber pot and slammed it down on his head as hard as I was able. He gave a gasp and slumped unconscious.

I wriggled out from under him and stared. He was out to the world. But I thought I had best make sure and gave him an even harder crack with the pot. He did not make a sound this time.

I leapt up and started to put on his clothes. They were a little too big for me but I thought the belt would pull them tight enough. I hesitated about the sword and dagger but then thought it best to wear them in order to look the part. I pushed my hair into his hat and pulled it down low over my forehead.

My fingers were shaking with fear as I pulled the clothes around me. At the last moment I remembered his paunch and stuffed my nightgown under his doublet. Then I saw his beard. It was huge and very noticeable. I would be found out as soon as I showed my face.

An idea flew into my head. I pulled the dagger from its sheath and began to saw at his beard. I managed to chop off about half of it, enough for my purpose. I stuffed it into my mouth, gagging for a moment, and pulled it low. It was enough to cover my chin.

Then I slipped out the door.

I hurried down the corridor, ears cocked for any sound. I paused at the top of the stairs and made certain that no one was on them before tiptoeing down. At the bottom of the stairs was the dark corridor which led to Dale's office and the alley. I debated whether to go that way or not. Dale's room was well illuminated and my disguise would not fool him. But he was an old man and I should be able to outrun him. If luck was against me, though, I would find some of my kidnappers with him and it would all be over.

I took a deep breath and headed for the door directly in front of me. From the noise I could tell that the room behind it was packed and thought it was probably a drinking room.

I pushed open the door and peered in. I was right. It was a large chamber with tables and chairs and men drinking wildly while they waited for the next available girl. It was ill lit and gloomy. A large door on the other side of the room was propped half open, and I could see it led onto the street.

I took one step forward and froze on the threshold in fear. Sitting by the bar was the pale man, Thorne, and another of my kidnappers. My heart hammered so loud I thought it might be heard despite the din in the room. But there was nothing for it; I had to get out. Thorne and his friend were deep in talk and with any luck I would be able to creep past them unseen.

I slipped across the room as casually as I could, keeping my head down to attract no notice. But when I was two steps from the door, Madge, the little serving girl, approached me. I was betrayed. She held out her hand, staring me full in the face, a knowing look in her eyes. "Good evening, Sir Edmund," she said.

I grunted as best I could and reached for the purse on my belt, thrusting the first coin I found into her palm. Her hand clenched upon it and she turned away, very swiftly.

I stepped through the door, out into the street. I felt wild with relief but knew that I was far from safe. I took a deep breath to try to calm myself and headed in the direction of the river.

Within moments I was in a labyrinth of alleyways and tiny courtyards. I hurried through them, taking a zigzag path. I feared I might get lost. But it would also make it harder for anyone to track me. I knew it would only be a matter of minutes before they realized I had escaped.

And then I saw it. The Thames was right in front of me and to my left stood London Bridge. The lights from the houses on the bridge were burning bright, normal and welcoming, a world away from the nightmare I had just fled.

I crept onto the bridge, willing my feet not to race too fast. I stared downward as I walked under the decapitated heads oozing from the spikes above me. Both sides of the bridge were crammed with higgledy-piggledy old houses which overlooked the Thames on one side and the crowded thoroughfare of the bridge on the other. I thought of knocking on one of them for help but soon dismissed the thought. My best hope was to get across the river and try to find safety there. I realized that I was chewing on Tint's beard in my anxiety and shreds of it were falling out of my mouth. I spat it out in disgust and pushed on for the northern side of the bridge. At last I reached the bank and made for the only place I knew: Walter and Margery Scrump's home. As I hurried along, I thought once more of the treacherous Art and wondered what I would do when I met him.

I turned into Offal Pudding Lane and headed to the Scrumps' house. I gasped aloud. The house was boarded up; no sign of life at all.

And then I heard it. Footsteps hurrying after me and a high voice crying out, "Stop, thief."

I looked behind and saw three men turning into the lane with Thorne in the lead.

Cunning swine, I thought. He would set up a hue and cry. I'd be caught and unmasked as a thief. How else would a girl dressed in a rich man's clothing and with his purse appear to the authorities? It meant prison for me at the least and possibly the noose. No, that would not happen. That would not suit Mr. Dale at all. His gang would make sure they got me in their clutches and haul me back to the brothel.

I turned and fled up the lane, nearly falling over Tint's sword as I did so. I turned into Eastcheap and almost collided with the first person I saw. It was Betty Dibble, Art's old girl, the hard, jealous Betty who despised and hated me.

But without a second thought I grabbed hold of her hands. "Betty, it's me, Alice," I said desperately. "Those men are chasing me. They kidnapped me and put me in a brothel. I've just escaped but they'll catch me again. Please help me."

She stared at me and my heart almost stopped. *She'll betray me*, I thought. She opened her mouth and let out a piercing scream.

"Girls," she cried. "Help me, help me, help me!"

A moment later half a dozen women raced out of the inns and onto the streets, looking about in alarm.

"They're after us," Betty cried, pointing to the men who had just raced round the corner. "They're going to take us to the stews. It's Alice Petherton and she's just escaped them."

The women cried out in dismay and raced towards us. Betty darted forward, reached down for a stone and hurled it at the foremost man.

The rest of the women surrounded me, fists raised high, yelling at the top of their voices.

The three men kept approaching, not fearing what they saw as a pack of foolish women. It was the worst mistake possible. The women surged forward and fell upon the men, slapping and kicking, their voices high in fury.

The men fell back, arms flailing, faces filled with sudden terror. They turned and fled down Offal Pudding Lane with the women on their heels, whooping curses and throwing punches as they chased after them.

"You all right?" Betty said as she returned to my side.

I nodded, unable to speak.

"They'll be back," said a familiar voice. It was Amy Pepper, the barmaid of the Shambles. "They'll be back in numbers and armed to the teeth. We won't be able to fight them off a second time."

"What will we do?" I asked, terrified.

"I'll send for my dad," Amy said. "He'll rouse up the Beast Keepers."

Pepper, I thought. *Pepper.* I knew that name from somewhere but could not place it.

"Jenny," she cried to a young girl. "Get off to the Tower and get my dad here with as many of the lads as he can. Tell him I sent you and tell them to bring their nets and weapons."

Jenny nodded and raced down the road.

"It's not far," Amy said to me. "They'll get here in time; don't fret."

My legs wobbled and I slumped to the ground.

"Get up, you silly cat," Betty cried.

I grabbed hold of her arm and tried to rise but I had no strength left to do so.

"I can't," I said. "I can't manage it."

"Bloody rich girl," Betty said. "Good for nothing but opening yer legs."

I panicked at her angry tone. "Don't leave me," I said. "Don't let them take me again."

Betty laughed and hauled me to my feet. "Don't worry about that. I'll let no brothel keepers get you." She looked towards Amy. "Should we take her to the Shambles?"

Amy shook her head. "The inns will be the first place the men will search when they return. Best wait for my dad and his friends."

She bit her lip anxiously and turned to peer down Eastcheap.

"But will he come?" I cried. "I won't go back to the stews." I fiddled with Tint's sword, tried to pull it from its scabbard, but my hands were shaking too much to even get a grip.

A moment later we heard the voices of women crying in fear and the noise of pounding feet. The women who had been pursuing the kidnappers came pelting back around the corner. Half a dozen men chased after them, some carrying cudgels. Thorne held a leather leash in his hand.

The women pressed around me, acting as a shield.

"Now don't be foolish, ladies," Thorne called. "We're only after our property. We're only after one of our whores."

"You can't have her," yelled Betty Dibble.

"But my master paid good money for her," Thorne answered. "She belongs to him. And do you know who sold her?" He gave a shrill and mirthless laugh. "It was Art Scrump, the heartthrob of the gutters. Or at least he was until yesterday."

I frowned at this and Betty shook her head, not understanding what he meant.

Thorne stepped forward, slapping the coiled leash in his hand as he did so.

"So, girls," he continued. "Just be sensible and let me have Alice Petherton. Unless, of course, you want to join her in Timothy Dale's little enterprise."

"You get her over my dead body," Betty Dibble cried.

"That can be arranged," Thorne said in a mild tone.

The rest of the men laughed loudly and stepped towards us.

Betty Dibble threw herself forward and kicked Thorne in the shin, making him snarl in fury. The men raced to his aid, and two raised their clubs above her head. But before they could lower them, the rest of the women leapt forward and began to battle with the men.

The noise was tremendous. Men appeared in nearby doorways looking on in amazement. Most went back inside and stayed there, but four butchers ducked into their shops and returned wielding knives and choppers.

"We're with you, girls," one cried.

They had only closed half the distance when a deep roar came from behind them.

A dozen men with long poles and nets hurried towards us. The roar came from their angry throats. But then a deeper roar sounded and four men pushed through their friends, wielding poles attached to the collars of two raging lions. The women screamed in terror and scattered at the sight of them.

"What the hell . . ." Betty said. I found my strength at last. I pushed her out of the way just in time. The lions leapt past us and hurled themselves on our assailants. Two men fell immediately and then the lions lashed out at two more.

With a howl of fear our attackers fled from the scene. One of the fallen managed to get to his feet: Thorne, his face running blood. It was that which did for him. The lions smelled the blood and leapt upon him. I heard the crunching of bone and Thorne cried out in terror and pain.

The Beast Keepers tried to pull the lions off but to no avail. One lion bit upon Thorne's legs and the other on his head and then began a tug of war with him. I stepped closer, terrified but unable to prevent myself from looking more. Thorne's arms thrashed in agony for a few moments longer before he slumped, all movement ended, and the lions began to rip at his flesh.

"What a way to go," said Betty, fascinated by the sight and unable to take her eyes from it.

"He deserved it," I said. "He well deserved it."

Chapter Thirty-Three

Salvation

I sank to the ground, shaking uncontrollably as if I had been walking for hours in the bitter cold. But at the same time my body was streaming with sweat. My nose wrinkled at a terrible sour smell and I realized that it was coming from me. *It must be the stink of fear*, I thought vaguely.

"She's all done for," I heard Betty say as if from a great distance. "Poor thing."

I tried to smile at her in thanks but my teeth were chattering too much.

"Do you think they'll be back?" Jenny asked anxiously. She was breathing fast from trying to keep up with the Beast Keepers.

"Soon enough," said one of the butchers, stroking his knife. "And with more men, I warrant."

Amy Pepper bent down towards me, a lantern in her hand. Her eyes stared at my face with growing alarm.

"We've got to get her to safety," she said. She straightened up and cried out, "Dad, come here."

One of the men holding the lions passed a leash to another and stepped towards us.

"She's in terrible trouble, Dad," she said. "She was taken as a prostitute and those men will be back from the brothel to reclaim her. Can you take her to the Tower?"

He shook his head. "I daren't do that," he answered. "A whore in the King's Palace. I'd lose house and job."

"But more men will come back for her."

He bit his lip and shook his head once again, crossing his arms across his chest as if to signify that there was an end to the matter. Then he looked at me and he gave a start. He stepped towards me and gestured for his daughter to hold the light closer.

"I know you," he said in wonder. "You're the girl who tried to save my Molly."

I stared at him blankly.

"At the Menagerie," he said. "You raced into the lions' den to try to save my little girl."

"Ned Pepper," I croaked. I glanced at Amy. So that's where I'd heard the name.

Pepper bent and lifted me from the ground. "Bugger home and job," he said. "I'm not letting this girl back in the hands of those bastards."

He whistled sharply and one of his men came towards us. It was the young Beast Keeper whose life I had pleaded for.

"Get the lads, Giles," Pepper said. "We're taking the girl back to the Tower."

Giles nodded and then peered closer to me. "I thought it was a man," he said.

"Never mind what you thought," Pepper said. "Get a move on; we haven't much time."

Pepper hoisted me higher in his arms, cradling me against his chest, and began to run along the streets with half a dozen of the Beast Keepers running alongside as guard. I marveled at his strength and stamina. It must have been more than half a mile to the Tower and he ran it at full pelt. Some of the younger men were hard-pressed to keep up with him, burdened with me though he was.

We reached the Tower and entered through a door which led to the Menagerie. I glanced down at where the beasts were sleeping, all apart from the lions which were, no doubt, contentedly digesting that monster Thorne.

We arrived at a little cottage and Pepper carried me in.

"Edith," he called. "Edith, come here and help."

A woman of about his years hurried over towards us, her face a picture of alarm.

"This is the girl Amy sent me to help," Pepper said. "She'd been kept as a prostitute and the brothel keeper is desperate to get her back."

"Gawd help us," the woman cried, her hand going to her mouth. "What if the King finds out you've brought a strumpet here? He'll have your head, Ned Pepper."

"I don't think so," Pepper said. "This girl used to be his favorite and I don't think he'd take kindly to her being kept prisoner in a brothel. Besides, she's the one who tried to save Molly."

Those were the last words I heard. I must have fallen into a swoon for when I awoke it was broad daylight and I was tucked into a bed with clean, fresh sheets.

I rubbed my fingers along the fabric. The weight of the coverings made me feel like a little girl once more: contained, secure and safe.

I looked round and saw Edith sitting in a chair beside me, busy with some sewing. She glanced up and smiled.

"How you feeling, dear? You've had a bad time of it. I'm Mrs. Edith Pepper and you're quite safe now."

"I'm thirsty," I said. "I've got such a thirst."

"It's the fear that's caused that, no doubt. A terrible bad time, you've had." Mrs. Pepper stood up and looked closely at me, concern visible on her face. "My Amy's here; I'll get her to bring something for you."

She went to the door and called out for her daughter to bring some ale.

Amy arrived a few minutes later with a large mug and a plate of bread thickly smeared with butter. "Once a barmaid, always a barmaid," she said with a grin.

She sat on the side of the bed and peered at my face.

"How you feeling, Alice?"

I shook my head. "I don't know. My head's in a swirl." I reached out for the mug and gulped down the ale.

Amy held out a slice of bread. "You'd best eat this," she said. "You look famished."

"They've been starving me," I said. "At the brothel. I only had one meal in half a week. The rest of the time it was a slice of old bread and a sip of stale water."

"You're safe now," Edith said. "Nowhere's safer than the Tower of London."

"But the brothel owner," I said. "He's bound to search for me. Timothy Dale, his name was. He beat me and allowed his men rape me. He's worse than a devil."

"Well, he won't get past my dad," said Amy. "And I don't think he'll try. Not after what happened to that man of his."

I gasped, remembering my last sight of Thorne. "He's dead, I suppose, the pale man?" I looked at Amy anxiously.

"I'd be very much surprised if he's still alive," said Amy. "Not with half his head and legs in the lions' bellies. Not sure which lion got which bit but they're still sleeping it off."

I shuddered, but not at Thorne's fate. If anything, I wished that the lions had chewed on him more slowly. No, I shuddered because of what he had done to me.

And then I remembered how I had come to be in that situation. I reached out for Amy's hand.

"They said that Art Scrump had sold me to Dale. That can't be right, can it, Amy? He wouldn't have done such a thing. Surely Dale and Thorne had been lying?"

Amy looked uncomfortable at my words and glanced at her mother, who sighed and shrugged.

"She'd find out the truth soon enough, Mum," Amy said.

She turned to me and took my hand. "Art did sell you, Alice. He owed Dale a pile of money and it was the only way he could think to buy him off. It didn't do him no good, though."

"What do you mean?"

Amy's eyes began to fill with tears and she shook her head.

Edith patted her on the arm and gave me a solemn look. "Art's body's been found on one of the waste barges on the Thames," she said. "Not his head, though. That was found on a spike beside Cross Bones Graveyard."

I gasped in horror. "They killed him? Even though they'd got me as a whore?"

Amy nodded. "Either you weren't enough to pay the debt or more likely they didn't want any witnesses to your abduction."

"And what about Art's parents? Walter and Margery?"

"They left town. The moment they heard about Art's death they left town. No one knows where they went, not even their daughters."

Tears filled my eyes. What a foolish, foolish man Art Scrump had been. But my loathing of him began to diminish even as I thought this. He was foolish, not truly wicked. A man who thought more of himself than the rest of the world did.

I lay in bed all morning, my knees tucked up under my chin, sucking the tip of my thumb. I stared at the window above me and listened to the roaring of the beasts in the Menagerie. *This is what I'm content to do forever*, I thought every so often. *Just stare out of the window at the passing clouds and not think of anything.* But I got out of bed for the midday meal. I was still shaking from the events of the previous week but I was absolutely famished and the smell of good cooking banished my trepidation.

A gown had been placed on a chair beside the bed. I guessed it was Amy's and slipped it on. It was a little loose around the bust but it would do well enough for me.

I found my hosts in a spacious living room. The Peppers were sitting at a little table in one corner with a fourth space already set.

"We hoped Edith's cooking would tempt you down," Ned Pepper said.

"I'd have brought you up a plate," Amy said, "but Mum thought it better if you ate with us."

"She was right," I said. I smiled my thanks at Mrs. Pepper.

I did not feel able to string more than a few words together. Nor did I care to, if I was honest.

I cannot recall much of that first meal beyond two things. The first was the taste of the food. It must have been some type of stew, for I remember chunks of meat and earthy-tasting lentils in a thick sauce. It was warm and filling and I believe that it tasted good. I was not certain of this for I was famished from being starved and I wolfed down the food.

Out of the corner of my eye I saw Mr. and Mrs. Pepper exchange glances and then Mrs. Pepper silently took my plate, disappeared for a moment and came back with a second plate brimming with food.

"There's nothing like a good dinner," Mr. Pepper said. "Nothing like and nothing better."

The other thing I remember was the constant chatter amongst the Pepper family. I cannot recall a word they said for I could barely focus at the time. But I do remember that they talked nonstop, when they were breaking up their bread to dip it in the juice, when they were spooning up their stew, when they were chewing on the meat. Nonstop chatter. And laughter. They laughed a lot, especially Ned Pepper. And as he laughed his food sprayed everywhere, on the table, onto his wife and daughter, onto their food and onto me. But nobody seemed to mind; he was in such high good humor.

I had never eaten with a family since being a child. My spirits were greatly lifted by it.

Mrs. Pepper insisted I return to my bed for the afternoon and I acquiesced like a lamb. I crawled under the bedcover, bent up my knees and put my thumb in my mouth. I took it out almost immediately for I felt stuffed to bursting with food and thought that my thumb might prove the last straw. So I stared out of the window at the passing clouds, drifted in and out of sleep, watched the clouds and drifted back once more into sleep. The roaring of the savage beasts seemed like a lullaby.

The next few days went by in a similar manner. I spent the greater part of the time in bed, rising only for meals. I felt like a thick skin had been grafted onto mine, as tough and unyielding as the shell of a cockroach. If anyone were to touch me I felt it would rattle and clack and they would be sure to draw back from me in horror. But this shell had its uses. As I lay in bed I began to think about what had happened to me since I had arrived in London. I thought about it quite dispassionately at first, protected by the shell, as though I were listening to some gossipy piece of tittle-tattle from Susan or Mary.

And then I began to feel it, feel it deep in my heart, and it hurt.

I wondered why these terrible things had happened to me, what I could possibly have done to deserve them. I wondered how people could be so cruel and vicious. How Timothy Dale could run a brothel; how the pale man Thorne could do his bidding, including kidnapping and raping innocent women; how the old woman who seemed so motherly could act as the brothel housekeeper and not worry two figs. Why men like Sir Edmund Tint could violate and flog poor women to satisfy their cravings. Most of all, I wondered how Art Scrump, the handsome, devil-may-care man who once had claimed he loved me more than all the world, could knowingly sell me to such a fate.

And then one night I woke in the darkness and began to wail. The noise came unbidden from me and I could not stop it. It was a cry of utter desolation, a venting of despair, a rant against my sense of betrayal. I howled like a wolf and in reply the beasts of the Menagerie awoke and cried in chorus with me. I could hear their bellowing beyond my wails. Their noise did not seem to be fearsome or savage anymore. It was as if they understood my plight and my despair all too well. As if they cried out in sympathy for someone who had suffered what they suffered daily. In sympathy and in fellowship.

The next day I awoke feeling drained and exhausted. But I managed a smile and got up and went down to breakfast.

"You had a bad nightmare," said Mrs. Pepper with a worried look.

"It was nothing," I said.

She placed her hand upon my shoulder.

"It was something," she said. "Don't dismiss it so lightly. Learn from it." She gave a fleeting smile. "It's all to the good; it's necessary for your healing. But it will stay with you all your days."

I nodded, although I did it out of courtesy for her concern. I did not understand what she meant.

Amy joined us for dinner that day. Apparently it was Sunday and she had an hour or two off.

"You look much recovered, Alice," she said. "You have looked so grey and lost. Now you look more like your old self."

"Do I?" I asked. I had no idea, for there was no looking glass at the Peppers' and, if there had been, I would not have wanted to use it.

"Much recovered," said Ned Pepper. "You had dark dreams last night. Edith sat in your room half the night, watching over you. It was like the breaking of a fever."

"You watched over me?" I said in astonishment.

Mrs. Pepper inclined her head and gave the smallest of smiles.

I got up and knelt at her feet, taking her hand in mine.

"That was such a kindly thing to do," I said.

I bent my head in her lap and felt her hand rest lightly upon it. The tears began to fall then. They were not painful tears, though, not tears to rack and shake my body. They were tears like rain, tears of summer rain that cleared away the torrid heat of summer.

The next morning I found Ned Pepper sitting in the living room on his own. He was mending a net and looked like a fisherman sitting by the banks of a river.

"We've been talking, Edith and me," he said. "We think that now you're on the mend, this place is maybe not the best for you. Too much clamor from the beasts, too much smell and jostle."

I had not thought this, although I had not yet left the house and walked close to the Menagerie. As soon as he said it I realized he was right. The sight of those caged beasts would prove a nightmare for me. They would remind me of his little daughter. And they would remind me of Timothy Dale's brothel.

"So, what we thought was," Ned continued, "and this was Edith's idea, not mine—what we thought of was that we'd take you up to her brother Robert's place. It's out in the country, far from London. Lots of fresh air and peace for you. It will do you good. We can't leave for a month, mind, because we've got some foreign dignitaries visiting. But we'll be able to go late August."

"That's very kind of you, Mr. Pepper. But I couldn't intrude on you or your brother-in-law any further."

"Can't you, though?" Ned said, putting down his net. "I say you can, Alice Petherton." He looked in my face for a moment and then turned away and stared at the window. "I'll never forget how you tried to save my Molly, never forget that as she lay there dying she was cradled in the arms of a caring woman, comforted and made more peaceful. I'll never forget what you did for her, Alice. And I'll never forget your courage."

He picked up the net and began to work at it once more, whistling with hardly any sound. His eyes began to film with tears. "Least we can do," he muttered. "Least we can do."

A month later I found myself in a little carriage on the way to a town called Stratford-upon-Avon. Ned Pepper had decided to take a few days from his duties and Amy had also determined to join us on the outing.

"A week outside of London," she cried. "What a wonderful thought."

Chapter Thirty-Four

To Stratford-upon-Avon

20 August 1538

As soon as we left London I felt my spirits begin to lift. It was like climbing out of a noisome drain. The air was fresh and moved with gentle breezes. The sky was a bright August blue, dotted with clouds like lambs on distant meadows. The sun blazed in the sky and there was not a threat of rain. The forests were bright and green, though here and there the leaves were beginning to turn to gold. Huge flocks of birds beat across the sky as if playing some delightful game, and the sound of birdsong was everywhere.

It took us only three days to journey from London to Stratford-upon-Avon. In the fields on either side, men, women and children worked from sunrise to past sunset to gather in the harvest. It looked hot, exhausting work. In some fields, the harvesters worked like a well-drilled army, heads down, cutting, stacking, moving on, cutting. Other fields looked much more haphazard, with little groups wandering about seemingly as the mood took them. Some gangs worked in silence. Others filled the air with song. Quite a few seemed to be teetering on the verge of drunkenness.

The summer heat had dried up the roads and made the going good for travelers on foot, horseback or on carts. A few horsemen hurried along on pressing business. Most seemed content to amble and enjoy the last of the summer weather.

Our carriage was an excellent one. As soon as I saw it I realized the advantages of being the King's Beastmaster. Ned Pepper had access to all manner of means denied to ordinary people. He had selected one of the better made of the Tower vehicles, chosen the finest horses to pull it and crammed it with good food and wine for the journey.

At one point he told a long story concerning a huge great bird from Africa which could not fly but could run faster than a horse. One of the Keepers had taken bets to see if he could ride it. He managed to keep his seat for several minutes before tumbling on the ground. He received a vicious peck from the giant bird and then the bird proceeded to chase the Keeper round the compound, pecking at the man's bottom with its vicious beak.

Ned told the story so wittily that I found myself laughing out loud. When I had finished, I wiped my eyes and glanced away, deep in thought. I could not remember the last time I had laughed. I thought it might have been with Art Scrump but I could not be sure. My mind flew back across the weeks and months. And then I had it.

Susan Dunster had given an impression of Thomas Seymour chasing after me. She wrapped one hand in a thick brown cloth and pretended it was his beard, but a beard with an independent, lusty life of its own which Seymour was powerless to control. It waved itself in the air, stroked and nipped at Mary, Lucy and me and even engaged in witty banter with its owner. That day I laughed until my ribs ached. Ned Pepper's story did not have that effect. But at least I was laughing once again.

We stopped the first night at the home of one of Ned's old friends in Aylesbury and the second at an inn in Bicester. Ned loved being at the inn; he was full of good heart and comradeship. Edith was less happy, suspicious of strangers and the dangers they might present. Amy spent most of the time scrutinizing the workings of the inn and the behavior of the barmaids.

"These country girls don't have a clue," she concluded. "But it's a goodly inn and well run." She glanced at one of the barmaids who was standing with mugs of ale in her hand, talking with a customer when she should have been on her way to our table. "The barmaids have it so easy here," Amy continued. "They don't know they're born." She gestured the barmaid to hurry along with our ale and the girl sighed for a moment and finished her conversation before sidling over to us. She plonked down the mugs with more energy than she had shown hitherto, spilling a great deal of the ale on the table.

Ned picked up his mug and took a good long mouthful. "The ale's good, though, Amy," he said. "Can't complain about that." And then he rubbed his hands together as another barmaid approached with a huge pie, steaming hot, and a dish of cabbage and broad beans.

We set off early next morning just as the sun was peeking above the hills to the east. We made even better progress than on the previous days for the roads were emptier and we were less delayed by slowly trundling wagons. We stopped briefly for a bite to eat and arrived at Robert Cooper's farm just as the sun was setting.

And what a welcome we had. Robert and his wife, Hannah, rushed out to meet us with their seven children. They seemed to be everywhere, chattering, laughing, hugging, kissing—a litter of puppies besieging their mother at feeding time. In a twinkling they had emptied the carriage of everything and I was swept along into the farmhouse.

I found myself in a long, wide room, with very low ceilings and whitewashed walls. A huge fireplace was set opposite the door. It must have made a goodly blaze in winter but today a scrap of a fire was all that was burning, just enough to keep hot a cauldron suspended above it.

"You must be starving," Hannah Cooper cried, directing us to take a seat. The children scampered to the table, pushing and shoving one another with fairly good humor. The noise was tremendous. Then Robert took his seat, folded his hands together and bent his head. The table fell silent immediately and he said Grace in a voice that seemed to fill the room. The moment he finished, the clamor started up again and Hannah ladled out a wonderful game stew onto our plates.

Later that night, Amy and I shoehorned ourselves into a tiny chamber with the four Cooper girls. It contained nothing but one large bed, which did service for all the girls. Three were quite small, but the eldest, Sissy, was fifteen years of age. She was a pleasant-faced girl and she had been struck by something about me as soon as we had arrived. Whenever I'd glanced in her direction I found her eyes upon me. She did not seem embarrassed at being discovered. She continued to stare and would finally give a little smile and glance away.

"There's not much room here, Alice," she said as I walked into the bedroom. These were the first words she had addressed to me. "But I'll shove up the others and we'll all be comfortable."

She pushed her younger sisters to one side of the bed and made room for Amy and me. *I'll never be able to sleep like this*, I thought. But I did.

I awoke next morning with Sissy curled into me and the youngest child draped around my neck.

The Peppers were tired by their long journey from London but I was exhausted, quite used up. It was as much as I could do to keep awake, and I swear I only did it because of the constant chatter and questions from the Cooper children. Where was I from, who were my family, how old was I, who were my friends, which animals did I like most, could I dance, could I sing, could I play any musical instruments? The questions were like a constant downpour. And then Sissy asked me where I lived and at this I stumbled for an answer.

"With your aunt and uncle," I said. "At least for the moment."

"But that's not been for long," Sissy said. "Amy told me that. Where did you live before?"

The thought of Dale's brothel settled on me like a flock of crows descending from the sky. I ran my fingers through my hair as if by doing this I could shoo away the memory.

"I lived in Offal Pudding Lane," I said. "For a little while."

"That sounds horrible," said one of the younger girls. "Offal pudding. Yuck, sick."

"And before you lived there?" asked Sissy. "Did you live with your family somewhere nice?"

I looked at her and wondered what her young life was like and what it might turn out to be.

"No, Sissy," I said, making up my mind. "I lived in a Palace."

The moment I said it the rest of the sisters appeared as if by magic.

"A Palace?" gasped Sissy.

I nodded. "Hampton Court Palace. Where the King and Queen live." *Or where Catherine of Aragon, Anne Boleyn and Jane Seymour used to live*, I thought.

"Never," chorused the girls.

"Oh yes," I said. "For three years I lived in one or other of the King's Palaces. I was one of the Queen's Maids of Honor."

Two of the littlest girls scrambled onto my lap and the others sat themselves at my feet.

"Tell us everything," Sissy cried, wild with excitement.

So I did. Except the bit about being bedded by the King.

I spent the rest of the summer at the Coopers' farm. The Peppers left a few days after arriving, but Edith, seeing how well being in Stratford suited me, was adamant that I should not yet return to London. I was still so troubled and exhausted that I did not have the strength to argue. And when I saw how happy the whole Cooper family were at the thought of my staying, I agreed. As soon as I had done so a thrill of pleasure ran through me.

The Coopers were the most generous of hosts and oftentimes I felt a little guilty at staying in their home and eating their food. I broached this once with Hannah but she dismissed my worries with a vigorous shaking of her head and a kindly smile.

"You've been through a lot, Alice," she said. "Edith and Ned have told me everything, but we needn't remind ourselves of it now. You're here to recuperate and I'm going to make good and sure that you do."

She turned back to her cooking. "Women can be treated cruel in this world," she said without looking at me. "I'm lucky because I found a good man. Not everybody has my good fortune." Despite her words, her voice sounded pensive, almost sad. I wondered at it but decided not to ask why. I never did find out.

Robert and Hannah were kept busy on the farm and in the house. The eldest son, Edward, spent most of his hours working on the farm and the few hours left over looking at me out of the corner of his eye. He was seventeen years old and a tremendous blusher. He was a good-humored, talkative soul except when I was near. Then his tongue would trip him and he'd babble like a baby, going crimson in the face. After a few moments it would get too much for him and he would beat a hasty retreat. His parents smiled indulgently and his younger siblings would cry out, "Edward loves Alice, Edward loves Alice." He would never respond apart from blushing even more furiously, though once I saw him cuff his younger brother, who had kept on with his taunting while stepping within Edward's reach.

The other children showed their approval of me in different ways. They followed me around when their tasks were done; they threw themselves into my lap and demanded that I tell them stories of the King and the Court. I obliged them as much as I was able and as much as I saw fit. I soon found out they were not my only audience. Hannah had no inclination to hear my tales but I sometimes found Robert listening, every bit as enthralled as his children. "Strange doings in the Palace," he muttered to me sometimes. "Strange doings." But he always wished to hear more.

Of all the Cooper family it was Sissy who was most fascinated by me. Whenever she could, she tried to stay close beside me. When we were all working preparing food she would summarily move any sister who had the temerity to sit next to me and would take her place without a glance at me. She was the most insistent in demanding that I tell stories. Although she loved to hear about the King and Queen she was far more interested in what it was like to be a Maid of Honor. What, in fact, it was like to be me.

She would hang on every word, slowing down in her work so much that her mother got exasperated and had to upbraid her. I apologized when this happened but Hannah always shook her head.

"It's not your fault, Alice," she said. "There's no harm in talk and stories. Only harm when Sissy can't use her hands at the same time as her ears."

Sissy would not answer, contenting herself with poking out her tongue when her mother turned her back. Then she would turn to me and put her finger to her lips with a conspiratorial grin.

Because I was not used to farm work I was not much help outside of the kitchen. But I was keen to do as much as possible, especially as the family were so busy with the harvest. The cutting and stacking of the wheat was much more complicated than it looked. I must have been very poor at it for I was soon assigned to a gang led by ten-year-old Rose, picking up the stalks the others had missed. It was backbreaking work and I was not much use at even this task, working at about half the rate of the youngest of the girls, who was five. But I was pleased to do it.

The other job I was given I performed much better. I was asked to tend to the hens, making sure they were fed and safe from foxes and collecting the eggs each morning. This was a wonderful task and I always took the two smallest children with me when I did it. I had not realized but hens were often prone to lay their eggs in strange and hidden places. We sometimes spent a deal of time searching out the eggs that had gone astray.

"I do believe these eggs have little legs," I said once. "They see us coming and run away, hiding their feet when they see us approach."

The children became convinced of this tale and earnestly told the rest of the family, and got annoyed when they laughed and would not be persuaded of the truth of it.

"Alice told me that eggs have legs," said little Annie. "And she knows the King."

That settled it, of course. I knew the King so whatever I said must be right.

The most useful job I did at the farm, however, had nothing to do with the Coopers' lives as they'd lived them up until that point. It happened by chance.

One day, about a week after arriving at the farm, I felt more than usually tired and picked up a book I had brought with me from London. All of my possessions had disappeared when Dale had abducted me and I was left with nothing I could call my own. But Ned Pepper had borrowed, as he called it, a dozen fine volumes from the King's library at the Tower and pressed them on me. I sighed when he handed them to me, thinking of how books had led to my liaison with the King. Would he resent me receiving them? I wondered. I knew I had fallen out of favor with him but surely he could not begrudge me the solace of a few books. Not after what had happened to me. So I quietened my misgivings and took the books.

The book I started to read that afternoon concerned a merchant's travels to far distant lands in Africa and the Americas. He wrote of marvelous mountains and dreadful deserts and how he had almost lost his life battling storms and the fiercest of winds. But more exciting for me were his stories about the strange peoples he encountered: pygmy men with jet-black skin, hairy little men who lived in trees and could not speak except with their hands and stately peoples conquered by the Spaniards, who wore cloaks made of feathers and had replaced every one of their teeth with gold ones.

He also wrote about the amazing creatures he had seen. Giant fish that swam alongside his ship, crocodiles with armor plate and razor teeth, and large cowlike creatures who lived in the river Nile and could open their jaws so wide a man could sit inside. He spoke of basilisks whose stares could strike a person dead and salamanders that lived in the fiercest fire. I almost began to doubt the merchant's stories but then he described birds as big as ponies that had no wings but could run faster than the wind. I recalled Ned's story of the giant bird in the Menagerie and realized then that the merchant spoke only the truth.

As I was reading, I became aware of someone watching me. It was Sissy. She was standing in the doorway, a pail of milk in her hand.

"Is that a book?" she asked.

I nodded, surprised at the question.

She put the pail upon the table and stood beside me, drooping on my shoulder, scanning the book intently. She pointed to the type.

"What are these for, Alice?" she asked.

"They're words," I said.

She shook her head. "But they don't speak, do they? Not like real words? Like words we're saying now?"

"No, they don't speak like that," I said. "But they do speak to me. A man wrote these words, as if he was telling a story, and when I read them it's almost as if I can hear him speak." I fell silent, wondering if I made any sense at all.

"But you can't hear him?" Sissy said. "You can't hear him speaking?"

"In my head I can," I said. I bit my lip. It was harder to explain reading than I imagined. Or it was to someone who did not know what a book was. I wished that Father Luke or Susan Dunster were here. I felt sure they would explain it better than I could.

Sissy put her hand upon my arm. "Will you teach me to read?" she asked. "Will you, please? I'd love it if you taught me how to read."

She came round and stared at me, her eyes big with pleading.

"Of course I will," I said. "I'd like to. As long as your father and mother agree."

When Sissy and I went to ask permission, we found that Hannah was reluctant. "It's not for girls to read," she said. "No good will come of it."

I wondered for a moment if she was alluding to me.

To my surprise, Robert was more enthusiastic. "Surely it can do no harm," he said. "The sons of rich men learn how to read at school. As sure as eggs is eggs it can't do Sissy much harm. Her head's enough in the clouds as it is. A little book-learning can't make her any worse."

So, despite Hannah's reservations, I began to teach Sissy to read.

She was a quick learner, even though her younger sisters constantly interrupted her, loudly declaring that they wanted to learn. In the end, I gave in and began to teach all of the younger children, as well.

"You're a regular scholar," Robert said to me one evening, "and it seems you're making little scholars out of my children." He came closer to me and put his hand on my arm. "Take it slowly, Alice. Hannah is not keen on book-learning. It didn't do her uncle and aunt any good from what I've heard." He shook his head at my questioning look. "She won't talk about it, got angry when I used to ask what had happened to them. So please, don't go making my children too fancy and above themselves."

"I won't," I said. "In any case I won't be here long enough to teach them more than their ABCs."

He shrugged. "You can stay as long as you like, Alice. It's a joy to have you here."

I watched him as he walked away, nervously wondering if there was something more behind his words. I told myself not to be so foolish. I must not think badly of every man, must not think the worst of them.

Sissy continued to work very hard at her reading, spending every spare minute going over the alphabet until one day she was able to recite it from beginning to end without a slip. I clapped with pleasure and she went as red as her brother did.

"Go and show your parents," I said. She was reluctant at first but then agreed to do so after supper. When all the plates had been cleared away she whispered in her father's ear and he smiled broadly.

"Sissy has a little trick to show us," he said.

Sissy stuck her lips out at his words. "It's not a trick, father. It's something I done for myself."

"Come on, then," he said, not unkindly. "Let's hear it before the stars come out."

She stood up and recited the alphabet, her hands behind her back and her head in the air as if she were plucking the letters from the ceiling. She made several mistakes in the order and repeated the letter *m* three times but I was the only one to notice and did not draw attention to it.

When she finished I led the applause. I cast an anxious eye at Hannah. At the beginning of the recital she had sat in stony-faced silence. But as Sissy proceeded her look began to melt and when the time came she clapped as loudly and as long as anybody.

"Clever girl," she said. Then she darted a quick, stern look at her. "But don't go thinking you're a lady like Alice. It's the cowshed you'll be working in, not a Palace."

Sissy laughed at these words but I sensed that she was a little hurt by them.

The next day, the weather grew very hot and sultry, strangely so for mid-September. Storm clouds massed far to the south and the heat grew more torrid. It was so hot that Hannah decided we would eat supper outside. The children got wild with joy at the news and our meal felt almost like a feast.

"Food tastes better outside, Mother," Edward said.

"I agree with Edward," I said. He blushed right down to his neck and I thought he might expire on the spot. "Your cooking is always excellent, Hannah," I continued, "but today it is the best I have ever eaten."

"Better than your grand feasts at Hampton Court?" she asked shyly.

"Much better. Much, much better."

The air grew hotter as night fell. The children were sent to bed and the adults and two older children sat under the stars a little while longer while Robert told them stories about the doings of badgers and hares. Finally, yawning with pleasure, everyone went to bed.

Sissy bundled her sleepy sisters into a tiny corner of the bed and fanned herself with her hand.

"It's so hot," she said. "I'd like to sleep outside but I daren't." She paused and then her words came quiet in the darkness. "Besides, I'd get lonely with only the old moon for company."

"It's better safe and sound in here," I murmured drowsily.

"It is better, isn't it?" Sissy whispered. "Even if it is hot."

I woke in the dark hours of the night feeling as if a heavy weight was smothering me. I realized what it was as soon as my eyes flickered open.

Sissy was lying on me, stroking my hair as gently as a mouse. I wanted to jump up but something told me not to. I did not want to alarm or upset her. Instead I lay still as she touched my hair. Then she moved her head and she kissed me gently upon the lips. I thought of my dreams of Anne Boleyn and could not prevent a sigh. I felt Sissy pause and listen, and then she kissed me on the cheek and lay back down beside me.

Sweet dreams, Sissy, I thought. I realized that she was having a girlish crush on me and smiled. I felt strangely flattered at her attention. For the first time since being abducted I felt loved and good and pure.

The very next day, as I was bringing eggs back to the house for the midday meal, there came excited cries and then the sound of the children calling my name.

I stepped out with my basket over my arm and squinted in the bright sunlight.

A hard-ridden horse stood in the yard, sweat glistening on its flank. A tall man stood beside it, deep in conversation with Robert Cooper. He glanced at me as I approached, a look of shrewd appraisal on his face.

"Are you Alice Petherton?" he asked.

A prickle of fear ran through me. Could it be possible that Timothy Dale had discovered my whereabouts and sent this man to abduct me once again? Or had I killed Sir Edmund Tint with the chamber pot and was to be dragged back to London for trial and execution?

"I am Alice Petherton," I said, though my tongue felt heavy and my mouth was dry as dust.

My legs wobbled and I would have dropped the eggs had Sissy not run towards me and held my arm.

"My name is Daniel Stokes," he said. "I've been sent by Lord Cromwell, Lord Privy Seal. You're wanted at once. I'm to take you to Greenwich Palace."

He turned and indicated a small carriage at the bottom of the drive.

"Get your things," he continued. "We leave immediately." He turned and led his horse towards the carriage.

"I'm not going," I said.

Stokes stopped and turned to face me. His face had a look of surprise but it was swiftly replaced by one of wry amusement.

"I think you are," he said, his voice quiet but firm.

"I am not."

He shook his head and glanced away as if he did not want to fully betray his reaction.

"It is the Lord Privy Seal who commands you," he said. "Thomas Cromwell."

"I know who the Lord Privy Seal is."

He stepped towards me. "Then you know that it is most unwise, most unhealthy, to disobey his commands."

I stared at him for a moment, my mind racing. But before I could even think of a reply Sissy raced to my side.

"Can I come with you, Alice?" she cried.

"No," I said, and her father and mother said the same even louder.

"Is this your maid?" Stokes asked.

I shook my head but Sissy called out, "Yes."

"Then get your things as well," said Stokes.

Robert and Hannah tried to argue with him but he brushed them aside. In any case, Sissy had dashed into the house, gathered up an armful of clothes and was back by my side in moments.

"I've got your things here, miss," she said to me, with a reasonable show at a curtsy.

"She's not my maid," I said, horrified at the speed at which events were unfolding.

Stokes paused and then glanced over a document he held in his hand.

"The Lord Privy Seal says to bring you and all your possessions," he said. "That must include your maid."

"But I've not said I'm going," I cried.

Stokes shook his head wearily before taking me by the arm and marching me towards the carriage.

When we got there he relaxed his hold and took me by the hand very gently. I looked at his face and saw a kindness there such as I had noticed in Ned Pepper and Mr. Cooper. He smiled and I felt a blush come to my cheeks.

The Coopers ran after us, complaining loudly. But it was to no avail. Sissy and I were bundled into the carriage by the tall man and the driver whipped up the horses.

"I'll look after her," I cried as we trundled down the track.

The Coopers ran alongside the carriage but it picked up speed and Hannah fell behind.

I leaned out of the window. "I promise I'll look after her," I repeated.

"Maybe," called Mr. Cooper. "But who will look after you?"

Chapter Thirty-Five

Cromwell's Plan

17 September 1538

I learned on that journey what it meant to be on the business of the Lord Privy Seal. While the light was good the horses were ridden at full tilt and changed every ten miles or so in order to keep them fresh. At these stops the coachmen swapped seats, food and drink was taken by the party and we were allowed to answer nature's call. Apart from that we did not halt, not even at night. Men on torches rode before and behind us and although we went more slowly we still made good speed.

Heaven be praised, the carriage was the most luxurious I had ever seen apart from the King's. It was slung on leather springs, which made it ride reasonably smoothly. Every surface was thickly upholstered and the seats had piles of bolsters and cushions heaped upon them. Even though we hurried through the night, Sissy and I were able to snatch a few hours of sleep.

I had given her a furious scolding when first we set off.

"What were you thinking of, claiming that you're my maid?" I said. "It's a wicked lie and look where it's got you."

"It's got me on a journey with you," she countered, unrepentant. "To a Palace." And then she gave a huge grin, quite taking the strength from my anger. I smiled despite myself. If truth were told, I was glad she was coming with me.

As the journey wore on, my mind returned to the same question: What did Thomas Cromwell want with me? At the first halt I approached the messenger, Stokes, and asked him the question.

He opened his parchment and quickly perused it. Then he snapped it shut and replaced it in his jerkin. "As I thought, miss, it doesn't say. The Lord Privy Seal doesn't have to say, of course. This document just orders me to collect Alice Petherton and bring her with all dispatch to Greenwich Palace." He glanced at Sissy. "With all her possessions."

She gave him a winning smile in return.

The journey from the Tower to Stratford had taken us three days and we'd thought that good going. The journey back to London was far swifter. We arrived at Edgware as the sun was setting and pulled into an inn to make the final change of horses. Sissy and I were so exhausted that Stokes ordered hot food to be brought to us. I begged to be allowed to eat at a table but he was reluctant to allow us to stray from the carriage. Seeing I was adamant he summoned the innkeeper and demanded that a table be brought out into the yard.

"Thank you for your kindness, Mr. Stokes," I said.

He gave me a broad smile as Sissy and I sat at the table.

"I can see the reason even more now," he said, almost to himself.

"What do you mean?" I asked.

But he seemed suddenly embarrassed and refused to say more.

We were soon on the road again and I fell asleep as we clattered through the streets of London. This was fortunate for I would not have wanted to see the rest of the journey. We must have crossed the Thames by London Bridge, which I had so recently fled across. And we passed through the streets of Southwark only yards from Dale's brothel.

"You missed London," Sissy said as I woke up an hour later.

"I'm glad," I mumbled. "I hope never to see it again."

Finally, in the small hours of the morning, the carriage came to a halt. We had arrived at Greenwich Palace.

I thought that Sissy might faint from joy at the sight of it.

Daniel Stokes helped me down out of the carriage.

"It is three of the clock," he said. "The Lord Privy Seal rises at four so there is time for you to eat and refresh yourself."

He took my hand and kissed it. "I am enchanted to have met you, Alice Petherton."

"Perhaps we will meet again," I said.

"Perhaps," he answered. "I should like that very much." And then he turned and hurried off into the night.

The torchmen, stumbling in their weariness, led us to the Palace. Once we were inside, a white-haired old man took over and led us up a winding stair. His joints creaked like old furniture when it is sat upon but he moved at a good speed nonetheless. He led us to a chamber with couches and a small fire, gesturing with one arm as if he were displaying some marvelous treasure. He bent to the fireplace, creaking still more loudly, heaped logs onto the flames and sat back on his haunches to make sure that it took. Then he creaked to his feet and left the room. He had not said a word in all this time.

He returned a few minutes later with two young servants. One brought towels, a basin and an ewer of steaming hot water. The other had a large tray with two plates, two glasses and a bottle of wine. The white-haired man shooed them out and then gave me a curious glance.

"Will you be needing anything more, miss?" he asked. His voice sounded as though he were calling from a tomb.

"No thank you," I answered. "But I am grateful for your kindness."

He gave me a cold smile and departed with yet more creaking.

I turned to find Sissy prowling round the room, as if in a daze.

"This is wonderful," she cried. "Is this the King's chamber?"

The walls were dark oak but with hardly a trace of decoration on them. The curtain on the window was a pale, plain blue. The couches were comfortable looking but without fine needlework or very much in the way of color. A nondescript room altogether.

"No," I answered. "This is not the King's chamber. That is a thousand times more wonderful. But you will never get to see the inside of such a wonderful place."

"Well, this is wonderful enough for me," she said, stroking the fabric of a couch. She went to the table and looked at the food.

"There's enough here to feed half a dozen people," she said. "As I'm to be your maid, I should serve you."

Before I could stop her she brought across an empty platter and a second one heaped with bread, butter, cheese, cakes and biscuits.

I shook my head. "No thank you, Sissy, I'm not hungry." How could I be when the whole of my heart was in my mouth?

"And you're not my maid," I said.

"Mr. Stokes thinks I am. He's very handsome," she said in a dreamy voice. "Do you think he's very rich?"

Only ten minutes in the Palace, I thought, *and she is already thinking like a Maid of Honor, appraising all the men and plotting out her future.*

"No, I don't suppose he's very rich. He's merely a servant, and besides, he has a wife and sixteen children to support."

Sissy's mouth fell open at that. "Oh" was all that she could say.

She looked so disappointed that I repented my words. "I was just teasing you, Sissy," I said. "I don't know if he's married or has a family. But I'm confident he is not rich. Servants do not get rich."

But then I thought to myself that Stokes was a servant to Thomas Cromwell. Perhaps, in that case, the old rules did not apply.

Sissy heaped food on her own plate. I thought it unfair that the sight of Stokes had fed her imagination so. If I was lucky Thomas

Cromwell would finish whatever business he had with me in a week or so and we would be returned to her father's farm. But at least I could teach her to read and write, I thought.

And then I smiled. I could see my future, for the first time since I had left Court. I would become the servant of the Coopers, if they would have me. I would help on the farm, make and mend clothes and teach all the children their letters. I sighed with pleasure at the thought.

Sissy turned to me with a frown. "You said I'd never get to see the King's Chamber," she said. "So how was it that you saw it?"

The question put me in a pretty pass and my face burned.

"I was a Maid of Honor to the Queen," I said. "I peeked into the room once."

"Which Queen?" she asked. "The one who got her head chopped off?"

"Her and one other," I answered.

"And what happened to the other one?"

"She died as well. In childbirth."

"And is the baby all right?"

"I think so. He was when I left the Palace, at any rate. He must be almost a year old by now."

"Perhaps I'll see him," she said. "Perhaps I'll be able to take him for a walk down by the river."

"Perhaps," I said. "But I don't think we'll be staying that long, Sissy."

She looked crestfallen but before she could answer, the man with white hair entered the room. "The Lord Privy Seal will see you now," he said.

A sudden fear gripped me. What would happen when I saw Thomas Cromwell? I took two steps towards the basin, flanneled my face with water and told Sissy to wait here for me.

I followed the creaking servant along a corridor and up a flight of stairs. He paused at the top, indicated a door as though it were a most amazing thing, and then rapped quietly upon it.

"Come," said a voice from within.

The old man opened the door halfway and signaled for me to enter, closing the door behind me without a sound.

Thomas Cromwell was sitting behind a desk, his elbows resting comfortably upon a leather document wallet, his hands clasped together as if in prayer. He looked at me with searching eyes, the faintest glimmer of amusement on his face.

"Well," he said, "you have led me a merry dance, Alice." He gestured for me to sit opposite him.

"What do you mean, my lord?"

"You disappeared," he said. "You left Hampton Court Palace in unseemly haste."

"That was none of my doing, my lord."

He sniffed and glanced at a document close to his elbow. "So I gather. I'm afraid Sir Richard Rich can act in a rather impetuous manner. Especially when he seeks to please the Duke of Norfolk."

"I had assumed that my leaving the Palace was on the order of the King."

Cromwell unclasped his hands a moment. "Not expressly." He clasped them together once again.

"You argued against the King, Alice Petherton," he said. "And that made him angry." He paused for a moment as if recalling the scene, then he gave a sniff and continued. "His Majesty made certain decisions that day. But they did not include banishing you from Court."

"But I was banished nonetheless."

Cromwell did not answer. As if to say that this was a topic now best forgotten. Then he frowned as if he were wrestling with some thorny issue. "I like you, Alice," he said at last, "and I do not care overmuch for Richard Rich. But he is useful to me, the most useful of all my servants. I will not chastise him but I will give him warning. While you are under my protection you have nothing more to fear from Richard Rich."

He stared at me for a little longer, which I found unnerving. Then he shook his head a little as if something perplexed him. He sighed and passed a glass of wine to me.

"The King has become morose," he said.

"I am sorry to hear it."

He held up one finger to silence me.

"He has grown morose," he continued, "distracted, melancholy." He paused and his jaws worked a little as if he were chewing over his words to find the most palatable.

"In fact he has grown so out of sorts as to be . . . ungovernable." He paused, his mind whirring like a clock, and I imagined that the word he had chosen was not, after all, to his taste.

"More exactly, he has grown turbulent, capricious." He smiled and I realized that these words were a gloss, that he had indeed chosen the word *ungovernable* quite deliberately. That, although he now amended it, he had, in fact, wanted me to hear it. It felt as if he had proffered me a precious gift.

"He has ever been masterful," I said.

"As is his right," he said. "As a King should be."

He unlocked his two index fingers from his praying hands and allowed them to play with his lip. "But this is somewhat different, Alice. It is as if he has fallen prey to a fever, as if he realizes it but does not yet feel inclined to recover."

"Then you must wait for him to recover, my lord."

"Alas, the affairs of a mighty nation can only pause a little while. Even for the highest in the land."

I could not help myself. I glanced around, alarmed in case anyone should be listening.

"We are quite alone," he said blandly.

I took a sip of my wine.

"To what do you attribute the King's disorder?" I asked.

"His melancholy?"

I bit my lip at his swift correction of me, feeling sick to my heart, and nodded.

"I attribute his melancholy," Cromwell said, "to you."

The image of Anne Boleyn leapt into my mind. I managed to blink it away but that was the most I could do for I was powerless to speak or even to think.

And then I thought, *I'm young, too young for this to happen to me.* I felt the icy edge of an axe upon my neck. The tears started in my eyes and I could no longer make out Cromwell's face.

"You are troubled to hear this," he said. "As you should be."

I wanted to wipe away my tears but my hand could not move.

"But I have a remedy for the King's melancholy," he continued. "You will return to Court and allow your presence to be known to His Majesty."

"I don't understand," I mumbled. "I thought you said that I had caused his melancholy."

Cromwell shook his head and frowned. "Foolish girl," he said. "It is your absence which has caused his melancholy. Had you not realized that? He needs you back, in his company, in his bed. To beguile him with your charms. He does not realize he needs you, not yet. But he does. And, therefore, I need you. The Kingdom needs you."

"And what if I don't wish it?" I whispered.

He gave a wintry smile. "Your wishes do not come into it. You will do as I say."

"And if the King does not wish it?"

Cromwell sighed. "Have you seen yourself in a looking glass, my dear? Henry Tudor is a King. But he is also a man."

He unclenched his hands and began to scribble on a piece of parchment.

"For the moment," he said, "I shall assign you quarters here in Greenwich. I shall require you to make yourself seen by the King within the next few days."

He finished writing, dusted the ink and folded up the document. "Give this to Isaac Jones, my servant. The fellow who brought you here. He shall arrange all."

"I cannot see the King as I am," I said. "I have nothing, my lord. No possessions, no clothes other than this gown and one other too tattered to be shown."

He frowned. "How so?"

I took a deep breath and told him all that had happened since Rich had me taken from Hampton Court. Cromwell listened impassively at first, then with growing incredulity and finally, with a sympathy I would not have imagined him capable of.

"You have suffered much," he said. "I am sorry for it."

He unfolded the document and picked up his pen, adding some swift sentences to the end.

"You shall have all the gowns you desire, Alice," he said. "And an allowance of forty pounds a year."

Forty pounds? I stifled my amazement at the huge amount. "How will this be paid?" I asked. "I am no longer a Maid of Honor. And I know that the King won't pay me anything."

"A friend will pay it," he said. He clenched his hands together as if to say there was an end to the conversation.

I glanced at him as he bent even closer to the document and realized who that friend was. I wanted to thank him but thought it wisest not to.

"Daniel Stokes tells me that you have a maid," he said.

"She is not a maid. She is the daughter of my friends the Coopers."

"Preposterous for a maid to have a maid," he said. Then he smiled like a wolf. "But not for the King's favorite. Your apartment has a small room to house her."

He waved his hand to dismiss me and bent once more to his documents.

I rose, gave a curtsy he did not see and made for the door.

"Timothy Dale?" he said. "One of the Southwark stews?"

"Yes, my lord."

He picked up the document once again, wrote something more in it and sealed it with great force as though he had never been more determined in his life.

Chapter Thirty-Six

The King's Great Anger

17 September 1538

I walked out of the Lord Privy Seal's office in a daze. I do not know what I had expected when I was summoned to the Palace but I had not expected this.

Isaac Jones led me down the corridor, his joints creaking like a horse in old harness, bearing aloft Cromwell's document as if it were a pennant heading towards battle. He went into the chamber where Sissy was waiting, scooped her up and led us, creaking furiously, through long corridors and down huge staircases.

At last we stepped through a door and found ourselves in the open air. It was still dark and the night had the deep chill that comes before dawn. Jones woke some torchboys who were slumbering in a porch and ordered them to bring a carriage.

He turned to me with an apologetic air. "The carriage may take some time. Boys seem unable to run as fast as they did in my youth."

I smiled and thought of him as a child, running like the wind to do some master's bidding and creaking even then.

"Where are we going?" I asked.

"To the castle," he said, pointing into the darkness.

"I can't see anything," Sissy said, peering into the distance.

"It's a quarter of a mile away," I said. "Too far to see."

"If it's that near we could walk," said Sissy.

The old man shook his head at this suggestion. "It is not fitting for your mistress to walk," he said.

Sissy turned to me, impressed by his words. She had never known anyone considered important enough not to walk on their own two feet.

A few minutes later a small carriage raced into sight, the poor horse whipped furiously by one of the torchboys, the other boy clinging perilously onto the back. Perhaps they'd heard Jones comment on their slowness and were determined to prove him wrong.

Jones held the door open for us and we climbed in. I watched as he hoisted his creaking frame beside the driver and we headed along the drive at a prodigious rate.

"Slow down, you fool," I heard Jones say, and the carriage slowed immediately. I was glad, for the movement was making my stomach churn. A few minutes later the carriage came to a halt. The door opened and Jones helped us out.

The two torchboys stood in front of us. They held their torches high to light the way. In front of us stood the castle. It was a very small castle, little more than a glorified keep with the addition of one tower and a fortified gatehouse.

"Are we being sent into prison?" Sissy asked, her voice trembling with fear.

Jones shook his head. "Not at all. The outside looks grim but inside there are plush and pleasant apartments. Your mistress will be quite comfortable here."

"But what about me?" she asked, her voice sounding panicky. "Where am I to go?"

"Hush, Sissy," I said. "You will stay with me."

The torchboys led us into the castle and up a large staircase. At the top of the stairs we came upon a long corridor. Jones overtook the boys and strode along the corridor to the right. Halfway along he halted and threw open a door.

One of the boys hurried forward to light the room. I stepped inside. It was a small chamber with two doors leading off it. Although it was small it was quite exquisite, quite beautiful. A low couch sat beneath a window, with a comfortable chair nearby. To one side there was a table, two chairs and a sideboard. Beside this was a large fireplace with a fire already burning. Sissy looked around and gasped in amazement.

"Are we going to stay here, Alice?" she asked.

"For the present," said Jones, lighting candles. "There is a bedroom through there, with a small alcove for your servant. The other door leads to a bath chamber."

Sissy's hand went to her mouth with joy.

"You may be moved into somewhere more suitable, more commodious, at a later date," Jones said.

I smiled and thanked him. That depended on me making my presence known to the King and him being pleased at my doing so.

"Is there anything else you require?" Jones asked.

I shook my head. "Nothing, thank you."

He bowed and made to depart but I caught him by his sleeve.

"There is one thing," I said. "Is there water in the bath chamber?"

"The Lord Privy Seal commanded that the bath be prepared with hot water, miss."

I closed my eyes in ecstasy. Thomas Cromwell thought of everything.

Although dawn was not far away we were exhausted so I insisted that we got some sleep. I hardly seemed to have shut my eyes when I was woken by a knock at the door.

"Who is it?" I called.

"The laundry maids," came the answer. "We've got some clothes for you."

I jumped out of bed, all tiredness banished at this news, and opened the door. Two young servants stood in front of me, laden down with gowns and other clothing.

"Come in," I said. "Put them on the couch."

The girls bustled in and gave me a dubious look. "On the couch, miss?" one asked. "We should put them in the wardrobe for you."

"No thank you," I said. "I want to look at them first. I will put them in the wardrobe myself." I paused. "I mean my maid will put them there."

The girls carefully placed the gowns on the couch, curtsied and left.

Sissy ran to the gowns and held one up to the window. It was a beautiful deep grey, trimmed with darker velvet and with a red linen partlet attached. She picked up a kirtle of light blue and held it against the gown. "This would go very well underneath it," she said.

"You have a good eye," I said. "Perhaps you would make a fine laundry maid."

She flung down the robe and came towards me, her face a picture of woe. "But I want to stay with you, Alice," she said. "I want to be *your* maid."

"I was jesting," I said, squeezing her hand to calm her.

She looked relieved and turned once more to the gowns.

There was another knock on the door.

"Put your clothes on and see who that is," I said. "Hurry now."

I went into the bath chamber, filled a basin with water and washed my face. I heard Sissy open the door and some clattering outside. When

I returned to the chamber the sideboard was laden with plates, glasses and three platters of food.

"Is this all for us?" Sissy breathed in excitement.

"If you want it," I said. "There's always more than enough to eat at Court."

She shook her head. She had lived on a farm and eaten better than most people but I don't suppose she had ever seen a table with more food than could be eaten.

"This bread is white," she said in wonder, holding up a loaf. "And these rolls." She held them to her nose and breathed in the fresh, doughy scent.

"Shall I serve you?" she asked, as delighted as a little child.

"If you wish," I said, taking a seat. I decided that for this morning at least, I would act out the role of great lady.

Sissy placed two plates on the table, a knife and fork the wrong way round and two glasses. Then she brought over a platter containing the bread and rolls and another with cold meats, butter, cheese and honey. She gave a doubtful look at the third platter, which was crammed with fruit.

"Leave that till later," I said. "And sit down with me, little maid. As there's no one to see us we shall eat together."

We ate our fill, Sissy seeming determined to eat up everything in sight. She almost succeeded. Finally, she gave a sigh. She waited for a while, grinning with pleasure, but could not contain herself long. She went to the sideboard for the final platter of fruit and brought it to the table, looking at it narrowly.

"What is all this?" she asked. "I can see apples, pears and blackberries but what are all the others?"

"Oranges, pomegranates and peaches," I said. "They come from far to the south."

"From France?"

"Possibly. Or Spain."

Sissy shook her head in wonder and started to bite into a pomegranate.

"You can't eat the peel." I laughed. "You must cut it and scoop out the seeds inside."

She put it back on the plate. "I think I'll have a pear," she said.

After breakfast I tried on a variety of gowns and finally settled on a russet one trimmed with velvet and a light green kirtle underneath. The foresleeves were cream, gathered in bunches tied off with dark grey trim. I chose a French bonnet with a coif of the same russet tone and a veil of midnight blue which hung to the small of my back. The shoes fitted well enough and I chose dainty ones of cream with thin bands at the ankle.

"You look like a Queen," Sissy cried, clapping her hands with joy.

I hope not, I thought. I wanted to live my life as I chose it. Not as I was ordered or coerced. I glanced at myself in the mirror. Yes, I had always wanted to live my life as I chose it. But now, after what I had experienced at Dale's and Thorne's hands, I was determined on it more than ever.

I insisted that Sissy dress herself in one of the gowns. Not as rich as mine, perhaps, but more fitting to a Maid of Honor than to an ordinary maid. She was so entranced that I could barely get another word out of her. I certainly found it hard to keep her attention. She danced and twirled in front of the mirror, bowing and curtsying for all she was worth.

Partway through this performance there came a sharp rap on the door.

I almost went to open it myself but then caught myself and ordered Sissy to do so. She stopped her twirling and walked towards the door with her nose in the air. I smiled to see this and her unbounded joy at being here.

She opened the door, peered out and glanced back at me in some alarm.

"It's a boy," she said.

"Not just any boy," came a familiar voice. "The only boy."

A head peeped in. It belonged to Humphrey the Page.

"It's good to see you again, miss," he said, pushing past Sissy without a word. "My, Alice, but you do look lovely."

"How dare you," Sissy cried.

"He's a friend," I said. "Or at least I think he is."

"A better friend to you than you realize," he said. "How do you think Master Cromwell found your whereabouts?"

I frowned. "Through you?"

He nodded. "I happened to bump into an old waterman name of Scrump who'd just got back to London. He told me that you'd been through some bad times and was residing at the Menagerie. So I took myself off there and found out from Ned Pepper that you'd been there but had left and was staying in the country."

He came towards me and touched me gently on the arm. "Ned told me something of what happened to you," he said quietly. "Not all, but enough. I am sorry that you went through such things."

"It is in the past," I said in a lighter tone than I actually felt. "And is Mr. Scrump quite well?" I asked. "And his wife?"

"They are. But not, apparently, his son. Bits of him are still turning up on butchers' stalls, so it's said."

I shook my head at his words. I could not forgive Art for what he'd done to me. But I could not bring myself to hate him either.

"Anyway, it's good to see you back, Alice. And I'm not the only one who will think that. The word is that the King is as savage as his lions without you."

Sissy stepped towards me when she heard this.

"Close your mouth, Sissy," I said.

"Yeah, close your trap," said Humphrey, turning to Sissy. "There's a draft in—"

He fell silent. Sissy blushed and she turned away. But then she looked back with a shy and wary glance. Neither said a word, which was great change for both of them.

I pretended a cough and they shook themselves out of their trances.

"This is Humphrey, a rude nuisance of a Page," I said dryly to Sissy. "This is Sissy Cooper, my maid and very good friend."

Humphrey bowed. "Charmed to meet you, Miss Cooper," he said.

Sissy's hand went to her mouth and she giggled. It was her only answer.

Humphrey turned to me but as he spoke his eyes kept returning to Sissy.

"Anyway, Alice," he said, "compliments of Sir Thomas Cromwell, he hopes you is settled here at the castle." He paused, glanced at Sissy once again, and furrowed his brow as if he had lost his thought completely.

A few moments later he clicked his fingers so sharply I almost jumped. "I remember now," he said, turning to me. "Sir Thomas wants to see you right away. He also wants to inform you that His Majesty King Henry, ninth of that name, will be arriving at Greenwich Palace an hour before noon."

"Eighth," I said. "King Henry the Eighth."

"That's what I said," Humphrey replied. "Sir Thomas says you are to go to the River Gardens, close to the entrance to the Palace. And you're to be in good time so His Majesty may happen, as if by chance, to see you."

"Happen, by chance? By the order of Lord Cromwell?"

Humphrey put his hand on his waist and shook his head ruefully. "Things that happen by chance and the orders of Lord Cromwell are much the same. As you should know by now, Alice."

"What about me?" asked Sissy, surfacing at last from her reverie. "Am I to meet the King?"

"I think that would be pleasant for you," I said. "If you can tear yourself away from your other concerns."

"I have no other concerns," she answered, although she kept glancing at Humphrey.

"And pray tell me what you will be doing, dear Humphrey?" I said.

"I shall be close on hand," he answered. "Close on hand to do any service you require." He spoke to me but his eyes looked at Sissy.

"Oh, Alice," he said, "there's one thing more. Lord Cromwell wants to see you before you see the King."

"Before I see the King?"

"Well, immediately, to be honest."

I picked up my cloak and headed for the door. "Thank you for being so alert," I said.

A coach was waiting for me at the driveway and hurried down towards Greenwich Palace.

Isaac Jones was standing in the entrance, swaying from side to side with anxiety.

"You must hurry," he said, leading me with swift pace and horrific creaking towards Lord Cromwell's office.

He was sitting at his desk, poring over some papers. *Does he ever get tired of reading and weighing arguments?* I wondered. *Does he never get tired of making decisions for the King?*

"Ah, Alice," he said. "Thank you for coming to see me."

I smiled but did not answer. We both knew well that I had no choice but to come.

"I wanted to make sure that you understand what I require of you." He paused and a half smile flickered over his face. "Or rather what the Kingdom requires of you."

"I did not know that I had come to the attention of the Kingdom," I said.

"The King is the Kingdom and you've certainly come to his attention."

"And been banished from it."

Cromwell shrugged. "That is what I intend to remedy."

"And is this a remedy that will really suit the King? Does he really wish to see me again?"

Cromwell laughed. "Of course he doesn't. Not yet, at any rate." He folded his hands together. "You must understand that though the King is a man of remarkable intellect he sometimes allows his great and generous heart to rule his head."

I feigned an innocent look. "Some people say it is Lord Cromwell who is his head."

He chuckled with pleasure at my words.

"That is foolish talk, Alice. But it is my burden to make many hard decisions for the King. His heart has too often ruled him in the past. As have the machinations of the old nobility. Now it is time for him to be guided by more simple people. Like us."

I laughed at his words. "You a simple person, Sir Thomas? You know that is not so. You are clever, Lord Cromwell. Perhaps the cleverest person in the Kingdom."

Cromwell nodded as if what I said was beyond argument.

Then he frowned. "Some people say I am too clever, Alice. But is it possible to be too clever? Cleverness is a gift that I have. I cannot hide it or undo it. It is the same with you, Alice. You have a gift although you do not know it."

"What do you mean?" I said, confused.

Cromwell's eyes narrowed as if marveling at something.

"Every woman," he said, "has the power to make a man fall in love with her. It is not an unusual power, and without it the world would end soon enough. Some have the power to make two or three fall in love with them."

He paused as if recollecting something, something which he swiftly put away as if he treasured it and would look at it again in a little while.

"But some women," he continued, "have the power to make not one or two men fall in love with them, but every man. Every man, every man who comes into contact with them. It is a rare gift. Perhaps one in fifty thousand women have it, perhaps one in five hundred thousand. You are such a woman, Alice Petherton."

I stared at him, not comprehending his words. "I don't know what you mean."

"Of course you don't. You are unaware of your power. But I have observed it, Alice. I have seen you in a room, reading a book or talking with some friends. Two men enter the room and pause. They feel it, something subtle and elusive but so powerful it cannot be ignored. They look around, searching for the source. And they realize in a moment that the source is you. Every man feels this. Every man.

"They have to seek you out, to get near to you. They are driven to see you more closely, to feast their eyes upon you. They yearn to get close enough to hear your voice. They want, of course, to get even closer. They itch to get close enough to smell you, to touch you, to taste you.

"For make no mistake, every man who comes into contact with you desires you. Every man becomes desperate to lie with you, to make love to you. They hold in their heads the conceit that by doing this they will conquer you, possess you. But they know, to the depths of their being, that in reality they will utterly surrender themselves to you."

He fell silent.

"You beguile men, Alice," he continued finally. "You enchant them. No, it is more than that. You cast a spell over them. Every man, Alice, every man. You snare them, hold them in a net, bind them to you with invisible threads."

My heart beat faster at his words though I did not know the cause of it. My thoughts leapt over the events of the past year, the pursuit by Rich, winning the favor of the King, being fooled and betrayed by Art Scrump, the brothel. Cromwell called what I had a gift. At the moment it felt just as much a curse.

"I did not know," I began. "Or I don't think I knew."

"Of course you didn't. It is not something you choose for yourself. It is part of your nature. As much a part of you as the color of your eyes or the sound of your voice."

He laughed quietly. "You see, Alice, even I am beguiled by you."

I turned from him and stared into the fire. The flames licked at a log like a dog licks at a bone. The crack of the burning wood sounded in my ears but could not still the whirling thoughts which Cromwell had awakened.

"Why are you telling me this?" I asked at last.

He leaned back in his seat and regarded me.

"I said that one in fifty thousand women possess this power, one in five hundred thousand. It was a guess. How could I possibly know the number? But I have known one other woman who possessed the power that you do."

The silence fell between us like a cloak dropped upon the floor.

"Who was that?"

"Anne Boleyn."

I gasped and my hand went to my throat in dismay.

"It is ironic that you reach for your throat," Cromwell said, "given what happened to her. For that is what the King did to Anne Boleyn. And the executioner reached out next."

I tried to swallow but could not. Cromwell looked at me, studied me, observed me as if I were some painting on the wall.

"That is why I tell you this, Alice," he said. His voice took on a gentler tone. "Anne Boleyn had this power. And with it she snared the King. But she did not know how to use it as she should. She used it capriciously, without thought, sometimes with malice. And she did not realize that different men respond to this power in subtly different ways. Most, as I have said, believe they want to conquer the woman who has such power, while knowing that they will abandon themselves to her."

He paused a moment and his quick tongue came out and licked his lips as if they had suddenly grown dry. "But some men," he continued, "want only to conquer. Still others foresee only the surrender and dread it. Both these types of men may prove dangerous to the woman. The last will prove deadly."

I did not answer for a long while. For now that Cromwell had said these words, the scales fell off my eyes. I could see the truth in what he said. And I feared it. I rejoiced in it and I feared it. *This is what a woman must feel when she gives birth*, I thought. *Overwhelming joy and a terrible, terrible fear.*

"So which of these types of men was the King?" I said at last.

"With Anne Boleyn? All three. At first he thought he could conquer her. Then he came to realize that in conquering he would be defeated. And in the end he came to loathe each surrender, to despise himself for it and to desire vengeance upon his mistress."

The silence lapped across the room, a ripple of water in a pond.

"Will the same happen to me?"

Cromwell shook his head and reached for my hand. "I hope not, for all our sakes," he said. "That is why I have told you."

I frowned. "Is that the only reason?"

His eyes glittered and he shook his head. "I said all men, Alice. You beguile and snare all men."

And then he leaned closer to me, pressing my hand tighter as he did so. His face moved close to mine and I heard him give a long, deep sniff. And then he bent and kissed me on the cheek, his tongue dipping out for the merest touch, the merest taste.

"All men, Alice," he repeated. "All men."

A little while before the eleventh hour struck, Humphrey, Sissy and I could be found waiting close to the landing stage in front of the Palace entrance. We were not alone. An army of servants lined the walls of the Palace on either side of the entrance, heads craning towards the river. An official who I took to be the Palace steward paced backward and forward, wringing his hands with anxiety and occasionally shouting at one or other of the servants. A dozen or so minor officials hung about on the riverbank, beside the steps which led up from the water.

We waited for more than half an hour and then there came a blaring of trumpets from the west. Every head turned in that direction, every eye strained. The officials by the bank stood straighter, their hands fluttering over their clothes, wiping and rearranging. The steward looked as though he might faint, scurrying to and fro with mincing steps, his hand on his mouth.

Suddenly, there came another stir from behind him. A figure appeared in the entrance, dressed in black, blinking in the autumn light. People fell back and bowed low as he walked past them.

"Is that the King?" Sissy asked, awestruck.

"No," I answered. "Almost. That is Thomas Cromwell, Lord Privy Seal."

Cromwell strolled closer to the river, the crowd of officials parting for him like the Red Sea did for Moses. As he came close to where I waited he shot me a quick glance. He was appraising me, making sure of me, commanding me. I did him a curtsy and he nodded, apparently satisfied.

The trumpets called once again, much louder now, and sweeping into view came a flotilla with the Royal Barge at the front. My heart went into my mouth at the sight of it. The last time I had been in the Barge was when I returned from the Royal Menagerie having just witnessed the death of Ned Pepper's little daughter.

But that was not the only reason my heart was in my mouth. For, even from this distance, I could see the overpowering figure of the King, standing high and mighty on the deck, waving at the crowds cheering enthusiastically from both riverbanks. The King was immensely popular with the English people and he knew how to encourage this; two small boats sailed close to the banks and officials hurled showers of coins towards the cheering crowds.

I saw this only vaguely, however. All of my attention was focused on the King and how he would receive me.

A few minutes later the Barge tied up and the King walked across the gangplank.

The steward flung himself close to the ground, like a hound that had done something to displease its master and was desperate to ingratiate itself. The King deigned to take a little notice of him and he rose, his hands wringing in ever more frenzy.

Then the Lord Privy Seal stepped close and gave the King a low bow. Henry touched him on the shoulder, once briefly, as if blessing him, and master and man turned and walked the few steps towards the entrance of the Palace.

And then it happened. Cromwell slowed his walk a little, enough for the King to notice the change in pace and slow down himself. And then he saw me. He paused for just a moment, turned his face resolutely to the entrance and strode forward. Cromwell gave me a quick glance and gestured with his head for me to follow.

My heart was galloping like a stallion and swarms of butterflies careered around my stomach. I followed after the King, with Sissy and Humphrey several steps behind. The steward tried to stop me but I ignored him and hurried on.

I had only taken half a dozen steps when I saw him. King Henry stood framed in a doorway, glaring at me. He crooked his finger and I followed him into the room beyond.

"What do you mean, coming here to Greenwich?" he cried.

His face was red with rage and he paced about like a bull about to charge.

I flung myself on the floor. "I beg pardon if I've displeased Your Majesty by being here," I said.

"You displease me by your very presence," he boomed. "Your very presence annoys and infuriates me."

"I beg pardon," I said. My head drooped to the ground and I gave a silent curse at Cromwell.

"Infuriates me, madam," the King continued. "Infuriates and enrages me."

He stamped his feet, close to my face, mere inches from me. I began to weep. I did not mean to but I did.

The King ceased his tirade and I sensed him step closer. His hand reached for my chin and he jerked my face up so that he could look at me.

His eyes were cold as the sea. "I am sorry you are weeping," he said. "Dry your tears."

I dabbed at my eyes, thankful that his rage had abated. And then he pulled a purse from his belt and flung it at my feet.

"I want my luncheon," he cried, disappearing from view. "I want my luncheon."

I stared at the purse. I could not believe he had thrown me a purse. The rest of the room seemed to fall dark and the only thing bright was the purse. It seemed to throb and pulsate with a cruel and mocking disdain. It was a vile thing and if I had the strength I would have plucked it up and flung it into a corner of the room.

Thomas Cromwell stepped into the room and gestured me to stay on the ground. He beckoned Humphrey to him, whispered in his ear and hurried after the King.

"Come, Alice," Humphrey said gently, helping me to my feet. "Sir Thomas says you are to return to your apartment and to make ready to depart."

I left the purse where it lay. I had no idea how I got there but the next thing I recall was Humphrey helping me into the apartment. I slumped down on the couch. I was exhausted, as though I had run ten miles and then been forced to engage in a fight with Philippa Wicks and Dorothy Bray. My tears had stopped but I felt numb from my feet to my head. More than numb. I felt as though I was not a part of myself any longer.

"Should I pack up your gowns?" Sissy asked.

"They're not my gowns," I answered in a dull voice. "Nothing here belongs to me."

"I don't think anyone will miss a couple more gowns," Humphrey decided. "Here, Sissy, choose two and pack them up. Nothing too fancy, mind, but nice enough ones."

I smiled weakly at his concern and his good judgment.

Within an hour everything had been made ready for our departure. When all was done it seemed suddenly to strike Humphrey that it would not be me alone who would leave. Sissy would as well.

"Where do you live?" he asked her.

"Hundreds of miles away," she answered.

"So I won't see you again?"

She glanced at me and then shook her head. "I don't think it will be possible. I'm sorry."

"Me too," he said. And then he turned away and whistled but with no discernible tune.

We sat like this for an hour longer until, at last, there sounded a knock on the door. Humphrey opened it to find a messenger standing at attention.

"She's wanted," the man said and crooked a finger at me.

I rose, straightened my dress and hurried after him. I supposed I had to see the Lord Privy Seal and be given instructions concerning where I was to go. I hoped he would show a little charity to me although I doubted he would show me overmuch for fear of annoying the King.

I followed the messenger, not paying any heed where I was going, and at length we stopped outside a large door. He knocked once, opened it and told me to enter.

I stepped inside and found myself face-to-face with the King.

"I have dined," he said. "And now I would make your acquaintance once again, Alice Petherton." He turned and led me into his bedchamber.

Chapter Thirty-Seven

Peering at the Future

17 September 1538

There was much passion in the King's lovemaking. Much passion but precious little affection. He ordered me to strip and then climbed upon me without a further word. He was hungry for me, right enough, and I felt him enter me at once. I was dry and yelped in pain, which seemed to act like a goad to him. He forced himself to ever greater exertions, the sweat coming off him like a river in flood.

All the time his face was like a mask. *His bedmate could be anybody,* I thought. But then the realization came that no, it couldn't. It could only be me. Only I could incite this mix of emotions in the King. For there was passion, anger, desire for revenge, desire to possess.

But over all of this I sensed, or thought I sensed, there was an overriding emotion of hurt.

I had stood against the King's wishes and I had hurt him. And now he was getting his revenge. And, as I gazed into his eyes, I saw he was enjoying his revenge in more ways than he had anticipated.

For as the act progressed, the anger began to melt in him a little. I felt his body relax a tiny drop from the rigid battering ram it had been at first. His eyes, those cold, cruel eyes, began to soften. And then he looked away, as if ashamed at what he was doing. At that very moment he climaxed and he sighed.

I gripped him harder. *We will see*, I thought, *we will see*.

I began to move against him, pretending to writhe with pleasure. I moaned and crooned, making my breathing sound fast and shallow. He blinked as if in surprise and then he stiffened once again inside me. I could barely move because of his bulk yet still I managed to stir and wriggle. I threw my head back and my eyes closed as if I were being catapulted to some far distant place. *If you will treat me like a whore, Henry Tudor*, I thought, *I will act like one.*

I began to purr like a cat as it licks cream, and then the purr became deeper and deeper, until it was more akin to the roar of those blasted lions that had proved so much trouble for me. Somehow, with incredible effort, I managed to arch my back as if in the grip of the most earth-shattering orgasm, raising him an inch or two above the bed.

And then I collapsed and moaned. This was no dissimulation. The act of lifting his monstrous bulk had nearly done for me.

But it had done for him as well. He gazed into my eyes and now there was no trace of anger, no trace of vengeance, no trace of hatred.

Now he looked like a moonstruck youth, snared by calf love, shot through with Cupid's arrows.

"Alice," he said, stroking me on the cheek. "My darling."

I held back his advances for two hours that afternoon. It was grim necessity for I thought my back would crack if I moved it too soon.

But my sweet resistance had the added advantage of heaping fuel upon the King's fire. Bit by bit, I added more. A twig here with a little kiss. A bundle of kindling when I allowed him to stroke my breasts. A small branch when I lay upon him and kissed him deeply, my tongue exploring his panting mouth. And then, with more twigs, more kindling and a strengthening breeze of murmurings to fan the blaze, I straddled him and threw on charcoal, logs and sea-coal with rash abandon so that his fire exploded and it was his turn to groan and shake, his turn to roar like a lion, his turn to be in my control, at my mercy. His turn to be subject and my turn to be mistress.

And to my surprise, I climaxed at the same time as the King. I was so shocked I could not speak. For, simultaneous with it, the thought shot through me that I did, a little, care for this monstrous man. I did, perhaps, even love him the tiniest bit. And that was when I knew I had both lost and won. Lost myself a very little. Won the King, now and forever. And, if I was more careful than before, won far, far more. Won the life I so very much desired.

"My darling," he cried, "my darling, my Alice."

Immediately the doors crashed open and guards raced in, swords drawn to find the foe who caused the King to yell out with such desperate tumult.

"Get out, you fools," he yelled, brandishing his fist at the men. "Get out and for once in my life, leave me in peace."

And then I lay upon his breast and stroked his face and calmed him and soothed him and crooned in his ear and all the while plotted out how to milk every last drop of advantage from the situation.

The King looked stunned next morning when I told him all that had happened to me since the day Sir Richard Rich had me bundled out of Hampton Court Palace.

I related it in the calmest manner. This was partly because I thought that this would have the greatest effect upon the King's now melting heart. But it was more because if I did not say it calmly, I might burst into tears of hurt and anger.

At length I finished. The King rose from his seat and filled a cup of wine, swallowed it down in one gulp and poured a second before returning to sit with me.

"Did you want one?" he asked suddenly, as if shocked that he had not already asked me.

I nodded and went over to the table.

As I poured the wine I peered at the King. He cradled his cup in his hands and stared moodily at the fire. I could see his mind working. I knew him well enough to know that there was genuine anger there, genuine pain at what I had suffered. But, at the same time, these emotions were running in tandem with other considerations. His own position, his wealth, the men who were most useful to him, the men who might be dispensed with.

"The Beastmaster, Ned Pepper," he said as I returned to my seat. "Ned Pepper was good to you?"

"He was very kind, my lord."

A shadow moved in the corner, picking up a quill. I almost jumped out of my skin, for in the hour I had taken to relay my story to the King, I had forgotten that the Lord Privy Seal was also in the room.

"A pension, Your Grace?" he asked in a matter-of-fact voice.

The King nodded, once, and Cromwell decided how much the pension should be and scribed it on a document.

"And the waterman?" the King asked. "The man who took you in and housed you?"

"He was equally kind," I said.

He glanced at Cromwell and, with that glance, Walter Scrump and his family became richer than they could have dreamed, so rich he did not have to work another day, could move from Offal Pudding Lane to Islington and buy a fine house. With the scratching of Cromwell's quill, Walter's unborn descendants succeeded to a life of wealth and ease.

"And this man, the one who ran the brothel in Southwark?" the King asked. "You say he was called Timothy Dale?"

"He was, my lord."

The King turned towards Cromwell who stirred himself and glanced sideways at the King.

"Everything, Your Majesty?" he asked. "Property, liberty?"

The King did not answer.

"Life?"

Again the King did not answer, which Cromwell took for assent.

"And perhaps we should put him to the test, Your Grace?" he continued. "To see if he has more accomplices we need to find."

The King waved his hand dismissively, a careless gesture that would cause Dale to be racked, broken, hanged and eviscerated.

Cromwell chewed upon his pen a moment as if a sudden thought had struck him, a thought which he found difficult to deal with. "Bishop Gardiner has, perhaps, been remiss," he said. "He appears to have continued to collect rents from the stews while at the same time neglecting to inform my office and remit the monies owed to the Crown." He opened his hands wide as if to indicate all the monies which were uncollected by the Royal Treasury.

"I do not like the idea of women being forced to live like that," said the King. "If they choose to do so, then well and good. But I do not want the existence of houses where innocents are kidnapped, assaulted and brutalized into the trade."

"The Bishopric of Winchester's control of the stews is very ancient," Cromwell said. "It's almost four hundred years since King Henry II gave the land to the Bishops. They continue to profit handsomely from rents and from fines upon the owners of the brothels."

The King looked away. I imagined he was calculating how much that profit might be. "It is wrong that the church should benefit from the weaknesses and corruption of man," he said at last with a pious look.

He leaned towards me. "That is why the abbeys and monasteries which indulged in vile practices have been brought to book."

Cromwell gave a little cough. "We can move against the stews, Your Grace, but we must be circumspect. Closing them would not be popular with the husbands of London. And if we scare the Winchester Geese they will just migrate. It may prove better to retain them all in one nest where we can keep a good eye on them. Otherwise they will spread across the city and the only ones who will benefit from the trade will be pimps."

"A fine, then, on the Bishop," said the King. "One which will remind him of his duty to the Crown and make sure he pays his future dues to the Treasury."

Cromwell took up his quill, rubbed the feathers against his lips for a moment as if pondering the size of the fine then bent to the manuscript and wrote out an amount with a decisive hand. He looked calm and businesslike, but Gardiner was one of his most intractable enemies and inwardly he must have reveled at dealing him such a devastating blow.

I turned my gaze from the minister to the King. They understood each other better than husband and wife. I could not fathom whether I had just witnessed a genuine debate about prostitution or a charade put on for my benefit. A charade leading, inevitably, to the further enrichment of the King and an increase in Cromwell's power.

"And what about the man who came to my chamber?" I said in a tone of greater demand than I intended. "Sir Edmund Tint."

The King nodded. "Thomas," he asked, "what do we know of Sir Edmund Tint?"

Cromwell opened a book and scrutinized it carefully. "Two manors in Essex, a larger one in Kent and one in Warwickshire. Annual income: four hundred and eighty pounds, twelve shillings and ninepence."

"Put him in the Tower," the King said. "Confiscate his properties."

As soon as he said this, an idea popped into my head.

"I am glad of this punishment," I said. "It is right that Tint loses everything for his crimes. It is also appropriate that the King, who he wronged by his infamous conduct, should benefit in this manner."

I left the words hanging in the air and waited.

The King turned to look at me. His eyes, still piggy from his hard calculations, grew wider with understanding. For a moment I detected real compassion for what I had suffered, then it was replaced by wry amusement.

"Of course, it was not only I who suffered from Sir Edmund Tint," he said, patting me on the knee.

There was a long silence, the only sound the shifting of a log in the fire.

"Perhaps one manor could appropriately be given to Alice?" Cromwell suggested.

I held the King's eyes in mine. I did not blink. But he did.

"Perhaps two," he said after a long silence. "I think that Alice would prefer two."

Cromwell scribbled a note. "I suggest the manor in Buckland, near to Dover, and Luddington in Warwickshire."

I gasped in pretend surprise, holding my hand upon my breast. "I am overcome by your generosity, Your Grace." I rose and gave a low curtsy.

As I did so, I heard the low rumble of Cromwell's laugh.

A few days later the King announced that I was to be accommodated in my own quarters in Greenwich Castle.

"You shall have the whole of the east side of the castle," he said. "From there you will be able to look down upon the Palace. And I will be able to look up to the castle and know that you are there, safe and sound for me."

"I am more than grateful," I said. I spoke no word of a lie. I was pleased to be the King's favorite once again but even more pleased to find that I did not have to share his bed every night.

"It is better that you are lodged in the castle," he said, almost as if he had shared my thoughts.

"Whatever Your Grace's desire."

He laughed. "Oh, my desire is for you, Alice, make no mistake of that. But my advisers' desire is that I get myself a wife, someone who will give me another son."

His face looked troubled. He reached out and took my hands.

"I have pondered whether to make you my Queen," he said.

My heart fell like a stone when he said it.

His eyes bored into mine and I struggled to find what to say.

"But I am of humble birth," I said. "All of your wives have been of exalted birth."

"Anne Boleyn?" he said. "Jane Seymour?"

"The daughters of gentlemen," I said. "And I am certain that noble blood must have run in Jane's blood."

"Her great-great-grandfather was King Edward III," he said with a shrug as if to dismiss such a distant connection.

"Well, there, you see. My great-great-grandfather was probably a shepherd."

The King laughed. "You underestimate yourself, Alice. He was probably a successful merchant. Or a moneylender."

I laughed at his words but felt a little chill of disquiet at their barbed nature. He understood me just as much as I understood him.

"Well, let us leave aside all talk of wives," he said. "For the present." He sighed. "My advisers would have me take a foreign bride. To placate my enemies and friends alike."

"I heard some talk of this."

He sniffed derisively. "Some would have me marry the young Duchess of Milan, the Danish girl, Christina."

"And would you have her as your bride, my lord?" I asked, hopeful that he would. "She is said to be the most beautiful Princess in the world."

He shrugged. "It is academic. Rumor has it that she is unwilling to wed me."

"And is she the only choice?"

He shook his head. "Cromwell seeks an alliance with the Protestant Princes of Germany. The Duke of Cleves has two daughters who are said to be pretty enough."

"Then I am sure Your Grace will find a suitable match."

"Perhaps I will. I shall not be forced to seek a bride from the Sultan or send to the Indies. Europe has enough pretty young Princesses it seems. I will send my painter, Holbein, to paint portraits of all of them so I can see who is the most suitable."

He chuckled to himself and I thought it best not to ask why. I was too busy trying to hide my relief that he had been advised to look abroad for a Queen.

He walked over to the window and gazed up at the castle on its hill to the south. I joined him. I could see why Cromwell had chosen it to house me. It was near enough to be on hand but far enough to remain discreet. No whisper of the secret concubine need travel to the courts of Europe to trouble the minds of thoughtful fathers. I wondered how permanent my position might be. I could not be sure that I would remain the King's favorite for long. I would have to make the best of it while I could.

"You'll need a household," he said. "In your apartments."

"I have a maid," I said. "Sissy Cooper, the daughter of the family I stayed with in Stratford."

"You'll need more than that," he said. "I'll arrange for my steward to choose some servants."

"Thank you, Your Grace." I was surprised by his generosity. "And would it be possible to have some friends with me?"

He looked bemused at my words. "You mean Maids of Honor?" He shook his head. "That is not possible. That is preposterous. A favorite with Maids of Honor. Preposterous."

"I mean friends. Companions."

He tilted his head in thought, considering. Finally he nodded. "Two only."

I took him by the hand and kissed it. I had two friends very much in mind.

Susan Dunster and Mary Zouche arrived at the castle a couple days later. It was the autumn equinox, when the day is exactly as long as the night, and I felt that the arrival of my friends would make me feel as balanced as this day. I hurried down to the Hall to greet them. We fell upon each other, crying like babies.

"We were so worried," Mary said.

"We thought you'd been murdered," said Susan. "Or worse."

I felt my face cloud at those words. "It *was* worse," I said. Then I shook my head. "No, it cannot have been. For I am alive and with the best of friends in all the world."

"And you are restored as the King's favorite," Susan said. Her eyebrow arched as she said it.

"I am. But I intend to be a more circumspect favorite this time. I shall dance upon eggshells."

They did not reply. It was obvious that they thought this a most sensible plan.

"And is this where you live?" Mary asked.

"It is," I answered, flushing with embarrassment and with pride. "And it is where you will live as well. You are to be my companions."

"So will we share a chamber with you?" Mary asked.

I shook my head. "Far from it. Follow me."

I led them up the stairs and through a wide oak door into a large chamber with a table in the middle and half a dozen chairs dotted around. "This is the reception area," I explained.

We then went through another door into a similarly sized chamber but one which was decorated with honey-colored oak paneling. A huge fire blazed in the fireplace, with four comfortable chairs placed in front of it and fire screens close to hand. There were two tall windows, both with a padded window seat, and other chairs dotted around the room with little side tables set beside them. On one table, in a corner of the room, sat a virginal. Mary clapped with delight when she saw this.

"I chose this for you," I said. "Go ahead and try it."

She sat at the table and began to play on the instrument. She played without music to read, from memory, a lovely lilting piece that gladdened the heart.

"She wrote the music herself," Susan whispered. "She made it herself."

A door opened and Sissy peeped in to listen. I beckoned her over and she came to me, head low with embarrassment.

We stood in silence and listened to the melody. I felt a warm glow begin to suffuse my body, warmer than the heat given off from the fire. It started in my heart and as I looked around at my friends the glow lapped up my breast, along my arms and to my head.

A reassuring calm swept over me, as if I were floating in a warm sea with the gentlest of waves. I felt transported to the safest of havens, to the place I always wanted to be. It was as if I were a part of everything around me, dissolved into it, and everything around was dissolving into me. A peace like I had never known before. And I was transported here not only by the music. I felt this way because of the friends I loved and because I knew that, finally, I was in the place I was always meant to be.

Thanks and Acknowledgments

No book is completely the work of one person and it is the same with *A Love Most Dangerous*. First and foremost I would like to thank my wife, Janine, who was a constant source of support while I was writing it and was the first person to read and comment on it.

I have also been fortunate to have a number of people who have read the book and suggested changes and amendments. They are too many to mention here but I would like to mention the following for their detailed comments and suggestions: Anne Shilton, Barbara Maria Patrizi, Dee Gillies, Erin L. Johnson, Julie Webb-Harvey, Sophie Six and Beverly Wyatt. I wholeheartedly agreed with most of the changes these eagle-eyed people have pointed out and incorporated them into the book.

I would especially like to thank Jodi Warshaw and her team at Lake Union Publishing for their support and unfailing professionalism. I have been lucky in having two superb editors, Marianna Baer, who offered insights and suggestions which greatly enhanced the novel, and Janet Robbins, eagle-eyed copy editor, who discovered all remaining errors and ambiguities and buffed and polished the final manuscript.

Any remaining mistakes are solely down to me. However, if you as a reader notice any typos, errors or jarring material which has eluded everyone's eyes, please let me know.

People in
A Love Most Dangerous

Alice Petherton. Maid of Honor to Queen Anne Boleyn and Queen Jane Seymour. Later the lover and favorite of King Henry VIII.

King Henry VIII. King of England. He was forty-five at the beginning of the novel and had been on the throne for twenty-eight years.

Sir Thomas Cromwell, Lord Privy Seal. The King's First Minister and one of his most important advisers. He was instrumental in the Dissolution of the Monasteries, in enriching the King and consolidating the power of King and State.

Susan Dunster. A Maid of Honor and Alice's good friend.

Mary Zouche. A Maid of Honor and Alice's good friend.

Philippa Wicks. A Maid of Honor who hated Alice.

Dorothy Bray. Philippa's accomplice.

Gregory Frost. The King's Groom.

Humphrey Buck. A Page and go-between.

Sir Richard Rich. Cromwell's assistant. Said to be the second-most-hated man in the Kingdom, after his master.

Peter Mason. Rich's manservant.

Lucy Burton. A young Maid of Honor.

Thomas Howard, Duke of Norfolk. Premier noble of the Kingdom. A useful servant to the King, though perhaps a grudging one.

Bess Holland. Thomas Howard's long-standing mistress.

Henry Howard, Earl of Surrey. Son of the Duke of Norfolk. An impetuous, rakish individual. A good friend of Sir Thomas Wyatt, he was one of the foremost English poets of the century.

Frances. Surrey's wife.

Sir Thomas Seymour. Brother of Queen Jane. A vain, ambitious, reckless man who reached far above his abilities.

Sir Edward Seymour, Earl of Hertford. Thomas's older brother. A man of much greater ability and wisdom than his younger brother.

Charles Brandon. Duke of Suffolk.

Thomas Cranmer. Archbishop of Canterbury.

Father Luke. A priest who acted as Alice's mentor in the new religion.

Father Ambrose. An old priest.

Walter Scrump. A Thames waterman.

Margery. Walter's wife.

Art Scrump. Walter's fast and loose son, who manages to seduce Alice.

Betty Dibble. A frequenter of the Shambles Inn and occasional bedmate of Art.

Timothy Dale. Brothel keeper.

Thorne. Dale's henchman.

Mrs. Barleyfield. Dale's housekeeper.

Madge. A young maid in Dale's brothel.

Jim. One of Thorne's accomplices.

Sir Edmund Tint. One of Dale's customers.

Ned Pepper. Beastmaster of the King's Menagerie.

Edith Pepper. Ned's wife.

Amy Pepper. Ned's daughter.

Robert Cooper. Edith's brother.

Hannah Cooper. Robert's wife.

Edward Cooper. Robert's oldest son.

Sissy Cooper. Robert's daughter who becomes Alice's maid.

Daniel Stokes. Cromwell's messenger.

Isaac Jones. One of Cromwell's servants.

About the Author

Born and raised in England, Martin Lake discovered his love of history and writing at an early age. After graduating from university, he worked as a teacher and a lecturer before he decided to combine his two passions and write a historical novel. Since then, he has written six novels and several short stories. When not writing, he can be found traveling, cooking, and exploring fascinating places. He currently resides on the French Riviera with his wife. Keep up with Martin at http://martinlakewriting.wordpress.com.